STEAL THE PLANET

RAY BLACKHALL

Sparkling
PRESS

STEALTH PLANET

RAY BLACKHALL

Original Publication 2006
Sparkling Press, an imprint of Dusty Spark Publishing.

ISBN 0-9763565-5-4
ISBN 978-0-9763565-5-4

Printed and bound in the United States of America

Sparkling Press / Dusty Spark Publishing
15821 FM 529 Suite #181
Houston, TX 77095

www.SparklingPress.com

Sparkling PRESS

I would like to thank my lovely wife Sally and my son Colin for all of their help and support while completing this work. Sally's assistance and suggestions were invaluable. Colin's desire to know what happened next was inspiring and gratifying.

Special thanks are also due to my first readers, Phil and Ross, whose praise and encouragement were major factors in my pursuit to see this work in print. I wish to express my true feeling of gratitude to Martha Whitacker. Without her inspiration, this book may never have seen the light of day.

I also wish to dedicate this work to the memory of Duane and Lloyd.

Contents

1 Discovery 9

2 Confirmation 15

3 Announcement 21

4 Decision 27

5 The Ship 33

6 The Crew 45

7 Launch 53

8 The Second Countdown 61

9 The Voyage Begins 77

10 Stealth Finder One 87

11 Second Chances 97

12 Full Speed Ahead 107

13 Disaster 121

14 Arrival And Orbit 135

15 Go For Landing 145

16 Base Camp 153

17 Exploration Sortie 175

18 The Surprise 191

19 Rescue 203

20 Escape 215

21 Reunion 235

22 Isolation 245

23 Departure 257

24 Returning 261

25 Hero's Welcome 269

STEALTH PLANET

1
DISCOVERY

JIMMY REMEMBERED every detail of the collision like it had taken place yesterday, the lady's arms flailing as she plunged face first into the snow, her gasp, a muffled cry, and her companion's look of agony as he realized what had happened. It still filled him with pride that he had been there to help, to chase down the perpetrators, to see that justice was served; and most of all, to meet his hero face-to-face.

Squeezing through the polished brass revolving doors of the space museum, Jimmy Pierce tugged his grandfather's hand, urging him onward, his older teen sister and dad following close behind. He had a single purpose, a youthful enthusiasm to reach the new museum displays that premiered today. Sheldon Pierce, Senior, was patient with his overzealous grandson. He understood Jimmy's anticipation and also looked forward to viewing the new exhibits. His granddaughter, Shelly, more interested than her body language suggested, showed her complete annoyance with her pesky little brother.

They all hurried past wonderful exhibits they had seen before, spectacular dinosaur fossils, interesting hands-on experiments in physics, passing it all until they found the crowded hall that opened today. Jimmy dashed ahead, clutching the silver Nastar ski medal given to him by the man in the life-size photograph at the end of the hall. Shelly was close behind, pushing her way through the crowd to stay with Jimmy. He stopped in front of the large photo of an astronaut, unhelmeted, standing with slack jaw and eyes agape, staring at a small photo above a mechanical portal. Jimmy had seen the picture before, many times. It had appeared in almost every newspaper and magazine all over the globe. Grandpa and dad caught up to the siblings, and the most senior Pierce could not help but notice the broad smile that appeared on his grandson's face. He heard the story about the chance encounter on the ski slope a hundred times; but could not wait to hear Jimmy tell it again.

The entire adventure had all started in the most innocuous way. Significant discovery is often the result of intense scientific scrutiny or at least serious search. In the case of David Striker, the man in the life-size picture, it was almost pure chance. The date was July 8, 2029, time: 8:05 a.m., place: the

Johnson Space Center, Houston, Texas. David Striker, young astrophysicist, had his encounter with fate. Little did he know how much his find would change his life or the future of human space exploration.

July 8, 2029 8:05 a.m.

Glancing up at the digital clock ticking off the seconds in the lower right corner of his far left monitor, David Striker could not believe that this day was already passing so slowly. David's position with NASA was not prestigious but a good one, and though the routine could be somewhat boring, he enjoyed it. The remainder of his left-hand monitor screen contained his desktop, listing his programs, shortcuts, and custom command buttons. A center monitor was festooned with all of the telemetry data streams normally monitored by him and his office mate. To his right, a third screen always retained the most recent high resolution image to arrive from his distant charge, a tiny satellite hurtling through the outer reaches of our solar system.

Absorbed in a game of paper-wad basketball with a miniature backboard perched atop the wastepaper basket across the office, David had been ignoring the data this morning. Since Margie Ritter, who shared their cramped office, would be arriving soon, he decided to gather up his few misses and to return the cluttered office carpet to normal. His office mate enjoyed his boyish games and, on rare occasions, also tried a few shots with her non-shredded prints.

At that non-scientific moment, it happened. David Striker was slouching absentmindedly at his terminal, awaiting Margie's arrival, sipping tepid coffee and downing his second donut when he noticed the slightly incongruent data. The present digital image on the right screen had a dull blur, a dark smudge, and the star he noted earlier was missing from this newest image.

At first, David considered it a data transmission error. Due to the vast distance from the source, telemetry glitches were common, almost normal, and the computer automatically corrected the majority of them. *Voyager 7*, the spacecraft that David monitored, was now many million miles from Earth. Signal problems were expected. David's distractions ended and his mind immediately refocused on his work.

Voyager 7 had been following its planned course flawlessly for over two and one half years, and was now heading directly for the planet Uranus, a bleak, frigid, cloud covered ball, also known as the seventh planet. This space probe was actually the seventh in a series of solar system exploration platforms begun with the launch of *Voyager 1* and *Voyager 2* in 1977. The Voyager series had been started anew in 2025 by NASA in order to test the latest state-of-the-art propulsion and data-gathering systems. The elapsed time to travel to Earth's distant neighbors was being drastically reduced with each new probe.

V-7 was David Striker's charge and she was fast and bristling with the best high tech data-gathering gadgetry the world could assemble. It had taken *Voyager* 2 over eight and one half years to reach Uranus, arriving in January 1986. Though primitive by comparison, *Voyager* 2 had discovered four new rings and ten new moons around Uranus. David's version would make the journey in less than twenty-two months and this new platform had far superior data-gathering capabilities.

Just think of what my craft can do, David often reflected. *Look at what we found out about Saturn on the V-7 pass, even more than Cassini sent us. This close encounter with cloud-enshrouded Uranus will give up some new secrets and I'll see them first.*

Until that moment, David was spending his uneventful six hundred and forty-second day watching the monitors, replaying the pictures and enhancing and checking the endless stream of images. The excitement had been over for some time. Jupiter had passed, a spectacle of swirling gas and moons. Saturn and its magnificent rings were far behind. The images were still fascinating, but for over a year, the results had been mostly routine scans and deep space mapping, until this day; because this glitch was different.

It appeared from his cursory look that something passed between the star and V-7's cameras. *What was this new smudge?* David moved his mouse furiously, clicking on the last series of pictures stored by the computer. These had been taken the day before, but due to the length of time for transmission from the satellite and decoding here at the NASA facility, he was evaluating them for the first time.

A heightened sense of curiosity gripped his overly inquisitive mind. David was ready for something more challenging than paper-wad basketball or attempting to defeat his computer at chess.

Sifting through the gigabytes of data comprising the never-ending stream of images from space often induced daydream reveries of places far away. Fantasies filled with beaches and palm trees, steep mountain crags surrounding high alpine valleys or subterranean crawlways filled with eerie apparitions kept his mind alert when his job became mundane.

He now feared that this piece of incongruent data might only be the latest; but the next image showed the anomaly again, only much clearer. David's heart pounded for just a few beats. He hit the enhance key to increase magnification and resolution. The latest image enhancing software provided by the spooks at NSA still amazed him. The new high-speed chips kicked in and the enhanced image instantly popped into view. David gulped and stared at this last image perplexed. He considered himself a competent and knowledgeable astronomer. He recognized the known stars, planets, moons, and comets on sight. He was also familiar with numerous large asteroids and much of the known and catalogued space debris. This new anomaly fit none of these "knowns" by basic description, and an occludal anomaly discovery this large seemed impossible in this day and age, and whatever it was, it had to be enormous.

David gulped another half cup of coffee, rubbed his eyes and decided to review the entire data stream for the last twenty-four hours. It only took him a few minutes and everything looked right. It was correct, there were no obvious data entry or data receipt errors. *Check another image.* He drummed his fingers on the desk impatiently waiting for more images. The new anomaly was there again, confirmed. At the highest magnification it appeared as a very dark orange-brown or more like deep reddish-brown, dull, nearly invisible orb.

David knew the *V*-7 cameras recorded an incredible array of scientific variables and, with the assistance of the computer, he could focus on one or virtually any combination of data sets. *Albedo,* he thought, *check for surface composition, reflectance as a factor of possible composition, infrared, I want to see them all!* David began imputing as much other sensor data as he could.

Margie opened the office door and noticed the sweat on his brow and the level of activity coming from her normally unruffled office mate. Several new printouts littered the floor, and David had placed three large photo prints between his desk and hers.

"What'd you do? Spill coffee on your keyboard again?" she laughed as she squeezed past him to her desk and console. "Anything interesting?" she added, half joking.

David said nothing. He just continued staring at the screen as his fingers literally flew over the keyboard.

I can't tell her yet. David glanced toward Margie. *Not yet. She'll laugh at me anyway.* He had conjured up a meteor once or twice as well as other jokes and inserted them in several early *V*-7 pictures in order to add a little fun to their normal day. He felt true excitement. *This could be something big! Down, boy. Control your excitement. This could be a hoax that Margie cooked up. You're overdue for a little revenge.*

A cold feeling ran through him, and suddenly he felt the hair on the back of his neck begin to stand up. He knew that Margie was an incredible computer hack and she did know the spook program better than he did.

Oh you son-of-a-gun. Burned my buns did you? Would she admit it? He had bitten and bitten hard; hook, line, and sinker.

"Margie, look at image number 73,862A," he said. *His original version, or was it hers?*

She clicked a few keys and looked at it for a moment. "What is it?" she said.

"I thought that maybe you could tell me," he countered.

"Give me a couple of minutes and maybe I can venture a guess."

But he stopped her. "I bit, Margie. You got me. I've been had. I admit it."

"Wrongo, donut breath," she returned and tapped her pencil on the image on the screen on her monitor. "What the hell is it? I didn't set you up. No jokes."

"OK, thanks," was his simple answer.

David's excitement returned. "Check the next image and bring up 73,862Ae, the enhanced version. You won't believe it, so take your time." He added new data and ran the advanced evaluation program. They stared at their monitors.

Silence filled the room except for the cooling fans on their computer towers for what seemed to David to be an eternity.

"My God!" Margie blurted. "It's huge and the computer analysis suggests increasing warmth inward from a strange, gaseous—but indeterminate—outer layer. Who put that planet there?"

Margie knew that it couldn't be a planet, but under the circumstances and with the preliminary analyses of the data at hand, it was the best description.

"We need to run a full diagnostic data analysis with complete integration of all sensory data from the entire series of photographs from the moment this was first detected in order to further evaluate this bogey." Margie was punching keys and running her fingers through her hair. Excitement brought beads of sweat to her brow.

"It won't take long," David told her. "I just re-aimed the onboard cameras two days ago to check out a different star group. It was purely by chance that we detected this new object, since it's barely visible at this distance and would be basically invisible to anything on earth. I have already started selecting all of the images since then. Let's check them all and load them for complete evaluation."

The computer whirred when they finished loading the group of images and they glanced at each other again. David pondered to himself. *We need to get this right, no mistakes, no unanswered questions. This could be a significant discovery and could bring us scientific notoriety—even fame.*

2
CONFIRMATION

July 9, 2029 9:14 a.m.

HANK WADKINS liked his job as director of the *V-7* program, but the high point of yesterday was when Margie seemed to flirt with him for a moment when she said, "Hi." She winked, he remembered.

Hank knew his job was safe. *Voyager 7* had a nuclear power supply and multi-redundant systems. The craft was a marvelous collection of high-tech gadgetry and the best technology the world could muster. Someone had to watch it, monitor and decipher the constant stream of data, and keep it running. He helped to design and assemble it and knew all of its idiosyncrasies. His job was as safe as the machine he had nurtured. David and Margie's jobs were another story. He loved them both, but his budget would take another hit this year. *God*, he thought, *I don't want to let them go, but come year end, we have to cut.*

He remembered when he hired them. David first, and one month later, Margie. They were a great team, experienced but young enough to face any challenge. David had started with NASA in the astronaut-training program, and had wanted to fly in space. His background was solid: He had great computer skills as well as technical degrees from Syracuse University and MIT.

Margie was a southern girl with a pretty face and a flair for scientific debate. What a brain; and beauty too: A Rice University and Sanford graduate with advanced degrees in physics and computer science, and a resume that would make anyone envious. They both were overqualified for what they did now, but never complained, and what a team they had been during the Jupiter Pass four months ago. They were awesome, their photo essays and briefings superbly done, and they thoroughly impressed the scientific community and the press.

The thought of having to let them go bothered him. Hank shook his head and picked up his coffee cup as he slid out from behind his desk. He walked out of his brightly lit office into the main corridor of their unobtrusive build-ing at the Johnson Space Center. *How would he tell them when the time came?* They were so dedicated, though he knew that computer games had to be filling part of their day.

As he passed their office he noticed the activity. David had either mastered some game or outsmarted Margie at something. He wasn't leaning back in his chair shooting paper wads at his wastebasket. As an undergrad, he made the Syracuse basketball team and was a fine athlete in several sports. It was unusual that Margie was not reading a periodical or scientific journal. Both were glued to their monitors and prints of photos were scattered throughout their office.

He tapped on the glass panel and smiled, they both looked up but hardly acknowledged his presence. *Oh well, I'll get my coffee and talk to them about the afternoon update briefing on the way back.*

Hank nodded at Betty Hurley, the Office Manager/Secretary, as he passed her in the hallway. Betty said, "Hank, you better get a donut early, or they will be gone because David and Margie grabbed another handful each and headed back to their sanctum. Hardly said a word, moving like crazy. What are they so excited about?" Hank thought first, then answered Betty. "Something is go-ing on, and my best guess says that it's not planning the next office picnic."

He entered the coffee room, filled his cup, dropped in two sugar cubes, and stirred with a plastic stick. He never quite made the switch to artificial sweeteners. Maybe a little creamer too—he liked the flavored creamers.

He glanced at the bulletin board, as he did everyday, and saw the new picture. Black, a few stars, and a blur with a hand-scribbled message on the bottom: "Do you know me?" It looked like a smudged coffee mark at first, but this was something different. He pulled the photo from the board, sat down at one of the tables and set his coffee down, holding the image so that the light hit it better.

Oh, here we go again. David had created another blip on the proverbial radar screen, a new bogie at ten o'clock high. The last one had a miniature creature hid-den in it like the children's search puzzles his kids had enjoyed. Hank spent nearly twenty-five minutes to find the darn thing. *What was this one?* Do you know me? *Was this supposed to resemble somebody or something?* He didn't have a clue, so he put it back on the bulletin board with a pushpin and made a mental note to query David. It looked like his handwriting, but he wasn't sure because so little was handwritten these days.

Betty interrupted Hank's second visit to David and Margie's office by an-nouncing a call from his wife, Helen. Hank knew Helen didn't like to be kept waiting, but he decided to have Betty say he would call her back in ten minutes. Little did he know that it would be more like twelve hours, as he turned the knob and stepped into Office 206.

"Hi, Hank," said Margie, speaking a little sheepishly.

"How late were you two here last night?" Hank asked.

"Pretty late," said David. "My eyes are burning, and I hope this coffee kicks in soon."

"What's going on? I know you two did not wait until the last minute to get ready for today's briefing," Hank paused.

"Can we cancel it?" asked David.

"Cancel it? I thought you couldn't wait to get it over with?"

"This is different," said Margie, we just might have something more interesting than anything we've had for the last five or six meetings."

"Interesting? How so?" queried Hank. "Does this have something to do with the new creation on the bulletin board? Let me guess. You have spied another comet or alien warship?" It was more of a statement than a question. They were not laughing.

David spoke first. He started out by saying, "Don't get mad Hank." *What did you mess up?* Hank thought to himself. David continued, "It is that picture, Hank, and all of these others we've been sorting and analyzing since yesterday afternoon."

David handed Hank one color-enhanced blow-up of the smudge with a detailed analysis of the data in two columns next to it. The bottom line under "computer analysis – object" caught his eye at once. "Possible planetary object."

Hank's eyes shot to Margie, who was simply nodding yes, then back to David, whose face was very serious. "We need this kind of prank stuff to make life interesting around here," Hank said as he reached to take more photos from David's hand. The second and third had "confirmation – all data" in caps across the top. "This is more convincing than your last tricks."

But this situation was different; the last picture had a level-3 priority-one code. It couldn't be faked.

July 9, 2029 9:54 a.m.

"Do you have confirmation from anyone else with the International Space Agency group? Have you contacted anyone?" The questions came out of Hank so fast that he had to catch himself. "Of course you haven't. You know the procedures." He composed himself and looked them both in the eyes. "One, is this a hoax? And two, has it gone out of here in any way?"

"Negative, both counts," said David.

"Same here," said Margie.

Hank studied the photos again for a minute as thoughts raced through his mind. "Contact Rob Martin at Berkeley and Martha Jackson with Euro Space Center Ops. Let's get confirmation and prepare what we can for this afternoon. We have people coming in from Washington, Japan, Russia, and Europe for this meeting. If we get confirmation from both parties, we give them the data, full show; you guys will have the podium. If we don't confirm, we don't discuss. Got it? David, Margie, this is your call and your show. If this is in any way a hoax, we'll get burned badly, so be careful."

July 9, 2029 12:38 p.m.

Hank rounded the corner and met David and Margie on the way back to his office. "We have positive confirmation from two parties who were given the data," said Margie.

"Both are sworn to secrecy for now," added David, "I promised to get them here for any press release or public announcement."

"We have to buy them dinner too," said Margie, "Their choice."

Betty heard the chatter in the hallway and joined Hank, David and Margie. Before she could ask a question, Hank cut her off. "We'll need lunch: Sandwiches, chips, and fruit drinks in David's office. Please bring some back from the cafeteria and hurry, we've got a lot to do before 2:00."

She didn't ask anything, didn't even ask for the money. Betty knew it was important. She had known Hank a long time and understood that something important was going on. Betty had not seen such excitement in a while around their *V*-7 Project group.

July 9, 2029 2:00 p.m.

They chatted around the conference room table, in the corners, and exchanged their normal pleasantries. This group of scientists consisting of one representative from each of the countries contributing to the *V*-7 effort was familiar with the briefing routine. Betty handed out new NASA photos and new data. "How's the family?" "Read any good books lately?" The group exchanged the regular questions. Hank, David, and Margie were not present.

The three hurried into the room and Hank proceeded to his place at the head of the table. David and Margie passed out envelopes to each person, and Hank started: "The projection photos are loading and the ones in your packets are for your use during and after the meeting."

Hank never beat around the bush. He always got right to the point, and the way the last few meetings had gone, he could have done everything for those by email. This group insisted on the formality of face-to-face meetings. And besides, they all enjoyed the expense-account trips. When Hank, David, and Margie entered the room, everyone sensed the change and more charged atmosphere. Curiosity was rising.

Hank waited until they had all opened their packets. "Ladies and Gentlemen, I trust that you all had comfortable trips. Welcome. We hope that the information before you will make the Jupiter Pass look insignificant by comparison. Please open your packets and look at the screen. The pictures are dated and continuous. Since these were taken, we have sent a new series of commands to *V-7*. They should reach there in a few more hours, and within 48 hours we should have an intensive investigation of this phenomenon in progress."

3
ANNOUNCEMENT

July 9, 2029 6:00 p.m.

THE BRIEFING lasted for four hours, but to Hank it seemed more like forty minutes. All systems of data transmission from *V-7* had been fine-tuned and transferred from the control room adjacent to the conference room. The control room for this project resembled a miniaturized Apollo mission room festooned with monitors and computers. All attendees could watch the technicians at work through the glass wall, and to a few, the entire scene looked surreal. Hank made the decision to put heightened security measures into place. No cell phones worked and no modems or outside connections were allowed. The technicians in the control room did not know any specifics about the new discovery, but interoffice gossip intimated the reason for the different tone in the conference room this time.

The conferees pooled their ideas, rechecked the programs and raw data, looked for bugs, leaks, and viruses, and the collective possibilities of a telemetry error or fake were pretty well exhausted. Their new primary task was to prevent the story from leaking prematurely and they discussed the possibility of waiting for more data before any announcement of a large new planet within the outer reaches of our own solar system. The lid would not stay on for long, since the *V-7* data went out to so many venues. Questions were beginning to arrive as to why the data was not being sent out as usual. Any interruption of the regular transmission caused near instant inquiries.

Most representatives at the meeting wanted to know why the new object had eluded previous detection. In fact, in many subtle ways, it had been detected, when other data streams from various sensors were analyzed more thoroughly. Astronomers were not looking for it and most did not have optics capable of detecting the well-hidden orb. Most were looking for planets orbiting distant stars, not their own. They were looking for fleas and had missed the elephant the fleas were riding on. It was well-camouflaged, and their focus was for much more distant planets. The newest data was irrefutable when taken as a whole.

With a programmed adjustment and a planned course change, *V-7* would be able to obtain a much closer look—but it was still going to be a long way off. Hank, David, and Margie programmed and sent directions to *V-7* to facilitate the course change maneuver. As the distance decreased, they would get much more detail and would be able to obtain better information from the onboard systems.

Hank and Lawrence Greenbaum from Eurospace made the critical decision. Hank asked if it was all right with the foreign representatives, respecting as much protocol as possible, to inform the President first. He proposed setting up a teleconference joint announcement for that evening. The vote was split with two strong dissenters, who were not pleased with this arrangement due to the time of day in their countries and the fact that the United States President would get the good publicity. Hank assured the dissenters that they could warn their news services in advance that a major story was breaking. They reluctantly returned to the fold, and after considerable argument, gave their affirmative support.

David and Margie almost had their hands shaken off and were overwhelmed by the repeated pats on the back. The crowd of delegates surrounded them, and Hank watched with a smile as they were engulfed by the group of smiling well-wishers.

Hank remembered the staff-cut problem he had pondered earlier that afternoon, and knew he'd never let them go unless forced. Not after this day; but he knew that he would never have let it happen anyway. At this moment they were again at their best; they were a magnificent team.

July 9, 2029 6:15 p.m.

David slipped out of the meeting, headed back to his office and closed the door behind him. He fielded questions for hours and was about OD'd on coffee. The sandwich for lunch was long gone. Margie was still in the conference room talking and socializing with the group. She sensed his stress level and whispered to him to slip away—he did so at the first opportunity. David was grateful and fatigued, but adrenaline was still coursing through his body and he felt himself trembling. He wondered if it was the excitement of the discovery, the caffeine, or simply exhaustion and decided it was probably a combination of all three.

Hank made arrangements to speak directly to the President. He respected all of his esteemed colleagues at the committee meeting, but could he trust them all to not jump the gun on the announcement? He didn't want to take that chance. While they were still Margie's captive audience, he began the task of setting the wheels in motion. Larry Greenbaum was completely trustworthy and was making certain that no one left the conference room. He was literally standing guard at the door. Restroom breaks required a security escort. So far no one had even tried to leave since the meeting began.

Hank Wadkins was efficient. As Project Director International, he made good use of his excellent organizational and communication skills, and was well-liked and respected by everyone in both NASA and Eurospace.

Wadkins knew the White House Press Secretary, Zeke (ZZ) Rogers and the President's personal secretary, Elizabeth Rainwater, fairly well. Zeke was perfect for the job: great credentials, total loyalty to the President, a big ego, and he enjoyed the limelight. Liz was Native American, straightforward, equally loyal and an impenetrable buttress when the President didn't want to be bothered.

He had decided to call Liz first and ask her if the president was available. Her initial response was a friendly, "Hello Mr. Wadkins. Is this important or a social call?"

"Liz, this is important, and I really need to speak to him as soon as possible," Hank returned. "Is he there now, and if so, can he be disturbed for a few moments?"

"He's here and not with anyone, I believe. Let me check for you." Just that quickly she was gone, and he was listening to nothing, no music or information, just silence on the line.

Hank was surprised when the president came on in only a few seconds. The president greeted Hank with a friendly, "How's V-7, Hank?"

Hank was always a little awestruck by President Walker's unpretentious and casual attitude.

"Fine, Mr. President," Hank replied. "Can you get a hold of ZZ fairly quickly and set up something?"

"What's up, Hank?" replied the President. "Do you have a problem with V-7 or with the press?"

"Well sir, we've have obtained a rather incredible piece of scientific information. Very soon, it will leak to the press or simply be announced somewhere. I, or we, figured that the initial announcement might be best if it came directly from you."

"Me steal your or Larry Greenbaum's thunder? Why Hank, what have you got? You usually only want presidential support when there's a tragedy in the program."

Hank chose his words carefully and delivered the message directly, but it still came out awkwardly. "We may have detected, well, we have detected—discovered a new large planet within the outer reaches of our own solar system."

"A new planet close to earth, not circling some distant star? How is that possible in this day and age?" President Walker inquired. "We've known about the other ones forever, or at least that's what my science education taught me. A new planet, not just an ice ball? "My God, just don't tell me that it's on a collision course with Earth! I just saw another rerun of the remake of *Armageddon* last night. I couldn't sleep."

"No, nothing like that," replied Hank. "It's an obscure little son-of-a-gun that just showed up on some *V-7* photos. From what we can tell so far, it has some amazing properties. I'll fill you in on what we know before the official announcement."

"I think I see why you can't keep a lid on it," the President countered. "Do you want to make the news this evening?"

"Yes sir," Hank answered. "Scientifically, this is big. Can you imagine the boost for the space program, morale, and the basic, mainstream interest?"

"I'm with you, Hank," the president shot back. "I'll have Zeke contact you ASAP. Eight p.m. prime time your target? OK, let's get it moving." Hank heard the click signaling their conversation was over.

July 9, 2019 6:50 p.m.

ZZ Rogers was efficient. His pager went off in the middle of dinner at The Empress Fine Dining. Zeke was especially fond of good Chinese food and was not pleased by the interruption. His mood changed with his surprise at the caller ID code, which he immediately recognized as the President's. The message read, "Big news, return ASAP." He asked for the check and saw the chagrin on his wife's face. He also felt the immediate sense of disappointment from his twelve-year-old twins.

His family rarely had the opportunity to have dinner together, and now this one had to be interrupted. When he explained that the call had come directly from President Walker, it only partially mitigated their disappointment. Zeke called a cab for his family, kissed them goodbye, and told them to enjoy dinner. He left the restaurant and trotted toward his car. The restaurant was only a half hour drive from the White House.

7:50 p.m.

Zeke was on the telephone the entire half hour after he abandoned his family at the restaurant. He knew that the press corps had been summoned and were waiting as he pulled into his private parking space. A lot of the regular press would be angry at this short notice and a few of the junior members would almost certainly be present. He had been briefed, but due to the lack of total security on the cellular systems he was still unsure of the exact nature of the announcement.

He was further briefed by the President himself, who was reading from a page marked at the top with the words "Secure – Urgent." "Ten minutes and we go live," Zeke thought aloud. "This is crazy." He landed this post due to his sharp wits, quick thinking, and ability to handle pressure. This situation was going to challenge all of these personality traits and then some.

8:05 p.m.

President Walker stepped to the podium as Zeke Rogers finished his ad-lib introduction. The President looked as distinguished as ever, and his poise was near perfect. He was connected by teleconference with NASA, Eurospace, and several leading scientists recognized as experts in the planetary sciences. Questions permeated the atmosphere of the hastily assembled conference. The murmur from the press contingent was slightly louder than usual due to their overwhelming curiosity.

The President began this special press conference by saying, "Ladies and Gentlemen and distinguished participants, I am honored to have been selected to deliver this startling revelation. I will be forced by my limited knowledge of the situation itself to limit questions until I am better informed."

"At approximately 8:05 a.m., central time, thirty-six hours ago, Mr. David Striker, Assistant Director of the NASA V-7 Program, made an amazing scientific discovery. A previously undetected large planet has been detected within the outer reaches of our own solar system."

He paused for effect and to let it sink in for a moment. An immediate buzz of excitement ran through the audience, and he could tell that his delivery had elicited the desired response from the press corps, who began shouting questions.

When they stopped, President Walker continued with a less dramatic intonation. "V-7 is being reprogrammed in order to make necessary course changes, the planned results of which should be to give us a much closer look. The discovery has been verified and independently confirmed by two other prominent astronomy teams as well as the Jet Propulsion Lab in Pasadena. Detailed analyses are continuing as I speak. Photos will be released this evening and, when I finish, I'll be turning this conference over to Hank Wadkins, the V-7 Project Director, for questions."

— § —

David was stunned. He sat in the conference room with the other members of the V-7 team to watch the formal announcement. When President Walker said his name, he had closed his eyes. Upon opening them he felt every eye in the room on him, even those in the control room through the glass. The silence in the room was nearly deafening. He felt trapped for a moment, and a sense of near panic raced through him.

It was Margie who let out the first whoop. Then the entire room burst into a crescendo of cheers, and Margie shouted above them all, "I've got the first round."

"Hank should be here," thought David. "He handles the press so well."

It was nearly 9:15 p.m. when Hank returned to the conference room. Chinese take-out was strewn about everywhere. A few of the foreign visitors stayed to celebrate while a few others left to call their respective agencies. Everyone with the V-7 Project was still there.

Hank was hungry. Betty had not left either and she handed him a plate with a warm smile. "Don't forget to call your wife," she reminded him. "I'll bet you forgot."

"Oh darn, you're right, I did," he said as Margie handed him a cell phone. "They work again." "We turned security down a bit. Hope it's OK, boss."

He grinned as he dialed the number. Betty noticed the glint in his eyes. He looked a little fatigued, but he was definitely beaming.

His wife answered as Hank shook David's hand firmly, sincerely and said simply, "Nice going."

"Hi honey," came from the earpiece.

"Sorry I forgot to call back," he said

"Congratulations to you, David, Margie, and the whole team. I understand," added Helen Wadkins. "That was a pretty impressive performance, and what do you do for an encore?"

Hank's response nearly floored everyone who was listening. "If I have anything to say about it," he emphasized. "We go there."

4

DECISION

August 4, 2029

NEARLY A MONTH had passed since the planetary discovery and life around the *Voyager* 7 Project was returning to normal. There were a few new personnel around, and everyone with *V-7* was more focused on the mission. In fact, the entire program had taken on a new aura of importance and pride.

The mid-course direction change instructions were sent to *V-7*. The craft acknowledged the instructions and sent a second confirmation to NASA upon initiation of the maneuver. The hope was to re-energize the ion propulsion system and send the craft on a generally intercepting course to send the *V-7* in the direction of the new solar system object and eventually use the planet's own gravity to swing *V-7* much closer.

The initial maneuver worked perfectly and the chase was now on over the vast expanse of space separating the planet and *V-7*, the pursuer seeking its quarry and the gap between the two narrowed rapidly.

New images came in as fast as the telemetry computers could send them. Upon receipt at various Earth stations, they were decoded, processed, and dispersed to the experts for analysis. Much more was now becoming known about Earth's mysterious new neighbor.

David and Margie were now well-known too, and were receiving near constant media attention. Everyone knew their names and faces as well as their new fixation, Enigma. The designation of Enigma was temporary, there was an elaborate plan to give this orb a permanent name. Eurospace and NASA started a contest to name it—a type of worldwide lottery. This lottery brought with it increased interest in the various space programs throughout the world, not to mention raising large sums of money needed for these programs.

David had made sure that Margie received proper and much-deserved credit too. This entire situation, which brought them considerable fame, also brought them much closer together. At first, they were completely overwhelmed by the publicity, but now they were learning to cope—as well as finding ways to hide from the press. They worked out some elaborate plans for avoiding reporters and traveling incognito. Whenever David went near his residence, reporters the curious, mobbed him.

David decided to move in with Margie during the last week of July. Although they had talked about it for quite some time, the decision became easy for both mutual support and mutual protection. They were hounded everywhere they went, and her townhouse provided more space, security, and privacy.

Hank did not like their decision. He patently disliked unfavorable publicity or intra-program gossip. Hank felt relief when David and Margie announced that they were living together to the entire V-7 group, and to the always hungry-for-news press entourage. Going public quickly cut down on the chances for negative feedback; besides, Hank had never seen them happier. They made a cute couple.

Enigma was slowly giving up its long-distance secrets. It was about the size of Mars, and preliminary analysis indicated that it had an atmosphere of various gases and suspended carbon or some carbon-like material. It did not give off much light and was almost completely invisible to most light gathering instruments, which included earth-based telescopes. This new discovery was a unique solar system object; a stealth planet.

This stealth world had even escaped the powerful eye of the Hubble Telescope still in Earth orbit. Though after intense review of Hubble files, this proved to be untrue. Enigma had passed through its field of view on at least three occasions, one of which was noted in a computer file as simply, "questionable photo reliability." Hubble had actually seen the planet, but the pictures focused on a distant region where stars were born in the Orion Nebula, a star in Orion's belt from Earth view.

Enigma appeared to have a solid to semi-solid core with a probable solid surface, although some data contradicted this observation. It was certain that it had a gaseous atmosphere fifty plus miles thick, held in place by a calculated, though fluctuating, gravity one half to one third of Earth gravity. Actual determination of surface morphology was almost impossible due to thick clouds and their strange low albedo characteristics. They were virtually impenetrable to even V-7's impressive array of sensors.

One thing was certain. This new planet was warmer at or near the surface, not very frigid like the other outer planets. Speculation ran rampant as to the source of this heat so far from the warming sun. Scientists suggested that nuclear, volcanic, or chemical processes were at work to make it that much warmer so distant from our sun. However, the exact cause remained hidden by dense, obscuring clouds.

The outer atmosphere was unique and the key to the planet's many secrets. Preliminary analysis indicated that the upper layers were very dense and stormy. The density diminished and the turbulence mitigated inward toward the surface. This was the opposite of the gas giant, Jupiter, and made the planet a little more Earth-like.

Every piece of data just fueled more speculation and debate. Guesses of mean surface temperature ranged from far below freezing to semi-molten. It was obvious from the beginning to everyone working on the project that Enigma, the new stealth wonder, was different from any other object in our solar system.

Everyone throughout the scientific community held theories as to how this interesting solar system resident obtained its unique characteristics. David and Margie, in conjunction with several colleagues, coined an interesting and credible explanation. Their premise was plausible because of its simplicity, and the public liked it because the theory contained no ideas that were too difficult to explain.

The theory began with a distant cold planet, perhaps looking much like Saturn which underwent a spontaneous change within the very core itself, caused by or causing a collapse of the planet's gravity. This gravity collapse was initiated by intense nuclear reaction deep within the globe. The core may have changed from solid to liquid. A veritable gravity explosion inward or implosion resulted, causing numerous rings of dust and carbon surrounding the planet to spontaneously collapse inward. The collapsing rings then combined to create the present thick, dark, tumultuous, swirling outer shell of opaque atmosphere.

The rebounding gravity wave would cause intense volcanism to break through the surface and trigger the release of numerous gases. This allowed for the creation of a new atmosphere. The outward rebound kept the rings from reaching the surface completely. It also helped explain the present non-polar, patchy gravity situation they had detected. Over time, the atmosphere underwent evolution into the present makeup, similar to the evolution on Earth.

There were as many scoffers as adherents to this theory, but it did have fairly wide support. David and Margie would at least have the unique opportunity to continue to study this planet and to plan and conduct the experiments that would solve parts of this puzzle. They had discovered this mysterious beauty and wanted to be responsible for answers to many more of its secrets.

Another group of planetary science specialists held to the notion that Enigma was in a state, not unlike the situation on Earth, when a meteorite impact caused the dinosaur extinction. A meteor or perhaps an ancient moon may have been pulled in by gravity and collided with the planet. The resulting debris formed a thick, choking, and sun-blocking cloud cover. Since Enigma was without obvious moons or rings, this counter-theory fit well and also explained active volcanism.

There was another factor about Enigma that was difficult to explain. If the dense shell-like clouds consisted of debris such as planetary surface, rock and dust, or meteoric debris, then Enigma should reflect light more like the other planets. Somehow the "shell" of Enigma absorbed light more than reflecting it back into space. It had to contain new, and as yet unexplained, characteristics or materials.

August 9, 2029 12:00 p.m.

A full month had passed since the announcement. Everyone, plus a few new faces, had returned for the monthly V-7 Project Meeting. Data had been disseminated to everyone associated with the V-7 Project, the usual scientific groups, and some new players representing astronomy and astrophysics colleges and universities worldwide.

Nothing had stirred such controversy in the history of the Internet. Everyone desired to know more, and theories now abounded from the strictly scientific to the profoundly absurd. One group dubbed it the black planet, a symbol of death, and proclaimed that the fires of hell caused the heat. David was particularly fond of this one and even added small horns to one of the photos. It hung on the bulletin board next to the coffee bar. Within an hour the photo was sporting a mustache and mischievous grin.

Hank Wadkins convened the meeting two hours early, and his plans called for a full day tomorrow. He was letting Larry Greenbaum handle most of this meeting since Larry had been low profile for most of the big day last month. Hank knew that Larry had an ego almost as big as his girth.

Larry was full of vigor and had a lengthy agenda planned for discussion and presentation of unreleased findings from thirty days of intense scientific scrutiny. Larry had just returned from Paris, London, and the Eurospace group meeting in Tokyo. His last stop on his itinerary had been at the White House for a briefing with President Walker. Rumor had it that something was up with the space station and the current plans for the Mars mission. Hank wondered why Larry visited with the President, but he knew that he would find out soon enough.

Greenbaum wasted no time in dropping his announcement bomb. After the meeting was called to order, he turned from his seat at the head of the table to Hank on his right and said, "Do you remember the last thing that you said to your wife on the night that we made the formal discovery announcement?"

Hank laughed and indicated that he had no idea. "Probably, 'see you short-ly,'" he said.

Lawrence Greenbaum just smiled. "That's not too far off. Hank, the last thing that you said was, 'If I had my way, we'd go there.' That thought hasn't left my head since you uttered it. Yesterday, Eurospace, NASA, and the governments of twenty-four countries agreed to do just that. We are to immediately begin the task of upgrading the Mars Project to send a manned probe to Enigma instead. Not to just study the feasibility, but to do it."

Hank's chin felt like it was somewhere near his lap. David and Margie showed signs of ecstasy shock. The "green bomb" stunned them all, but the spontaneous burst of questions that ended the momentary silence was overwhelming. David never dreamed that he would see seventy-eight-year-old professor "Bow Tie Carson" jumping for joy, but there he was, hopping around like a four-year-old with a new puppy. Hank was hugging Greenbaum, another sight David would have bet the house that he would never see.

That evening, David and Margie slipped away inconspicuously and had a quiet dinner away from the group, splitting a bottle of Merlot. It was a warm, beautiful evening, so they went for a stroll along the beach near Galveston. Neither had said much about the project all evening. They had to clear their heads. Larry adjourned the meeting at just past four, and a huge dinner celebration was scheduled at six thirty.

It was now almost nine. David and Margie stood together looking up at the sky over the Gulf of Mexico in the general direction of Enigma. David said it first. "I want to go. I trained to be an astronaut. I had the right stuff. I dreamed." He covered his eyes with his hands and Margie heard the slight sob.

Margie put a hand on his shoulder, then faced him and put a hand on each shoulder. "Then go," she said in a kind but strong voice. "Go for it, make the team—give it a shot."

He uncovered his eyes and gazed into hers. "I couldn't leave you, and besides, they'll probably want a bunch of young kids."

"You won't be leaving me. I'm going too. If you can make it, I can too. Besides, she confidently added, they will have to take both of us or put up with our constant harassment."

"Let's walk," he said and they continued back toward the car in silence. David loved this woman. She always made him think and never ceased to amaze him. He also knew that when she put her mind to something, it could become an obsession.

He remembered their first close encounter. It had been their fourth or fifth date. They had gone back to her place to have coffee or tea and ended up having tea on the terrace. They'd watched the clouds of steam rising off of her hot tub. The stars had been beautiful, the air crisp and clear, adding twinkle to the heavens. He remembered again that the forecast had called for the possibility of a light freeze by the next evening.

He had remarked that the hot tub looked inviting. She said that it was nicest when it was cool like this. She disappeared and returned with two gigantic fluffy towels. Without hesitation, she slid out of her clothes and slipped into the water stating simply that clothing and swimsuits were not good in the hot tub.

David was comfortable with nudity. He piled his clothes on his chair and started to get in, only to find her blocking the steps from below.

"You stay in great shape," she commented as she sat back and moved to one side of the tub. David had said the first thing that came to his mind as he felt a cold breeze on his back. "If you block the stairs, I'm going to have to hang around out here."

He remembered those words so well. They had both roared with laughter and he had nearly fallen getting in. The rest of the evening had been a dream. He could never have imagined a better fantasy. He still thought about it, and he always felt that special warmth for her whenever the thought returned.

They were approaching the car, and he squeezed her hand gently. They embraced and kissed with the passion of new love. The joggers across the street winked at each other and panted on their way.

5

THE SHIP

O N August 19 NASA, Eurospace, the Japanese, Canadians, and Russians all agreed in principle, with some reservations, to change the Mars mission to the Enigma mission. Plans for the exploratory vessel to reach Enigma and return were ambitious if not almost unrealistic. NASA and Eurospace engineers began putting components together and creating the most unwieldy space vehicle ever devised. They planned a twelve-month building phase, including ground based and in-orbit fabrication. It became readily apparent to the planners that this schedule would be unfeasible. They wanted an October 2030 date for the earliest possible launch time. If not for the incredible early success of the ion-drive propulsion experiments, and the fact that the Mars Project was already sixteen months into production, the Enigma project would have taken five-years at a minimum. Fabrication seemed untenable and the results of cutting corners haunted them at every turn.

The first components of the Mars vessel had been launched into orbit and tethered together there for storage and assembly. Mars One was nearing the point for actual assembly of the first sections when major design changes were initiated in order to add a whole new array of components. Retrofitting the new components would present some serious problems. New sections for hydroponic gardens, supply, and fuel storage were needed for a longer trip. The crew size also necessitated considerably more space for personal quarters and supplies. On a trip of this duration, some basic comfort was a necessity. To be ready on time, with a dependable vehicle, the engineers and fabricators needed a miracle.

— § —

Workaholic, yes, addicted to his pursuit, completely, the wiry frail-looking scientist, Ishmael, slept a few hours here and there, but sporadically at best. His complete devotion to his government-sponsored experimental nanotechnology work was commendable; but attention to small details, safety protocols, and standards established when the project began over four years ago started to slip. He became focused on his goal of perfecting nanotechnological fabrication from raw materials. Because he had designed the system, he was confident in its reliability and the banal details of quality control wasted precious time. Ishmael spent more and more hours, many very frustrating, forcing his submicroscopic nano machines to do his bidding.

His lab was a remarkable assembly of supercomputers, glowing hemispheres, and conduits of all shapes and sizes connected to each other in ways which only he understood. Part of his plan was to make himself indispensable, so that he alone understood all of its intricacies. When anything did not work as planned, broke, or failed completely, Ishmael was the only person who was able to repair or restart all of the procedures. This situation was perfect for his sponsor, a covert government agency connected to several space research groups, and made it easy to conceal funding from close scrutiny, but this factor also proved to be its near fatal flaw.

Ishmael was working with one of his closest and most intelligent lab associates when the glitch occurred, when the crucial mistake was made. A safety valve on a transfer conduit temporarily stuck in the open position. Volatile liquids were mixed with the wrong raw material. When Ishmael's latest concoction of nano builders was introduced the computer registered the alert, sounded a warning, and immediately started to shut the procedure down, but it was too late. The resultant explosion killed the lab assistant standing nearby in an instant. Ishmael, preoccupied on the far side of the lab, was protected by a bank of computers and desks and shielded from the worst part of the blast, but not from the materials turned loose by the explosion. The double-redundant lab containment features prevented further escape, but Ishmael was inside, exposed to the unknown dangers of his own creation and trapped to suffer the consequences.

Contamination dangers were planned for in the design and function of the deeply-buried facility. Because the dangers of prolonged nano exposure were still largely unknown, contingencies called for extreme measures. His team had conducted numerous experiments with lab animals and created many scenarios that approximated his present situation. In general there were few serious health problems unless materials used in the research had toxic characteristics. The nano builders simply stopped replication and the process shut down and ended. In experiments with warm-blooded animals and prolonged exposure the builders remained active and subtle physiological changes were detected. Human volunteers were exposed to minute traces and showed only mild reactions.

Ishmael's exposure was extreme. He was well aware of the consequences of his situation and knew his own carelessness had caused his partner's death and his own total isolation. High-level contamination called for the lab to remain sealed and the contents to be incinerated. He also knew that the lab tech was expendable. He was not.

— § —

The International Space Station was finished in 2008, more than a year behind schedule, due to the world economic slowdown triggered by 9/11 and the shuttle tragedy. Begun with the launch into orbit of the first modules in last quarter of 1998, the station had slowly taken shape. Cost overruns had been horrific, nearly causing the project partnership to fall apart. But the station was finished, bigger and better than originally planned and was functioning better than anyone anticipated or expected.

Passenger flights were now a reality. The first commercial passengers were selected dignitaries and VIPs. These VIPs were strictly those who could pay enough and pass the rigorous physical fitness tests. Non-scientific passengers began visiting the station for the first time in February 2025. They were allowed a two-day stay. Seats were based on a lottery system, followed by the same rigorous physical examination and tests.

The project directors decided on a radical new spacecraft design. The new ship was based on a design resembling a modified "Hoberman" sphere or oval. Compact at the time of launch or acceleration, the ship could be expanded to a larger size for more comfortable travel. The expanded state created a much larger surface area, which would be covered with solar energy gathering materials. In its compacted state it somewhat resembled a rounded flying saucer. While expanded, it would also rotate to even out the temperature and create a sense of gravity. The rotating modified Hobermanesque design was still intact, but the entire project scale was very much enlarged.

Plans called for a launch from orbit. The vessel was to be fabricated from pieces shuttled into orbit. Assembly personnel would live aboard the International Space Station. Not having to escape the gravity pull of the Earth's surface would save on fuel expended during launch. The ship would be hurtled into deep space using a combination of computer coordinated propulsion systems.

Ion propulsion drive was the newest system. Its use would make the voyage many times faster than the conventional space travel methods used in early space exploration. Instead of years, this trip would take only months; thirteen to fifteen months duration was expected. With orbital, landing, and exploration time, the entire voyage, and return, would be less than three years if all went well. The return part was the primary uncertainty, but no one expected not to return. Without ion drive, moving at the speed of the early Voyager platforms, the trip could take almost thirty years.

The ship plan was amazing if anyone could figure out how to actually complete it. It was designed to rotate, creating a sense of gravity. With the new magnetic suits, quasi-gravity was obtainable. The benefits of magnetic fields on the body were well known. Coupled with a magnetic field in the craft and the semi-magnetic boots and suit the crew would wear, the body could be coaxed into believing that it was experiencing gravity. Early tests aboard the space station had proven successful, but there were still problems to work out.

The new ship was soon dubbed the *HobieKat*. Components were built in factories around the world. More people were working on it in some way, worldwide, than the numbers that built the pyramids or dug the Panama Canal.

Lee Tanaka, a fast-speaking Japanese electronics wizard, was the project manager. No one knew if he had ever slept or where he derived his intense energy, but he never slowed down. Lee claimed it was an herbal concoction his mom prepared from a traditional Japanese holistic medical treatise. Most of his co-workers believed it was his hereditary work ethic supported by pure genius.

It was also Lee's genius that led to the development of the ultra-light, ultra-strong, electronically conductive, and solar energy gathering material that would form the outer shell of the *HobieKat* when in its expanded form. Made of Kevlar and titanium and interwoven with his electronic mesh, this material was finding more uses every day. The invention of the material brought Lee immense wealth, which he hardly noticed, given his complete dedication to his work.

In its collapsed configuration, the *HobieKat* formed a compact shape, and the ion propulsion system and particle beam propulsion system accelerated it like a bullet fired from a gun. In its expanded form, it would be an immense energy-producing, rotating labyrinth moving at incredible speed. It could be secured and collapsed and prepared for an acceleration phase or course correction. The biggest problem in its design to date was slowing it down and controlling rotation, but these problems were being conquered. Several miniature, unmanned versions had passed their tests, and a two-man version was rolling around helplessly in orbit. A space plane was launched to retrieve it and rescue two very disoriented cosmonauts.

Space planes would be launching monthly from the Kennedy Space Center, the Baikonir Cosmodrome in Kazakhstan, or the Eurospace Launch Facility. Ferrying various components to the space station, each would return for another load, like trucks at a supermarket. The manned contingent of technicians in orbit aboard the space station was doubled for two-month shifts. Their job would be to put the components together like a giant jigsaw puzzle. Fortunately for the technicians, components built on the ground were trial fitted on Earth several times, prior to launch, in order to make their jobs a bit easier.

Security was beyond anything ever devised. Lee Tanaka knew it if someone burped too loud on the ground or in the air once the pieces had been delivered for launch. When he took over, he wanted passenger shuttles stopped immediately. He was overruled by the directors, who quickly pointed out that the lottery to pick the passenger list had already raised more than 380 million dollars for his project. But Lee was still concerned about overall project security. At least he had complete control over everyone on the Space Station, and no one was going to sneak anything aboard. He had devised a security and quality control system that worked, even though it was laborious and stringent.

But even with Lee's guidance and the massive human effort, the *HobieKat* could not be finished on time, without innumerable bugs, not without cutting many corners—and that was not Lee's style. High standards and no cutting corners were the reasons he was a near unanimous choice for the position of Project General Director.

His troops and crew were led and directed by Hank Wadkins and Hank's Chief Engineer, Larry Kraft. Lee expected hard work and undying dedication, and Hank and Larry were good at their jobs, but at this point, even Lee was praying for a miracle, because without one, his mission was headed for a spectacular and expensive failure.

— § —

Hank called Larry into his office in Houston. They were discussing Lee's construction dilemma. "My God, how are we gonna build something big enough and bad enough to carry ten sky jockeys to the end of the solar system? Hank, the Mars mission is in its earliest stages. We've been building that beast for over a year, and are still having problems with the design, and with making enough fuel on the surface of Mars to bring our people back. The logistics of going that many times farther just seem untenable. The lathe monkeys in the shops can fabricate just about anything you need, given enough time and with plenty of our most precious commodity, large piles of bucks, but what you're asking us to do will take a miracle. Can we do it? Eventually.

Good old American know-how and international technical support can build your ship. The freakin' world may go broke doing it, but yes, we can. Now, making it safe enough, and giving the crew a realistic chance of coming home, that's where it's going to be tough.

"Larry, what if I told you that there might be a way to build parts of the ship, faster, cheaper, and safer than you've ever imagined?" Hank let his thought sink in to give Larry's questioning demeanor a chance to look for the how response. Larry Kraft was the senior development engineer on NASA's prestigious staff of fabrication and development specialists, a man who could envision, design, and physically create the most extraordinary parts, and then make them all invisibly mesh into the perfect final machine. He was a workaholic, overweight, and terribly in love with Margie; a fact he didn't hide, even though he knew she was infatuated with David.

"Hank, I know your background. I know how you think. I know what you eat, where you live, and even a few of your bad habits. If you're playing mind games, I wouldn't like it, and you know that. What have you got up your sleeve? Unless you're planning on usin' a little red sled and eight tiny reindeer, you gotta' be talkin' about something I don't know anything about." And Kraft took great satisfaction in knowing everything about every project at NASA.

"Exactly, Larry. You don't know anything about it because only a handful of very special people do. I'm one of the lucky one's who just got in the loop. Buried deep underground beneath a mesa in New Mexico is a top-secret government project labeled, "Ishmael". What I say about this was classified until only a few hours ago. Ever heard of nanotechnology?"

"Yeah, colleges and industry have been working on it for years, little bitty materials engineered atom by atom, microscopic self-replicating machines, or shit like that. I've read about it and even heard the rumors about a secret government project to make it work. Very expensive and lots of potential problems like: what happens if they get loose, what happens to the environment? I guess they'd have to keep it deep under ground to lessen the potential for letting the things loose in nature before they know the ramifications. People still remember the old movie *The Andromeda Strain*."

"You've done your homework, Larry, and already know a lot more than the average person. It's time you learned a little more. These things apparently can now be programmed to self-replicate a material and follow a computer design to build things. Specifically, they've been programmed to make Lee Tanaka's fabulous material from the basic elements. It comes out perfect, iridescent, near-translucent and can be done most efficiently in weightlessness. The last shuttle mission with the 'special scientific experiments' proved it would work.

It was the dry run test and everything worked better than the computer simulations and models. Get the picture?"

"Holy shit!"

"That's what I said. Now, we can safely move the materials into space, in orbit, feed in the raw materials, and turn the nanos loose to do their job. The little sons-a-bitches thrive under those conditions and work until they're outta food. Then they sit there dormant until you start the process up again."

"Hank, you make it sound like they're alive."

"Machines, submicroscopic self-replicating tools to do just the job you need. And, best of all, cheap!"

"When do I get to see this for myself?"

"Tomorrow, if you can sleep tonight. We leave to go see the lab and get the first demo open to those not directly involved in the project. If that goes well, the public gets another incredible scoop to go with our last one. We're on a roll here, and we got some great people involved all the way to the top."

"Hank, you never cease to amaze me. Guess that's why you got the job. If you think I'm going to be able to sleep tonight, you're wrong. Man, I want to see the little things work. If they can help me build my, I mean our ship, I'll kiss their micro-miniature asses."

"Well, I can't tell you a lot more cause that's about the sum total that I know about it to this point. I can't wait to see the demo either. We're both in for a real treat. We're on a Lear headed for Los Alamos at 7:30. I'll pick you up on the way."

— § —

Lulled to sleep by the rhythm of the pavement grooves slipping beneath the tires, Larry is startled awake by the sudden fishtail lurch of the car, and the sound of rubber on gravel. "God damn rabbits!" Larry realizes that Hank may have dozed off too, but a look over his shoulder at the road kill disappearing in the heat mirage on the hot pavement behind them proves him wrong.

"Too many of those varmints anyway, Hank," Larry groans while rubbing his tired eyes. "Nobody's gonna miss him."

Hank was slowing down in the middle of nowhere USA. Larry didn't know how long he'd been asleep but the dash clock indicated at least a half hour had passed since he'd last glanced at it. The scenery was a nice change from home, but he'd slept little since Hank's revelation. They were slowing to turn into a small innocuous side road with no markings except for some rusted and bullet-riddled no trespassing signs. Wide enough to handle two-way traffic, the gate, set back one hundred feet or more from the road, was a single twisted bar, held to a leaning wooden post by a small, weak-looking chain. The dusty road on the opposite side was little more than a single track through the rugged high desert terrain.

Pulling up to the flimsy gate Larry opened his door, but Hank was already stepping out to undo the chain. No lock, just a few well-oxidized chain links hung over a bent nail kept the gate in its closed position.

A quarter mile past the gate the road dropped into a small cobbled arroyo and turned abruptly to the left following the channel of the dry streambed. At another sharp turn parallel to a meander Hank braked hard and swirling dust momentarily obliterated their path. When the small cloud cleared they both read the larger sign directly ahead: "Warning, bridge out, road closed, no vehicular traffic beyond this point." Below that in freshly painted red letters: "U.S. Government property, all trespassers will be stopped and prosecuted to the fullest extent of the law. The use of deadly force is authorized."

Hank smiled, started up again and just kept on going. "Damn, Hank, the sign said bridge out."

"I know what it said. I hope you smiled for the cameras. That's the first checkpoint. If you're not authorized to pass that spot, the security boys would already be on their way and the sensors would have you pinpointed, identified, and locked for intercept. They're real sensitive about who gets in and exactly how far they get. They don't mess around here. We were under scrutiny when we pulled off the highway."

A mile or so farther on they came to the first sure signs of human presence, a imposing security fence with a clear perimeter in front of it. Beside the road stood a bunker-like cement structure with heavily tinted glass. Stepping out of the small building, a uniformed guard waved them forward, and smiled as they pulled up beside him. "Hello Mr. Watkins, Mr. Kraft, we've been expecting you. The other two gentlemen joining you just pulled off the highway and should be with you two soon. Would you mind stepping out for a moment after driving your vehicle onto the concrete pad?" The guard was quite polite. His companion remained in the doorway, with a nasty looking gun leveled directly at them.

From outward appearance, the entrance to the underground lab looked like nothing more than a small outbuilding on a former hardened ICBM base. Hank knew that this had been a launching site, but newer ones, and a mobile strategic nuclear submarine fleet, had rendered it all but obsolete, and its current use was far more potentially productive.

Once inside the entrance, they rode a small elevator down to another level, and then proceeded through an elaborate security checkpoint. They donned clean-suit coveralls, and another plus one-minute elevator ride brought them to a dimly-lit foyer before immense blast doors. A single heavy steel door in the right hand blast shield glided silently open, and a frail-looking little man standing within motioned for them to enter.

"Greeting Mr. Watkins, hello Mr. Kraft. They call me Ishmael. Welcome to the project that bears my name. Mr. Tanaka and his assistant will be joining us shortly. Yes, I see that they have arrived."

Larry offered a handshake but Ishmael withdrew his tiny, gloved hand. "Let me show you around a bit while we wait for the others," Ishmael continued. Larry was a little miffed at the refusal of the handshake. "Don't worry about the handshake Mr. Kraft. Proper procedures and contamination prevention protocols necessitate the elimination of some things."

Larry had not given a clue about his feelings and was very careful with his body language, especially his oversized body, *"So how had the little man known what I was thinking?"*

Hank ignored it all and was already intently studying the contents of the room. In a few minutes Tanaka and his associate joined them. Ishmael was touting the wonders of his research, expounding upon his secret project. "Gentleman, I can show far better than I can explain. If you would be so kind as to follow me into the lab, I'll demonstrate the wonders of nanotechnology."

Through another set of steel doors, the four guests stepped into a cavernous room filled with an array of computers, containers, ductwork of all sizes, miles of wires, and numerous Plexiglas-like domes.

"Rather than explain each step of the process, I'd rather just show you how it works." Mr. Kraft would you please allow me the use of one of your blueprint diagrams? Perhaps the G-652 strut brace would be a good start." Ishmael waited expectantly while Larry shuffled through the one file he'd been allowed to bring with him. Larry wondered, *"Hank didn't even know what was in my file, so how did Ishmael determine what parts specs I'd brought along?"* Larry was beginning to feel a bit uneasy about Ishmael. He couldn't place the accent, couldn't see any telltale facial features or get any feel for this man's origin. Larry prided himself on telling a lot about a person's background by his features, but this one he could not place. Handing him the part diagram, Ishmael just looked him in the eyes and smiled.

"Let me first show with this part what we have achieved here. Mr. Tanaka, I will then demonstrate just how easily we can fabricate your experimental material."

Ishmael placed the blueprint on a large device that looked very much like an oversized antique flatbed scanner. Pushing a few buttons the computer attached to it whirred to life and the process began. They all gathered in front of one of the clear domes to watch. Within the clear hemisphere stood a small raised countertop that looked like it was covered with a glistening liquid metal. The contents of the dome began to glow a shimmering purple-blue. Shafts of multicolored light shot from all directions, illuminating the center table, shooting from it and converging toward it in a fantastic display. The outline of the G-652 plan appeared in the shining countertop, first in two dimensions and then in a spectacular three-dimensional holographic image.

In only a few more seconds the amorphous metallic countertop began to move. Tiny dendrites of shimmering liquid metal streaming over the lines of the blueprint in ebb-and-flow patterns of incredible beauty and iridescence. Before their eyes the form of the strut brace began to take solid form in less than two minutes; the piece was completed in under five. The glowing dome fell silent. Fan motors whirred briefly and the computer screen soon read: Task Completed. Slowly the clear glass dome rose as slack-jawed incredulous observers moved in for a closer look.

Larry was captivated and reached for the piece without thinking or asking, suddenly realizing his foolish mistake. *"I could be burned badly if its still hot,"* he thought.

"Go ahead, Larry, pick it up, examine it. It won't burn you, it's not even hot." Ishmael sounded triumphant. Larry was dumbfounded again, this time because Ishmael had seemed to read his mind again, more so from this fact than the object now firmly in his hand. He hefted it in a mock gesture of weighing the piece, examined the details, traced it and fondled G-652 until Hank decided to take a closer look for himself. Satisfied that it was the real thing, Hank passed it in turn to Tanaka.

Tanaka's new material was the next test. This one went as smoothly as the first; Lee testing the material in every way he could in Ishmael's lab. Questions and answers continued for another hour, when Ishmael informed the group that Larry was hungry. Larry hadn't said a thing, and was caught up in Lee's work at the time. Larry looked at Hank and said, "I hadn't even heard my stomach growl," he laughed at Hank, but caught himself in mid-sentence. It had happened once more; it was as though he'd read his mind again.

Hank had been paying little attention to Larry but noticed his colleague begin to sweat in the cool lab. Larry leaned toward Hank and whispered a quiet, "Look at his finger where it shows through his torn glove. He ripped it a few minutes ago helping Lee and hasn't noticed." Hank turned to look at Ishmael as the tiny scientist covered his right hand with his left in front of him, obscuring the gloved hand with the tear. That was the acid test. Larry knew that Ishmael was mind reading somehow. Ishmael knew that it was time to send his guests up for their luncheon.

"Dinner is served back at the second level," he announced. Gesturing toward the door they all fell in line and headed for the now open exit door. At the outer portal in the blast shield, Ishmael stopped just short of leaving and bid his guests good day. "I must prepare my equipment for shipment to the Cape. Don't want to keep the NASA folks waiting." They were anxious to ask him more questions over lunch, but he said he seldom ate anymore, and waved farewell as the portal clicked shut.

Larry said nothing as they rose up the first elevator from the depths of the secluded laboratory, preferring instead to think of the lyrics of his favorite songs. Refusing to even answer a question from Tanaka, he hummed aloud and smiled back. "Ever seen anybody so happy about or preoccupied with the noble avocation of eating?" Hank inquired.

At the top, when the doors opened, Larry nearly burst forth like he was holding his breath. "Hank, he was reading my mind. Not once, not coincidence, he was reading my thoughts. You see how he covered his hand as soon as I pointed it out to you?"

"Larry, he probably had some pretty sophisticated listening devices planted in that room. Believe me, they can pick up the slightest whisper."

"Then what about knowing I'm hungry before I do?" Larry shot back.

"Larry, you're always hungry. It wouldn't take a clairvoyant to see your girth, the time, and hear you gurgling, as well as being a good host."

"He knew I thought the G-652 was hot."

"Larry, we all read that from your reaction."

"You saying they're all coincidences, Hank?"

"Sure could be, Larry. We're also dealing with an incredible mind down there. To him, reading people may be kind of a game."

Tanaka had heard enough. "Hank, he did it to me too. Several times he answered my questions before I asked them. Didn't think anything of it the first time, but the second was a complex question I'd been toying with in my mind. He answered it before I got that far, and looked sheepish when I looked at him in amazement. I shrugged it off and went on, but coupled with what Larry just said, I find it wholly credible.

They walked to the security area and found a nice meal prepared for them on the table. Little was said through lunch and Larry barely touched the food. Noticing, Hank suggested leaving and stopping on the way back to town. Larry agreed and they were on their way back out the gate and onto the highway in less than fifteen minutes.

Not until they were clear of the gate and heading north on the highway did Larry talk about the rip in Ishmael's glove. "Did you see his hand, his finger, Hank?"

"Just a glimpse, but it looked a little strange."

"Hank, it had an iridescent look."

They drove on without another word until they came to a friendly-looking roadside café on the outskirts of town. Both ate well and compared thoughts quietly in a corner, where the locals could not overhear them.

A briefing was scheduled for the morning and both would have much to say. Nanotechnology was breathtaking and invaluable to their present project. The design requirements of the ship were now tenable. The eccentricities or oddity of the inventor could be tolerated.

— §—

When the fabrication of a clean duplicate laboratory began in a large, isolated hanger at the cape, Hank and Larry knew exactly what was happening, but few others understood. Margie and David were not yet in the need-to-know loop. Larry was given the assignment of making sure everything was prepared to meet the specs of Ishmael. He wondered why the little man didn't come to supervise this himself. He was told that Ishmael had to prepare the transfer of a few unique pieces, the keys to what made the nanotechnology work. What he didn't know was that Ishmael was already at the cape awaiting the first available shuttle ride to the ISS. He and his precious and most essential pieces had been secretly flown to the cape and moved into absolute quarantine. The potential for any kind of environmental problem from nanotechnology was a serious reality and every precaution was being taken to completely isolate the scientists and secret equipment involved. Security was total and impenetrable.

In only a few days, the duplicate lab was built to the rigid specifications and packaged for shipment into orbit. It was then also sent to the ISS, and assembled within one of the already fabricated sections of the orbiting ship. Once functional, the nanotech "builders" started their magic; duplicating needed parts one-by-one. These many parts were then added to the existing pieces and the whole then assembled by robotic helpers and floating space walkers.

With the help of Ishmael's technology, the ship took shape quickly and parts were always perfect. The small scientist's arrival aboard the ISS was uneventful until those onboard noticed that he never removed his flightsuit and helmet. He took up residence in one small module and came out only to inspect new parts. Always suited up, he never mixed or socialized with the other workers or crew.

6

THE CREW

DAVID KNEW that the odds were not in his favor. There were at least four crews training for the Mars mission already, and they were the best of the best. He had gotten up the nerve to think it really was possible and walked into Hank's office, took a seat, and simply said: "I want to be on the crew for the Enigma mission." He expected Hank to say, "Dream on," but Hank simply said, "Are you still good enough? Do you think that you still have what it takes?" When David did not respond he added, "If you want my honest opinion, I think that with you they'll be getting their top guy." David was flattered and felt the blush on his face. For a few seconds he was actually at a loss for words—a rarity for him.

It was the second bit of news that he was more hesitant to tell Hank. "Margie wants to go too," David forced out the words. He knew his statement would catch Hank by surprise.

Hank was visibly upset for a moment, but his face changed almost immediately. "Of course," he said. "What a great idea, and besides, you two need to be together. What happens if only one of you can make it?"

"We thought of that and hope to cross that bridge when we get there. My sitting here while she's out there is not comforting. I'm going to have to work extra hard to make sure that doesn't happen. You know how she is once she sets her mind to something." Hank extended his hand, and David was relieved at Hank's support and genuine friendship.

Before he left, Hank added, "You have my full blessing, but you had better finish what you start."

"Count on it, sir," David said as he gave a military salute, turned on his heels, and headed out of the door with a broad smile on his now relaxed face.

David and Margie immediately stepped up their intensive physical fitness program. They pushed each other hard and worked each other's minds as well. Although they always stayed in great shape; working behind their desks, sorting and analyzing the endless images on the monitors burned few calories.

Their daily exercise regimen now doubled.

Hank decided that he would call in all his markers in order to get them on the list for the mission. What he didn't tell David was that he was already on the list for consideration. Margie, on the other hand, was not, at least not yet.

— § —

The early astronauts had all been test pilots; jet jockeys with flight jackets and sunglasses. With the shuttle program, before the turn of the century, came crews with scientists and teachers. Eventually the private flights had begun. The crew for a new kind of specialized mission such as this one would have to be much larger, and would be an interesting cross-section of multitalented individuals with compatible personalities.

Margie was a brilliant scientist and a top physical specimen. She could still run David into the ground, but tended to be much more excitable and didn't handle stress nearly as well. Eurospace was exerting a lot of pressure for a very cosmopolitan crew. At least the numbers gave them a chance. Plans called for an unprecedented crew size of ten space travelers and a ship almost twice the size as that called for in the Mars mission. What were their odds? Crew selection would not be finalized until the last days before the actual mission, and that was still a long way off.

David thought of space pioneer, Alan Shepard and his first sub-orbital flight in 1961. He thought about his hero, John Glenn, NASA's first orbital flight in 1962, February 20; he knew all the dates. October 29, 1998, John flew again at age 77. October 2030, David wanted to be on that flight.

— § —

When word came down that the Mars mission was on hold, Phillip Allen had been beside himself. His frustration turned to anger; all those years of training, a few months to launch, and now this. He had been selected primary pilot and that made him "A number 1" in the astronaut training program. He had basked in the limelight, and now the program was essentially being scrubbed.

Roberto Ortiz, "Orbit" took it in stride. Orbit was Phillip's co-pilot. After calmly listening to Phillip's tirade, he simply said, "New bus, different trip. Come on, Phil, we'll still get the ticket." His optimism was infectious, and he and Phil had set out to get a cold brew and lay out a battle plan to assure them of a trip to this new world.

The competition between the potential crewmembers was fierce, but Phil and Roberto's close friendship and combined talents set them on a course for flight crew #1. They were well versed on the new ion drive propulsion system and had been in on its testing and development for over four years.

— § —

This voyage to Enigma called for a much larger crew than had ever been sent out of orbit in space exploration history. The crew would include a pilot and co-pilot, multitalented systems specialists, a well-trained medic, propulsion systems engineer, a cook or food prep and disposal tech, a geologist, communications expert, EVA specialists, and a human relations specialist.

As in the Mars mission, at least four full crews were being prepared. This time the reason was more critical. The trip to the Stealth Planet was going to be a very long and confining journey, and crew compatibility would be a major factor. The loss of one key person from a crew could potentially force the switch to an entirely new crew. Several particularly critical positions and talent capabilities could only be substituted for by replacing the need with an entire new crew.

This mission would be different in other ways too. The ten-person crew would be shuttled to the space station where they would join their craft already in orbit. All crewmembers were to be carefully trained in multisystem capabilities. Everyone must be versatile in repair and replacement of critical components. As well as being near perfect physical specimens, they would need to be the most mentally competent and compatible group of individuals ever assembled. Close proximity for long periods could bring out the worst in almost anyone. This group would be cooped up in subnormal gravity for more than two years. The space station had proven this feasible with the routine, protracted stays of some of its inhabitants.

A special camaraderie would need to be established within each group. The crews would be teams selected, by not only skills, but also psychologically interlaced by personality, personal habits, sense of humor, phobias, and various other criteria. NASA and Eurospace were training and preparing candidates as thoroughly as possible.

April 2030

David didn't find out about being on the Potential Crew One list until April, and never varied his routine or strict training regimen. He worked even harder to prevent being a late scratch. His personality profile, psychological analysis, and compatibility file fit very well with the other Primary Go Team. David did not do anything to push for Margie to get on that list because of the simple fact that it would not have done any good—and she would have been infuriated if she found out.

Margie's temperament and slight claustrophobia definitely worked against her. Early in the training, the crew selection committee had noticed these traits as well as her insistence on perfection and her intense personal drive. When intense training began, David feared that she would be an early scratch, but her quick thinking and mastery of virtually every system had been a major point maker. She impressed the crew selection committee continually. She even rescued her entire training group from certain disaster during one simulation when the specialist in life support was baffled.

David also knew that the shrinks were interested in couples or pairs due to the longevity of this mission. Their close personal relationship and ability to work together as a team were definite assets. Work in the simulators could have been routine, but not for this mission. The perplexing array of glitches and what-ifs made every day a new challenge.

The Potential Crew One list included forty-eight names. In addition, the backup list included about forty more. From the first list, twenty-four were selected for Crew One with three alternates and twenty-one were cut. Crew Two would come from those left from list one and a few from the backup group. David and Margie both made the first cuts, he in the middle of the list, she as the last alternate.

Once the Crew One group of twelve was selected, if more than three couldn't go for any reason, or any became a late scratch from Crew One, then backup Crew Two would become the Primary Go Team. The compatibility factor was too important to allow anything else. There was also a rumor that at least two from the backup group might still be moved to Crew One. They trained together twenty-four hours a day, five days a week, but were allowed some free time on the weekends.

The shrinks and analysts watched their every move and noted every reaction, every emotion, taking notes constantly. Nothing escaped their watchful eyes. If you didn't enjoy life in a fish bowl five or six days a week, then you were an early scratch. Of the original candidates, nearly one third failed to complete the first six weeks, and NASA trainers became concerned they would not have enough trainees left by launch date.

Primary Crew One was announced on July 1 so that their picture could appear on the front page of every major newspaper on July 4. Most had been secretly informed well before that date. Crew Two was also announced. There were no hard feelings, no bruised egos, and an exceptional camaraderie when the final cuts were made. The sense of duty and dedication to the program was the greatest asset of the entire group, and they all knew the dangers of failure and the inherent risks in the mission. This was the world's best, all the right stuff, just as NASA usually described them. The international pride in the teams fueled a seldom seen sense of brotherhood.

David knew he had made it a few days before the public announcement. Margie did not find out until the last day and was ecstatic when she finally learned that she was on Crew One. She controlled her excitement and maintained her composure better than she expected. She and David were together, would stay together, and continue to work together.

Crew One also included pilots Phil Allen and co-pilot Roberto Ortiz. Phil was a cool-headed, handsome, Air Force top gun with nerves of steel. His faithful sidekick was a Hispanic wonder boy from Mexico with equal skills and the brains to match. Their abilities on the simulators, alone or together, were legendary in the program. Only time would tell if these abilities transferred to the real ship far from Earth. At this point the entire crew had incredible faith in their prowess.

The doctor selected was Dr. Ann Pritchard, a highly skilled general practitioner and surgeon from England. Her credentials were outstanding. She had a perfect figure, clever mind, and great physical skills to go along with her neatly-trimmed blond hair, smooth skin, and piercing blue eyes.

The team scientific officer and geoscientist was geologist Norm Mailer, who graduated at the top of his class and never looked back. He had multiple scientific and computer-related skills. Tall and lanky with a wisp of wild hair, he played his part like he played poker: betting with skill, frustrating his opponents, and always winning the best pots. He would be in charge of selecting the final landing site, if one was attempted, and conducting any subsequent surface scientific experiments.

Communications specialist was Rod Amerigo, their "Italian Stallion". At six-foot-six this two-meter specimen was a tower of power. Trainers expected him to be an early scratch because of his size. Instead he was a consensus pick due to his incredible ability to ferret out even the most inconspicuous problem and fix it with amazing skill and speed. Rod also had to be Systems Analyst and only secured his position over Kahil Said, an extremely competent engineer from India, when Kahil injured his hand during the last week of training. If you had a problem develop anywhere on the ship, Rod's job was to find it and do something about it. He and Margie were a formidable force when it came to soothing the glitches and gremlins that popped up continuously during training.

The man in charge of their equally important energy source was the dashing Russian cosmonaut hero and engineering whiz Sergey Vosorov. He was charming, witty, and conversant in six languages. His dedication to this project earned him the highest respect from everyone involved. As Propulsion Specialist, Sergey was a graduate from Moscow's best applied-propulsion school and a top-notch cosmonaut. Everyone was impressed with his credentials, training, and dedication and wanted him to be part of the team. It was rumored that he could have built their entire vessel alone if he had enough time. He could fabricate nearly anything and had selected the essential replacement parts and backup materials for the voyage.

Their exterior vehicle activity specialist was Moses Brown. He was a warm and friendly fellow with the strength of an ox and the patience of a saint. He had been a good football player making second string All-American at Stanford as a receiver. Everyone in the training program agreed that he was the best choice for any critical extra-vehicular work and a great leader for the descent team. If a landing were to be made, he would be the man in charge.

Life support, the crew's number one concern, was in the capable hands of Margie. Keeping life support systems in delicate balance would be her biggest responsibility and David would assist her. As Security Officer and computer/systems specialist, he would help her inspect the ship and monitor all critical systems.

Casey Ramirez had the title of Dietitian and Onboard Supply Specialist. She was pretty, moved with a grace that David marveled at, and was extremely efficient. She was actually often quite shy for all of her looks and pedigree. She was in charge of their hydroponic gardens, as well as all food supplies and meals—basically chief cook and bottle washer. She had quickly become "Cookie". It was not a title she liked at all at first, but she accepted it and grew tolerant of it with time. She had the job of keeping supplies in order and to somehow make meals both interesting and palatable. For cleanup and preparation of meals she would have the assistance of the entire crew. Casey was an extraordinary young lady with innumerable skills. Born in Argentina and raised on a sprawling cattle ranch, how she ended up in this project was quite a tale. She had the almost uncanny ability to grow anything with success, and success followed her everywhere she went.

Perhaps the most interesting member of the crew was the serenely spiritual Oreen Nadu. An expert in all subjects religious or spiritual and beyond testing on the intelligence charts, she was said to feel things no one else knew existed.

Her sixth sense, undying sense of humor, and ability to analyze psychic, psychiatric, and even paranormal phenomena earned her a place of respect and great adulation. Oreen was not exactly sure how she had made the crew; but her sixth sense told her that with hard work she would make it.

Mission Commander was Air Force Colonel Jason Kidd. He was a military man with a military mind for leadership. Jason had a charisma that most people found hard to explain. A few gray hairs sprouted from his crew-cut head, but his body was honed sharp by intense physical workouts. His quick decision-making showed great self-confidence and the obvious ability to lead. The respect of his crew was earned—not taken for granted or supported by rank. Jason had become an early favorite of the entire group working on the mission, and a true standout in a school of overachieving experts.

7
LAUNCH

November and December 2030

NOVEMBER was an easier month with brief time scheduled for the crew-members to visit family and friends prior to isolation or for some R&R in any way possible. Margie and David decided to fly to Colorado for some skiing and fun in the snow. They completed a short stint with both immediate families and were in turn visited by distant relations. Now it was their time to do what they wanted and to get away from the routine of training.

NASA warned against any risky behavior. In the case of David and Margie, that pretty much ruled out most of their forms of outdoor entertainment. Because they were recognized nearly everywhere they went now, they chose skiing. With masks or goggles they could remain incognito on the slopes. Meals could be prepared in the kitchen at the condo. It seemed the best chance they had to be low profile but enjoy the outdoors.

They planned to be extra careful and to stay on relatively easy terrain, since an injury at this point would spell disaster. Their parting orders, though not direct, were mostly common sense. No risky behavior was expected and, "Please don't catch a cold for heaven's sake," was the doctor's final order. They knew that they would have to pass a last battery of tests and complete stringent physical examinations. Hank Wadkins gave them the final warning. They were still part of his team, even on the mission, and if they got sick or hurt, they would be back at their desks at NASA.

Conditions on the slopes at Vail were nearly perfect; fresh early snows brought good powder over packed base, and the crowds were not bad. In their ski clothes and goggles they were unknown faces in the vacationing crowds. The weather was gorgeous, with a slight breeze and only a few sparse clouds drifting aimlessly across the mountain sky. Fresh powder had fallen the night before, and conditions just didn't get any better. They were both laughing and enjoying the fresh air and open spaces, away from the confined spaces of training.

Simba was an easy, relatively flat, long run that allowed for a side-by-side cruise. David did not see it coming. The young snowboarder was clowning around with his buddies. He heard the collision and saw Margie going head over heels, literally flying through the air. She landed hard as the kid sprawled face down to her left. Oblivious to the collision, the young snowboarder stopped long enough to clear the snow from his face and took off to catch his friends.

Margie did not move. David's laughter turned instantly to sheer panic. David was out of his skis and running back up slope to her. Another skier stopped to check on her. David's heart was pounding, not from the uphill run in fresh snow, but the fear that gripped him from within. He knelt down beside her and brushed a few fresh flakes from her face. "Margie, darling, are you hurt? Don't move. Can you hear me?"

Her voice came back. "That sucked, did you get his license number?" She smiled and rolled over delivering a kiss to his terrified face.

He hugged her and asked again: "Are you hurt? Take your time. Be sure."

This time her answer came back more slowly and pensively. "I am OK, I think, but my leg hurts where he hit me. I may have a bruise, but I think all parts are functioning." She was slow to get up and to compose herself.

A small crowd of skiers had stopped to see if she was all right. A young boy about eight or nine by his size said: "My sister saw the whole thing. She's after them; they'll never outrun her. She's going to report them to the ski patrol." Almost in the same excited breath he added, "Hey, I know you. You're that space guy." The secret was out and several others showed instant recognition. Margie slipped on her goggles. David said thanks to all, adding, "Please help keep our secret."

The father of the family surrounding them said, "Your secret is safe for an autograph for Jimmy. He idolizes you." David was happy to oblige. The dad handed him a pen and trail map to sign as David bent down and peered into Jimmy's face. "Thanks, pal," he said. "What's your last name?"

"Pierce, Jimmy Pierce," he squeaked.

"Well, Mr. Pierce," David said, "if your dad will give me your address when we get to the bottom, I'll send you a mission pin and autographed crew photo. Follow us."

The dad quickly spoke up again. With a broad grin spreading across his face he said, "When we get to the bottom, I'll dig a business card out of my wallet and buy the hot chocolate."

David watched as Margie skied ahead. She was tentative but seemed to be OK. His heart was still in his throat, and he knew what must have been going through her head.

When they reached the bottom, Shelly Pierce was waving wildly to her brother who was skiing to David's left. Three teenage boys were sitting dejectedly between two ski patrol members. Margie recognized the clown hat lying in the snow beside one young man. She skied directly up to the three and made a sharp hockey stop which, even at her slow speed, managed to throw snow and slush on the perpetrator.

"Are you OK, Miss," said the pony-tailed ski patrol member to the right. He was in his twenties, face well tanned, and obviously in great shape.

"I think so," said Margie. "No thanks to that bozo." The young boarder did not even look up.

The well-tanned countenance looked down at the disgruntled boarder and rattled off his sentence. "He's busted, third complaint in one week, a new record. Won't be boarding here any more today, or for that matter, this season, if I have anything to say about it."

David's anger began to subside. "Thanks," was all he said to the ski patrol. David turned to Jimmy, reached into his unzipped pocket, and pulled out an amateur NASTAR ski medal he had won that morning. Pinning it to the boy's ski jacket David said: "Thanks pal, you've been a big help." The boy said nothing; he was awestruck. David turned and kissed Shelly. She smiled and her rosy cheeks blushed even more. Margie took his gloved hand and said, "I'm done for the day. Let's head for the condo. That hot tub is going to feel good." Jimmy's dad handed David a piece of paper and a business card, which he slipped into his pocket as they exchanged good-byes.

With mild hope in his voice, the dad said, "The offer for the hot chocolate is still good. Maybe even something a little stronger if you'd like." He recognized the look on their faces and simply added, "I'll bet you two just want to relax." Without another word to them he said, "Come on, you two. Let's let these folks unwind a little." Jimmy and Shelly waved goodbye and joined their dad as he turned away.

"Don't worry, we won't forget you, and thanks again," were Margie's parting words.

They spent the evening in each other's arms on the large faux bearskin rug in front of the fireplace. She had a bruise on her leg but nothing serious. The mental strain had actually been worse than the physical pain. They put an ice bag on the bruised areas and decided that the most effort they would put out tonight would be starting a fire and popping some popcorn. This evening brought back memories of that incredible night that David often reminisced about.

They spent the next day in the condo, leaving only for a quick brunch. Reading, soaking, and pampering each other had replaced standing in the lift lines, riding the chair lifts or gondola, and whisking down the slopes. It wasn't a bad trade, since their training had been vigorous, and just sitting was feeling therapeutic as well as a nice change. They returned to Florida feeling good, refreshed, relaxed, closer, and Margie's bruise was now only a yellowish discoloration on her calf.

David suggested that they stop in Houston on their way back to the training facilities in Florida. They planned to visit Hank and Betty at NASA. Hank was pleased and proud of them, and Betty cried when it was time to leave. Everyone with the V-7 program gathered for their last official face-to-face meeting before launch day.

The crew was restricted to base after December 1 and was prepping for shuttle launch to the space station on December 22. There would be a few more runs on the flight simulators, but as of the 23rd, the tests and simulations would be on board the *HobieKat*. Actual launch from the vicinity of the International Space Station was scheduled for Christmas Day. The launch, along with the endless fanfare, was to be beamed to more than two billion people worldwide. V-7 had long since passed Enigma and was hurtling on beyond the outer reaches of the solar system.

December 20, 2030

Final preparations were now underway around the clock aboard the *HobieKat* and Space Plane *Pathfinder*. The Space Plane had been modernized from end to end. It was a beautiful sight, now having logged more missions than any other NASA vehicle. The countdown clock would be started late today at 100 hours. Crewmembers were now sequestered, undergoing a final battery of strenuous physical tests and complete examinations. All twelve were still intact as a group, with no late scratches, substitutions, or replacements. They had beaten the odds to get to this point and were primed like a well-oiled machine to go forward with their mission.

Aboard the *HobieKat*, final preparations included checks of food inventories, final systems inspections, double checks of multiple backup systems, etc. This list went on and on. Everyone knew their jobs, and thanks to Project Director Lee Tanaka's diligence and Ishmael's incredible technology, they were ready ahead of schedule, and had plenty of time to test and retest many times.

The glitches had been there, but none were serious or mission threatening, and all were worked out.

December 22, 2030   T-Minus 20 hours

Pathfinder was rolled out and fueled for launch. The sky was a magnificent clear blue, with little wind and freshness that only a cold front could bring. She was resplendent on her pad with trails of vapor rising from her sides.

Crew One was awakened early, had a good breakfast, and boarded the bus for the pad at 9:00 a.m. They stopped for the final requisite photos, made their brief speeches, and waved for the sea of cameras. The interviews seemed endless, and the photo sessions were far too numerous. At this point the feeling of starting the real thing was pervasive among the entire crew. The whole world was watching in reality this time, and they were ready to oblige, ready to start the show.

Everyone donned their launch suits and took their seats for last-minute checks. They would be switched over to onboard systems shortly. All twelve were in their seats in the cargo bay, and the Space Plane crew went through their final checklists. Phil Allen and Roberto Ortiz wanted to be driving but had to trust their compatriot, Captain Bob Bennett, this time.

At 2:07 p.m., December 21, 2030, the *Pathfinder's* engines roared to life, and the mighty vehicle rose from the pad in a cloud of steam and exhaust gases. The rollover went flawlessly, and the exterior fuel tanks used to accelerate the vehicle toward orbit sputtered out and dropped away at precisely the prescribed moment. Main engine shutdown went exactly as planned, and *Pathfinder* slipped into orbit in only a few minutes. It would take several orbits to catch up to the International Space Station and play the game of maneuvering into the docking space. Captain Bennett, pilot for this mission, had done this seven times this year already and felt extremely confident in handling his precious cargo. He planned to deposit them on the *HobieKat* doorstep at exactly 6:00 a.m., December 22.

The liftoff and flight into orbit went very smoothly. David and Margie enjoyed an adrenaline high and agreed that it was more fantastic than anything training offered. Most of the rest had experienced a flight aboard a shuttle before. Of the twelve, only four had not made a flight. Allen and Ortiz piloted several runs with major *HobieKat* components. Most of the rest either got to ride on one of those trips or had spent time on the space station at some point. Casey Ramirez and Oreen Nadu were the only others besides David and Margie who were flight rookies.

Spirits ran high, and conversation among the group was incessant. Anticipation and excitement were morale boosters, so flight control did not interrupt but listened, mildly amused. The regular *Pathfinder* crew was very quiet. This was just one more run of many for all of them. They would join the team aboard the space station for final checks and last-minute maintenance.

Pathfinder glided into the docking position with the International Space Station at 5:58 a.m., December 22, two minutes ahead of schedule. With the sound of the hatches engaging, they knew the Space Plane achieved docking. Beside their seats in the converted cargo bay, they were surrounded by several containers of all of their personal gear. It was not easy to plan for nearly three years of space travel, especially with near weightless conditions and limited storage space for personal gear.

While they waited for the green lights to come on, indicating pressure seal and equalization, Margie and David chatted through their direct communication channel setting. Margie had remembered young Jimmy and Shelly Pierce. Upon arrival back in Florida, David made a point of getting the autograph of every crewmember and that mission pin for him and a second pin for his sister. He even included a brief special thank-you message for the dad. They should have arrived at the Pierce's home just in time for the launch. Jimmy and Shelly would have bragging rights from wherever they were watching. David still winced when he remembered Margie's collision and was still thankful that she had not been injured.

The red light above the exit lock changed to green and the door opened. Two smiling space station techs entered. Everyone was busy removing their helmets and assisting one another out of the safety harnesses.

"Welcome to the ISS," said one of the techs with his list in his hand. "Commander Kidd, will you please follow me? The rest of you, please follow Mr. Griggs. He will show you to your quarters on the *HobieKat*. Your gear will be delivered later."

Connected together, the shuttle, space station, and *HobieKat* were a maze of components and modules, easily visible from earth at night. Even with all the briefings, the arriving crew would be lost without their guide. When they reached the connecting tunnel to the *HobieKat*, there was a reception committee lining both sides, floating and clapping. They had the station equivalent of the red carpet rolled out. It was a spontaneous reception since none was planned due to the tight schedule.

The twelve members of the Primary Go Team, Crew Number One had plenty of fanfare and flashing cameras, but this meant something special. Each knew in his or her heart that once they passed through this portal it would be as much as three years before they returned through it. Eight men and four women were boarding their coach for the most spectacular journey in human history. They felt like the crew Christopher Columbus led across the unknown sea, looking for a new route to the Far East.

Above the portal was a group of pictures with the word "Pioneers" in large block letters above. Below the photographs were the handwritten words: "God Speed, Crew One." David recognized each face in the photographs at once. A sense of humility rose through his body, and a feeling of pride filled his chest. Everyone stopped speaking as all eyes focused on that open portal and the figures above.

From left to right were Yuri A. Gagarin captioned with: "April 12, 1961, The first man in space." Next to him was the smiling face of Alan B. Shepard, with the date 1961 and the words, "First U.S. sub-orbital flight." Next to them was Lieutenant Colonel John Glenn, February 20, 1962, the first U.S. astronaut in space. Beside them the strong face, resplendent in her flight suit, of Valentina Tereshkova, Vostok 6, 1963, first woman in space. The final photo was that of the first crew to reach the moon, Neil Armstrong, who stepped on the moon on July 20, 1969, Buzz Aldrin, and Michael Collins. Recognition of the last photo above the portal was immediate—it was the entire crew of this mission.

Very few words were exchanged. The crew of the ISS saluted in military fashion, and one waved a small American flag. Led by Commander Kidd, who waited for his crew to exit, each crewmember shook hands with the station personnel and passed through the opening in subdued silence. The reverie of arrival aboard the *Kat* was replaced with a more solemn rite of passage. Each sensed the sudden feeling of loneliness.

8

THE SECOND COUNTDOWN

DAVID WAS BOTHERED by the fact that the last person to leave their vessel prior to the sealing of the hatchways between it and the ISS was the odd little man he had heard so much about. Ishmael, the wiry mystery man, was an idiosyncratic anomaly among the more robust and fit group of personnel who had assisted in assembling the *Kat* in orbit. David was concerned that, as Security Officer, he knew surprisingly little about him. It was common knowledge that Ishmael had free reign of all parts of the *Kat*. Word had leaked that he had almost been killed in some kind of explosion. They all knew that he seldom spoke to anyone, except to give instructions, and that he never removed his helmet. It was David's job to not trust him and his body language was almost indecipherable.

Curious, David began his tasks by checking the duty rosters to see where Ishmael was working at particular times. Every person that had moved within the orbiting station and the *Kat* was meticulously scrutinized and their work checked and re-checked by Tanaka and his team. Everyone but Ishmael; the roster contained an abundance of information on every step and each person, but a decided dearth of information on Ishmael's particulars. It was strange, but David noted that Ishmael's level of clearance was the highest and that he had facilitated construction of the incredible vessel around him. He made a mental note to scan the database for Ishmael's badge location and to have the computer track his movements and create a log. David was not certain that this would alleviate his uneasiness about the little man, so he logged his thoughts into his personal system and went on with his duties.

Crew One settled in and unpacked their gear. Time for rest would be very scarce between arrival aboard *HobieKat* and the planned launch on Christmas Day. This particular day was chosen not for its religious significance, but for the feeling of peace and international brotherhood associated with it. The various space agencies would also benefit from a huge television audience. With so many people at home or sharing time with their families, virtually everyone in the U.S. television audience would be watching the launch live.

A busy schedule was planned for complete final systems checks and to keep the crew's minds fully occupied. The psychological factor was important; there would be plenty of time to relax and think during their journey. It was now necessary to maintain peak efficiency and a keen mental edge.

Everyone on the crew attended a brief orientation and then toured the entire ship, with stops at all duty stations. The mock-ups had been perfect but walking through and working in gravity was considerably different from doing the same under extended weightless conditions. Due to the proximity to the shuttle and space station, the magnetic fields and gravity simulators on the *HobieKat* were in a standby mode or a very low working status. For now, floating and moving horizontally through the passages was almost a game.

The first meal came at a few minutes before noon, and everyone was famished. David and Margie were experiencing mild space sickness, and Oreen could not stomach the thought of eating. Space food had come a long way since the early days of space exploration and the new packaging designed for this mission worked well. Everyone ate together in the cramped spaces of the mess unit. Food and supplies were stowed everywhere. Miles of Velcro held supplies of food, water, and other essentials. As these were used and compacted during their journey; space in the *HobieKat* would at least increase, but initially, extra space was non-existent and the crew would be cramped.

Food and water for two years for twelve people, even with the water filtration systems, used more area than was available. They were expected to grow and produce a limited supply of a few food products in the onboard hydroponic gardens, enough to supplement their rations. If these gardens failed, they could stretch their foodstuffs, but it would be difficult. The mission also called for the launch of supply vessels with which the *HobieKat* could rendezvous on the return leg of the journey.

An adequate supply of energy would not be a problem as long as the nuclear power supply remained in good working order. The *HobieKat* carried two self-contained nuclear-fueled power systems and fuel and parts for a third. These were meant to supply electrical power for all onboard systems and were an integral part of the propulsion system.

Water and oxygen were the most critical necessities. Water would be cycled through and recycled from the hyrdoponic gardens, onboard storage supplies, and waste. Breathing gases would be recycled through converters and the gardens. It would be compressed and conserved in order to create an adequate amount, even in the event of serious leaks or small hull punctures.

In theory, the *HobieKat* could travel along for years longer than this trip called for. It was designed to be a versatile vehicle. Individual sections of the overall structure were designed to function independently. Certain sections could be detached from the main ship and attached to the landers. Hooked together in this configuration, these components could form another fully functional return vehicle in the event of damage to a section of the main ship. If or when needed, the Descent Excursion Vehicles or DEV modules would have to be partially assembled while in orbit around their target.

One characteristic of the *HobieKat* was the amount of living space compared to its predecessor craft. Unlike earlier exploration vehicles, this one had a number of components comprising the overall ship. Each crewmember had or shared a small personal module. Various units were also set aside for recreational activities aimed at alleviating the potential boredom of a two-to-three-year journey. The physical conditioning section was a wonder of ingeniously designed training equipment. Everyone recognized the necessity for the maintenance of healthy physical conditioning during such a protracted period of semi-weightlessness. This component of the ship had been planned with that in mind. Part of every crew person's daily schedule called for some time to be spent in this area.

Margie and David were assigned adjoining units in one section. Relative to space for crew aboard a nuclear submarine, their areas were comparatively spacious. All surfaces were covered with micro-Velcro and underlain with magnetic mesh. Once on their way, they could float in the partial simulated gravity semi-weightless or adhere to any surface. Comfort would not be nearly as much of a problem as their predecessors faced. All major structural components of the *HobieKat* had automatic or manual pressure-sealing hatchways. Each crewmember's compartment was also equipped with the luxury of a window-like portal.

The first night aboard went well and was semi-comfortable for the entire crew. They initiated their rotating shifts, though somewhat modified until launch day. Everyone was in good spirits. It was now 8:00 a.m., December 23, fifty-two hours until planned departure. Today was a day of continuous tests including the propulsion systems. Technical helpers were to depart by the same time the next day, and then the *Kat* was to be sealed and separated from the International Space Station by 1200 hours on Christmas Eve.

Commander Jason Kidd had tended to his crews' arrival and then gone directly to the main control unit upon arrival aboard the *Kat* in order to speak by teleconference with Hank Wadkins, Lee Tanaka, and Margie's mom, Cynthia Ritter. He was sickened by the news they gave him. Margie's dad, her greatest inspiration, and her younger sister, who was home from college on Christmas break, had been involved in a tragic car accident.

Her dad had survived with only relatively minor injuries, only to have a heart attack in the emergency room. His condition had been downgraded to extremely critical. Both were in the intensive care unit at Methodist Hospital in Houston. Her sister, Becky was on full life-support. Her prognosis was poor, and her survival depended on making it through the first night.

They discussed whether to inform Margie now or to wait until after launch. They agreed that she had right to know, but also wondered if they should wait to tell her until after the departure. Should she be given the choice to leave the ship and return to Earth on the returning shuttle or ordered to stay aboard? They discussed these questions and their ramifications on the secure communication channel.

Margie's mom was now alone to face this crisis. She was visibly shaken but holding up well under the circumstances. The conferring group, including Jason, Lee Tanaka, and Hank Wadkins, decided that it was Cynthia who should make the ultimate decision. Margie's mom thanked them for their concern. She asked Lee Tanaka if open communications could be maintained between them if Margie went on the mission. Hank explained that they could teleconference as often as necessary. Cynthia asked Hank if he thought that she should tell Margie now. Hank answered without hesitation that, knowing Margie, it would be best to wait a few days. Jason commented that he thought her choice was much more difficult than any decisions he had faced recently. Cynthia thanked him again for his support and personal interest.

She made her decision. The strength was evident in Cynthia Ritter's voice. "If she stays, what can she do but hold my hand? I can handle being at the hospital. And, Hank; it will be great to have you and Helen there with me. If she learns of this now, gets distracted, or misses the mission, it might make her dad and sister feel worse. No way! She goes. Don't tell her, not yet. Jason, if one of them dies, I want you to have David tell her, but don't let David know just yet either."

Everyone wished Cynthia and her loved ones all the best. Hank reiterated that if there was anything else she needed, she could call him any time, day or night. He gave her a code. President Walker had already contacted the hospital and encouraged the staff to provide the Ritters the best care possible and even spoke with the specialists involved.

Cynthia thanked them all and said goodbye. Lee Tanaka said the direct hookup to the *HobieKat* would be prepared, ready to use when she was ready. They set up another update call for later that day.

Jason's heart was in his throat and deep concern etched on his brow as he turned away from the monitor. He knew that he had to put this aside and get on with the business at hand without emotion, but his heart ached for Margie. Casey Ramirez's dad had passed away without warning during the last phase of training, and it was a difficult time for everyone because she chose to leave. She was only gone for a couple of days and quickly caught up. It was a period of review exercises anyway. This situation was different and so close to final launch.

When he caught up to the rest of the group, everyone was curious as to why he left so suddenly upon their arrival. Ironically, it was Margie who had been the most inquisitive and kidded him about it. He brushed her off with a weak smile, making the excuse that he had to talk to Lee Tanaka about something, which was the truth.

After dinner on the twenty-third, the last group briefing was held. This marked the completion of the final series of pre-launch tests. All systems were given a "go" with the exception of a slight computer malfunction in Life Support System A. Margie had cleared it up in less than two minutes. Several simulated system failures were handled by the computers. Everyone on the ground, on the space station, and aboard the *Kat* was pleased with the results. The countdown clock passed forty hours with all indicators signaling go for launch.

December 23, 2030 10:00 p.m.

The emergency alarms blared at 10:01 startling everyone on board. No mistaking this sound. They all were programmed to it: depressurization, exterior hull breach. In seconds the ship would be automatically sealed at all major control points. Pre-programmed to automatically seal any minor hull breach, the nanotech enriched outer skin material developed by Lee Tanaka should self-repair. It had worked fairly well in tests, but the efficacy of a repair was dependent on the start up time for the process and the size of the opening. Micrometeorite debris punctures would seal almost instantly. A catastrophic failure could only be contained by sealing off the entire section immediately, thereby minimizing the area involved.

In the fully-packed, confined passageways, getting to emergency stations was difficult for those off station. While the green lights were on between or inside any components, one could pass through. These doors closed automatically in emergency situations and doors between major component sections of the ship were always in the closed position.

Margie had been on duty at her Systems Analyst station monitoring numerous read outs and statistics. The hair on her head almost stood up when she saw and heard the alarm. It was pinpointed in one second as a hull breach in component B-6, the Medical Infirmary and Lab. The component had sealed, and Doc Pritchard's locator monitor indicated that she was still in there. Every component on the *Kat* had emergency breathing apparatus as well as life support and filters, but this looked bad. She was still in there.

David did not react fast enough to escape the exercise module. His training caused him to react instantly, without panic, but he was strapped to a machine. They drilled on this, and he had always made it, but not this time. He checked on his communicator and listened in his earpiece for crew reaction and for any special emergency instructions. He said nothing until instructed to do so during the immediate crew location check, which was now in progress. One by one they sounded off to the list already generated by the computer and in Commander Kidd's hands. "Eleven accounted for, all systems shipshape. Breach in section B-6 sealed off and localized. No additional problems apparent except the security officer, David, is isolated in the gym."

"Way to go, David!" The pained words came from Jason. David winced and finished tapping the security door override code into the number pad beside the door. He prayed he had the correct code. It opened, and he was moving toward Doc's section as quickly as possible. He ditched his magnetic boots and was hurtling himself forward through the compartments. With his remote control, the doors opened automatically as he approached them, but only if the green light was lighted on the access control panel.

Jason's voice in the earpiece told him that he and Sergey were on their way from opposite directions. There were no life signs from Doc, no pictures from the monitor in the lab. Everyone else was to remain vigilant at his or her station.

David reached the infirmary first. He looked through the glass portal in the lab door, expecting the worst. Instead he saw Doc's pretty face peering back at him with her tongue sticking out and her eyes crossed, not in the agony of sudden depressurization death, but in profound laughter. She was enjoying his agony.

Lee Tanaka's voice suddenly broke his stupor. "Nice job, team. You all handled that unscheduled drill very well."

— § —

It was now midnight on the 23rd. Christmas Eve was beginning, and the countdown clock was down to T-Minus thirty-six hours. There was no arguing with those off duty about getting some sleep. They sought out their personal pods and lapsed into deep sleep almost immediately. The day had been exhausting, and rest was welcome.

Margie and David were both off duty. It had taken David awhile to calm down after the excitement of the too-real drill. He reflected that he hadn't panicked. He had functioned professionally and with a clear head in a situation he had deemed totally real. He was a little ticked off at Doc, though. Until he realized that she was laughing, her look, with crossed eyes and protruding tongue, had appeared for a moment to be a gasp of death.

David decided to join Margie in her quarters for a few minutes before they both turned in for the night. At their present orbital position, bright sunlight poured in through the portal. She closed the cover. Both took a few minutes to contact their families and Margie noticed that her mom was not at ease. And where was her dad? She wanted to blow him a kiss on the telecom screen reminiscent of when she was a little girl. Dad always enjoyed that.

When David came in, she looked at him with her big, blue, weary eyes and remarked, "David, Mom looked tired and troubled, but she would not say why. She can hide her emotions, but I can read her pretty well after all these years. Something was bothering her."

"She's probably nervous about her firstborn heading for deep space," said David. "She is going to miss you terribly, you know, and maybe your Dad was upset and wanted strong Mom to talk to you."

"You're probably right," she replied. "I am going to miss them too." She hugged him close and let out a tiny sob. He patted her back and ran his hands through her hair.

"We've got each other for a while," he said as he held her tight.

They remained that way in silence, gently moving to and fro in their weightless state for least five minutes. Finally, she looked up at him and said, "You are my strength for now, and I love you."

Before he could speak, she slid her hand down the front of his flight suit and felt him through the fabric. At that moment the telecom screen above her bed beeped twice and began blinking. Every compartment on the ship had a complete two-way telecommunications system. In their personal quarters it beeped twice and flashed red for five seconds before coming on. This was designed to provide the occupant enough time to hit the privacy setting. This would keep the screen blank and allow only voice communications. If not activated, the occupant needed to prepare for two-way video and audio feed.

Margie and David simply moved apart and watched the screen leap to life. It was Doc Ann Pritchard. She was smiling a little nervously. She said, "Hi, Margie. Oh. Hi, David. Say, I'm sorry I scared you, but they told me to make it look real, and well, I could not quite finish the effect. David, you went white for a second. I was calling Margie to see if you were angry before I called you."

"Angry? Heck no. I'm not mad or upset, but I'll get you Doc," he chortled. "I always get even."

"I'm just glad that you got there that quickly," she confessed. "They set you up, knew that you were strapping into an apparatus in the gym. It's nice to know that we can react that quickly in a real emergency. I won't cry wolf unless ordered. See you both at breakfast at 0700. Better get some shuteye."

"Bye, Doc," they answered as the telescreen went blank. "You tell me how she can do that," David said.

"Do what?" Asked Margie.

"How can she sound more American than you or I when she was born in London?"

"She knows seven languages, at least five fluently," Margie observed. "She's quite a linguist."

"How come I didn't know that?" he wondered aloud.

Margie patted him gently again and said, "See? You don't know everything. Have a good night. See you in the morning."

David couldn't get to sleep for a while. He conjured up visions of their voyage and the New World they would explore. He remembered the discovery day, the fanfare, the training. He thought of Margie's touch, and that wonderful evening came back again. He felt his warmth growing and decided to put his thoughts aside with some music. It worked. The visions became more subdued. He relaxed and soon drifted into a dream about Margie and playing in the snow, but everything was strangely different.

He awoke with a start to Jason Kidd's voice saying, "Rise and shine, sunshine," on the telecom. He had not even heard the beeps as the telecom came on. "It's 6:30, the grand salon dining room opens at 0700, and your reservation has been made. Oh, by the way, I need a full security sweep completed by 10:00 and full lock down of all compartments by 11:00 sharp in preparation for final separation."

"Got it, sir, as prescribed," David returned as he loosened himself and floated out of bed.

"Sergey will be joining you for the scan. He'll meet you at chow time. Let's get this baby shipshape for de-dock and move out."

"I'm on my way ASAP," said David. He watched Jason's face fade from the screen.

Margie was already awake, freshened up and heading out of her compartment when he clicked open his door. "Meet you there," he said. "I've got to get ready. Wow, you look great."

She smiled, winked, and disappeared through the hatchway. David was hungry and had slept so hard that he was still a little groggy. It was probably good that he had slept so soundly, since the last night before launch would probably be sleepless. He was ready in a short time, although personal hygiene, taken for granted on earth, actually took a lot more time and effort in space. He did enjoy spitting out his tooth and gum cleaner and watching it float around in a large globule. He was just making a spit ring when the telecom beeped again. He barely had time to use his suction sweeper to suck it up as the face of Sergey appeared.

"Are you prepared yet?" said the Russian-accented voice.

David tried to think of an answer in Russian, but he knew just a few phrases, and he could not think of it. "I'm ready and hungry," David countered.

"You will be speaking Russian when we return and we will have plenty of time," Sergey added. "My English is very good, Da?"

The telecom went blank again. David wondered what the Russian would have thought of his spit ring.

He made his way to the galley and met Sergey there. Margie was finishing up and savoring her space coffee in the ingenious coffee sippers designed by the French aerospace program. Sergey made a comment about the day's weak American coffee, but they were all used to it by now. He preferred his own blend. Co-pilot Roberto Ortiz and Casey were also finishing their breakfasts.

The next breakfast shift would be arriving shortly, and everyone needed to be fed and out of the mess hall by 0800. Their next meals would come after the ship was made secure and moved away from the space station.

Casey, the dietitian, cook, bottle washer, and official food handling and nutrition expert was one busy lady. Cookie had a tough job ahead to make food interesting and appealing during their long voyage. No one envied her job, but everyone hoped to keep her happy and to stay on her good side. She had a temper and an unusual sense of humor; but she had a wonderful creative ability with almost anything edible—and some things almost inedible. Casey had come to them from Argentina by way of relatives on the west coast. Her family had a long history of restaurant ownership importing the finest beef from their ranch in Argentina. The family cookbook was over 200 years old, at least the parts written down, with some traditional dishes being much older.

Cookie had also been an outstanding athlete on the ladies' soccer team at Stanford. She became interested in space-food research and decided to try for a job with NASA. Cookie spent three years in the International-U.S. space exploration group and became well known for several innovative methods to preserve and store food for use in space. At least there would never be a dull moment in the galley with her onboard.

David and Sergey began their routine checks on all telecom links and backup systems first. They plugged in their handheld computer systems analysis units and got a green light from Margie. They would repeat this process throughout the vessel and then retrace their path as each compartment was secured for separation. They had done this exercise, it seemed, a hundred times or more during simulation and were sincerely hoping for no bugs or problems. They had sixty-seven major systems to scan with backups, bypasses, and rechecks. Something almost always went wrong somewhere.

— § —

Sergey moved ahead to the next compartment to start another check. Margie came back on audio and then appeared on the telecom in Norm Mailor's compartment. "We've got something here," he said to Andre.

"What's up?" David inquired.

"We've got a fire-heat sensor showing excess heat in a storage compartment," Margie warned. "Some very weird readings."

"Darn, we've only covered two compartments so far," Sergey said as David slid through the next hatchway.

"Look's like a bad heat sensor in the door control," Margie intimated. Sergey nodded in agreement. "Wow, the techs checked those yesterday and replaced one up in the computer backup area," added David. "And I thought these nano machines and our supercomputer were supposed to fix things."

"Let's check it again, test it, and move on," replied Sergey. "We have a lot of manmade things here mixed with what the nanos built. Let's keep hoping that they all intermesh. I keep wondering what might happen if they aren't all congruent."

But Margie added that Ishmael would take care of it since he and the last techs were essentially done and almost ready to leave the *Kat* for the space station. Sergey and David moved on. David wondered why Ishmael made that decision, but his only comment was, "It didn't take long to find something wrong."

But that was all they found during the scan. The rest of their search-and-destroy-the-bugs mission went smoothly, without any other problems or repairs. When they completed their rounds it was after 10:30 and nearly time for lockdown and final ship and station securing. Every compartment section of the *HobieKat* was now ready.

At 11:00 a.m., Florida time, on December 24 the last techs aboard the *Kat* bid farewell and the hatches on the *Kat* and International Space Station were closed. A few waves were exchanged along with a blown kiss or two, and a few more pictures were taken through the umbilicus attaching the two space creations. The hatches and airlocks were sealed, and the umbilicus moved away slowly. EVA specialist Moses Brown, Commander Jason Kidd, and David were the three peering through the hatch on the *HobieKat* side.

Several faces appeared at portals on the ISS. David's eyed were pulled to one in particular, and intrigued by its faint blue-purple glow. Tiny eyes glowed from within deep pockets in a too-small face. The upper half of the frail frame of Ishmael filled the portal, still in his helmet, an idiosyncrasy that David did not understand. This vague little man, who often said nothing, but always anticipated every question, perplexed him. David had noticed how uncomfortable Oreen and Ishmael had been in their one face-to-face meeting. Oreen was not spooked very easily, but their mutual mind games had been a bit disturbing. Oreen did not like him, and had told both he and Margie that she sensed something different about Ishmael. David remembered his own uneasiness and his promise to himself to check on Ishmael's movements while onboard.

With the final click they looked at one another and smiled. It was Jason who broke the silence: "Gentlemen, start your engines. Let's get this baby ready to rock and roll."

Moses let out a huge sigh, clasped the shoulders of the other two men and winked adding a deep, "Let's go."

— § —

Press Secretary Z.Z. Rogers was ready for the mega-extravaganza that was about to take place. The press had gone off the deep end on this one. Coverage was endless and omnipresent. Cameras were on the President, NASA, Eurospace, the astronauts' families, friends, teachers, and heads of state of every country involved in this program, more than any other single event in history.

The initial liftoff of the *Endurance*, which put the crew into orbit, had received fabulous blanket coverage, but in this case the press had to point cameras at people and places other than a vehicle on a gleaming launch pad. Of course there would be myriads of cameras pointed at the vessel from the space station and satellites in orbit in order to cover every conceivable angle during the second launch.

Twenty-four hour coverage had started well before separation. The logistics of press coverage required one incredible director. There were connections with all twelve crew positions by telecom. Connections were also needed between ground control, space station control, every family, and all directors of the individual space programs as well as the various heads of state. President Walker had a tough decision to make. It would not be difficult to keep Margie Ritter insulated from the press and a possible leak of the story about her sister and dad until the last two hours before launch. At that time the press wanted everyone on the crew to make goodbye statements to the public. All contact could be secured until then. He knew only too well that the press could be too overzealous. He also knew that the news was out, and it was a great human-interest story.

The crews were going to be far too busy to watch all of the hoopla leading up to the launch. They would be watching the show on videotape at a later date, a date after they were on their way.

Liz Rainwater came into the oval office with a small pile of papers. "Still thinking about Margie and the press?" She asked.

"You can read my mind like a newspaper, can't you?" President Walker shot back. "We can secure the hospital ward and keep Mrs. Ritter there with her husband and daughter. Margie can talk to her again, but she will want to say 'Hi' to her dad and her sister. We've got to plan something better than that or tell her."

"Zeke thinks we can bypass it by calling for no communications for the last few hours in essential systems, like what was done for earlier missions. This circus that the press has planned is too much, anyway, and Lee Tanaka is furious about it."

"Yes, Liz, that's what everyone around here thinks and what Lee Tanaka wants for his crew. The less personal coverage there is, the better it is, at this time. It's what he thinks is best. I agree. Call Zeke, and let's cut this media crap down to size. I know that we half-heartedly agreed to it, but we can change our minds, especially when crew security is at stake. Let's shut them down."

"With great pleasure, Mr. President."

— § —

The call came in on the President's personal line at about 4:00 p.m. on Christmas Eve afternoon. He was watching a little football, as a diversion, trying to find something that was not pre-launch coverage or another interview. It was from Cynthia Ritter, Margie's mom, and he cringed before taking the call. Her voice was warm and friendly, not an emotional tremor that signaled bad news. To the contrary, she was bright and cheerful, starting with, "Merry Christmas, Mr. President."

"Happy Holidays, Cynthia. You sound pretty cheerful." He awaited her response with guarded optimism.

"Mine just got a lot better." She sounded genuinely happy.

"Good news?" he inquired.

"Yes, sir. John is off the resuscitator and breathing on his own this afternoon, and according to the doctors, is doing remarkably well today. The trauma to the heart from the impact of the collision also caused the mild heart attack. Luckily it happened when it did, in the emergency room. They recognized it immediately and kept him from having serious problems. Apparently, his cardiovascular system was not seriously damaged. He's heavily sedated but should regain consciousness as it wears off. Otherwise he is pretty much OK. His broken ribs will be sore, but the prognosis has gotten much better, in fact down right good."

"Oh, that is great news, Cynthia." President Walker did not want to spoil her mood, since she was obviously doing so much better. He considered changing the subject, and decided to go ahead and ask while she sounded like she was in good spirits. "Any update on your daughter?"

"No change at all but in some ways the doctors actually think that's good, Mr. President. At least she's hanging in there. The greatest concern at this point is swelling of the brain. She's one banged up little girl."

He could hear the tremor returning to her voice and interrupted her before she could go on. "Are the doctors doing everything you want, Cynthia? Is everything to your satisfaction there so far?"

"Yes, sir, I couldn't ask for more. Thank you again. She appreciated his support and understood why this man had been elected to this lofty position. He was a true leader and his compassion was genuine. She could tell that he really cared.

"Get some rest, and take care of yourself, Cynthia. Thanks for calling." He hung up feeling a lot better about everything. In only twenty hours the crew of the *Kat* would be on their way. He hoped things would be bit less hectic for him, if that were possible considering his normal schedule.

— § —

Aboard the *Kat* things were going fine. An afternoon pre-Christmas, pre-launch party was in progress, and spirits were exceptionally high. Oreen Nadu, the crew's secular leader, was leading a group singing Christmas carols. She was then planning to read a short message of inspiration to the crew, which was to be broadcast later. It would touch upon almost every imaginable major religion. Oreen was a scholar of most beliefs and had a wonderful charismatic personality, which endeared her to nearly everyone. She also had a special gift, almost a sixth sense, for things—a sense that went beyond normal to paranormal in nature.

Her energy was boundless, her intelligence renowned, and her abilities sometimes almost scary. It was said that in an oral test for one of her degrees, she answered several questions before they were asked. There were several other similar legends concerning her mental prowess. She would fill many roles during this voyage from psychologist to inspirational leader to mechanic, if necessary. And when any crewmember needed someone to talk to, there was no one better.

Numerous last-run-through systems checks were in progress. The *Kat* was now completely on its own power, and all propulsion systems, including nuclear, pulse ion drive, and conventional, were ready to be made fully operational. Everyone would be far too busy to worry about anything except the tasks ahead. There would be little time for any final goodbye messages. Most of the crew had taken time earlier to send special messages and had prerecorded a brief holiday wish for the press and friends.

Rod Amerigo had taken the messages from everyone and relayed them to Earth. All communications between Earth and the ship would go through him or Commander Kidd from now on. Rod had also been informed that Margie was to be incommunicado for another day. The final send-off press show was to be strictly screened. Only very limited two-way communications between the crew and the ground would be allowed until well after launch. These communications were restricted to only those between Rod, Commander Kidd, Pilot Phil Allen, and Mission Control.

At T-Minus twelve hours, a short hold in the countdown was planned if every system was not functioning perfectly. At midnight NASA expected the crew to rest. That would be tough for every crewmember due to the adrenaline now coursing through their bodies. The launch was be the most dangerous time for the ship and crew. Everyone was ready, but the butterflies were there.

At T-Minus three hours or 9:00 a.m. EST Christmas morning the final press show was held. It went smoothly, much better than expected. The President and his counterparts from fifteen nations sent their collective wishes for a safe and wonderful journey of discovery.

Lee Tanaka, whose coordination of this effort was truly remarkable, made a brief speech, followed by Larry Greenbaum and Hank Wadkins. Almost everyone involved in the top level of the program had a brief chance to express their gratitude and pass along a few words of inspiration. As usual, Ishmael was mentioned but not seen or heard from. The press only had enough time left over to ask a few questions. The President just smiled when the First Lady remarked that everyone seemed to be running over his or her allotted time.

At 11:00 a.m. or T-Minus one hour the final countdown began. The collective eyes of more than two billion people were glued to their TV sets or computer screens watching the image of the *Kat* ready to pounce.

Everyone on board the machine was secured and ready as the clock ticked down on the second countdown. The engines and drives were brought to full power during the last five minutes. Moved to a safe distance from the International Space Station, the ship would accelerate out of orbit at an incredible rate and be able to maintain the rate, at a level safe for the crew, for as long as needed. Without the strong effects of gravity to overcome, the ship and crew would actually be exposed to less stress than during a conventional liftoff from the ground. But things could still go wrong. Once the ship was fully expanded and operational, it would become even more comfortable.

The final seconds ticked off as the ship was slowly brought to full power and the propulsion systems all synchronized by the computers. Jason Kidd yelled, "We're outta here," and in a few minutes the ship was pulling away from the space station, heading for a tiny dot at the far reaches of the solar system.

9

THE VOYAGE BEGINS

A JOURNEY of this magnitude was more of a norm two or more centuries ago. A close analogy to the crew of the *Kat* was the early journey of frontier settlers in the old American West, or the voyage of Christopher Columbus. These earlier explorers, adventurers or travelers banded together in order to cross the sea or the great expanse of the continent. The travelers sought each other's company for security, to share community skills, and to assist one another for the mutual benefit of the whole.

The stealth planet mission was an effort of this sort. The crew's mutual cooperation, interaction of skills, and joint efforts were aimed at one goal; success. In the space program success meant completing, or very nearly completing, the mission as planned. To obtain success on this mission meant not only great scientific discovery but also survival. Earth's greatest modern technological creation was whirling through space, carrying its finest, most highly trained explorers on a mission with relatively low odds of total success.

The analogy did not go much further. When a wagon broke down, or a ship was damaged, it was repaired from materials at hand. In the case of the *HobieKat*, a breakdown could be infinitely more complex. Only so many parts and only so many raw materials could be brought along or fabricated in space, and the nano-tech "helpers" did have limitations. Unlike the pioneers, the crew of the *Kat* could not step out on the ground to facilitate repairs.

This is where nanotechnology added an insurance factor. These micro machines could build virtually anything, as long as the driving computer was properly programmed, and there were adequate raw materials. Their handiwork was everywhere; they were an integral part of every section of the ship. Just exactly how much was an unanswered question.

Fresh air, sunlight, walking, swimming, gravity, fresh fruits, vegetables and room to get away from everything were all luxuries that were left behind. Sensory deprivation was a well-known problem. Long-term exposure to weightlessness was another. Claustrophobia was at least well studied from submariners, but still a serious potential problem. The crewmembers would have to deal with all of these problems, some of which were certain to appear eventually. As the trip grew in duration, something as simple as boredom could have deleterious effects.

The first few days out went well. Everyone functioned like the proverbial well-oiled machine NASA trained him or her to be, and the ship performed perfectly. Acceleration out of orbit went as planned. The moon's gravity was used to assist this propulsion. It worked well. The specialists and planners ran countless simulations and tests with the smaller scale versions, but the launch of the *Kat* was literally a first try. Computer coordination of the propulsion systems went extremely well.

The second day out, Margie had an incoming message from her mom. She had just gotten off her duty rotation and was returning to her quarters. Margie and her mom set up a prearranged time to communicate, when Dad could talk too. Between her time on duty, the time of day on Earth in her parents' time zone, and her Dad's normal work schedule, they needed prearranged times. It was also necessary to schedule during NASA's allotted transmission windows.

This was not the expected time, so Margie was a bit surprised and curious about the transmission. She clicked on the telecom two-way button and her mom appeared sitting with a man who appeared to be a doctor.

"Hi, hon. How's your day, or night, going?" said Cynthia Ritter.

"OK, Mom. What time is it there? It must be 10:00 at night," Margie responded.

"It is 10:00 o'clock here. Let me introduce Dr. Robert Leslie."

"It's nice to meet someone I've heard so much about," the doctor said politely.

"Is something wrong, Mom? Where's Dad? Where are you?" Margie realized something wasn't right. Mom was sitting in a room with a doctor. She should have been at home with Dad getting ready for bed. That was exactly why they planned their calls for a certain time, so both of them could be there to visit with her.

"He's here, Margie. Dad's been ill. I will fill you in with Dr. Leslie's help."

"Oh no," Margie hesitantly replied.

"Let me explain, dear," Mrs. Ritter cut in. "Don't get upset yet. Dad was in a car accident. He was in pretty bad shape for a day or two, but he's improving fast. Dr. Leslie says his prognosis for a full recovery from this point is very good."

"Oh, Mom, what do you mean, 'from this point'?"

"Just listen a little more," Cynthia continued. "He was actually on life support for a while, but he's now doing fine on his own."

Dr. Leslie interrupted. "Your dad has a couple of broken ribs and a few other bruises and contusions, but he's a tough guy. Our biggest concern was a brief cardiac arrest in the emergency room that left him in a mild coma. But he is out of it and probably out of danger and is beginning to really bug the nurses. So we think he is going to be fine."

"You said that he was in bad shape for a day or two. When did this happen?" came the inquisitive and now slightly irritated response from Margie.

"It happened a couple of days before you left orbit." Margie's mom's face had now taken on a look closely akin to a little girl caught with her hand in the cookie jar. "I'm sorry, Margie, a lot of people agreed not to tell you until now, but blame only me, since I made the final decision."

Dr. Leslie added, "It was for security and your presence of mind at this late stage of launch preparation. Even President Walker got involved."

"Wow, I'm shocked, flattered, and a little pissed off, but I'll get over it. Please excuse the expression. I think I'll understand when I get a chance to think about it a little more. May I talk with Dad?"

"Actually, that's why we called. He wants to talk to you too. He's still a little weak, and don't be shocked by the shiner and bandages on his head." Cynthia Ritter was preparing her for the more difficult part of this message as best as she could.

"It looks worse than it is," said the doctor. "He's sitting up in bed in the next room. We'll go in when you are ready."

"Mom, I can't believe that you didn't tell me, but I'm not mad. I might be later. You did a good job of not showing it, but I remember telling David that I sensed something was wrong. We were just so busy that I didn't think about it."

"You didn't need the distraction and there wasn't a lot you could do at the time."

"I could have been there for you, but at least Sis was."

"Oh, I had lots of support under the circumstances," interrupted Mrs. Ritter. "Are you ready to talk to Dad?"

"Yes, please. May I now?"

"Give us a few seconds to plug the telescreen in. We'll move it into his room next to his bed."

In a few minutes the screen cleared again, and Margie winced at the image before her. Mr. Ritter's bandaged face and black eye filled the screen. She did her best to hide her shock, but she didn't do a very good job. She could tell by his reaction.

"Hi, sweet thing." Allen Ritter spoke first when he saw her troubled look. "Quite a shiner, huh? This one's worse than the one I got as a kid. They said that the air bag caused it, but the darn thing probably saved my life. Got a pretty good bump on the noggin too, and a few stitches. None of that hurts at all, but these broken ribs are a real pain. Before you get all worried about me, Doc says I'm going to be out of here in no time."

She smiled, "That's great, Dad. "There's no way they'll keep you there very long if I know you and how much you dislike hospitals. You look like hell, though."

"Gee, thanks. That's my girl. Trying to cheer me up, are you?" he said as he started laughing in tandem with his distant daughter's face on the screen. He winced in pain as he remembered his very sore rib cage. In fact, they were all laughing—even the doctor who had given him orders not to laugh if he could help it. The strain of tension had disappeared from the hospital room.

Margie could see Dr. Leslie on the telescreen. His body language and face told her that he had more to say. Dr. Leslie and the Ritters had gotten by the easy part. What Allen Ritter had to say next would change the entire tone of the call. He had rehearsed it in his aching head. He discussed at length the subject of exactly how to reveal their other daughter's grave condition to Margie. Dr. Leslie and Cynthia made suggestions, but there was no easy way to do it. From the beginning, he insisted on being the one to tell her.

Margie was talking about the launch and their first couple of days, but he was only half listening. He returned to concentrating on what she was saying just in time to focus on the words: "Dad, are you OK? Would it be better to talk later when you're feeling better?"

"No, Margie. There's something else on my mind, and there's no easy way to say it." He pondered one last brief moment and started. "Margie, Sis was in the car with me, and she's here in the hospital with me too. She was on the side of the car that got hit when we were hit broadside. I'm afraid that she got it worse than I." It was all he could say. Tears welled up and burst from his sore, swollen eyes.

Cynthia Ritter was at his side holding his hand as he sobbed and went on. "She survived, but just barely." But he could say no more. The emotion choked off the rest of his words.

"Oh my Lord, not Sis too!" came Margie's alarmed reply. "But you said that she's there too, so she's all right."

Cynthia Ritter and Dr. Leslie both began to speak at once, but Cynthia gave way to the doctor. Dr. Leslie began in a professional voice. "Miss Ritter,

I am one of a team of specialists that are doing everything possible for your sister. I will be absolutely frank and truthful with you. The jury was out on her surviving the first night. She was pretty banged up and her right hip was shattered. She also had several serious internal injuries and we were worried particularly about peritonitis, a secondary internal infection, which often happens in cases like this."

He paused for a moment but began again before letting her respond. "She made it through the first night and we have controlled the infection so far. That is a major step in the right direction. She is in a deep coma at present but that is probably best for her at this point. All of her vital signs are showing stability and as of today, some noticeable improvement. I saved that last comment for your mom and dad too, because I had not even told them about the slight improvement until now."

"Is there hope?" Cynthia cut in. "Did you say improving? I know you did."

"Only slight at this point, but any improvement is a step in the right direction and a cause for optimism. Our prayers are with your sister, her wonderful family, and you, dear space traveler." Dr. Leslie was smiling when he finished his remarks and wanted to leave them alone to deal with their situation as a family.

"Is she going to be messed up or crippled?" Margie interrupted. "I mean she is so beautiful and talented." Dr. Leslie could see the fear and sorrow on her face.

"Only time will tell on those counts, but her angelic face is hardly bruised," Dr. Leslie added. "I'm going to slip out of here and let you visit, but please, only a few more minutes." He waved, turned, and was out of the door to the room before anyone thought to say goodbye.

"He's a good doctor, and I like him." Mrs. Ritter looked at her daughter's face on the monitor. "The President sent him. He said that he's one of the very best. All the doctors at this hospital have been great. They really care."

"Keep your faith and don't be too distracted. That's an order," Dad said. "We'll take care of her, and rest assured that she'll pull through. You got that?"

"I do, Dad, and you get better quickly. I'll have to let Mom get you a card. Sorry I won't be able to bring flowers myself."

"I think that's enough shock for one call, don't you, honey?" Cynthia interjected. "Let's all get some rest, and we'll update you in the morning. I've got to find some way to get grumpy comfortable or he's going to drive the nurses crazy."

Margie blew a kiss to Mom and Dad and waved a cheery goodbye. She smiled as brightly as she could but felt helpless when the screen went blank. She sobbed for a few minutes. Under the circumstances, she couldn't wait until David could join her. She needed to talk to someone, and he was always a good listener.

She was startled and turned quickly around as the door opened and David entered. He immediately wrapped his arms around her and held her tightly as spasms of sobs began to shake her entire body.

"Did you know?" she asked through tears.

"Jason told me you were getting a call about an accident at home concerning your dad and sister," he replied as he looked in her teary eyes. "Tell me about it when you feel like it."

"I will, but for now just hold me, and don't let go." He held her to him and let her cry on his shoulder. Pent up emotion from their arduous training and the shock of this new information just poured out.

— § —

As the first days turned to weeks, the voyage remained far from routine. Everyone at Mission Control and onboard expected more problems than had occurred. Margie conferred daily with her mom. Dad had gone home after a week in the hospital and was almost fully recovered.

Margie's little sister had pulled through. She made it through the most dangerous period. Her body fought off infection and began to mend. She remained in the coma for nearly a month but finally awoke one day in a near amnesia-like state. The news was wonderful to Margie, and everyone onboard the *Kat* felt her relief and joy.

When Cynthia Ritter uttered the words: "She's awake," Margie's mind and body were nearly overwhelmed with happiness. She was ecstatic that Sis had made it. The coma had actually been good for her in some ways. The original damage to the back of her head was severe. Brain swelling became the chief concern. Most of the medical team agreed that the coma was the direct result of the swelling. They had been able to mitigate and relieve it without serious problems, but the road uphill for little sister was going to be steep and long. Her injuries were healing, but her hip was shattered by the impact of the wreck. She would be weak and would need an extensive physical rehabilitation program. If anyone could do it, Margie knew that her sister could. At least her parents were going to know exactly where their daughters were for quite some time to come.

— § —

David and Margie's days were full as the ship neared the critical point, at which time the decision would be made to either continue on the present course or redirect the *Kat* toward Mars. If anyone had free time, it certainly was not them.

Hank Wadkins talked to David and Margie as often as possible. He relayed news from the old *V*-7 Project and the latest gossip from NASA. Since a final decision on the mission destination was still up in the air, they often discussed the potential landing areas on Mars. Both were well aware that a solid contingency plan was an absolute necessity if they were unable to continue on to Enigma. Margie was almost reluctant to finalize the Mars plans. She thought that it was unlucky to think of anything but their true final goal. But the scientist always came through, and she tackled the task with the same ferocity and fervor she normally displayed.

The biggest obstacle was obtaining a consensus of opinion from the vast number of specialists working on the problem. There were so many potential landing sites, each with its own particular reason for being the most important. Betty Hurley had suggested putting all the places in a hat and drawing out the lucky winner. That was not going to happen. Everyone involved in the program had reasons for insisting that his or her site be selected. The final candidate was the site that yielded the most common factors. David only hoped that he would have as much data and the same dilemma when it came to selecting a point to land on Enigma. Mars had been radar imaged, photographed extensively, and mapped in considerable detail. He only wished that he had the same luxury with their stealth target.

David had begun the project of reviewing all of the available data from the *V*-7 pass. He had done this on many occasions before, but always with distractions at the office. Now he had time to ponder over each photo and compare them anew. He was sure that, even with their inherent similarities, he could find something new.

David had just begun studying a select group of photographs while listening to his favorite music collection when he heard the yell. Even over the music, it came in loud and clear. He stuck his head out of his module and removed his earphones in time to hear another burst from the direction of Casey Ramirez's compartment. The second was louder and more emphatic and sounded distinctively like, "Dammit!"

As security officer David knew that he should investigate. He laid down his earphones, switched the music off, and started in the direction of the shout.

Upon arriving at Casey's compartment, he was greeted by another tirade.

"Where are you, you little shit?" she screamed. "You're in big trouble." A cushion from her chair spun by. "I've got to find you before you get me in big trouble." She began frantically turning things over and searching her cabin. Casey turned in time to come nose to nose with David, who was watching her with mild amusement.

"Oh, hi, David," she said as she looked right past him, nervously searching the corridor.

"What is going on?" he asked, smiling broadly. "I heard you in my cabin with earphones on and loud music. At first I thought that you were in real trouble. Did you lose something?"

"The little shit got out! He's gone!"

"Who? What are you talking about?" David asked as he followed her search and began to look for whatever it was too. He began to figure out what was going on just about the time she told him.

"Orion is gone. He was right here a minute ago, and when I turned around he had disappeared." Orion was one of Casey's biological experiments and also one of the crew's many "pets". In fact, Orion was just about the entire crew's favorite critter and the unofficial ship's mascot, a two-year old African tortoise that loved his heat lamp and liked to be petted on top of his head.

Orion was not supposed to be out of the bio-lab area, and especially was not allowed to be loose.

"And just what was Orion doing in here, and why was he outside of a safe container?" David inquired, this time with his duty as security officer in mind.

"I glued Velcro to the bottom of his shell and stuck him over here so that I could pet him. I made sure that he'd gone to the bathroom in his container before I took him out. He loves to float around in here and push off of things with his feet, but I velcroed him in place while I was reading. I'm hoping that he's still in here because my compartment door was open. I don't like it closed."

It was all David could do to keep from laughing. She noticed his amusement and looked at him with guilty eyes. "Look, I know it was dumb, but I like that little creep. Are you going to help me find him or not?"

David had seen Orion in action. This turtle was anything but slow in space. He took to semi-weightlessness like no other creature he had seen. He could flap his feet to get moving, bounce off of anything, and fling himself around at a very un-turtle-like speed. If he had gotten out of the compartment, he could cover a fair distance by now, and that could present a real potential problem.

David switched on Casey's telecom screen and uttered the words, "Bridge, David here." Casey cringed.

"Go ahead, David." Commander Kidd's responded.

"Commander, I need a search party for an escapee."

"Would you like to run that one by me again, Mr. Security Officer? Just what do you mean by an escapee?"

"Sir, one African tortoise by the name of Orion is AWOL. He has flown the proverbial coop over here in Casey's module. We are currently hot on his trail, but he's a crafty one, sir."

The bridge was an instant roar of laughter. "Do we need to secure ship and go to battle stations, Mr. Striker?" Another roar.

Moses Brown's familiar voice came over the speaker. "I'm off duty and stand ready to volunteer, sir. I can track that little sucker down or my name isn't Moses." Still more laughter.

Meanwhile and to escape the laughter, Casey squeezed past David and headed in the opposite direction of David's compartment.

"He'll be headed for the hydroponics section, won't he, Casey?" It was Sergey Vosarov's voice from the galley. "If he shows up here, we'll have turtle stew for dinner tonight."

The crew was having a great time tossing around turtle stories and suggestions for how to capture him. Sergey suggested forming a posse and heading him off at the pass, using the traditional American method. Coming from the Russian with his accent, this painted an even more hilarious picture for the others.

A search party did form and began combing that section of this ship, to no avail. A four-inch-long turtle had a lot of room to hide in the many spaces of the *Kat*. Especially when he had the kind of multidirectional capabilities that a floating turtle possessed.

After about three hours the search was halted and Casey and David began to worry not only about the safety of their quarry but also the kinds of problems he could potentially cause. Casey Ramirez was beside herself. She called herself stupid at least twenty times—and so far no one had disagreed.

David and Casey decided to call off the search temporarily and hoped that Orion would get hungry and come out to eat. Casey had not fed him that day, but African tortoises could go a long time without food or water.

David returned to his compartment and resumed his photo work and listened to his music before he had to go back on official duty. He had decided that no one at NASA needed to know about this yet. As he settled back into his chair, out of the corner of his eye, he noticed a flash of movement. Floating into his cabin came a small, reptilian head, followed by a squat-shelled body. He simply reached up and grabbed Orion and petted the top of his head, saying, "I ought to kick your ass."

"Captain, after a valiant struggle, I have captured and secured one prisoner named Orion," he relayed to the bridge. With that, he spun Orion on his horizontal axis, and let him float spinning for a few seconds. When he stopped him, the turtle's face showed the dizziness. "Oh shit, turtles puke!"

Laughter carried throughout the ship. After recovering his composure the captain uttered: "Well done, Security Officer. Lock him in chains and throw him in the brig. Over and out."

10

STEALTH FINDER ONE

March 16, 2031

NASA HAD SENT the two probes to Enigma during late spring of 2030. In mid-May the first roared into space from Cape Canaveral, Florida aboard the Eurospace Shuttle *Valiant*. Released into orbit, then moved to launch position, it was fired toward its distant target in the same manner the *Kat* was later launched. On June first, the second was sent on a different trajectory, which would time its arrival just two Earth days later.

These probes were sent to gather more data for the Enigma mission. Voyager 7 had returned an amazing amount of rather startling information about the "Stealth Planet," as the crew and Mission Control now affectionately knew it. David and Margie had the task of translating and deciphering most of the data. Other scientists from around the world made their own observations, additions and deductions. The sum total of their multiple hypotheses was the conclusion that the planet had certain characteristics that made it different from every object in the solar system except for one, Earth.

Enough information was obtained to convince an impressive number of important people that they should approve the joint manned mission to further explore the New World. The key factor was sending humans, not rovers. The only planned long-range mission with a larger crew had been the Mars mission. NASA and the Russians always sent unmanned robotic probes to do their initial exploration forays far in advance of sending anything with people.

The logistics and risks of this mission were carefully appraised. Due to the distance, overall elapsed time, substantial costs, and sheer number of missions needed to produce the desired results, the joint space exploration powers-that-be had decided on one comprehensive, unprecedented, peopled project. At first, many considered it an absolutely untenable, unrealistic, and just plain dumb idea. But before too long, most scientists agreed that it would be humankind's greatest project. The incredible sense of cooperation between and among so many countries and their respective governments, scientists, and workers made it worthwhile. The risk of failure was great, but the rewards of success were immeasurable.

Because the probes could maintain a higher rate of speed than a craft with a human cargo, they would be arriving during the third month of the *Kat's* voyage. The basic premise of this reasoning was that, if the probes totally failed or sent back data indicating that the planned mission should be aborted, this mission could be re-directed toward Mars. It was always in the back of the planners' minds that the probabilities were such that the mission would most likely end up with this scenario.

In every crewmember's mind there was not any chance that this voyage was going to end up at or have Mars as the first stop. The entire initial training group had adopted an Enigma-or-bust mentality. Under Lee Tanaka's dictatorial direction, anything less was unacceptable. Any mention or discussion of Mars was strictly secondary to the primary direction of all efforts.

The first vehicle nicknamed, *Stealth Finder One* was due to arrive on March 16, 2031. It would obtain a high orbital position, deploy two exploration descent probes, and remain in orbit around Enigma, mapping and photo imaging a good portion of the cloud cover and whatever it could decipher from the surface. Due to the unknown total thickness of the outer, radar-dampening layer of the atmosphere, it would drop to successively lower orbits until it could hopefully see through the muck.

Voyager 7 had detected the layered atmosphere, and scientists were able to do some chemical analyses of its composition. Radar imaging was disappointing due to the radar-dampening characteristic of the carbon rich outer layer. This characteristic also dampened any light reflectance, enhancing the planet's ability to stay hidden. Photoreconnaissance by Voyager 7 had been wonderful, but the closest point it had come was over a million miles. Astronomers and scientists learned enough from other sensors aboard *V*-7 to convince them that the surface probably had traces of liquid water. The insulation of the atmosphere and active volcanism made the surface well below freezing but relatively warm compared to the other outer planets with wide aerial surface temperature variations. It was just too tempting a target and not completely inhospitable.

Stealth Finder One and *Two* were meant to complete the puzzle. Not only were they programmed to orbit and sense a broad spectrum of variables, but if all went as planned, they would land on and plunge into the surface. If they completed their missions as prescribed, there would not be much about the atmosphere and surface chemistry that would escape their myriad sensors.

The ides of March were barely passing when *Stealth Finder One* reached orbit around Enigma. It had been sending a steady stream of telemetry for almost a week during its approach and rendezvous. Sensors were automatically activated one by one in order to preserve precious energy. This far from the sun, a very large array of solar cells would be needed to generate even a small amount of solar energy. The nuclear generator onboard was extremely small due to the compact size of the spacecraft. Energy conservation and use allocation needed to be carefully controlled. This proved to be the tragic shortcoming of *Stealth Finder One.*

David was ecstatic when he received confirmation that the craft had indeed obtained a stable orbit. He was still the man in charge of data absorption and assimilation. He was also the first to receive and interpret it due to the additional time it took the data to travel from them back to Earth. He was primed and ready for new telemetry.

Margie was working directly with David again. Oreen took over some of her Systems Analyst chores. Margie was just as anxious to be monitoring and interpreting the new data stream from *Stealth Finder One.* The correct analysis of this data was critical to the overall success of their mission. Now it was up to Stealth Finder probes to supply the information and for David and her to put it into proper perspective. Only then could Commander Kidd and the decision-makers back on Earth put their final OK on proceeding to the planned destination.

David was watching the multiple telescreens built into the walls of the communications module. He was glued to the new images from the high-resolution camera on *Finder One* when Margie silently drifted in. She watched him staring with almost maniacal intensity and decided to wait until he finally noticed her rather than disturb his reverie, and in all likelihood, almost scare the wits out of him.

"David, David, darling," she said softly when he failed to notice after a few moments. She knew that he didn't scare easily and was not jumpy.

He finally turned to her and said, "Wow! This is great! I can see so much more than our best *V-7* photos. There are things showing up in the atmosphere that were just not clearly discernible in the earlier pictures. The upper part of the outer layer is harsh, and shows high wind velocities. We aren't going to get accurate readings of what's underneath until we get down through it. And that worries me. Those winds are strong, though only in a relatively thin layer, and there are elements in that layer that could be abrasive and corrosive."

"Tell me something that I'm not already worried about," Margie responded.

"These are known major problems. What new have you got to add to this concern?"

"Look at this sequence of pictures, and look at the motion of these individual cloud masses. What do you see?"

"Oh, I think I see what you are getting at," she frowned. "Those clouds are not just traveling along. They look like they're literally imploding in large convection cells or something."

"That's about it," he sighed. "I just hope that the probe remains stable and can get through that mess before retro fire or the first breaking parachute deploys. The two descent probes will get shaken a lot harder than we originally thought. They will be going in blind with most sensors temporarily shut down or idled, and we're too far away to make any emergency changes. It will literally be a shot in the dark. I'm afraid that our target's blanket is going to continue to make exact analysis of the surface difficult until we get through it."

She joined him at a console and began typing in some commands. She kissed him softly on the cheek and was surprised by his nearly overwhelming response. He pulled her close and hugged her while giving her the most sensually intense kiss he had given her in awhile. She blushed and kissed him back with equal intensity.

David had forgotten that the two-way telescreen connection to the bridge was still activated. Commander Kidd interrupted Pilot Phil Allen's concentration on his next chess move with a gentle nudge with his elbow. Allen looked up and smiled, adding a whispered, "You dirty old voyeur, you." Cappy Kidd, as they sometimes called him behind his back, couldn't stifle the laugh that escaped, and David suddenly remembered the telescreen.

David was about to give them the finger when he remembered to whom he had been talking and quickly abandoned that thought. Instead he went on with his kiss, and reached around Margie to wave a pleasant goodbye and flick on the privacy button.

The screen on the bridge went blank, and the two chess players resumed their game. Phil laughed and commented, "That might have gotten interesting if you hadn't laughed so loud."

Commander Kidd said, "And you referred to me as voyeuristic? We had better let them have some privacy for a while." They both laughed and went back to their series of chess confrontations, which Commander Kidd now led forty-one to twenty-six.

— § —

Every component was working well within acceptable parameters when the first stealth finder craft reached initial orbital position. Two smaller surface and atmospheric exploration probes were deployed as planned, and the main orbiter began its initial descent to just above the thick, black clouds.

The first surface exploration descent probe plummeted downward at high speed through the upper atmosphere, its heat shields working well. As it entered the dense upper cloud layers of Enigma the tumultuous clouds whipped it about wildly. Built to withstand almost anything, it broke through the clouds into a dim and fiery world. A tremendous down current in the dense layer had increased its downward velocity instead of slowing it, and the sensors aboard the craft began awakening and calculating when to brake and deploy slowing drone chutes. The radars were working properly and began to make necessary adjustments to trajectory and speed, and to scan for a safe place to land. Onboard cameras clicked to life and began taking pictures, but all too late. The probe detected water while searching for a hard landing area, but all for nothing.

In a few moments the unlucky probe encountered part of an immense volcanic cloud containing ash and sulfuric acid. Again blinded, the first probe plunged, confused, into a valley filled with molten rock and debris. Its usefulness was extinguished in seconds after its long and dangerous journey.

When the telemetry ended it was a profoundly silent moment for the entire crew. David and Margie watched it with a sickening feeling of loss. They could only hope that the few moments of telemetry they had received would be of some significant help to the overall mission.

Commander Kidd's voice was loud and obviously agitated. "Does anybody know what happened? Did we lose the signal or the craft? David, what's your assessment?"

"It's gone, sir, not just a transmission loss. The bird is dead."

"How soon until the second one goes in?"

"About five more minutes to release from the mother bird. It's still attached by a thin fiber-optic line," added David dejectedly.

"Did we get anything from the first one?" was Jason Kidd's next query.

"We should have that data analyzed and decoded in a ten minutes or so, but from the length of time it was operational, I don't think that we can expect too much. But I'm sure as hell hoping we got something. The second descent bird is slightly more solid and pretty tough," David added. "As you know, it's supposed to descend rapidly and burrow into the surface to analyze the soil or water or whatever it lands in or on. There were more cameras on the first bird. This one isn't blind, but it won't send us any color glossies. OK, everybody, cross your fingers and toes. Bird two should have just broke with mother bird and is dropping in on the host."

David knew that what they were watching had actually all happened some time ago due to the time it took for the data to reach them, but they were treating it all as real time.

David did not have the heart to look at the data from the first descent vehicle from *Stealth Finder One*. He saw that Margie was busy at her console and figured that she was evaluating the last data. He wanted to focus on the second probe and concentrate on what happened to it. In a few minutes, when it began the planned descent, he would soon know if they were going to learn much from this second bird.

Margie knew that the communications blackout with the second descender would last for a few more minutes. She was feeling the same disappointment that was written all over David. When the first processed image came into view, her disappointment only grew.

"I've got the first image on the screen here, David," she started. "It's pretty dark and blurry, even with the maximum enhancement and image re-stabilization."

"Is it worth looking at?" he droned. "Can you make anything out?" he added, moving from his status board to hers.

"Bridge, Margie here. We've got the first photo image up and an infrared image to go with it," she said before acknowledging David's questions. "Look for yourself," she added pointedly to David. "The photo looks pretty useless, but the infrared says a lot about our quarry. I'm adding other wavelengths and going to assimilate some of the other sensory data to make a composite and do it to both pictures."

"Both?" came the simultaneous responses from David and Commander Kidd.

"Yes, both. Two complete sets from all sensors are all we got, and from the last data, it seems we were lucky to get that. The probe took a terrible beating in the initial descent stage, and the temperature measurements went through the roof as telemetry ceased. I'm guessing that our bird dropped into turbulence like a mega-storm, like being hit by a force-four tornado, and maybe was incinerated on impact or before. Either we were incredibly unlucky, or that planet is far more inhospitable than *V-7* led us to believe."

"Commander, I concur completely with Margie's initial evaluation."

"Did everyone on board get that?" was Jason Kidd's next question, but it was more of a comment. "Let's relay your findings and complete evaluation back to Houston ASAP. Let's also hope like heck that the second probe survives a little longer and gives us something positive. I also suggest that we re-evaluate the programming for *Stealth Finder Two* and see if we can't improve our chances for success. If we don't, people, I don't think I have to tell you that it will mean an abort and course change to Mars. Good luck."

The pictures were poor at best and told David and Margie little. Darkness with a distant reddish glow and a very faint horizon was evident. The infrared photo data showed the hotter spots, and the ultraviolet information was marred by a strange spotted glow, which David and Margie could only shrug off as bad data. Even the composite images revealed little of concrete value, nothing they could depend upon as totally accurate.

— § —

Probe two from *Finder One* faired only slightly better, but what it relayed back sent elation and excitement throughout the *Kat*. It survived the plunge and encountered far less turbulence from its gyroscopic data and radar. What it landed on was not rock or soil but ice—frozen water! It was true; the planet had water vapor in the atmosphere as well as frozen water on part of the surface.

Unfortunately for the second probe, it was damaged on impact and cracked at several seams. Internal heat dissolved some surrounding ice, and its communications telemetry sender drowned and shorted out. The rest of probe two continued to function perfectly as it went about its tasks but communications with the *Kat* were terribly downgraded and eventually were lost completely.

The second lander lasted just long enough and sent back just enough usable data to replace the crew's dejection with new hope. There was usable temperature data indicating that at least some areas of the surface were not too extreme for landing. Radiation, though high, was within acceptable ranges. Winds were potentially navigable and survivable. The atmosphere, though thick and unbreathable, was at least not poisonous. And there was water, precious water, in the form of ice.

Telemetry from the second probe had lasted long enough to whet their appetites for more. When the data stream just stuttered and then winked out, David and Margie were stunned.

"Oh no, not again," were Margie's exact words as David was marveling over the magnetic and radiation readings. "Shit!" she screamed. We've lost bird two."

"What happened?" cried David. "Everything looked fine, and all systems were go. Give me a diagnostic analysis of the last few seconds of transmission."

The computer was simply blinking 'Transmission Error – System Failure' over and over.

"Go to backup," he shouted, but immediately reminded himself that any command they sent would still take some time to get there. "Can't we have some luck?"

"Should I send the 'go to backup' command?" Margie asked. "You know as well as I do that it will shut down the primary transmitter. The backup isn't nearly as strong."

"Do it, Margie. It's probably our only chance to re-establish any kind of communication. If that fails we'll at least know that it is a complete data-transmission failure."

She sent the command, and all that they could do was hope that the probe could receive it, make the manual switchover and start talking to them again. They both were disturbed by their initial conclusion, and it was later confirmed by the computer analysis. Bird two was probably still functioning but could not talk to them.

David let Jason know immediately. Commander Kidd had instructed them to give him hourly progress reports and patch through anything interesting directly after they confirmed landing and a good signal. He had then signed off to get some rest.

Sergey and Roberto Ortiz were on duty on the bridge. David decided that Margie could be the bearer of bad news this time.

"Bridge, Margie here."

"What's new with you two," Roberto responded.

"Is Commander Kidd awake?" she asked.

"No Senorita, he's been asleep for awhile and his screen is blanked. Do you need him or can we be of service?"

Margie really liked Roberto's style and Hispanic charm. He was incredibly fit and handsome and always flirted with her. This time she had to dispense with the pleasantries and get right to the point. "I've got some bad news for Cappy and everyone else. The bird winked out and basically stopped sending."

"Man, what's with these tweeties," Roberto responded. "I thought that this one was running fine."

"It was, probably still is, except for sending," she added. "Better wake up the boss. We have sent some commands and hope the probe will switch to backup, but it's probably a long shot."

Sergey added his input to the conversation. "Wait until base finds out. This is not good. They will not be pleased. Jason will have to let them know right away."

"We are all too aware of that," Margie ended and signed off.

— § —

The news was received at Mission Control in Houston, the chosen primary data-decoding station. Hank Wadkins called Lee Tanaka, Lawrence Greenbaum, and Press Secretary ZZ Rodgers immediately as the news came in, and they hastily convened a meeting of all of the directors to evaluate the new data. Rodgers had called the President and passed the pertinent information to Liz Rainwater so she could let him know.

As director of Eurospace and coordinator of the international assembly effort, Greenbaum was going to be in charge of this meeting. Besides, Tanaka had laryngitis, and Hank was going to review the data piece by piece.

Greenbaum kept it simple. He introduced the topic to the group by saying: "Ladies and gentlemen, both lander probes from *Stealth Finder One* were dispatched to the surface and were lost almost immediately thereafter. A limited amount of telemetry was received but an insufficient amount to make any final assessments in the eyes of those aboard the *Kat* and our experts here. The second stealth finder craft will arrive tomorrow and begin its experiments. We hope to receive more data from its landing probes due to several minor changes sent to the craft. The handouts and CDs given to you as you entered will provide you copies of all data sent by the probes and our assessment of the chances for the second craft. Based on the information before you, we would like your independent assessment of our chances from here. I will add one personal note. What we have gotten so far is absolutely fantastic and indicates, in my humble opinion, that we made the correct decision a year and a half ago."

Instead of disappointment, the feeling of excitement and a general sense of success were relayed to the *Kat* from Houston. Mission Control remained positive and sent the collective feeling of making the best out of the situation.

Back aboard the *Kat*, the entire crew was tense and nervous and preparing for the arrival of the second make-it-or-break-it *Stealth Finder Two* and its all-too-important rendezvous with the now slightly less mysterious Enigma.

11

SECOND CHANCES

March 18, 2031

SINCE THE LAUNCH from Earth orbit, this was the most important day in the mission, day number eighty-four. Everyone's attention on board the *Kat* was focused on *Stealth Finder Two*, the second orbiter, and its two descent vehicles poised for release. Minor orbital entry angle and orbit-attainment instruction changes had been transmitted to the craft. Confirmation of receipt and initiation of the instructions had just been received. While everyone gazed at the telescreen monitors, the computer was simulating exactly what was taking place near Enigma.

Finder Two was captured by the host planet's gravity, swung in a low arc into a very high orbit and made final course changes to line it up for probe one release. It established a communications link with *Finder One*, which was still circling the planet at a lower orbit. *Finder One* had established an orbit well above the tops of the highest raging storm clouds and was busy mapping cloud tops and weather phenomena. Its ability to see through the clouds was minimal, and onboard systems had warned it to drop no lower.

David and Margie asked Oreen Nadu, their medium and spiritual leader, to join them for the day. Oreen had told Margie that she had a bad feeling about *Stealth Finder One* three days ago, a full day before they lost the probes. She even said that she had a dream about lost and blind baby birds. David and Margie always referred to the probes as birds. They were afraid to ask her about the second set of probes, but they knew that Oreen would tell them anyway.

"Margie, you ask her, please," David whispered to her.

"Are you still afraid of me, David or just what I might tell you?" Oreen chimed in, in her inimitable style. She had the ability to sound like a Voodoo priestess when she wanted to. In the next moment she could be more charming and refined than a Hollywood hostess. She did scare him, though only because of her uncanny abilities that he could not explain using pure science.

That was exactly why she was on this mission, that and her ability to understand, soothe, and control even the most dispirited human. She had unseen, inexplicable powers that science was still struggling to decipher. They were her gifts, and she used them well; never abusing them. Margie just loved her; David was wary of her, but trusted her decisions completely.

"Oreen, I'll always be afraid of you for my own good," David answered. "You might turn me into a toad or change my brain into Jell-O."

"Negative on the first charge, star boy. You already is a toad. And make that jelly on the second, not Jell-O."

Margie cut in. "All right, you two, let's call a truce and get down to the business at hand."

"I'll makes you a mouse," Oreen continued, now laughing at Margie. She was obviously enjoying the act and they were all now laughing. In her simple way, Oreen had done it; she had broken the tension that permeated the module.

David and Margie had sent an entire series of new commands to *Finder Two*. They received confirmation of receipt from the *Finder*, and now it was following those new instructions to the letter. Through the communications link with *Finder One*, *Finder Two* was now basically telling *Finder One* to abandon its mission in orbit and commit suicide. The very complicated instructions reprogrammed the orbiter to become a terminal descent vehicle.

The specialists, crew, and Mission Control all had agreed that they needed the maximum amount of reliable information about their target below the impervious clouds and turbulent upper atmosphere. If the second pair of descent probes met final demises similar to the first, Mission Control could not approve the complete mission. One orbiting platform, out of harm's way at an upper extreme orbit, would suffice to relay needed data upon their approach, if there was to be an approach.

Stealth Finder One was going in with all guns blazing. Brought up to full power, and all systems turned on to maximum efficiency, it was aimed and sent crashing through the torturous atmosphere. It would blaze a path for the optically specialized first lander probe from *Finder Two*. If successful, the risk to this first descent module and its specialized optical equipment would be minimized. At least that was the theory. This contingency was always part of a backup plan anyway; so, the programming, though difficult, was semi-cookbook.

Assuming the plan was successful, *Finder One* would continuously send data back to the descent module it was leading to the surface, allowing it to make course and landing changes, in order to aim for the best possible landing site. Descent Module One was further instructed to deploy slowing parachutes at a lower elevation and to employ a hovering style of flight. *Finder One*, meanwhile, would send data until it burned up, disintegrated, or plowed into the surface at a very high rate of speed. It had no heat shield, no brakes other than its maneuvering pulse rockets, and absolutely no chance of survival for very long.

Everyone understood that the machines would communicate, but no one knew how long *Finder One* would last. The theory was to break through the thick cloak of dense black clouds and get a few pictures of what was underneath, since it was at least now confirmed that there was a less thick layer below. They all knew that the orbiter, by design, was not as strong as the descent modules. Cognizant that the first descent vehicle from *Finder One* had not fared well at all, this next move was a long shot at best, but any assistance rendered to the next descender would be invaluable.

David was convinced that this time this stealth planet was going to give up a few more secrets. The layered atmosphere was confirmed and the outer shell had been analyzed extensively now. Stealth Planet was definitely a unique scientific objective in many ways at this point. Dense, light-and-radar-absorbing outer layers were thick and rapidly moving and a raging tumult of storms or vortices. The atmosphere thinned considerably and calmed down somewhat below this layer. It then thickened and warmed toward the surface, a property unique to any body in the solar system. There were many gases in this atmosphere, and the outer layer contained several elements that could not be clearly identified. David was sure that this gave the outer layer its unique properties.

The planet's surface had numerous hot spots, thermally and radioactively, with many signs of active volcanism. Gravity was variable and strangely patchy. Water was present in the form of vapor and ice with some traces of free oxygen. Bits and pieces were being added to the puzzle since *V-7* made its historic pass, but they would still need to obtain more extensive, higher-quality data and information if they were going to get clearance to proceed to the Stealth Planet with this mission.

"Margie, we should be under way with our next foray according to the mission timer," David stated. He whispered very quietly and a little lower than the last time as he leaned toward her. "Ask her now, please."

Margie glanced at Oreen and Oreen raised her eyebrows and peered back. Margie wondered if Oreen had super hearing too and knew David was now convinced that she did. Before Margie could say anything, Oreen said, "What are you two whispering about now?"

David just had to say it. He couldn't resist the chance and took it while he was in a great mood. "Oh come on, Oreen, why would you need to ask? Aren't you reading our minds? Don't you know what we're thinking? Come on, you aren't losing your touch, are you?"

"Of course not," she quipped. "In your case there just ain't much to read. Kinda like looking at the comics when you're sittin' next to a great novel."

Margie was still trying to get a word in edgewise and ask Oreen about her feeling concerning the next phase of her present operation. Instead she was now thinking: *Here we go again.* And she could not help but laugh again too. David shot her a quick glance.

"Hold on, young lady, I'm not done with the young gentleman yet," Oreen continued. "You wanted her to ask me what I thought about the chances for success for the next phase of the Stealth Finder mission. Didn't you? And Margie was going to ask me before your cute little slippin' comments. You should have asked me more before you reprogrammed your babies to sacrifice *Finder One.* It will not work. Everything tells me that *Finder One* won't help *Finder Two.*"

"You mean to tell me that you've waited until now to tell me this if you felt this strongly about it?" David pleaded. "You mean that this whole Stealth Finder stuff is doomed to failure?"

"Calm down, David," Margie interjected. She noticed that Oreen was taking on the role of voodoo priestess again, something she loved to do to taunt David.

"Yeah, astronut, calm your ass down," Oreen added with even more character. "I'm cogitating on your stuff right now, at this very instant, and I feel a big old dream coming on."

Margie was now out of control and tumbling about the module laughing hysterically. David didn't see what was so funny.

Oreen went on: "I didn't say anything about the mission failing. Actually, I think we're going to get some very pleasing information, and you might end up real happy." She let the y at the end of happy trill from her lips. It was obvious that she was enjoying this game. "Oh, I'm cogitating, I am," she squealed as she spun around next to David.

He finally realized what was going on and let out a small laugh. "Man, I am uptight about this. Sorry that I got so shook up. You two can stop playing whirling dervishes now."

But the other two were enjoying this moment and just kept on. "Are you cogitating too, Miss Ritter?"

"Oh, yes ma'am I am." Margie spun on using her best little-girl southern drawl. She found their word "cogitating" to be hilarious at the moment.

David seized the moment to get even, just a little bit. He silently and carefully switched on the two-way telescreen button, being watchful of their glances. He opened their channel throughout the ship with the flick of a second switch and calmly went back to work at his console.

"What's wrong, honey, is your ass still mad?" Oreen taunted.

"Yeah loosen up a bit. This is fun," added Margie.

"May I inquire as to what the hell is going on in the Data Assimilation and Control Module?" The familiar voice of Commander Kidd came over the two-way speaker.

"Just a couple of loose screws, Captain," David responded, without taking his eyes off of his work.

"That's a pretty apt description," added Doc. "We may have some serious space sickness there. Do you need some assistance, David? Maybe a couple of straitjackets?"

The reverie was over just that quickly for the whirlers. Laughter was coming in from everywhere throughout the ship, along with wonderful tidbits of descriptive verbiage.

Now it was David's turn to laugh, and he hugged them both in their moment of light embarrassment. "That was fun," he added. "We need to do this everyday."

"Did you mean it, Oreen?" David asked.

"You bet I did, David," she responded. "Cross your toes and fingers, but I feel good about *Finder Two.*"

David smiled and hugged her again even harder.

— § —

The probes from the *Stealth Finder Two* were about to have a much better chance for success for one other reason. When *V-7* attempted to image through the tough outer shell of Enigma, its attempts were stifled. Most forms of energy striking the outer layer were simply absorbed. *V-7* provided only clues due to be being hampered, but just enough was garnered to whet more appetites.

Though the resources for analyzing this problem using *V-7* had been limited, the probes were designed to overcome the obstacles. The problem of penetrating through the layer to image what was below it was a two-way street. Once the probes were below the surface layer, sending data back through the layer would be just as big a problem. Lasers were useless, radio energy absorbed, microwaves or radar dampened except for a few wavelengths. But the data transmission specialists had come up with some ingenious ways to overcome this problem.

Unfortunately for probe two from *Stealth Finder One*, the solution had not worked very well. The incorrect assumption was made that the probe had completely lost the ability to transmit. In actuality, it was sitting on the surface transmitting some information. The data transmission was simply not penetrating the planet's shroud. Part of the reprogramming of *Stealth Finder Two* was meant to cause the probes to attempt data transmission bursts using various methods that might be at least potentially successful. A computer analysis of the partial transmission from the first probes had suggested a possible answer. The solution worked during several computer simulations. Since the exact nature of the outer layer was still conjecture, the models were of limited value.

David and Margie added their own ideas and could now only hope that one of them worked. Their ultimate goal was to get a good look below the shroud, particularly at the surface. A landing could not be chanced unless a clearer picture was obtained. The clearer picture would simply not happen unless the data was successfully relayed through the layer and back to them. The scientific community following the mission on Earth was enjoying the challenge presented by this problem.

Stealth Finder Two deployed her two charges and sent them on their way. *Finder One* signaled and the first probe from *Finder Two* responded by following, dropping out of its orbit. Cameras carried by *Finder One* blinked to life. The radars all powered up at the same time as ordered. Every system of sensors came to life at once rather than sequentially, as in a normal power-up. The fact that this would overwhelm the power supply rather quickly was well known, but of little consequence, since the craft would soon be destroyed anyway.

As *Finder One* dipped into the foreboding clouds, many of its systems were already badly overloaded and rapidly failing. Onboard cameras snapped several good pictures that were instantly transmitted rather than being stored. The pictures were sent to orbiting *Finder Two* for relay back to the *Kat*. In order to minimize the effects of the atmosphere, this precaution was used, rather than direct transmission. All sensors continued to function although *Finder One* was very badly jostled by the whipping atmospheric currents, and began heating up very rapidly. To the dismay of those aboard the *Kat*, *Finder One* was now basically blind but could use the merged data from various sensors to detect a path through the atmosphere with the least destructive potential. Before *Finder One* emerged from the outer clouds, its underpowered energy resources were expended and most systems had failed. The craft was in pieces and was incinerated by the heat of friction with the atmosphere and quickly burned up.

David and Margie's plan was bold but left only one possible outcome for the craft. *Stealth Finder One* was sacrificed, but the plan worked. *Stealth Finder One* lasted just long enough and was able to steer clear of the most dangerous and potentially destructive disturbances.

The first descent vehicle from *Finder Two* followed the same path and was spared the destructive forces encountered by its predecessors. But it did not come through unscathed. The optical sensors were left with a soot-like covering, except for one camera, the lens cover of which, by design, would not open until on the surface. This camera survived to transmit after landing. The parachutes deployed correctly, and the retro rockets slowed the craft, as planned, for a relatively gentle and successful landing. It came to rest on the surface of a rugged and rather barren alien world and began the task of sending data. David and Margie's decision to transmit data in bursts, in the specific manner they hoped would allow penetration of the atmosphere, worked. Descent probe one from *Finder Two* was on the surface and successfully transmitting.

Descent probe two from *Finder Two* was in trouble almost immediately upon its encounter with the dense cloud layer. It was hit by several very strong tornadic vortices. By basic design, it would land by a controlled, low-angle crash, cushioned by inflated bags. It would then measure ambient surface conditions using numerous sensing devises. In addition, it would then probe the surface for up to three meters, analyzing all of the materials encountered.

Functioning as planned, it hit the surface, skipped on its cushioning air bags, and came to rest half-buried in a sand dune. Probe two obtained success again, but not without some damage. Both probes from *Finder One* essentially failed, whereas both probes from *Finder Two* functioned well within the design parameters. The true measure of success was still dependent on the quality and quantity of useful information garnered and transmitted back to the *Kat*.

Probe one was the photographer and was a sensory monitor of a broad array of surface conditions both close to the lander and toward the distant horizons. Probe two, by contrast, would analyze the immediate area of its landing in minute detail. It analyzed soil and rock samples, atmospheric gases, temperature, winds, light values, and various other properties of the surface. Its auger was designed to dig into the surface and test in several ways for composition, chemistry, and biology from the first scratch of the surface to a maximum obtainable depth of about three meters. It also measured gravitational values and effects. This probe was a miniaturized scientific laboratory, and it was now on the surface of Enigma and functioning.

The landing sites were fairly close together, less than fifty kilometers, incredibly only thirty miles apart after a multi-month journey. Both had landed on opposite sides of a low mountain range, thus allowing information gathering from two entirely different sites. Unfortunately the machines had the obstacle of mountains between them, which would cause interference with inter-craft communications.

David could hardly wait to see the first images gathered by probe one from *Stealth Finder Two* from the surface. Images from the hovering and landing were very blurry and poor, in spite of the technology used to capture them. Conditions on the surface were very dark on final approach, and the landing lights were almost completely obscured by the strange soot coating the camera lenses and everything else.

Once the craft was stable on the surface, a second camera system became operational. Its main lens and fiber-optic vantage points allowed much better coverage. This main camera rotated three hundred and sixty degrees, zoomed in or out, and was supplemented by several other lenses connected by fiber optics. Several additional views were obtainable using these other vantage points.

Sending commands to the craft was expected to be extremely difficult once on the surface; so the lander was designed to run a pre-programmed, general reconnaissance sequence of photos. The first photos came into the computer on the *Kat*. These were non-zoomed, color photos of a few degrees of arc from the main camera. The next images were views of the surface below the lander. None were bright enough for David and Margie to make out much detail of what was there. Disappointment returned following David and Margie's initial perusal. Frowns and impatience were the general consensus of the crew.

Everything in the program operating the cameras was designed to follow sequential steps; each built from computer analysis of the first photos. Each step would be slow and tedious for the impatient analysts. Margie was the most disgruntled. David had more patience, as usual.

The initial photos were at least thought-provoking. The immediate landing area was a dark, somber place. They wondered if it got any brighter. There was an obvious red glow in the distance. Could an active volcano cause it? When zoomed telephoto shots began to come in, they would have an answer.

The surface below the lander appeared to be a coarse, sand-like material. Margie and David expected light intensity from the lander's limited lights to be considerably better. Pre-programming of the onboard computers would slowly adjust the light intensity and exposure duration for subsequent digital photos. As time on the surface passed, a spotlight would add illumination and definition to the pictures. Its use had to be limited because of the energy consumed.

As each photo came in, it was quickly analyzed, saved, and disseminated to everyone onboard for his or her analysis, curiosity, and comments. Relayed to Earth, these photos were also analyzed by myriad experts, none of whom really knew exactly what they were examining.

Breakthrough number one came at 0200 ship's time while David was sound asleep. Margie's excited voice came through his intercom with a distinctive character that he immediately recognized. "David, wake up and switch on your monitor. You'll want to see this."

He rubbed his eyes and glanced at the clock. He had only gotten about two hours of sleep. His eyes were heavy.

"Come on, sleepy head, switch on your monitor," she insisted.

He yawned and groped for the switch. The picture appeared instantly and he stifled a second yawn. "Wow, that's neat!" he exclaimed. "Any idea what it is?"

"It's green and looks like phosphorescence," she replied. "Looks like a spill from a light stick or a firefly's butt."

"Great description, and it does," he said through a yawned laugh. "How far away and how big? Can you tell yet?"

"Get up and join us up here in data processing," Margie stated emphatically.

"Aye, aye, my captain," he returned. "That looks awesome."

David arrived in the processing compartment in time to see Margie, science officer Norm Mailor, and copilot Roberto Ortiz pointing at what looked like another view of the glowing phenomenon. The conversation occurring was one of excited speculation.

"David, join us. Look at this one," came from within the compartment. He slipped inside.

"This one shows more as the camera swings toward it," said Margie. "It's a patch on a rock. Could be a mineral within the rock or a coating on the rock. It's not quite clear enough yet." She was so excited she was almost babbling.

"If it's a coating, it could be chemical or bioluminescent," stated Norm Mailor. "It might be a lifeform."

David realized this as he said it. He felt gooseflesh, and the hair on his arms was standing up. The ramifications were enormous, a lifeform, possibly.

If the material was alive, the discovery constituted one excellent justification for the completion of their mission.

Subsequent pictures showed the landing area appeared solid, non-threatening, and potentially favorable as a choice for their landing. Excitement was replacing the earlier disappointments.

12

FULL SPEED AHEAD

WHILE THE PICTURES continued to come into the *Kat* and to the various agencies and specialists on Earth, Mission Control debated but made the decision to allow Jason and his crew to forge ahead with the primary mission, that is, if the crewmembers were also unanimous in their decision. Mars would officially be bypassed just short of the absolute final decision point. The ship and crew were functioning to near perfection, so now it was up to them.

"You are go for the long trip," were the simple words in the message from Earth. Commander Kidd read the brief message from NASA Mission Control. He then continued with the official version. "You are hereby authorized to bypass the Mars Mission, the secondary backup target. You must all agree that you are ready for a mission of more than double the duration. If in complete agreement, repeat complete, you are further instructed to reconfigure the ship and to enter a new course. Immediately prepare for propulsion on said new course." This was followed by the new calculated trajectories and technical information. The message continued, "Please advise as to when preparations will be completed," and ended with, "Good luck, God speed, good hunting."

They had done it, had passed the critical point, had received enough necessary information from the planet, and had been given the "go" to proceed with their mission. Morale was at its peak again. They were now completing the third month of their voyage and embarking on the next leg, which could take another eight months, if all went as planned.

As David reflected on the first three months, he recounted his activities and their progress. It seemed more like only three weeks. The time had literally flown by. What had seemed like routine, he realized was more like nervous energy. All efforts to this point had focused on one objective: heading for the Stealth Planet. They had now achieved this goal; the mission was an official success so far.

President Walker surprised them all with a long personal message. Zeke Rogers briefed him well, although the President's personal interest in the project was obvious to the crew from the start. The President had taken the time and effort to focus on each member of the crew. He picked out a few anecdotes or idiosyncrasies and produced a special tribute. Everyone was caught by surprise and touched.

Lee Tanaka also sent his heartfelt congratulations and said he wished he could be there a dozen times. Hank Wadkins and Lawrence Greenbaum added their best wishes and lauds. They were proud of the *Kat* and its twelve travelers.

Ishmael did not send any message. David noticed this and was now convinced that Ishmael was purposely avoiding contact. He went back to his file and log to review it again. The computer had long ago generated a map with traces and a spreadsheet log of Ishmael's whereabouts throughout his time during the fabrication of their vessel. David had looked for something obvious, some pattern out of the norm for the reclusive little man. He wondered if maybe he needed to look again and decided that yes, he most certainly did, and began to scour those records again.

Margie's conversations with her family became less frequent as time sped by. She actually had more free time to communicate, as the obsessive analysis of the lander data became less critical. The frequent calls home left her with a genuine feeling of homesickness. It became more obvious everyday to the crew that she was suffering and struggling with her emotions.

Doctor Pritchard had summoned David for a consultation during the latter part of the fourth month. It was Doc's job to notice and monitor everyone's behavior. She had seen the subtle changes in Margie and consulted with Oreen Nadu, because she knew that Oreen was aware. Doc knew that Oreen and Margie had forged a strong intellectual bond. They also both enjoyed picking on David.

Oreen made the observation that Margie was not getting enough rest. She was sleeping, but not really resting. Her close relationship with her sister and the continuous worry for her well being were slowly taking their toll. Her brief elation with the *Stealth Finder* probe photos was replaced shortly thereafter by a period of depression.

David noticed it and was as supportive as possible, more than anyone else could be. He was becoming a bit frustrated by her denials that anything was bothering her. Their relationship remained warm and wonderful, but his feeling of being helpless was growing.

Doctor Pritchard's job was the easiest on the voyage thus far. She had a super healthy crew with virtually no complaints, but she observed her crew, and did so very well. Not much escaped her gaze. In her own inimitable way, Doc had zeroed in on the problem. Her reason for a consultation with David was to first investigate the potential for some type of problem between David and Margie. Beyond that, she just wanted to find a way to cheer her up. Doc was never one to waste a word, so she came directly to the point. David said, "Hi," and settled into a comfortable position in the infirmary.

"I've seen some subtle changes in Margie," Doc began. "She seems a little depressed. Is everything fine with you two?"

"Yes, Doc. We're getting along great, but she does seem a little down; still feels bad about her sister, even though she's recovering well, considering how severely she was hurt."

"That was my prognosis too," observed Doc. "A bit depressed, nothing physical, but it is a bit protracted."

"Yeah, I keep telling her to snap out of it, but I can't seem to get her to shake it."

"I'm going to suggest a checkup with me, and we will go from there."

"I've got a better idea, Doc," David smiled. "Are we private? Two-way communicator off? I know how to cheer her up."

"Yes we are, David. Your conversation in here will be private unless we've prearranged any two-way communications."

"Well, Doc, I've decided to ask her to marry me. We'll get married in space on the way to Enigma and honeymoon in orbit. How's that for wild? She's wanted to get married for almost two years, and I've been the biggest fool in the cosmos not to have done it already."

You could have knocked Doctor Pritchard over and sent her tumbling with a feather.

"I haven't asked her yet, Doc, and I'm hoping she'll say yes. I've never been afraid to ask her anything before this. Jason can marry us, as the captain of this ship. He should have the power. Oreen could probably do it too, or they both could."

His excited sputtering did not let Doc get in a single comment. "Wow!" she said. "What a great idea and a super event for the entire crew to plan for. She'll say yes, or I'm a poor judge of relationships. You better ask her soon, though, because I'm lousy at keeping secrets."

He was beaming. "Thanks, Doc. I had to tell somebody. I am going to go ask her right now. I've rehearsed how I'm going to do it."

David headed out of the infirmary with thoughts whirling through his brain. He could not believe that he had told Doc, the chief gossip on board.

But he knew that she was a professional first and never talked about anyone's personal business, just everything else. It was Oreen he was worried about. She could see right through him. Her knowledge of eye reactions and body language was beyond belief. If he ran into her, she would figure it out. At least, that was what he feared.

Margie Striker. It sounded good. She had said so several times. He considered asking her on several previous occasions. Even before the discovery, he at least tossed around the idea. During their training it had troubled him. *If one or the other of them didn't make the crew,* he often wondered if it would be better to be married and be apart or not? *If he had made the crew and she hadn't, would she want to marry him? Would he want to be married to someone who would be gone for two to three years — someone who might never come back?*

It was all a moot point. They made the decision long before the final crew selection, that if one did not make it, the other would not go either. They thought that this idea made them work that much harder. Fortunately, it was a bridge they never had to cross.

His reverie was suddenly interrupted by a hunger pang accompanied by a tap on the shoulder. His stomach growled. He did not even realize where he was; he was so deep in thought. It was Oreen, smiling broadly, her hand still gently resting on his shoulder.

"Somebody is really hungry and very pensive," she said, raising her eyebrows. David turned toward her.

David was shocked at her appearance, but his stomach had temporarily rescued him. "I'm starved," he answered. He suddenly saw the potential to test her again. He had made up his mind that he would ask Margie soon, very soon. Maybe immediately if Oreen guessed or somehow figured it out.

"Care to join me for a quick snack, Oreen? I haven't eaten yet and would enjoy the company if you haven't eaten already."

"I haven't," she answered, adding, "I'd be delighted to join you. We don't talk enough."

They made their way to the dining module expecting to see Casey, but she was off tending to supplies. Her latest culinary creation was waiting for them. Rod Amerigo was just leaving. After they were gone, Oreen checked the intercom and whispered to David, "I think that the relationship is good between those two."

"Leave it to you to pick up on that," David said, testing the waters. "What else have you picked up on?"

"Me?" Oreen grinned. "I thought you weren't much on gossip and hearsay? It must be boring if you're asking me about our floating dormitory."

"Just trying to make conversation, Oreen. What would you like to talk about?"

They spent the meal in quiet conversation on several non-controversial subjects. David carefully avoided anything about him and Margie. Casey returned, looked around for Rod, and said, "Hi," before going back to work on some culinary concoction. She was preparing something special for Roberto Ortiz, since it was his birthday.

David prepared to leave feeling confident inside that Oreen did not sense anything about his plans. He felt good, more confident that he finally outsmarted her or at least kept something from her. He was just leaving the mess area as Oreen sipped her second measure of hot tea.

"David," she spoke softly. "Ask her."

"Pardon me?" David responded.

"She loves you very much. Ask her, David."

"Oreen, you're amazing." David was stunned and bewildered. Oreen was smiling at him and then turned away with a wave of her hand.

"Thanks, Oreen, I will," was all he said. He left the mess hall, his head still spinning inside.

That evening both he and Margie would be off from duty at the same time. He carefully prepared a small sign saying simply, "Margie, will you marry me? I love you!" He morphed it into the most recent photo of her favorite rock with the phosphorescent patch. She would notice the difference in the picture and enlarge it immediately. He could not wait to see her reaction as he finished adding it to the photo. It blended in almost perfectly. Margie studied the photos of the peculiar yellow-green discoloration with a passion. Several other patches had been located, and they now had a few good close-ups of the rock and immediate area around it. One altered photo would serve his purpose well.

When she arrived at her personal compartment, he was waiting. He was fidgeting.

"Hi, honey. How was your day? You didn't come up to the photo-recon area."

David said that he was fine and had been busy with other things.

Margie continued by saying, "Oreen told me that you two had a long, enjoyable lunch together. She even said that it was probably the most that she has ever enjoyed talking to you one-on-one. I was pleasantly surprised. You two aren't known to get along that well."

David's heart sank a little. He couldn't imagine that Oreen could have or would have said anything. Margie also had just said that she was in the photoreconnaissance area, which also meant that she had, in all likelihood, already seen enough of the new photos for today. He truly wanted her to see one more.

She noticed the photo on her computer screen. "Is that the last one?" she asked, and then quickly answered her own question. "Oh yes, I've seen enough of that to give me a headache."

This was not going as planned. She was about to turn off the monitor when he stopped her hand. He brought it to his mouth and kissed it softly. He kissed up her arm, all the while never taking his eyes off of the monitor. He continued to stare at the picture until she followed his eyes to the screen and the eerie picture. A questioning look slowly appeared on her face and she began staring hard at the bright screen, their faces now side by side.

"How did I miss that?" she asked. He did not let go of her hand. "David, what is that speck? I must have missed it." She used her free hand to move her mouse, placing the cursor directly over the tiny new speck. She enlarged it once. David smiled. It was still too small. He tried to get her other hand, but she enlarged the area again. This time, tiny print appeared. The next enlargement brought the tiny letters to a legible size, in nearly clear focus. He began to quiver.

"Yes, yes, David, of course I will." She smiled and hugged him to herself as tears streamed from her eyes. "Whoever the little green man is who planted that sign there, I'm going to marry him. I've waited long enough for you to ask me."

Laughter replaced her tears and he joined her. He anticipated that he would be happy and relieved to hear her say yes, but he had never expected to feel this good.

"Can I tell Oreen? Please, David, she'll be so happy."

"Sure you can, but I'll bet that she already knows. You may announce it to the entire universe. I'm the happiest guy in our tiny piece of it."

"I've got to tell everybody." Margie was excited. David was elated. "May I go now?" she asked. "I want to tell the rest of our crew personally. I'll be back as soon as I can, and then we'll have a special evening. I want a print of my proposal to take along."

Margie went throughout the entire vessel spreading her message of good cheer. Every crewmember expressed total delight. Oreen, of course, was thrilled and wanted to start planning that moment. Commander Kidd shook Margie's hand and was somewhat perplexed at the news that he and Oreen would be performing the ceremony.

Jason had one question for her. He politely inquired, "Margie, who is going to tell Mission Control? They are going to be surprised. You also know they are going to milk the PR for all it's worth."

"You're right," she answered. "You can tell the folks at NASA and in Washington, but I'm going to tell my family first. I don't want them hearing this from the media. David will want to let his folks know too."

"Of course you know that we can keep this our little onboard secret," he interjected.

"No, I don't think that will be necessary," she continued. "I'll check with David, but I think that he wants the entire world to know. Come to think of it, so do I."

Jason had waited for a second confirmation from David and Margie. He then relayed the message through Hank Wadkins, their friend and mentor. Mission Control was surprised and delighted. It was exactly what they needed to keep attention directed at their mission: a marriage in deep space, millions of miles from Earth. Hank was also very pleased by the news. He summoned Betty Hurley into his office and announced they would need some champagne. They immediately contacted David and Margie with a personal congratulatory message. Margie told Hank and Betty to look for an invitation, and she expected them to show up. It left Betty feeling a little sad that she would not be able to be there. She did promise to save some champagne for the special celebration dinner they would all have when the newlyweds returned.

Hank contacted Lee Tanaka and Zeke Rogers. The message could be properly prepared and the news release timed to everyone's satisfaction. It would not take long for the news to spread.

— § —

At the midpoint of the fifth month they were nearing the halfway point of their journey. The ship and crew were still functioning smoothly. NASA, the crew, and all involved hoped the second half of the journey would be as successful as the first half.

David and Margie set a date for the wedding. They picked June 26—a traditional June wedding in the bleakness of space. This date would also mark the passage of the mission's sixth month, another milestone.

Each member of the crew would be an integral part of the wedding party. Oreen and Margie were having a great time organizing their plans. To everyone's surprise Rod Amerigo wanted to be involved in everything. He was having fun and treating David like a little brother. Oreen offered a simple explanation: Amerigo just had more free time on his hands than the rest of the crew. She was preparing to take care of that little problem before he became a pest.

Casey took it upon herself to design and fabricate a fairly elaborate wedding dress for the bride-to-be. At first Margie wanted no part of her idea. A simple exchange while wearing her uniform would have suited her. Casey and Oreen would not hear of it. Casey sketched some basic ideas and used a pattern-designing program to put together a simple, yet elegant dress. When Margie saw it she liked it. David thought it was great. For Casey it was a mission accomplished.

On the twentieth of June, while working on the dress with Casey, Margie was summoned to the photo-recon area. She was perturbed, but Casey said, "Go ahead," since they would not have called her unless something interesting came up.

She wanted to make sure David did not see her dress, so the telescreen was in the intercom position only. She checked twice before saying, "David, what have you got? Is it another miniature signpost? I'm already taken."

"No sign this time, but the inhabitants left the post behind," he returned.

"What exactly do you mean by that?" Margie was now curious. "Can you patch it through to me here?"

"I can, but I thought you might want to help run the diagnostic analysis. We haven't seen much new for a while. The lights have been off for several days to conserve energy. They were slowly being covered by that mysterious soot too."

"I know all that," she stated emphatically. "What is different?"

"This is the first photo since the lights came back on." David's tone was more serious now. "I really think you should see this."

As she headed toward the recon area, Margie passed Rod Amerigo on his way to get a snack. He wanted to talk to her about the dress and Casey's work. Margie had noticed his ever-increasing interest in everything Casey did. It was Oreen who first noticed it, then David on his security rounds. Rod and Casey spent several nights together during the second month. It was expected and only human to cohabitate, so David ignored it. Romantic encounters were expected, and one of the reasons for final crew selection was the factor of compatibility. She knew that they slept together often. At this moment she was not interested in social chatter and suggested that Rod go check on Casey's progress himself. He stated that he was on his way to do exactly that. He smiled, turned, and headed for Casey's compartment.

When Margie arrived at the recon area, David handed her a printout with the original photo the computer had downloaded. She stared at it for a few seconds before making the correct observation. "Whatever it is, it is in the foreground and extremely out of focus."

"Exactly," David said. "There's not much hope of deriving a clear image from this data, but the camera should adjust the focal length automatically and give us a better image on the next one. Right now the computer is extracting the foreground data and reprocessing it to create a good three-dimensional projection. We should get an excellent holographic image. I'm also processing the data for composition. I knew that you would want to be here when that data came out."

The composition data came out first. Bitter disappointment was written all over David's face as he scanned the composition analysis data on the screen. "Unknown" was repeated several times. He typed in the command, "make best fit," telling the machine to take its best guess. He knew that the computer would try to refit the data to the best analogy from the vast library of possibilities stored within. The hair on his arms stood up and his eyes widened as a brief result appeared beside the blinking cursor: Possible organic compound, source, and composition unknown. The answer continued to blink on the screen. No one uttered a word.

The low hum of the primary recon analysis computer broke the silence. A fuzzy image appeared on the right screen of the dual high-resolution monitors. A holographic three-dimensional image had formed. David leaned over, selected a new color bar, and changed the color to one more subdued. The chosen shading rendered an excellent view of a stem-like object with a bend near the upper edge of the frame. The fact that the object in the original was so much out of focus made surface detail of the image untenable. Therefore any more detail would have to wait until the next image.

David, Margie, Roberto, Sergey, and Jason, who had joined them, began to speculate. Could it be a stick, a hair, or possibly be a dried piece of something organic? It certainly left plenty of room for guesswork. It was Margie who made the observation that, since the first photo, they had not seen anything remotely resembling anything from Earth, or anything that moved except for the sky above the lander and some blown dust.

The next photo was expected to arrive within a few hours. They would be able to draw some more scientific conclusions. It had been an exciting afternoon already. Commander Kidd and Phil Allen watched a repeat as the object formed on their monitor. They filled the bridge area with conversation, arguing about what they had seen. They both wondered where Amerigo was. He seldom missed a new recon photo and always enjoyed relaying them to Mission Control.

When Jason reached the bridge, Roberto had a message waiting for him.

Roberto handed him a paper with the new information from Control. "Where's Rod?" he asked Jason and Phil. "This communiqué came in, and he wasn't here to take it. I had it sent up here to the bridge."

"Interesting. Rod wasn't at the recon lab either." Jason decided to find him. "Rod, please contact the bridge." Jason double-checked to see if he was on duty. Their schedules had all become more relaxed. "He might have decided to go to sleep."

"Rodrigo, here," the Communications Officer interrupted his thought. "I'm in the Bio-Lab. I was down here checking that Orion's restraints were still working. Casey has him out of solitary confinement."

"Cute, Rod, but you missed an interesting little news tidbit that came in a few minutes ago. Roberto picked it up for you."

"I know," said Rod. "I picked it up on my pocket unit, but it didn't seem that important."

Jason relayed the brief message to the crew. Rod was right. It was not that important, but it added to a day that started out normal but was getting very interesting. Enigma had been officially designated the Stealth Planet. It was the name everyone on the ship already used for their quarry.

Rod was enjoying his time alone with Casey. She seemed to like him, and he was growing very fond of her. He had been spending more and more time in the Bio-Lab. Today's meeting generated more vigorous heat between them. Rod just decided to kiss her when Orion came paddling by. Before he could move closer to Casey, as if on cue, Orion decided to deposit his calling card pellet, which came floating toward him.

"Casey, your beast is trying to run me out of here."

Casey looked up and immediately snatched Orion out of the air, stuck a Velcro patch on his bottom and deposited him in his open container. "How can you go so much?" she scolded.

"Thanks for the help, Rod," she said as she captured Orion's gift and disposed of it. She kissed his cheek and returned to her sewing. He was caught by surprise by the kiss.

"See you later." He smiled and headed toward the Communication Center feeling good about the afternoon with Casey.

The next photo came in a few minutes past seven that evening. A small crowd of crewmembers formed to see the photo first hand. Jason decided to patch it through the ship to everyone's personal compartment as well as to the fitness center and dining area. The camera had not focused on the foreground. The object, whatever it was, had vanished. Wind and atmospheric-turbulence data indicated that there was a slight breeze, a strong air current moving through the area around the lander. Strong winds and storms in the vicinity of the lander were fairly frequent.

Margie was a bit dismayed but did not dwell on it. The object was something new and different and had succeeded in causing a fresh round of speculation. A tiny fragment, barely a spec in the foreground of a larger picture, had caused quite a stir. The computer proclaiming it "possibly organic" was the culprit responsible for their new perplexed state.

Moses Brown suggested that a mosquito had landed on the lens and had gotten blown away by the wind. Margie feared that wind. Each time it blew, a new coating of that mysterious soot further obscured the camera lens. Margie had thought that the tiny object would become breakthrough number two.

— *§* —

Days passed without much additional information. The newest photos yielded new vistas and new objects to study, but little else. Data from the second lander added to the photo information from the first. The machine analyzed the soil, which ended up being loose and variable in grain size. No hard rock was encountered in the borehole to the depth of 2.6 meters. Norm, as geologist, identified a number of common rock-forming minerals, typical of volcanic rocks on Earth. He isolated several unknown constituents.

The lander sampled the atmosphere several times and thoroughly analyzed the constituents. Temperature fluctuations were noted, gravity mapped, and sounds recorded. More organic-like compounds were identified in the upper soil layer. A clearer overall picture of conditions on the surface was slowly forming. The second probe apparently came to rest in a very dry, dune-like body of wind-deposited surface material. Ice crystals were observed and that piece of data conclusively proved that water was present—possibly abundant.

Rod Amerigo and Doc made the next discovery. Rod decided to listen more closely to the monotonous sound bits recorded on the surface. The computer had already broken down the sounds by several analytical procedures. Rod discovered a rhythmic tapping on one bit. This again piqued everyone's curiosity. It was very faint but isolated and not generated by the lander itself. This only became another piece of a growing mystery.

David and Margie's counterparts back on Earth made another interesting observation. Hank Wadkins was given an enhanced fragment of a photo taken by the low-light optical system carried aboard Lander One. The image had been captured during the descent. The low-light system would have been invaluable on the surface due to the generally darkened conditions. It was damaged and the optics badly coated prior to landing. Since damage was detected and the system normally consumed energy fast, it had been automatically powered down after landing.

Hank was glad that his people found this one. He contacted David and sent the fragment to him for his comments. The picture had been captured at an elevation of just over thirty kilometers, eighteen and one half miles, just less than one hundred thousand feet.

It showed a portion of the surface with several obvious valleys and sinuous patterns of patchy color within the valleys. It showed a dendritic pattern resembling veins in a leaf. Color corrected from the night-vision captured image, the valleys displayed traces of the same phosphorescent green color that had been detected in the vicinity of the lander. It was unmistakable. And these were large concentrations, much larger than the traces on the rock near the lander.

David was very pleased with this new data. He could not believe that they had missed it. Margie added it to their growing store of data, thanking Hank for his persistence. To be visible from that elevation above the surface, this new green pattern had to be quite extensive.

After a brief discussion concerning the technical merits, Hank, David, and Margie agreed to take a chance and try to send a new command to the lander. An attempt would be made to power-up the low-light enhanced optical system in the hope of using it to capture non-illuminated images. They recognized the inherent danger of damage to other components, but thought that they would be able to isolate the system just enough. It was going to take some time to set up anyway. Now that they were in mid-June and closing in on the planet, it seemed like a reasonable idea with acceptable risk.

Plans for the fast-approaching wedding went smoothly. Jason and Oreen put together a simple exchange of vows and a brief service. It had taken Jason a few hours and some research help from NASA to determine his official capacity. Oreen did not care about an official version; she was making her own plans.

Casey Ramirez and Sylvia Braddock grew flowers in the hydroponic gardens off the Biology Lab. Among Casey's many supplies were numerous types of seeds. The flowers had been her idea from the start. They were part of the original selection of supplies and provisions. They had enough blooms to fashion several bouquets and even boutonnieres for the gentlemen. Orion had the luxury of dining on one damaged bud.

An eager press, and an equally fascinated public, followed developments pertaining to the wedding. Margie and David's romance in space was a major event. NASA and the International Space Agency were basking in the coverage. Liz Rainwater kept the President aware of every detail. She was totally enamored with the story.

Margie was tired of the notoriety. David didn't mind as much this time, since the press was millions of miles away. NASA directed a steady stream of stories, magazine covers, and Internet gossip to the couple. Most of it was treated with mild amusement and generally accepted tolerance. Both Margie and David were very pleased that the event was not taking place on Earth, although they both knew that the story would not have been nearly as sensational. Their only disappointment was the fact that their families would not be present, except for videofeed coverage.

When the big day finally arrived, everyone was ready, even the young couple about to be the stars of the nuptials. Margie was nervous but looked resplendent in her gown. Casey and Doc did a beautiful job of making it. Rod spent a lot of time looking over their shoulders and making suggestions. Margie and Casey also arranged their precious blooms into beautiful floral decorations. Everyone else on the crew was involved in some way, making each feel a special part of the event. Casey and Moses Brown even made a quasi-cake, a feat only she knew how to create.

The service was beamed back to NASA for tape-delay broadcast to every network that had requested it. Interest seemed almost universal.

Commander Kidd was officiating and began the ceremony. Oreen would take over after the exchange of vows and complete a brief but elegant service. Rod had rigged up cameras at several angles and planned on making a first-rate production of the celebration.

The bridge had enough room for nearly everyone. Duty stations could be monitored from this location and by using hand-held remote controls. David waited nervously beside Jason as his bride-to-be was gently floated in by her attendants. Sergey had selected nontraditional music and a brief few stanzas of the traditional wedding march for effect. Margie was beautiful.

As Margie joined David at his side and Oreen moved beside Jason, the commander recited the service pausing when he came to the vows.

"Do you, Margie Ritter, take this man, David Striker, to be your wedded husband?"

"I do," she said softly.

"And do you, David Striker, take this woman, Margie Ritter, to be your wedded wife?"

"I do," he smiled.

"Then by the power vested in me by the United States government and as commander of this ship, I now pronounce you man and wife."

It was done. Jason finished his remarks and Oreen started hers. As she nudged Jason aside, Oreen added, "You may now kiss the bride. Jason forgot to tell you that." As she finished those words, the rest of the crew raised a congratulatory cheer. Strongman Moses wiped aside a tear. Oreen went on and on about what great people they were and how happy they were going to be, but David never heard a word. The kiss had sent his mind elsewhere, and he was filled with pride. Margie cried during the service, but was now cheering with the rest of the crew.

When Oreen finished, each crewmember added a few personal remarks, including humorous stories, shook hands with David, and kissed Margie. Each also gave them a small gift, virtually all hand-made, even though Margie and David had said no gifts. The ceremony concluded with a series of taped congratulatory messages from their families, dignitaries, and a few close friends. The newlyweds would have endless recordings from others to listen to later. The ceremony went beautifully; storybook style, with a special flair.

13

DISASTER

THE CREW spent several uneventful weeks following the excitement of the wedding. Anticipation of nearing their goal began to replace a sense of tedium. It was business as usual but with a more charged atmosphere among the crewmembers.

David was resting comfortably in his compartment, drifting in and out of dream-filled sleep, when his dream took on a familiar pattern. His subconscious remembered the ear-piercing sound of the general alarm and repeated blasts indicating fire. During sleep he often relived some of the more memorable drills and tests from training. He often recalled the one drill that really frightened him. It had been unsuspected, all too real, and the first glimpse of Doc Pritchard's contorted face left an indelible impression.

He was nearly awake and the dream would not go away. David sprang from his bunk fully awake. As his conscious state took over, he propelled himself from his cocoon with such force that he crashed against the far bulkhead of his cabin. It was not a dream. The general alarm was sounding, and he could smell the distinctive pungent odor resulting from an electrical fire.

Training clicked in, his reactions were almost pure instinct. David secured his portable communicator to his wrist, placing the earpiece receiver in his left ear. He grabbed his flight safety suit and pulled it on in one motion. Releasing his emergency breathing apparatus, he put it to his face, being careful to start the airflow. The entire procedure, including adding his helmet took only seconds.

As Security Officer, David had a multi-purpose fire-fighting backpack in his compartment. He was slipping it over his shoulder as he exited, quickly checking in on Margie's compartment next door. She was wide-awake, suited, and motioning for him to go. Gone was her dream of a wonderful evening alone with her husband—that bliss was replaced by sudden chilling fear. Margie connected her helmet and began checking the alert status information flashing on her monitor.

Margie was one step ahead of him, as usual, and it was not even her emergency duty assignment. David had not wanted to take the time to check his monitor. The fire was obviously close, very close. His nose had relayed that piece of information. He was heading in the direction of the smoke, which was wafting toward them from past Margie's area. It seemed to be emanating from the supply storage unit just beyond.

Sensors quickly detected and pinpointed the heat, smoke, and gases emitted by the combustion. These sensors alerted the main computer, which in turn activated the alarms, automatic fire isolation, and extinguishing systems throughout the ship. After scanning for crew location and activity, the compartments or sections involved would be automatically sealed, isolated, and evacuated of combustible gases. The fire would be snuffed out because it would be deprived of the oxygen needed to keep it burning. A source of combustion could also be manually blanketed with special foam to smother it. David was prepared for this by means of his special backpack.

Immediate containment was the first objective. The greatest dangers to the ship and crew were fire, the choking smoke, and the potential release of toxic gases. David's earpiece was filled with a staccato of shouted comments and questions. Jason Kidd was repeating his name. He called for the channel to be momentarily cleared.

"Striker here. I'm in section C. It's pretty smoky but safe so far," he stated.

Emergency protocols took over. The Commander and Security Officer had communication priority. Everyone else remained silent while assuming his or her emergency duty stations, standing by for information. Time was now critical.

Jason's voice remained cool and confident. David could hear Roberto's excited voice in the background. "David, can you see what it is yet? The camera in that section is obscured by smoke. Is it isolated in the supply area? The master control and ship's guide unit on the computer highlight it there."

David heard a cough behind them. Margie had turned to see its source too. Casey was following them without her emergency breather.

"Get your breathing gear and suit up now!" he shouted. She turned and headed back toward her pod. David could not believe it. *All that training*, but he quickly forgot the thought, returning his attention to the partially closed hatchway ahead.

It was not secured. The red lights above the door were blinking continuously. Smoke was pouring out of the storage component, filling the corridor ahead. The computer checked for crew location and determined that it was safe to close the hatch to isolate the component, but the hatch did not close completely.

"Jason, we've got serious trouble. The hatch isn't closed all the way. Unless it's secured the evacuation fire-control system can't work. Smoke is pouring out. Get more help down here. We are going to need it."

"Help is on its way." In fact Jason had barely uttered the words when Moses Brown and Norm Mailor appeared.

"David, we have to either manually close that hatch or open it and fight the fire by hand. Assess and make a choice, but be quick about it. Doc, stand by for life support readouts, and give me numbers on breathing-mixture levels and any toxic buildups. Isolate all unaffected sections, and stand by to snuff the compartments if and when we can. We might have to do it manually with that many people down there."

"I'm watching all breathing-mixture levels and monitoring for toxic pollutants. I'm ready on all counts, sir." Margie's life-support tasks took on a whole new character.

"Jason, Moses and I are going to try to free the door. There doesn't appear to be active fire, only slow smoldering on the panels inside, door left."

"Be careful," Jason cautioned. "It could burst into flames."

Moses and he were at the door. Margie and Norm were a few feet behind, holding the fire fighting packs, ready to unleash the contents. The smoke was getting thicker, making visibility poor in the area of the smoking door.

Moses could see why when they surveyed the hatch through the ever-thickening smoke. A roll of silvery safety tape used to secure supply containers was jammed in the hatchway. It wasn't much, but the safety material was enough to jam the door and prevent it from closing securely.

Tape was wedged in just enough to leave a crack, and the heat inside was pushing smoke out. The internal door control panel appeared to be the source of the fire, but David was rendering a guess. How the tape had gotten wedged in there bothered David, but the task of un-wedging it was the immediate problem. He touched the tape, but it felt like steel and would not budge. For a moment, the thought flashed through his mind that someone placed the roll there on purpose. It was a sickening thought; one that he wanted to dismiss. He knew his fellow crewmates too well; it was out of the question.

The redundant door control panel on this side of the door was undamaged. Margie was taking no chances. She had already rigged up an override relay through her handheld unit and was ready to operate the door from her position, if they could get it un-jammed.

Moses moved close enough to test the door for heat. "It's OK," he signaled to David. "You get ready to pull that junk out of the way when I open it slightly by hand. You ready?"

"Ready," David answered, grasping the rolled mess of tape and bracing his leg against the edge of the hatch. Moses strained, but the door did not move. It should have turned easily. Norm nodded to Margie and moved forward to help. She let her unit float on its tether and aimed the fire retardant, ready to shoot.

"It's jammed! It's not moving! This should not be happening," Moses lamented.

"Let me try, too," Norm Mailor added, grasping the release.

"Captain, give me another readout on the door circuitry status. Mine showed everything operable before I put it down. I can't see it now."

The last few words from David sounded strained. Jason could hear it in his voice. "We show normal. How about you, Margie."

"Can't look, Commander. I am aiming this fire killer and want to cover the whole area in case anything goes wrong."

"Do you need more help?" Jason's voice had taken on an uneasy edge.

David came back with a no almost immediately. "Don't open anything connecting this section. That means no one else in or out as long as it's isolated, unless you detect structural damage. If we can't close this thing in a few more seconds, I want you to snuff this entire section. We've got our breathing gear and plenty of extra air. Give us another thirty seconds. Then evacuate the air and exhaust the smoke."

"The entire section, David? That could be dangerous." Jason was now concerned for his ship and crew. "All right, David. I'll give you twenty seconds. Get ready. You know the drill."

David heard the crack. He wasn't sure if the door had moved or Norm or Moses' back had popped. He saw pain on Brown's face through the choking smoke, but he also felt the hatch move. He was now looking through the crack between the hatch and the portal it sealed. There was no fire, only smoke. The smoldering had apparently been unable to ignite into flames due to consumption of the limited air in the component. He yanked hard at the roll of tape, it softened and seemed to change shape and then he pulled it free. David put his shoulder to the door as Norm and Moses turned the handle and the hatch eased shut. Brown secured the hatch. Margie shouted wildly into the communicator.

"Jason, wait. They got it. It's closed."

Commander Kidd was about to flip the switch to initiate the fire-control system when he saw the indicator for the compartment C-3 "fire control" illuminate. The computer had been quicker on the draw.

David heard the fire-control system initiate and the venting of the compartment; its contents replaced with non-combustible fire-retardant gases.

They had won this round but still faced considerable danger. The fire was contained; limiting it to the storage area in this section, preventing damage to personal quarters and property. Removing the smoke would take time, but once the air-circulation system could be restarted, the air-supply scrubbers would remove smoke and particulates, as well as potential toxins. Since each section of the ship was a separate, linked module, the chance of the fire spreading through ductwork of any kind was remote. But David knew that it was possible; fire was unpredictable. They would have to re-enter the fire-damaged area as soon as possible in order to check for additional danger potential and to assess the damage. David hoped the hatch would still be operable.

Jason's voice broke the momentary silence. "David and fire team, listen up. We have another problem. Only eleven crewmembers are presently accounted for by voice. Casey is not answering her page. Her locator indicates that she is in your section. Is she there now, or have you seen her?"

Margie answered before David or anyone else had a chance. "She was following us without her emergency air pack, suit, or helmet. We sent her back to suit up and figured she evacuated this section. We're on our way to check."

Margie didn't wait for orders or accompaniment. She turned and headed back toward Casey's module as fast as she could propel herself. The smoke was thick. No one had really noticed how thick during the battle with the door and enemy behind it. Now they all realized the danger to anyone not breathing contained or filtered air who still remained in the fire containment area. Margie hoped that Casey had at least gotten to her pod and sealed herself in.

Moses shouted, "I'm going too." He followed Margie in her frantic search. David was ready to head out with them when Jason's steely voice reverberated through his earpiece. "Stay there, security officer! You too, Norm! They'll find her by her locator. She appears to be in her compartment, but the signal is weak. You two need to stand by and watch for more trouble in that storage room. Margie has you on my screen so we can observe from here."

David wanted to join the search. Casey might be in need of real help, and it was his job, but so was this. He listened intently to the constant chatter in his earpiece. Finally he heard Margie's voice, "We've found her." The next words chilled his blood. "Doc, get down here quickly! She's down and out on the floor and bleeding from the mouth. She's not breathing!"

Doctor Pritchard's voice followed immediately with a sharply delivered order. "Do not, under any circumstances, remove your breathing mask! Do you read me? No one in that section remove your masks! Even if she needs CPR, you are to put a mask on her and start the air, but do not uncover your mouth or nose! I'm on my way. Commander, I will need to enter that section alone through the isolation tube. Do not open any hatches to that section under any circumstances. Damn it, Oreen, tell them!"

Oreen spoke next. "Jason, listen!" She hesitated, and then followed Doc's lead. "I'm monitoring for Margie. I show high levels of toxins in that smoke. I . . . I also show nano contamination, both materials and builders. It must be scrubbed or evacuated from the ship as soon as possible."

"Shit, how serious is that?" David feared something like this would happen sooner or later. He had numerous security problem models and simulators to study on his computer. These included several with inhalation or ingestion of builders or materials, or nanos as the crew referred to them. Nano, by definition, means one billionth. To all of the crew that meant real small, and on board a spacecraft, real small meant real easy to lose.

David stopped to think of the way that nanotechnology worked. The supercomputer linked a series of nanotubes, conduits formed by and containing the submicroscopic builders, throughout the ship. These tubes connected every space, no matter how small, literally linking all parts of the ship like veins in a human body. Both builders and prefabricated raw materials for every conceivable part for the ship coursed through those inhuman veins. In theory, if something broke, and the computer detected it, having the computer project a virtual electromagnetic field grid on the object could facilitate a repair. The virtual image was created in the ship database. The tiny nanotubes were computer programmed to respond to the virtual grid by directing a new artery to the corresponding real point. Projecting a real electromagnetic grid anywhere within the ship would have been dangerous and almost impossible. The computer fooled the conduit nanotube material, another composite created by Ishmael and Tanaka. The tubes responded to the computer-simulated grid and were drawn to that point. Once in contact, the nano builders and their raw material building blocks were supplied directly to the problem and with direction from the computer brain, repairs were facilitated.

David was worried. Everyone within the sealed area was using a helmet or full face-covering breathing apparatus, everyone except Casey, when she'd come up behind him and Margie.

"We're already venting and replacing as fast as we can. It will take a while, but it should start clearing in a few minutes if we don't have any more smoldering."

Jason wanted more information. "David, can you see through the glass portal in the hatch? How does it look inside?"

David flipped back the cover on the observation slit in the door and peered inside. The smoke was gone, sucked out of the room and vented to space. The charred panel behind the door showed no signs of further heat or smoke. The contents of the room looked blackened but relatively intact, except for two or three storage containers near the origin of the smoke. He recognized the containers. They were mostly food, but one was Norm's chemistry set for use on the surface during the landing phase, and one held emergency explosives. Next to those were Norm's most valued possessions, the rest of his laboratory equipment for analytical use on the planet. David immediately realized that if this equipment was badly damaged, the loss could seriously hinder their exploration efforts.

Then David noticed something else. The nanotube leading into this room was damaged. Somehow self-repair in the fire had gotten mixed with repairing damage caused by the fire. The result was a silver-purple sheen on parts of the area around the fire damage. He knew what to look for, and there it was. No doubt about it, nano material, and therefore builders, were loose in the ship. Consequences were unknown; only time would tell.

Margie knelt beside Casey and turned her head, attaching the breathing mask. She felt for a pulse. It was there, faint but steady. She was alive and seemed semiconscious. Moses checked around her cabin and realized what had happened. Casey tried to save one of her pets, a tiny finch. Casey was overcome by the fumes while trying to seal it in a container and give it clean air, but it had perished. It was typical of kindhearted Casey.

Doc Pritchard entered the sealed section through the hatch at the end. Rod Amerigo met her on the way through the pressure lock. He insisted on accompanying her and would not take no for an answer. After consideration, and knowing how he felt about Casey, she decided to enlist his aid. Rod's size and strength would come in handy.

Moses Brown was essentially forcing Casey to breathe. She was lapsing in and out of consciousness. Doc arrived by Casey's side, checked her vital signs and told the others that they had to get her out of there and back to the infirmary as fast as possible. By the time they were ready to move her, the air in the section was beginning to clear noticeably.

Rod was visibly upset. He was gently supporting her head as they moved Casey through the section. Deep concern was etched on his face. They were no longer hiding their fondness for one another from anyone. Doc decided that the air had cleared enough to open the hatchway and get them all out. She checked on the toxin levels with Jason and Oreen to be absolutely sure.

Upon receiving the OK confirmation from Jason, Doc directed Margie, Moses, and Rod out of the contaminated section to safety, sealing the hatch carefully behind them.

Moving Casey was easy in the near weightlessness. The most care had to be taken to make sure that she was not moved too quickly or bumped into any equipment. Doc moved ahead to prepare for her arrival in the infirmary. Moses and Rod followed with the precious, floating beauty.

Back in the slowly clearing section, David and Norm were entering the blackened storage compartment that was re-pressurized and refilled with clean air. Norm was nervous and upset about the potential damage to his experimental gear. He knew extra provisions were stored in the compartment. If destroyed or contaminated, their loss could pose additional serious problems to the mission.

The hatch opened easily. It was not seriously damaged. David went in first, with Norm close behind. There was no sign of smoke or fire activity. The computer had directed the nanotube back to its original position, and the contaminating sheen had been gathered up by the receding tube. They each removed their helmet and breathing apparatus, placing them within reach nearby. The room wreaked of burned plastic. David removed his gloves and felt for warmth. There was none. The sensors in the room were damaged but could be replaced.

"Jason, there is no sign of heat or any remnant of the fire. It looks like it started in the door control panel. It's totally destroyed. The wall panels are melted and a couple of storage containers right by the door are damaged."

"How about contents? Can you tell yet?" Jason asked.

"We'll check in a minute. Let me see if the camera in the corner is working so that you can have a view of the room. If not, Norm will rig one up." David checked the camera, which was properly aimed, but the lens was blackened. The smoke residue rubbed off easily, and Jason acknowledged that they could now see.

Norm went about the task of opening one of his instruments. The case was badly warped, the plastic having partially melted, so he gave up on it and tried another, which was less misshapen.

David opened one of the food containers, the contents of which were toasted but looked edible. "I hope that everyone likes smoked, dried food, with extra-tight shrink wrap. The food inside doesn't look too good, but if it's not contaminated, we will probably be able to salvage most of it.

David noticed the blackened container between the food and the cases with "Mailor" stenciled on them. He knew immediately what the box was because he had been present when it was secured there. This receptacle was the most dangerous container on board in the event of fire. The case held explosives to be placed in explosive bolts in the event of the emergency separation of parts of the ship. It was plain bad luck that, of all places aboard the *Kat*, the fire had started here. They were blessed by good fortune that the fire had not affected this case, even though this type of explosive was not easily detonated. Had the explosive been involved, the results would have been catastrophic for the ship. They had escaped and averted a complete disaster.

"Jason?"

"Yes, David?"

"Before I opened this compartment, the wall was partially covered by what looked like nano material. It looks like it's all gone now, but it was there before we evacuated.

"We know. Oreen did what the drill called for. She monitored it by computer and fed in the fix."

"Hope it worked," was all David said.

Jason wanted to know more than he could see, so he left the bridge area and was on his way to join in the investigation. His greatest concern was finding out how this could have happened. Most of the materials used in the interior of the ship were fire retardant. The electrical systems were tested and supposed to be fail-safe. No combustible materials were stored together. He had many questions bouncing around in his head and they demanded answers. When he reached the room he was at first shocked at how little damage had occurred.

"Here's where we think it started, Sir." David pointed to the hatch control panel as Jason entered. "I have a good idea of what must have happened, Commander. I've put two and two together and have come up with either real carelessness or possible sabotage. Before you go wild, I think it's the former. I'll show you what I think happened; but it shouldn't have happened. You can take it from there."

"Proceed, Mr. Security Officer. I'm all ears." Norm was now listening intently too. He had been busy rummaging through his precious instruments looking for damage.

"Sir," David stated, "we found the hatch jammed by some partially unrolled strapping tape used to secure the stores. The hatch was stuck in one position, and the control motor apparently overheated, since it couldn't open or close. I think it shorted out, taking out the warning circuit with it. I know that it's not supposed to happen, but that's my guess so far. The panel caught fire and dropped to the floor as it melted. My big question is how did the door get stuck?"

Jason considered the situation and ramifications and answered, "My question exactly, David. You could be right, it could have been done on purpose, but I find that hard to believe."

"Me too," added Norm. "But I think David's prognosis for how the fire started is a damn good one. We can easily trace who was in here last."

David did not like the word sabotage. All he could think about was indirect sabotage. A mistake by the nano program—perhaps an attempt to repair a problem that instead overwhelmed a man-made circuit. He remembered for a moment that Ishmael had said the techs would fix that last minute glitch in this same door circuit. It bothered him again, even worse this time.

"David, hand me your handheld unit and let's patch in to life support and see whose bio-locator was in here last. Someone was, and any saboteur certainly would not have worn it in here." Jason typed in a few words and immediately had his answer. He did not use verbal commands since the handheld unit was programmed specifically for David's voice. He held up the unit so that Norm and David could read the name: "Amerigo."

"I think we need to talk to Rod. He went to sick bay with Doc and Casey." Anger was now evident on Jason's already strained countenance.

Norm stayed to clean up and was joined by Sergey and Phil Allen. They had work to do to replace what they could and facilitate human repairs. David followed Jason to the infirmary.

Amerigo was holding Casey's hand and wiping her brow with a cloth when they arrived. Casey's eyes were closed, and an oxygen mask covered part of her face. Rod had a look of trauma on his face, but she looked relaxed.

"How is she, Doc?" were the Commander's first concerned words.

"She will be fine, but she scared us half to death. I've sedated her, and she'll be here for a while. You don't think that I'm going to let go of my first patient very easily, do you? She breathed in some of the fumes and just passed out. I'm worried about the big guy over there, though, he might not make it." Doc expected a smile by trying her best to interject a little humor. Jason's face was not smiling, and he was staring at Rod.

"Mr. Amerigo, we need to talk. Right now." Jason was stern and persistent without making it a direct order.

"She'll be fine, Rod. Go ahead." Doc took the cloth and nodded for Rod to go.

Once outside of the infirmary, Jason came directly to the point. "Rod, were you in the C-3 storage bay earlier today?"

He answered with no hesitation. "Yes, sir, I went to get some things for

Casey. She needed a box of supplies for dinner tonight. "I damn near smacked my head. Got my feet tangled up in the tape as I left."

"Rod, that strapping jammed the door and almost ended this mission." Jason's voice had lost all traces of friendliness.

"What? Oh no! You mean I caused the mess down there? Oh Jesus, I almost killed Casey. I could have killed us all!" With that the giant man simply went to pieces and wilted against the bulkhead.

Jason grabbed his arm and shouted in his face. "Straighten up, get control of yourself, and get down there and help clean up. That's an order!"

"Yes, sir. I'm sorry," was all he said as he pulled himself together and turned away.

After a few seconds Jason looked at David and said, "I wasn't near hard enough on him. Things have gotten too lax. We have got to get this mess cleaned up and make sure that absolutely nothing like this is allowed to happen again. Do you understand me, Mr. Security Officer?"

"Loud and clear, Sir," David said with a sharp military salute.

"And keep an eye on Rod. From now on he won't have time to flirt with Casey. We're going to keep him so busy that he won't have time to sleep, much less time to screw up."

Just then Doc rushed from the infirmary. "Christ, she's pregnant! Blood analysis shows it clearly and I wasn't even looking for it."

Now Jason was even more angry. "Are you sure, Doc? Of course you are. Rod is in some deep shit here."

"Jason, mission rules state that everyone take contraceptive pregnancy inhibitors. Who didn't take it, Rod or Casey?"

Casey's muffled voice got their attention, and they went to her side to listen. She was conscious and trying to speak through the mask and sedative.

"Rest, Casey." Doc was insistent but Jason was trying to make out what she was saying.

They both understood the words before Casey nodded off. "I didn't take them. It's against my religion. Please don't take my baby."

Neither Doc nor Jason could believe the words. "Jason," Doc whispered, "She inhaled a lot of smoke and had silver-purple sheen on her lips. She and the baby are both contaminated."

Doc and Jason knew that the mission protocol stated emphatically that no pregnancies would be allowed. It was clearly understood that an unwanted pregnancy could cause too many problems. Any mistake called for an immediate abortion. But final decisions always rested with the man in charge, the mission commander.

"Doc, how far along is she?"

"She is still in the first trimester, Jason, and until today, she's been as healthy as they get."

"This is one decision that I never thought I'd have to make, and one that I don't like."

"I can do it while she's out, but it could have bad psychological ramifications." Doc was trying to help him.

"Today has been a mess. I'll speak to Rod. Don't put any more stress on Casey right now." Jason could read Doc's body language and it was obviously in favor of letting things go for now. "If the fetus has problems or seems to be developing with any complications caused by today, Ann, you must take the baby. That's an order."

"OK, Jason, I'll monitor things very carefully and let you know." When Jason left, Doc was ecstatic—first a wedding, and now a baby.

Once the smoke had cleared, figuratively and literally, David could not get the cause for the incident out of his head. He played back his security recordings from the C-3 area. He watched Rod enter, open a case and extract some food containers. He watched him trip over the tape, almost bang his head, curse his own stupidity, call himself clumsy, and put the tape roll back on the box behind the door. Rod had not purposely placed it in the path of the closing hatch and there was no evidence that it fell off, or rolled, into the path of the closing hatchway. David did see a flash of silvery movement through the crack before the hatch closed, or almost closed. He played the brief stored video back over and over. He realized what it was. It was time to look at the pre-launch sequence for just this area again, and to have the computer analyze its own code for the compartment. He would find the archive video and compare everything from C-3. Something was wrong.

David also resumed his studies of the Stealth world with renewed vigor. The goal was growing nearer, and the data files were steadily increasing in volume. The acceleration away from the Mars decision point had been tremendous. They covered the first forty million miles to the vicinity of Mars in about ninety days. This distance was less than one astronomical unit, an astronomical unit being the distance from Earth to the Sun, a mere ninety three million miles, or about one hundred and fifty million kilometers. The distance from Mars to the Stealth Planet was another thirty-plus astronomical units, a distance of nearly 2.8 billion miles. If the propulsion system continued to work, they were to reach the goal in a total elapsed time of about ten months. They were well ahead of schedule.

They were now nearing the end of their eighth month. The ship and crew had now endured a voyage of almost 2.2 billion miles. Communications with Earth suffered from the time delay for the signal to reach them. The delay had only been about three and one half minutes while in the vicinity of Mars. Their communications, traveling at almost the speed of light, now took almost four hours to go one way. Normal two-way conversations had become a thing of the past months ago. All messages now were indirect, generally in the form of a memorandum.

David spent much of his current time reviewing celestial mechanics, the study of planetary orbits resulting from gravitational forces. Nearly all of the previously known planets had circular orbits in a flat plane. The exceptions were the slight deviation of Mercury and the wide, elliptical, non-planar orbit of Pluto. Astronomer Percival Lowell had postulated the existence of Pluto in 1905. He suspected its existence because of perturbation or slight irregularity in the orbit of Uranus. Another American astronomer, Clyde William Tombaugh, did not confirm his hypothesis until the actual discovery of Pluto in 1930.

In 1847 Neptune was discovered in much the same way. Its existence was postulated in 1846, a year before, again due to perturbation in the orbit of Uranus. When it was actually first seen, the location was almost exactly where it had been previously predicted to be. David was convinced that the same situation should have given away the Stealth Planet. He was convinced that this evidence existed somewhere. He had made sure that the entire archive of astronomical data available at NASA had been downloaded to his system prior to launch. His training schedule and intense studies of their craft had precluded his study of this subject back on Earth.

Now David had time and he poured over the data. He knew that in the 1840s, Pluto could still not be seen due to its small size and the limited power of optical instruments of the time, even if it had been detected mathematically. Neptune, on the other hand, was huge by comparison to Pluto and Neptune also has a very high albedo or ability to reflect light. Neptune, a gas giant, has an albedo of eighty-four, meaning that eighty-four percent of the light striking it is reflected back into space.

All of the outer planets were basically formed by the condensation of gases, except for the ice ball, Pluto. The Stealth Planet did not fit the gas-giant category at all. It also had by far the lowest albedo of anything yet detected in the solar system. This phenomenon had helped it to stay very well hidden. In addition, the orbit calculated appeared to be elliptical and not in the same plane as most of the rest of the solar system. It also had no rings or moons. Except for Venus with none and Earth and Pluto with one, all of the remaining planets had multiple moons. This planet had its own set of particularly unique characteristics.

David was as curious as any scientist about the many unique properties of this distant world. He had postulated as to how a planet at this great distance from the sun could retain heat. Uranus, at a distance of 1.68 billion miles from the sun, had a surface temperature of approximately two hundred and eighteen degrees below zero Celsius (-360 Fahrenheit). Neptune, almost one billion miles more distant, had about the same surface temperature. Scientists believed that this could only be possible due to internal heat within the planet. The Stealth Planet, at an even greater distance from the heat of the sun, had much higher surface temperatures than either of its closer neighbors.

Astronomers worldwide had studied the nine planets, sixty-three known moons, and more than sixteen hundred identified major asteroids, and the Stealth Planet had escaped detection. To David it was still amazing. He was convinced that he could find additional evidence that it had been detected or postulated some time or somewhere before. He had found a brief reference to an unknown factor that had caused a temporary irregularity in Neptune's orbit. This gave him another avenue to explore.

The outer shell of his Stealth discovery still baffled him. Spectroscopic data should have identified the composition of the outer layer completely. In 1814, German physicist Joseph Von Fraunhofer had invented the Spectroscope. He discovered that every chemical element exhibits a unique set of spectral lines when analyzed using his methods. NASA used this analysis method to identify the constituents of the other distant planets with great success. The puzzle of the new solar object defied this form of analysis too. Spectroscopic data from Stealth Planet showed several anomalous peaks of unknown composition.

David continued his studies and prayed that everything would go smoothly from here to the end of the voyage and beyond. He wanted to sample the atmospheric mystery material that defied analysis and hid the planet for so long and take a good look at what was underneath it. In spite of their recent mishap and near tragedy, he felt renewed confidence that there would be additional great discoveries ahead. He also suspected that Ishmael was involved in this mission in more ways than met the scrutiny of everyone in the program.

14
ARRIVAL AND ORBIT

MONTHS TURNED INTO weeks, and weeks into days. What the crew expected to be a long and arduous journey passed with only a few difficulties or problems. At the beginning of the tenth month, the distance to their target was closing rapidly. The probes from *Stealth Finder Two* gathered enough information to paint a relatively clear picture of surface conditions. Much to everyone's chagrin, the power source on probe 2 was beginning to fail. David and Margie's demands pushed the tiny craft to its limits, and considering the circumstances; it had performed up to and beyond expectations.

Aboard the *Kat*, the mood had changed from just wanting to get there to eager anticipation of arrival. Several of the crewmembers, who had waited nearly ten months, were ready to assume the new responsibilities required of them once in the vicinity of their goal. Pilot Phil Allen, propulsion specialist Sergey, and navigator Roberto, were working together as a team. They now needed to determine the best approach path, speed for capture by the planet's gravity, and position in orbit. At this point no one had any desire to either overshoot the target or get pulled in too close. The pilot and navigator faced a tricky maneuver with no room for error. Jason gave the command to reduce their forward speed, and the computer began calculating the final course corrections and maneuvers for braking and capture.

David, Norm Mailer, Moses Brown, and Oreen assumed the task of organizing the parts needed to assemble the two landing vehicles. The primary parts of these specialized descent excursion (DEV) vehicles were neatly folded and stowed in several adjoining compartments of the mother ship. Once in orbit, the main part of the vehicles would be swung out of their berths and the remaining pieces assembled by space-walking teams. Moses was in charge of this phase and eager for a chance to demonstrate his talents. Moses was leading the first team to the surface. If his team made it, this African American strong man would be the first human being to set foot on another planet. He was the EVA specialist. When it came to opening the door, he had the job.

Moses was like a kid in a candy store. He had been doing support tasks since they left Earth. Now he was in charge of the most critical phase, if this mission was to succeed. Commander Kidd would still be making the final decisions, but Moses would call the shots once they departed for landing. Moses had patiently waited for his opportunity to shine and was preparing to make the most of it.

Choosing the remainder of the Primary Descent Team was at Jason's discretion. Norm Mailor was an essential member, since he would be conducting many of the experiments on the surface. He had spent a good part of the voyage studying every piece of available data about Stealth Planet and was eager to have the chance to explore. Jason could not go; it was crucial that he maintain his command from the *Kat*. Everyone else volunteered to go except for Phil Allen, who was also expected to remain in orbit. Roberto was a natural selection since he was an extremely well-trained pilot, and the landing craft would need someone capable of handling any problems, though everyone had pilot training. The fourth potential crew person to join the team was as yet undecided. Jason wanted all nonessentials to have a chance, so he wanted to wait for a short time before making a final decision. He had plenty of other things to worry about between the present and any attempt to land. He had evaluated every one of them since they left Earth.

In addition to the first descent team, Jason would select a second, backup team. The second group would be sent only if the first team's landing went without a serious problem or could be sent in the event that the first team had problems. The use of the second team was at Jason's discretion. Risking four of his crew was a big gamble. If the first group encountered a serious problem, Jason was not ready to even consider whether to put others at risk. The Captain understood this burden of command.

Jason decided to not worry about the final selection of the last team member until the *Kat* was safely in orbit. He had had plenty of extra time to mull it over during the voyage. NASA decided before launch that he would make the final picks when and if they arrived. He would base the selections on behavior, performance, and psychological profiles compiled during the trip. Except for Rod's mistake and a few flare-ups of temper and frustration, his crew had performed better than he expected. He took great pride in every one of them.

For months the computers balanced propulsion and speed, and followed the intercepting course with the distant planet to perfection. Now Jason and Phil allowed the computers more limited control. They would follow the guidelines laid out by the machines but final positioning would be in the hands of this group. Pilot Allen was ready and eager to do some real flying.

The two *Stealth Finder* crafts had sent copious amounts of information regarding the conditions at various orbital altitudes. They planned to park the *Kat* in orbit well above the limits of the mysterious outer layer of the atmosphere. Their selected position would be higher above the surface than the orbit still maintained by *Stealth Finder Two*.

— § —

Final approach came on October 16, 2031, in the early hours of the day. Clocks and calendars were almost irrelevant for the crew, except for maintaining schedules. But everyone onboard wanted to know the exact moment of orbital capture. NASA control and the scientific community could only hope that the time of orbital attainment went well. Their verification would not arrive until well past the critical moment of capture. NASA had reviewed Jason and Phil's final approach plan and given it their complete blessing. Now it was up to the pilot and his assistants to lock onto their goal and complete phase one of this incredible ten-month quest.

Jason and Phil counted down the seconds as the conventional retro-rockets ignited for the final breaking maneuver. The planet loomed ahead like a massive, reddish-black ball. It was now only two hundred kilometers to the swirling outer shell and under four hundred kilometers to the surface. The focus of their attention looked dark, eerie, and very inhospitable. It was not a pleasant blue ball as the Earth appeared from the moon. Instead the foreboding black orb inspired both awe and fear in the hearts and minds of the arriving Earthlings.

The entire crew studied it with intensity during the final approach, searching the outer shell-like surface for signs of breaks in the turbulence, breaks that could facilitate safe entry. The pilots needed to study these breaks in detail in order to understand when and why they occurred. Nothing looked very promising during much of the initial observation. Once the *Kat* got close, the chinks in the armor began to appear. *Stealth Finder Two* compiled large files of data researching the shell phenomena. This outer layer still appeared very dangerous and turbulent to the arriving crew.

"We are here, people." Jason was jubilant as he relayed the moment of orbital capture to his crew. "The captain has turned off the seat belt sign, and you are free to move about the cabin." He was shaking Phil's shoulder and expressing more emotion than anyone could remember. It was infectious; the entire crew began cheering in unison.

Rod Amerigo made sure that he got it all on tape, combining pictures from every duty station throughout the ship. They had made it, covered the immense distance faster than anyone thought, and were cruising in orbit.

Each crewmember watched the monitors intently as the final seconds ticked off the flight plan clock. Margie and David were not on station. They were holding hands and watching through the exterior-view port in David's compartment. Commander Kidd had offered them the helm, but they had declined, wanting to share the moment alone, together. This event held an even more special meaning for the two of them. It was a dream come true, this time to be shared intimately.

Margie waited until the message had come through from Jason. She squeezed David's hand hard and joined in the loud cheering. Jason's words brought tremendous emotional relief to the entire crew. When the cheering subsided, she and David smiled broadly and listened to the strains of training songs now echoing through the ship. After joining in for several stanzas, Margie reached over and turned off the two-way telescreen switch. David was transfixed. He was staring out the port at his destiny.

"David, honey, I don't want to ruin this moment or disturb your reverie, but we are now in orbit. Do you know what that means?" She turned him to face her while wrapping her hands around his shoulders. "It means that we're now officially on our honeymoon. Remember?"

He smiled and caressed her cheek. "I do remember, but we've been unofficially honeymooning since we got hitched."

"Yes, but this now makes it official." With that she flipped the switch, closing the compartment door and typed "do not disturb" into the illuminated information panel beside it. She pulled him to her and kissed him deeply saying, "Right now, Mr. Striker, I want to capture you."

The computer systems confirmed capture, and the ship's propulsion systems were temporarily powered down. Phil was watching for orbital decay, but the *Kat's* position and orbit looked perfect.

A burst message was sent to Mission Control upon confirmation of a stable orbit. The crew knew that the celebration would be starting on Earth in a few hours. Rod was also compiling a file of the onboard celebration. If all went well from here, exploration of the surface could begin in as little as a few days.

By afternoon of the first day in orbit, the scientific team was busy preparing clusters of sensors that would be dropped from the *Kat*. These small bomblets would be fired directly at the surface. Each bomblet carried varying arrays of sensors intended for gathering additional data from the outer shell and the atmosphere below. These sensors were designed to activate at different elevations, pressures, and wind velocities. Coupled with the *Stealth Finder* data, the bomblets were expected to contribute the final critical data to determine if a human landing was possible.

Norm Mailor headed this scientific team. Margie, Casey, and Oreen were all his direct assistants. Casey made a quick and full recovery from her problems during the fire. She had been embarrassed more than hurt and took a lot of ribbing for her foolish actions. She wanted very badly to do well during her present assignment, but she was now in the third trimester, eight months pregnant. Doc checked her often and saw no reason for her not to go full term and Casey had done exactly as instructed. Jason made the final decision to allow her to go through with the pregnancy. The crew took the news of her condition in stride, and fussed over Casey like expectant grandparents. NASA and the international space community were shocked at first, when they received the initial report from Jason, but ended up supporting his decision, and were pleased with the new scientific value. At times Casey felt like a guinea pig, but in a sense, they all were, she just most of all. Time even tempered that excitement, except for Doc. Casey became her fixation, worse for Casey than any doting grandmother. At this point, she was very restricted in what she could do. Her duties were the same as always but her helpers, always including Doc, were in abundant supply. For her, things were becoming very uncomfortable at the time that the others were getting very busy. For Casey, this was a difficult time.

The baby appeared to be perfect and Doc was very pleased with its progress. It was Casey she worried about. Casey had indeed inhaled nano material, and the nanos were prevalent throughout her system, showing up in every urine and blood sample, appearing on occasion in her saliva. None of the rest of the crew showed any traces or abnormal symptoms. Signs of the nanos were restricted to only Casey and Oreen so far, and it had been quite a while since the incident. A few times Doc spotted a silvery iridescence on Casey's fingertips. Oreen's nano traces appeared in a corner of one eye during a routine vision exam. Everyone knew about Casey, but only Doc carried the knowledge about Oreen.

Casey was not isolated from the rest of the crew, but she and Rod had to cease their visits after the problems caused by the fire and their foolish decision to not follow orders. Jason had been adamant. If they wanted to keep the baby, they would respect the decision to not have contact. Casey did not want to take a chance of spreading the nanos to Rod, so they all agreed.

Casey and Rod talked about it and wanted to wed in the future, but things cooled down between them following the ordeal, though she was still quite fond of him. It took her several weeks to convince him that the accident was not entirely his fault. Commander Kidd made a point to keep their work details separated when possible, but Casey did need assistance, and Rod was diligently there.

Moses began preparing the descent team and their equipment. He was anxious to begin assembling the descent excursion vehicles or DEVs from the sections in storage aboard the *Kat*. He and his assistants would be spending considerable time doing exterior vehicle activity (EVA). A walk in space, no matter how inhospitable, would be a welcome change from being cooped up inside the *Kat*. No attempt would be made to explore the surface until both of the DEVs were completely fabricated and tested.

The first sensor clusters were released by the end of the first day in orbit. Others would be released daily until the DEV team was ready to go. *Stealth Finder Two*, which was still orbiting below and behind the *Kat's* path, also gathered telemetry from all sensors. This allowed the maximum amount of data to be obtained and assimilated. *Finder Two* could track any break or hole in the ever-present storm clouds below. By the time that break passed beneath the *Kat*, the DEV could be sent on its mission through the weak point in the shell, if the weaker area still existed.

Sensors also measured the strange, omnipresent, very dull-reddish lightning in the thick outer cloud layer. This faint lighting gave the planet a characteristic barely discernable glow. So far, this strange phenomenon had not seemed to cause damage to any of the other vehicles that passed through it on their way to the surface. The low, umber glow appeared electrical in nature, similar to lightning on Earth, and the crew feared that it would cause additional interference with communications to and from the surface.

The second day in orbit was busy for the teams preparing for the much-anticipated trip to the ground. Moses was unable to get much sleep. He gathered the first EVA team and discussed logistics of opening the cargo bays and swinging out the first DEV. Internal assembly was completed and the vehicles were thoroughly checked over numerous times from inside their hangars. Extra gear and supplies were stowed aboard the DEV during the voyage. The crew meticulously unloaded and rechecked each item one last time. Norm made some final adjustments to his equipment and loaded it into DEV One last.

Moses picked the EVA teams to do the final vehicular tests. They worked in shifts in order to facilitate all final system checks. Once swung out of the hangers, the descent ships would be completed and then would be ready to power up and test all systems at the first available chance.

The DEV was a beautiful bird. In Earth-based flight tests and countless simulations it performed admirably under close scrutiny of the NASA and Eurospace directors. Unlike the LEM vehicles used by NASA in the lunar landings, these were sleek craft; closely resembling jet-fighter aircraft. A vehicle like the early LEM was far too fragile and would be torn to pieces by the anticipated turbulent initial descent. These super-strong, highly maneuverable DEVs were built to withstand extreme stresses and temperatures. The entire exterior of the craft was coated with a continuous, thick-but-lightweight ceramic shield. A DEV was designed to make a quick, high-angle drop and level out as altitude decreased. It could hover and land similar to a conventional jump jet. This fact made the final selection of a suitable landing zone much safer for the craft and crew inside. The pilot could search and enjoy more discretion as to where he set the craft down.

Moses fussed over the birds like a mother hen with her prized chicks. The exteriors were polished clean, the interiors sanitized to perfection. No Earth-originated foreign microbes or materials would be let loose on the unsuspecting host below. The flight suits and equipment received the same intense scrutiny.

Norm's equipment presented the biggest problem. Several of the containers had been warped and thus destroyed in the fire. Norm and David had to assemble makeshift containers by borrowing from other onboard equipment. It had taken time, but he was well satisfied with the final results.

By the morning of the third day in orbit, Moses, Phil, and Jason were ready to swing out the first DEV for exterior tests. The cargo bay in which it was stored had a long manipulator arm similar to that used on the space shuttles and space planes that replaced the aging shuttle fleet. It took several hours to move the craft and position it for the tests. Phil was in charge of operating the manipulator arm. Moses was to be in the bay and accompany the craft out of the hangar. Roberto and David conducted the engine and flight tests. Initially the craft remained tethered to the *Kat* by the arm and an umbilicus. For the final tests at full power, the craft was released to a safe distance, and the crew was on its own. After tests were completed the tricky part came with recapture and reloading of the DEV into the hangar.

The second DEV was then tested in the exact same manner. In total, the tests took well into the next day. By the end of the fourth day Jason expected that, barring unforeseen problems, both vehicles would be ready to go. Whichever one had the highest performance rating during the tests would be the one used for the initial descent. That decision depended on computer readouts and the pilot's feel for the craft.

By the middle of day five, both DEVs were thoroughly tested and prepared. Roberto selected the first vehicle, though the differences in the computer evaluations of each were negligible. DEV One was ready to go. Roberto was ready, Norm was ready, Moses was more than ready, and Jason was now faced with the last selection. He waited until the last moment to finish his personal evaluation of each potential flier.

It was necessary that he, Phil, Rodrigo, Doc, and Casey remain aboard the *Kat*. The soon-to-be-mom was essential to maintaining the life-saving hydroponic gardens. They had ended up using more food supplies than expected, and some had been damaged in the fire. Jason wanted Doc Pritchard to remain in orbit because of her importance to the general health of the crew, and to watch Casey. He wanted Margie present for re-docking of the craft upon their return to the *Kat*. No one had the ability to operate the arm better than her but Phil, and Phil would be very busy.

Jason considered allowing Margie to co-pilot the DEV but scratched her off the list. She and Sergey had done a perfect job of maintaining and balancing the critical systems while getting here, and he wasn't going to chance not having them around for the return trip. He knew that they both would be disappointed but would also understand. Oreen was showing a few symptoms and having some trouble with the protracted near-weightlessness, and some time on the surface might help. She worked well with Moses and their chemistry was good; so, he made Oreen and her sixth sense the choice to fill out crew number one for DEV One. Jason wanted to know not only scientific information from the landing but also Oreen's overall impressions and feelings.

He struggled a bit with this choice because he felt almost obligated to send David on the first attempt. He discussed the situation with him personally, offering David the position if he really desired it. Jason personally wanted David and Margie to be part of any second crew. David said that would be fine without hesitation, making Jason's choice of Oreen logical. In addition to David, Jason selected Sergey to pilot the second DEV to fill out that roster.

Jason announced his final decisions to the entire crew during the evening of the fifth day in orbit. There was little discussion, though he offered the floor for comments. This was a duty bound crew and they idolized their leader. Not a single comment was made other than Oreen's, "Holy crap," when she realized she was on crew one.

Jason then read the battle plan for launch of the first DEV. The entire crew worked tirelessly for three days pre-flighting the vehicles and had spent countless hours preparing before that. They were ready to launch, but he wanted them to spend a day resting and relaxing. They had certainly earned it and were a full day ahead of schedule anyway. He wanted them revitalized and ready for launch by 0700 on their seventh day. They would go at the first acceptable break in the shell.

Oreen was awestruck. She was truly happy with the prospect of being a part of the first landing crew and wanted very much to be with Moses. She hugged him with tears streaming down her cheeks. It was an unusual display of emotion by this normally stoic woman. The four crewmembers of Crew One decided to dine together and review their tasks and strategies. Alternate crew two had all already eaten so they retired to the recreation room for discussion. Sergey as pilot and leader wanted to go over some details with David. If for some reason they were needed, he wanted to cover every contingency.

They all slept long and hard on the sixth day. Jason's decision was a sound one. He had noticed signs of fatigue in several of the crewmembers. He wanted no one to be at less than peak performance levels when he released the first lander.

On the morning of the seventh day, everyone on the descent crew ate a hardy breakfast and suited up. They wore full space suits like they normally used in the EVA activities. They anticipated that they were in for one rough ride. Lighter flight suits could replace these on the surface if conditions were within acceptable limits. At least they could switch to the lighter suits once they had a base camp established and their habitat fully functional.

Once suited up, Jason and Doc Pritchard scrutinized the bio-feed data on the four. They wanted no onerous stress levels or potential anxiety problems. Nervousness was to be expected. Crew One boarded the DEV and was secured in with no problems. The craft was pressurized and unshackled from its restraints in the hold. The umbilicus was disconnected, and the ship switched over to onboard power. Next, the hold was depressurized, and when the monitors blinked green, Phil was ready to gently lift the bird from its nest.

"I'm ready here, Commander," Phil said as he finished his checklist.

"How are your onboard readouts, Roberto?"

"I'm five by five on all systems, sir. Ready to swing out and prepare for release."

"Phil, you may swing out the bird," came the words from the commander.

Phil began the slow task of raising the DEV and skillfully moving it out of the hold and positioning it at the extreme reach of the arm at its maximum distance from the *Kat*. This laborious task took almost one half-hour. It required a keen eye and great skill to move the bird from the close quarters of its berth.

Once at the end of this last connection to the *Kat*, Rod Amerigo ran one final systems check of the onboard telemetry and communications and reported that everything was perfect.

"Roberto, are you ready for release? I show all systems go and green lined."

"Ready, Captain. We are prepared to power up engines and perform move-out maneuver."

"On my count you may disconnect, Phil, and retract the arm. Three, two, one, release!"

Phil flipped the release switch, and the lander was free, floating beside the *Kat*. In the spotlight beam directed toward her, DEV One looked resplendent, proudly displaying the national colors of every country involved in this mission. Carefully stenciled below the flags were the names of the crew.

"You may initiate move-out and go to full power at one thousand meters. Commander Kidd nervously delivered his final instruction and send-off from the entire crew. May your flight be steady and your mission successful in every way. You are hereby go for landing. God speed and take care. We'll see you in a few days." The bird's engines began to glow, and it moved slowly away from the *Kat* to the starboard side. He could see the smiling face of Roberto through the windshield and his helmet visor. With a final wave, Roberto initiated the first slow turn, and his face disappeared from Jason's monitor. The unexpected feeling of loss crushed Jason's insides, and Doc leaned over to grasp his chilled hand.

15

GO FOR LANDING

STEALTH FINDER TWO and Margie, monitoring its info, detected a fair-sized weak area in the turbulent outer shell. It looked good under close observation by *Finder Two* and, if still intact, would pass below the *Kat* in less than forty-five minutes. This gave Roberto time to locate the anomaly, take additional readings, and attempt the descent if it looked good. If the opening closed or worsened, they could remain in orbit to await the next one or return to the mother ship, without expending too much precious fuel.

Once the crew embarked, only time, fate, and rigorous training would determine whether they ever returned. They were doing fine except for Oreen, who was breathing heavily, but her readings were well within acceptable limits. Roberto moved DEV One to a safe distance slightly ahead of and below the *Kat*. They were well out of illumination range by even the *Kat's* most powerful spotlights.

Jason could still just make out their running lights at a high magnification through the infrared telescope. Through the other optical systems, the crew of the mother ship scanned the roiling clouds for the more open, less violent area.

From the vantage point provided by *Stealth Finder Two*, the weak point resembled the eye of a compact hurricane on Earth, only much smaller. It was very open and relatively calm compared to the storm surrounding it. The only problem was its limited aerial extent and rapid, somewhat unpredictable, movement. Another unknown was its exact direction and duration.

This eye in a vortex presented an unparalleled opportunity for a smooth ride at least part of the way. Roberto had to find it, aim for it, and time his entry perfectly or be buffeted badly by the surrounding storm. He would have to hit the bull's eye if and when the bull's eye appeared, but this was an unprecedented chance to penetrate the shell with the least initial resistance.

He and Moses were seated in the front of the cockpit area, with Norm and Oreen at the rear. The DEVs had six seats, but the rear two seats were packed with gear for this flight. They were prepared for a seven-night visit with adequate supplies for at least seven more as a contingency. These supplies could be stretched for much longer if the need arose or in the event that problems forced a longer stay.

Roberto dropped the nose of the craft, assuming the position for rocketing out of orbit. The computer had given them a most likely target scenario and the necessary trajectory data. This system continuously updated all projected flight path information. It was now standing by waiting for initial detection of the target by the *Kat's* computers. Once seen, the computer would feed Roberto audio data and project a heads-up display in three dimensions. He needed to aim his craft and fire its thrusters. For a pilot as good as Roberto, this was still one tough shot, even with the assistance of the powerful artificial intelligence allies guiding him.

Fuel use was a major concern for this mission and Norm was monitoring this critical element intently. The fuel consumption for the nosedive maneuver had to be no more than about two percent of capacity. Once the lander started toward the ground, the planet's gravity would accelerate their fall. The DEV was designed to dive in at a steep angle. It then would attain an ever-decreasing attitude while gliding. Once relatively flat to the surface, the rockets would reverse for braking and then rotate for a soft, vertical landing. This left a only a small margin for error and little extra fuel for use while searching for a suitable landing site, but it did allow the pilot some discretion. The pilot and crew would not be able to sightsee for long. Maneuvering in orbit had used only a negligible amount. If they were forced to abort the dive and climb again, a second attempt to land would depend on total fuel expended to that point. If the fuel level dropped below eighty-five percent while orbiting or attempting a descent, it was mandatory to rendezvous with the *Kat* for refueling. At least seventy-five percent would be needed for leaving the surface and climbing back into orbit.

Roberto wanted as much extra fuel as possible for selecting his landing point. He would either make it through the shell on the first try or refuel. If they were caught in a maelstrom, he planned to climb out as fast as possible or ride it out. He could not afford to use fuel fighting through it. One thing was sure, either way, he wanted to be able to get back to the *Kat*.

With a short burst of activity, the cursor on Norm's monitor began tracing a shape, and in a few seconds, it became a three-dimensional color image. Green and orange contrast, medium hues, depicted a moving green mass with a plunging orange funnel. The approaching vortex was not a perfect circle but shaped like an oval torn at one end. The target was there; the data beamed directly from the mother ship.

"Roberto, it looks good, ominously good, but a little turbulent inside," Norm encouraged him.

At the same moment, Jason Kidd's voice broke in from the *Kat.* "You have acquired the target, and it looks good."

"We concur. I'm going in. We'll call you from the ground." With that, Roberto looked around the cabin of the DEV and nodded. "It's a go crew. Check your restraints and hold on tight."

"We're ready," Oreen said.

"Let's go," added Moses.

"Fire away. This ought to be one hell of a ride," Norm finished.

Roberto flipped a few switches on the panel in front of him, tightened his grip on the control stick, and pressed two small buttons labeled, "Shield." A front panel covering the windshield began to close. The shield was made of the same materials as the rest of the craft. Roberto would use the computer image and follow only colorful patterns on the screen until near the surface. Outside it would be pitch dark, and they could not afford to have their windshield covered by the same black soot that obscured the lens of the *Stealth Finder* Probes. Roberto would need clear vision to select a final point to set down.

While the shield closed, Roberto locked his view finder mask with its visual heads-up display on the target to obtain a third set of locking coordinates. Lastly, he fired his thrusters and aimed the DEV directly toward the center of the fast approaching vortex.

The four astronauts watched the monitors on the front control panel as the small yellow cursor on the screen, shaped exactly like their craft, began to descend toward the opening. It was a frightening moment. Oreen broke the silence with a calming voice that only she could muster at this moment. "Into the jaws of the cyclone rode the four intrepid explorers."

Norm picked up on it. "Go baby, go. We're in."

"Ride 'em, cowboy," Moses whispered, barely audible to the rest.

DEV One moved swiftly and smoothly into the vortex. They braced for turbulence, but there was almost none, a few initial shakes going in and a growing G-force pushing them as the planet's limited gravity began to take its grasp. Slowly, but perceptible, it was palpable to their heightened senses.

Down the axis of the funnel they plunged, each following the slow but steady progress of the tiny yellow ship on the screen.

"Outside hull temperature rising rapidly," Norm added.

"We have an eighty-degree down angle, encountering unstable atmospheric layer, distance: twelve thousand meters. Severe turbulence expected." Roberto's pilot voice came through their earpieces. "Hold on for real: We're going through. We're over halfway through the shell."

The cabin shook violently. The craft tumbled hard, and Roberto again broke the silence. "Easy, Baby."

It shook again, harder this time. The crew strained against their safety harnesses. "Breaking right!" Roberto shouted.

"Watch that patch to starboard," Norm yelled.

"I see it," Roberto countered. He wildly corkscrewed the ship through patches of violent atmosphere. "I'm afraid we'll have to hold up on the complimentary beverage service."

"I put us at seventy five percent through." Norm paused, "Coming up on eighty percent."

"We're go for landing as far as I'm concerned," Roberto said as the craft was buffeted a third time.

"Bad stuff ahead all over!" Moses exclaimed from his rear seat.

"Eighty-five percent, wall ahead!" Norm's voice took on a different tone. The computer images of the vortex were changing constantly, but in an instant the wall of the vortex touched the descending cursor.

Roberto instinctively pulled the stick hard to the side as the DEV was pounded again, this time the hardest yet.

Roberto reduced his down angle and switched off his engines, ready to start them again if needed. He fired them only seconds before. Everyone felt the mind-numbing forces within and out.

"Great move, Ace. You earned top honors." The words strained from Norm as the forces on their bodies began to ease. "Ninety percent." Norm only squeezed out the last word.

The pounding sustained by the DEV began to mitigate, replaced by a few shakes and a slow rumble. Norm watched the gauges through strained eyes as Roberto worked to control the DEV. "Ninety-five percent." Norm listened to the strained sounds of his crewmates.

A few more seconds, and the shaking reduced to slight vibrations typical of a dive test from training.

"We're through, people!" Roberto was excited. "What a ride! That's the tough part. We're under the shell."

The computer screens showed the DEV still plunging, but the 3D projection showed the eye of the vortex was disappearing above.

"Switch on ground acquisition radar and get an atmospheric sample," Roberto urged.

Norm pointed to his touch screen controls as he reactivated them with his right hand. "All radar active. I've got your sample. Let's see what we have."

The analysis printed out on the screen. Roberto looked at it, checking several columns of figures. "Particulates are within safety range, non-abrasive. Let's open the window."

They descended more than halfway to the surface. "Opening screens for visual," Norm said excitedly.

The super-heated screens moved out of view, and an alien panorama appeared. It was almost as if they were still looking at the computer screen with a dark background; an area of reddish, obviously molten surface to one side and a contrasting black area with dendritic yellow-green ribbons to the other.

Oreen uttered her first sounds since the start of the plunge. "Where's the sunshine? Did we have to land at night?" All four laughed.

The view was fantastic. They sat mesmerized by the strange beauty of contrasting brighter areas against the stark black.

The ship descended steadily, the angle changing in tandem on the monitor. Roberto was flattening their trajectory. "OK, people, let's get busy looking for a place to set this baby down." Roberto was leaning toward the windshield.

Norm continued to study the monitors.

"I think the red stuff is hot," Oreen said.

"No shit," Moses quipped.

"Coming up on twenty thousand meters." Some good looking flat terrain at twenty degrees," Norm stated.

"I'm on it," Roberto concurred. "Uncover landing lights, and give me one hundred percent illumination," Roberto ordered.

Norm moved his hands and said, "Locking on to target area, distance twenty-six thousand meters."

His target appeared on the monitor as a three-dimensional flattened landscape. "There's a plain area above that valley, just below the mouth." Norm pointed at the spot as vectors appeared on the screen. Roberto reversed the thrusters and powered them up. He was flying parallel to the ground—which was rapidly approaching. Five thousand meters and rotating engines," Roberto acknowledged, watching his gauges closely. "Gears are down and locked."

Norm's voice was machine-like. "Fuel level ninety-two percent and normal."

"Hold on once more." Roberto stated emphatically. "I'm going to set her down."

They slowed, hovered shortly and saw dust rise as the DEV settled gently toward the alien surface.

"Watch that little ridge," Norm advised.

In a moment they were solidly down and listened to the sound of the engines decrease and disappear. It was 4:01 p.m. Zulu October 23, 2031.

Silence. No one spoke. "Welcome to Enigma, the Stealth Wonder," Moses broke in as he released his safety restraints. "Please check around the cabin for personal belongings. I'm going to get ready to take a close look at this new world."

All four began to move around the cabin. "Get off a burst message and continue as we planned. Moses, you have the communicator."

Moses uttered the first official acknowledgment of landing. "As humankind embarks upon a new world, may we come in everlasting peace. Mother *Kat*, the kitten is safely down."

"It's sent," Roberto said. "We'll know if they got it it they acknowledge They'll have to send a response many times to get it through, but the computer will add up the fragmented pieces. Let's hope they got ours, the signal is pretty weak. We need to set up the transmitter and main antennas first thing. Shall we grab some lights and look around? Norm, Moses, you get ready. Oreen and I will get the first equipment ready and take all the outside readings." Roberto was wasting no time but was also not in a hurry.

Oreen and Moses pushed the lighted buttons to uncover the side window ports. They peered outside into the darkness, and then went about their other tasks.

Roberto rotated his landing lights shining them at the side ports and under the wings, checking his landing struts. They were straight and level, having only sunk a few centimeters into the surface layer. "Looks good," he smiled.

"Fabulous landing, Roberto," Norm hailed as he clasped his shoulder and thrust his gloved hand toward the pilot. "I can't believe we are here."

Within ten hours of touching down, Norm and Moses passed through the outer hatch, and Norm helped Moses as he swung around and began backing down the ladder. He stood on the last rung and looked back at Norm. "Now I know how Neil Armstrong felt. That's a second giant step for a man and a greater leap for mankind," he uttered as he dropped from the bottom rung and landed on the planet. Norm handed down several cases of equipment and followed carefully. He waved at the faces of Roberto at the windshield and Oreen at the side port.

Norm and Moses moved around the base of their craft, training their lights at the underside and landing gears. Satisfied by their inspection, they proceeded toward the rear of the craft. "You know, it's beautiful," Norm said as they reached the back.

"Outside temperature minus sixteen Celsius" Moses said. "Almost sweater weather." It was above zero Fahrenheit.

"Look, Moses, there's some of that green stuff over there by the little rocky ridge." It was only twenty meters away. Roberto landed a little close. The craggy black ridge was about the same height as their craft with a dune of coarse debris piled against it and what looked like windblown sand material at its base.

They moved closer and trained their lights on the ridge. "Roberto, give us some more illumination," Moses said.

The lights from the craft shed plenty of light on the area, but Roberto aimed one landing spot at the ridge, switching to broad beam. The ridge ended abruptly to their right. They followed it to the left in the beam, where it disappeared into a darkened valley, with ever-brightening green patches coursing up into it.

"Look at this flat protected spot to set up a base camp." Norm pointed to and was interested in the sheltered, leeward side, "Roberto, Oreen, can you see this?"

"Looks great," Roberto responded from the DEV.

"We'll finish the look around." Moses moved next to Norm as they aimed their lights at the sheltered alcove just beyond the ridge. "We'll set up here tomorrow if everything checks out. Let's assemble the antenna and send another high-energy burst transmission."

Moses and Norm returned to the DEV to complete the task of putting together a better communications link. They unloaded cables and the collapsible antenna from an underside, recessed compartment. After stretching out the cords, and connecting the antenna, Norm plugged the cables into the exterior receptacle. He had to wipe off a thin veneer of black soot. Norm was eager to get on with his experiments but knew well that this day called for only a rudimentary look around and cursory survey. He and Moses finished securing the antenna and anchored it, re-checked the connecting cables, and finished work on the high-energy transmitter. He would have plenty of time to look around later.

Their second message using the burst antenna got through. Aboard the *Kat*, the entire crew breathed a sigh of relief. They were safely down, uninjured, and in good spirits, if they could judge from Moses' message. The hours waiting for word had been excruciating.

Jason and his crew toasted their comrades. Jason relayed Moses' message to Earth, adding all data readouts the computers obtained from DEV One before the communication blackout, which occurred during the descent. He knew that a mighty celebration would begin on Earth in a few hours. He also sent the acknowledgment of receipt of the message from his crew on the ground. He was truly very proud of them.

Once the link was completed, it was time for Moses and Norm to return to the lander and wait in the pressure-lock area for suit checks. The lock was armed with an assortment of scanners ready to analyze their suits. These sensors would check for contaminants and constituents, whether chemical, solid, gas, liquid, or biological. They would remain in this hold for hours while being scrutinized from head to toe by the sensors. Decontamination provided a good break from the tension, which had filled them both since their EVA started. They touched as little as possible outside. An amazing amount of detail could be gained from what might be stuck to them. Floor scanners passed over their boot bottoms repeatedly.

Moses and Norm closed their eyes and listened to the soft strains of music Oreen selected for their stay in the lock. "Get some rest," she said gently. "We have the first watch."

Roberto added, "They know we're here; they got the message. Congratulations all around."

16

BASE CAMP

D AY TWO on the surface began with analytical evaluation of what the landing party had learned so far. This was a day to observe, watch, listen, and garner what they could from the minute particles of dust clinging to Norm and Moses upon their return to the pressure lock. Both outside explorers had experienced fatigue and imbalance due to their return to gravity. Even though only a fraction of Earth's, they all felt it, even though their days aboard the *Kat* had prescribed daily, two-hour, resistance exercise regimes.

All four rotated watches. Only two of the crew rested at a time. They scanned the area with the landing lights and probed the soil with sensors on the landing struts. Preliminary analyses showed no dangerous toxins or other contaminants, but there were still unknowns. Only Norm's laboratory could unravel more of these secrets. He could not wait to collect more samples of the dark soot covering nearly everything. The partial analysis by the sensors of the material coating his boots left him with incomplete data.

Awash in the floodlights of the DEV, the immediate surrounding area looked rocky and rough. They had landed in a flat valley between opposing ridges. From Norm's preliminary look, he reported that the rocks appeared to be volcanic, resembling night landscapes he had visited in Hawaii. He didn't see much layering; the familiar signature of sedimentary rocks or those formed by erosion and deposition of layered grain stones. Norm stated that the barely discernible valleys could have been formed by erosion and therefore should yield more information. He planned an exploration sortie into one of these as soon as Moses allowed him to go.

Nothing moved, with the exception of a few gentle gusts of wind rolling small black grains toward the nearby rock ridge. The wind came steadily from the same direction. Today they would observe the local meteorological conditions, too. They had no desire to be caught outside on the surface, setting up a base camp, in an unexpected alien storm.

The distant red-orange glow of volcanic activity added strange hues to the omnipresent dark sky. Roberto had steered well clear of this potential threat. The contrasting phosphorescent green patterns in the valleys in the opposite direction added slightly to the low-level ambient light. White light from the lander added an unfamiliar white dot to the landscape.

For the first thirty-six hours on the planet, virtually nothing changed. The air outside remained just above zero degrees Fahrenheit, varying little. Numerous gases formed the atmosphere. Norm ventured the observation that they could eventually extract a breathable mixture over time using available technology. He wanted to set up a small unit to test his hypothesis and potentially extract a mixture for a generator. Oreen was already assembling pieces and was fabricating a prototype of the breathing apparatus.

Roberto checked and rechecked his machine. If anything did happen, he wanted to be able to blast off and jettison weight in an instant. Even though the gravity was about one-third Earth gravity, the climb back out of here was still his chief concern. He wanted his craft primed and flight-worthy.

Moses was readying his surface equipment. On his approval, they would all embark from the craft and begin assembling their habitat. He again reviewed the computer simulators and directions for each step. The transition to the outside had to be smooth and efficient—he expected clockwork precision.

— § —

Aboard the *Kat*, the entire crew remained glued to their communications monitors, awaiting the next bits of information. Incoming bursts were slowly deciphered by Rod and passed directly to Jason Kidd or Phil Allen. Jason wanted it that way. His crew and NASA would receive any communiqué only after it had passed through his hands.

Subsequent data transfers, which followed each progress update, were downloaded for Margie and David's analysis. Margie fed these bits of information into their computer system for complete break down.

Jason received a plethora of congratulatory responses from Earth-based colleagues. The news of the landing on Earth touched off wild celebrations all over the world. Their short celebration on the *Kat* paled by comparison to the most conservative visions Jason's eyes beheld on the digital videos. His crew watched them with both mild amusement and amazement. Each received numerous requests for personal stories from the relentless press. Even billions of miles were not enough to insulate them from the ravenous media. Most of the crew prepared responses in order to satisfy the lust for news.

Jason was bothered by one thing. He had selected Oreen because of her ability to perceive and feel things that the rest of the landing party would miss. She had sent comments, but they were strangely devoid of personal observations.

Jason clicked his communicator. "Rod, get a burst off to Oreen: 'Need your personal perceptions; what do you feel so far?' Send it now and let me know as soon as you get something back. Thanks."

"Message prepared and I'm starting to send," Rod answered. "Will stand by for response."

When Roberto received the message in the DEV, he pointed it out to Oreen, adding: "The boss wants to know how you feel." Roberto had also noticed how quiet Oreen had been. Her normally affable personality was noticeably different, but she had been preoccupied with the equipment.

She looked up at Roberto while helping Norm box up a fragile piece of equipment, including connectors and cables. Roberto wasn't sure what it was and was not ready to ask just yet, but decided to take a more personal interest in her present disposition.

"I've been busy and haven't had much time to think or feel," Oreen said, not looking up.

"Oh, come on, Oreen, you're making me nervous," Roberto insisted. "You must be getting some vibes, you always do. This place must be rendering something."

Moses stopped his work and looked up. Norm had placed his object in the box and fastened it securely. He also waited for Oreen. All eyes were on her, and each now realized that she was acting differently, not strange, but not the normal, outgoing Oreen.

"OK, time out, let's talk," Moses broke in. "Oreen, Roberto is right. You are not saying much. Tell us what you feel."

Oreen straightened up and turned around. They all took their seats and awaited her speech, as she seemed to search for the right words.

"I don't feel anything clearly," she began. "Just bits and pieces, kind of like the messages we send. Maybe it's the foreign landscape. Maybe it's being enclosed in this DEV. Maybe it's this jump suit. Maybe it's this whole situation. My head is messed up again, now that we are back under real gravity, even if it is only one third of Earth's."

With that she paused and closed her eyes, saying nothing for what seemed to the others like five minutes. No one else uttered a sound. When she began again, her demeanor had changed, barely perceptible, but she was quieter than before. "I feel things that I can not describe. You won't like everything I'm about to say. I feel trouble, but I can't put my finger on it. I feel pain, but I don't know why. I feel a strange presence, but just can't focus on it. I'm trying, but it won't come through."

"Trouble for us?" Moses inquired, breaking her thought pattern. "Sorry," he added quickly.

"That's OK, Moses. I wish I could tell you more, but that's about all. When we all go out that door, I want you to have a lot of light and, for me, a big stick. Something tells me that we need to keep our eyes and ears open, and keep it bright."

"Do you think that we should not go back out?" Roberto asked nervously.

"Oh no, nothing like that," Oreen assured. "We should be OK. I just feel that we should be alert and prepared at all times."

"Advice well given and well received," Moses said as he stood up. "We'll take plenty of lights, and I'm going to take my laser cutter since it's almost a weapon. Remember, everybody will always buddy up. No one will be alone for any reason. And watch your backsides at every step. I'm hungry. Let's eat, and get ready to hit the surface. It should not take more than a few hours to unload the equipment, the Habitat, and set up. Norm and Oreen, you take a break too. Get a little rest. Roberto and I will finish up and keep the watch."

"Food time, I'm starved," Norm said as he stood up yawned and stretched.

"Oreen, I'll send your comments to Jason," Roberto added. They all felt the hunger of hard work and stress.

In a few hours they were ready for EVA Two. The plan was to unload some equipment and the Habitat. Next, they would set up additional lighting and finally assemble the inflatable Habitat, anchoring it securely. One would continuously be on guard or observing while the others put things together carefully, but as quickly as possible. Then they would again return to the DEV to wait, monitoring all activity, or lack thereof, by remote video surveillance.

Moses knew how badly Norm wanted to poke around, and cautioned him to stick to today's duty. If all went well, Norm could be working on his experiments by the next Earth day. Norm acknowledged his caution and assured Moses that the few samples that he planned to collect today would be obtained in the immediate area of the Habitat site. At least he would have these if anything went wrong or they had to leave before he could gather more.

Moses opened the hatch for the second EVA. He cautiously surveyed the entire area before stepping onto the ladder. He slid down and moved to one side, checking around in all directions, shining his halogen sealed-beam spotlight with his left hand. His other hand was at his side, in close proximity to his laser tool. He wasn't quite sure why. The next one out of the DEV was Oreen. She gazed about, swinging her head from side to side and, seeming satisfied, joined Moses at the base of the ladder on the opposite side.

Roberto appeared third. He nervously began to descend and suddenly slipped and fell to the surface with a soft thud, dropping his light. Norm, who was just stepping out, didn't even chuckle. Oreen and Moses helped Roberto straighten up. Roberto pulled his flashlight back to his gloved hand using the tether, clipped it to his suit, and switched on his helmet lamp.

Moses' voice broke the silence that had been maintained since the hatch opened. "Oreen and I will unload the Habitat, you two start unloading the rest of the gear." With that said, he and Oreen moved beneath the fuselage and began unclasping recessed fasteners in the underside of the DEV. When all of the clasps were opened, Moses used his handheld remote unit to open the double hatch and begin unloading the Habitat.

"Oreen, you keep your eyes open, and I'll get this thing unloaded." He didn't have to ask. She was shining her light in all directions, not really knowing what she was looking for. Oreen knew that she had scared herself and them. As psychologist, it was all a part of her plan. Nothing would keep them on their toes better than a little fear. Moses pushed a few more buttons, and the sound of electric motors indicated that the Habitat was being lowered. Before it reached the ground, Moses stopped it to give it a full inspection. He released the recessed bulbous wheels, and they gently moved into place.

In a few moments it was on the ground and ready to roll. The Habitat was a fully self-contained, mobile unit. It unloaded itself, drove by remote to wherever you wanted it, and completely unfolded itself in preparation for inflation.

Next, Moses unloaded a small trailer that he attached to the chassis carrying the Habitat. He drove the entire setup with his handheld unit, similar to remote-control vehicles enjoyed by children, young and old. The trailer carried all of their gear. Once detached from the Habitat, the chassis became a surface-rover vehicle. The trailer became Norm's laboratory workbench. It would be some time before the chassis would be used as a rover. For now, Moses just wanted it to do the task at hand. Roberto was pleased because their escape craft was now that much lighter.

Norm handed box after box and numerous slings of equipment to Roberto. Lastly he handed down powerful spotlights and extra batteries. Each crewman had at least three sources of light, not including the helmet-mounted spot. Roberto stacked the supplies away from the base of the ladder. When they had finished unloading, Norm secured the hatch and began his descent.

At the same moment, Moses started up the Habitat driver and began the meticulous task of rolling it toward the boxes. When parallel with the stack,

Norm and Roberto began piling them on the trailer. Moses continued to scan the area with his light. The super-powerful beam could illuminate an object at a distance of almost one mile.

Very few words were spoken during the entire unloading procedure. When they were satisfied that everything was secured, Moses restarted the Habitat and began rolling it toward the sheltered alcove behind the end of the ridge. They all trained their beams on the alcove and the rock walls surrounding it. Satisfied by their inspection, Moses moved the Habitat to the end of the ridge and stopped it there.

"OK, everybody, let's get our motion detectors and lights set up as quickly and carefully as possible," Moses ordered.

Norm and Roberto unfolded the light standards, and Oreen attached the floodlights. For today, they installed one solid perimeter of motion detectors. Eventually, when the entire system was installed, they would be encircled by three rows of sensors capable of detecting virtually any movement within the perimeter and out to a distance of more than three hundred meters.

"Norm and I will place the sensors while you keep watch and help light our work area," Roberto said as they finished the light stands. These were placed at various distances from the proposed location for the Habitat. They supplied adequate low power illumination for the entire area surrounding the DEV and the new base camp.

They were all nervous until these lights were fully operational. The DEV lights were on, but not at full power. At the highest illumination values, the DEV lights drained considerable power from the already overworked electrical system. A small, high-efficiency, self-contained generator operated the surface lighting. Each crew person could operate the DEV lights and the surface illumination system using only a handheld remote.

The sensors for the motion detectors were set up next. Roberto and Norm placed the remote sensors at various angles and positions in order to create a web of coverage surrounding the entire base camp area. When completed, they returned to the Habitat cart. Moses activated the system. One by one the sensors blinked to life. The monitors on the handheld units showed the overlapping vectors of coverage. Moses moved several sensors and realigned two before Oreen signaled that the job was finished.

"There isn't anything that can move over, under or through that net without us knowing about it, and we'll feel the faintest quakes. We'll add outer circles later, but for now, we're in good shape." Moses was more relaxed and proud of their accomplishment. Between the sensors, which constantly scanned the area from the DEV, and their new array, the perimeter of their base camp now felt and appeared more secure. There was a general sense of relief, but a great deal of work still lay ahead.

Their next task was to set up and anchor the inflatable Habitat. They criss-crossed the selected location, moving a few pieces of coarse rock debris and prodding the ground for firmness. Rolled into position, Moses again used his remote unit to unfold the self-contained Habitat. It automatically unfurled and spread the unit out upon the ground. The vehicle also contained the air tanks and a complete recirculating rebreathing system. Each corner contained an auger for setting the important anchor system. Moses and Oreen again kept a vigil as Roberto and Norm used the drills to secure the rounded corners.

Opened, the Habitat measured five by seven meters. Its four-ply construction consisted of four layers of Lee Tanaka's miracle, ultra-light, ultra-strong material. The quadruple plies could stop a high-powered rifle bullet fired from point-blank range. These multiple plies also added an insulation factor as well as complete wind and fire protection. Properly anchored and enforced, the habitat could withstand a hurricane-force wind with minimal damage.

Moses flipped a switch, and the nearly silent inflator began the task of filling their new home. It would be further braced from within and without by telescoping poles. As it rose, Norm and Oreen attached the outside corner braces and inspected the entire exterior. Satisfied with the final product, the crew reassembled beside the trailer in front of the Habitat.

"It's time to get the equipment unloaded and placed inside." They all knew the drill, but as he directed them, Moses was relentless in his desire to get things done and get back inside the DEV. This part of the operation left them most blind and vulnerable to any emergency need to liftoff from the surface.

Bladders separated the four plies of the Habitat keeping the interior section isolated from the outside as much as possible. Moses remained outside, Roberto between the first plies, and Norm, between the next and Oreen inside.

The boxes of gear and supplies were unwrapped between the first two and the double-wrapped contents passed through to the second. One inner wrap was then removed and the contents again passed to the inside. The containers held food, water, medical supplies, chair-beds, and various other essentials. There were equal and adequate supplies aboard the DEV as well. Passing everything to the inside was a slow and laborious task, taking well over an hour. The entire operation went as planned. Oreen separated and stacked the equipment, started the filtering system, and exited the Habitat last. The entire operation since leaving the DEV took over two and one half-hours. They were finished a half-hour ahead of schedule. Moses again assembled the team in front of the Habitat, and they all gathered the empty containers and moved them to underneath the trailer. They detached the now empty trailer and extended bracing legs, converting it to Norm's laboratory workbench.

Moses addressed his crew, beginning with a compliment. "Nice job, everyone. We got that set up in an amazingly short time. We have a little time left. Oreen and Roberto, head for the DEV. I'm going to let Norm get some good samples from this immediate area. That way if we do have to pull out of here early for any reason, we'll have some samples to take back."

Norm said a thank you and did not wait for a second invitation. He began to shine his light toward the end of the small ridge. He picked up several rock specimens and placed them in the used, plastic, packing bags. Moses watched his every move, trying to decide just how Norm selected his samples. They circled the Habitat, never leaving the alcove. Norm filled several sample containers and placed them in a box he carried by its strap handle.

As they were rounding the last corner of the Habitat, Norm stopped in his tracks and shined his light at a small depression in the surface material. He looked at Moses and asked, "Have you noticed these small impressions?"

"Yes," Moses responded, there's been a bunch of those around. What do you think caused them?"

"I'm not sure," replied Norm. They could be from something falling, kind of like raindrop imprints. Possibly tiny craters from falling volcanic debris." He bent down and dug around in a group of several pockmarks. "If something hit the ground it should be in the hole or under the debris, but there's nothing here."

"Did you notice the big ones?" Moses asked.

"No. What big ones?" Norm was growing more curious about the scattered tiny pits.

Moses directed him to the front side of the ridge, the side facing the DEV. Behind two one-meter-square-sized boulders were some detritus-filled pits measuring perhaps one-third meter across. On the leeside of the rocks, the pits were protected from erosion or filling. If there had been any others on the windward side, they had been erased by the occasional winds.

"This gives me another piece of the puzzle to solve, and I've got a lot to learn," Norm said as they turned and headed for the lander.

When Norm had filled two boxes with samples, they sealed them carefully and placed them in the cargo area once filled by the Habitat. Secured in the hold, Norm felt great relief that he had something to eventually study. Both Norm and Moses noticed that the wind had started and was growing stronger. It was time to get back to the security of the inside of the DEV.

Moses and Norm returned to the outer air lock just before the total EVA time reached three hours. Everything had gone without a hitch. The base camp was established and provisioned. The rover was ready, and the laboratory could be set up quickly during the next EVA. For now, they would again have to wait, watch, and listen. Nothing had changed in the character of the environment or weather, except for the wind and steady increase in its velocity. Otherwise, all remained calm and uneventful, just the way Roberto wanted it to be. They were nearing the midpoint of their third Earth-time-measured day on the surface, and so far, so good.

After almost a half-hour in the decontamination lock, they felt the DEV begin to move slightly in the breeze. Roberto was anxious to get back to the controls. He could operate the craft and everything else from within the lock, but he wanted to be at his console. A warning light erased that thought. The scanners detected a chemical combination very similar to a quasi-organic pathogen. They would now have to wait for complete decontamination.

For what seemed like an eternity, they waited, huddled and cramped together in the close quarters of the pressure lock. When the all-clear green light finally appeared, everyone ducked as Roberto propelled himself through the door in one motion. They watched in horror as one of the newly placed light stanchions crashed to the ground, shattering one lamp.

They all scrambled from the lock, leaving their heavy EVA suits behind. Each grabbed a seat and began assessing the growing storm outside. The dark had gotten much darker. Black soot was swirling through the air along with pieces of charcoal-colored debris.

"Close the window covers," Roberto screamed. "That damned soot is sticking to everything. It's like black snow!"

Suddenly the motion detector system went wild. Alarms and flashing lights began filling the cabin with a cacophony of confusion.

"What the hell is it?" Moses asked looking at the monitors.

They were losing visual signal as the intensity of the approaching storm increased. Warning indicators were flashing everywhere.

"Turn the alarms off," Roberto shouted.

Norm's eyes were fixed on his monitor. "There's so much junk flying around out there that the sensor system is overwhelmed," he said. "We're blind right now and the cameras aren't getting much." Even the Doppler radar was confused and painting an unclear picture of their surroundings.

"Wind speed rising steadily," Norm reported. "Present velocity fifty knots, with gusts to sixty knots."

Roberto now faced a perplexing dilemma. If the winds increased too much, he could not safely leave the surface, even under maximum liftoff fuel use. If they stayed, there was no way to know how strong the storm would be or how long it would last.

"Strap into your seats!" Roberto warned.

Everyone had already done so, except for Norm, who was re-securing several bundles of his lab equipment. The storm raged outside. Light stanchions toppled, and debris buffeted the DEV from several directions. The crippling soot covered almost everything with a fine, barely translucent coating. Oreen suggested shutting down the motion-detector network and relying on the more dependable data from the DEV scanners.

Oreen saw it first, and then Moses caught it out of the corner of his eye while watching Norm finish securing his bundles. A large object appeared on the screen as an unidentified blip. It was moving slowly toward the ship.

Roberto followed Norm's gaze to the monitor and gulped. "What is that, and where is it headed?"

"I have no idea what it is, but it's headed straight at us, bearing one-eight-five degrees, distance seven hundred meters," Norm said as he began tracking the object. It was slowly approaching the DEV from almost directly behind them.

"Norm, Roberto, the wind is blowing in the opposite direction." Moses' voice was deep and steady but he sounded very concerned. He was right. Whatever it was, it was moving almost directly into the wind and appeared to have come from the higher elevation of the nearby valley.

"Could it be a landslide or a debris flow of some sort, Norm?" Roberto inquired as he squirmed in his seat. He had lost his normally cool composure and Oreen noted signs of stress.

"I don't think so," Norm answered. "It's moving too slow, and the radar shows it to be solid."

"Give me closing distance and ETA," Roberto barked. I'm going to uncover the super beams and light it up even if they get covered with soot. We have to get a look at it."

"Roger that," Norm answered, sounding jittery.

Oreen understood that she must calm the group. Norm had triggered her thoughts. She had been transfixed by the incredible efficiency and bravery of the others. She had also been overcome by a tremendous feeling of another presence. It had seized her attention completely for a few moments.

Roberto was following emergency EVAC procedures and was ready to uncover the engine ports, activate, and blast off if the situation warranted it. He feared the black soot and potential damage to his engines from the flying debris. "Get off a message to the *Kat*, Moses. Say: 'Base Camp completed, have been hit by storm. Assessing risk of remaining on surface. Emergency evacuation potential real.'"

Oreen watched the approaching blip on the screen along with the others. Just as Roberto was about to hit the switch to uncover the high-intensity landing spots, the motion of the object stopped, and it then began moving back in the opposite direction much faster. In a few seconds it disappeared in the direction of the valley and was gone.

"Well, at least whatever that was is gone, and we seem to be holding up OK." Oreen's most calming voice soothed their ears. "Take it easy, Roberto. You're doing a great job," she added.

The crew sat in silence, watching and monitoring the storm through garbled sensors. It lasted only twenty minutes and reminded them all of a fast moving afternoon thunderstorm back on Earth. It had seemed like forever. Moses wiped his brow. The sweat was just pouring off, and his thirst was approaching unbearable. He knew he would dehydrate if he did not ingest some liquid very soon.

Oreen unbuckled her harness and moved to his side, wiping his brow. None of them had put their flight helmets on. The tension had been so thick that they had all overlooked them or had not wanted their encumbrance until they were airborne. The storm dissipated as almost as fast as it had started. It was time to assess the damage.

Evaluation of the problems produced by the storm required that they make another quick EVA. They had to at least clean off some soot and remove debris from around the landing struts.

Norm was exhausted and upset by the storm damage. He was so pumped up to set up his lab and begin his experiments that he could not rest—as tired as he felt. They were all fatigued from the combination of hard work and tension. Moses fell asleep almost as soon as the storm danger abated. Norm insisted that Roberto get some rest too, since he had burned a lot of energy and earned a respite.

They reopened the front window covering and used the cleaners to remove the clinging soot. The landscape had changed little except for a few new dunes of black sand. To their initial horror, nearly all of the lights were down, and several were obviously broken. It was much darker than Oreen wanted it to be. They also switched the motion detector field back on. It was working but with considerable interference caused by partially-buried sensors. The antenna looked fine.

Their Habitat came through almost unscathed, still standing straight, with a small dune of sand piled against the front. The sand helped to hold it in place. This fact brought at least a partial feeling of relief. They were dirtied and had lost some lighting, but everything else had survived the storm intact.

Moses and Roberto slept for several hours. Oreen and Norm kept a silent vigil at the windows, keeping one eye on the monitors. Oreen could barely keep her eyes open. She was tired, very tired. She caught herself dozing once and realized that she could not afford to not be fully alert. "I'm going to wake Moses to see if he's ready to relieve me for a while."

Norm acknowledged her by nodding, hardly taking his eyes off of the front window. He was seated in his copilot chair, staring blankly. "Better get them both up. I could use a break too. We all need some good rest before we go back out. I'm not too pleased with our lack of light. I'm beginning to see things and am getting a little jumpy."

Oreen woke Roberto, but Moses was already stirring. "How long have I been out?" he wondered aloud, rubbing his eyes.

"Almost three hours," Oreen answered, handing him a cup of water and several vitamin capsules.

"Three hours!" He was on his feet and replaced his boots. Recollection of the storm raced through his head. He suddenly remembered the surrounding darkness and fallen light stanchions. "We've got to get more lighting and clean up."

His raised voice awakened Roberto. He had been snoring and looked disheveled, slouched in a rear seat. He didn't look very comfortable, but no one wanted to wake him. Roberto at last woke in a combined yawn and stretch, and rubbed his eyes with both hands. "Did I hear three hours? That's enough for me." He moved forward, picking up a packaged food bar and container of water on the way. Once in his pilot's seat, he looked at Norm and said: "How's everything look, Norm?"

Norm's answer was a monotone, "We're still primed and ready to fly. All systems are reading normal."

"Have you seen anything interesting lately?" Roberto waited, but Norm did not answer right away.

"Yes," he said after a moment of reflection.

Oreen was just about to lie down on the fully reclined rear seat but stopped her progress, rising again. "How long ago and what did you see?" She was curious because she had seen nothing, didn't want to miss anything, and she had felt that strange presence again about an hour ago.

"About an hour ago, on the radar, another blip, smaller and faster." Norm's words were choppy. "It appeared, started toward us, retreated back in the same direction when it came within the range of our spots. I was about to alert the rest of you when it just disappeared. I didn't have a chance to hit it with the landing spots."

"I felt it, really felt it this time." Oreen settled onto the reclined seat as everyone turned their attention to her. "There was something out there that gave me that same uneasy feeling. This time I figured that it was just me, but Norm says he spotted something at about that same time. Can't really tell you what it is, though. I'm not getting any of the feelings that I can attribute to something tangible."

Moses spoke next. "Oreen, get some sleep. Norm, buddy, go get some shut-eye too. Roberto and I can handle things for a while, and then we all hit the surface again to get our lighting back and have a good look around."

"Roberto was wide awake and refreshed. "Moses, can you rig up another one of those laser cutters? We can light up something on the top of that mountain with it or use it to zap almost anything."

"You know that I can, Roberto. It's always been part of the overall contingency plan for exploring. But you also know the primary mandate: 'Destroy nothing, disturb as little as possible, do and leave nothing harmful.' We don't shoot the things at anything unless we absolutely have to, not even a rock."

Moses continued, substituting a new train of thought. "This time when we go out, we repair our lighting and then switch it to low power. We may have no choice if too many of the lights are damaged but they should be OK. Once at low power, we switch to all low-light facemasks. With light-enhancement visual equipment, we can save our batteries and still be able to see just as much. We can also get a good look at what we illuminate with the red-beamed lasers."

Roberto said nothing. He continued straining his eyes, checking in front of the DEV. Moses began working on a second pulsed laser for the next EVA, at the same time scanning alternately through the side ports. Norm was settling down to rest after freshening up. Oreen was lying supine on the sleeper, staring wide-eyed at the ceiling. A few gusts of wind shook the DEV again, but then subsided to almost complete calm.

Three and one-half hours had passed when Roberto roused Norm and Oreen and announced that it was time to perform their next EVA. Moses allowed the extra half-hour because Oreen's eyes hadn't closed for at least that long after she lay down. They were both ready in minutes, and then all four feasted before they donned their heavier EVA suits. It had been an uneventful three-point-five Earth hours. Moses converted the laser and he and Roberto rigged up a back harness.

Once again they prepared and exited the DEV in an organized and orderly manner. They dug debris and sand away from the ship's upright struts. They salvaged the unbroken lights and replaced several lamps. They cleaned soot where they could and adjusted the motion-detector web. Once the DEV chores were completed, they switched their attention to the Habitat, which needed little other than removing sand by the front entrance.

Roberto gave Moses a ceremonial salute. "Mission completed, Sir. I think that we have everything shipshape again."

He was right. The storm damage was repaired, and they were ready to begin their look around. Today called for reconnoitering the immediate vicinity and collecting samples for Norm. The four explorers began true scientific evaluation of the surface of this Stealth Planet.

They assembled in front of Norm's workbench. Norm had prepared color-contoured maps from an area of about one square kilometer around the DEV. He used side-scan radar images obtained on their final approach to land along with surface radar, combining the images into a representative topographic map. He had also input three dimensional cube displays into their handheld units. All data could be displayed on the heads-up visor display within their helmets too. The positions of the DEV, Habitat, and each explorer were shown by different colored pips. Distance, directions, and identities were also displayed with each marker.

They paired up. Norm and Oreen began a broad sweep of a semicircular arc from the DEV toward the valley to the rear of the DEV. Moses and Roberto watched and tracked their progress from between the DEV and the small ridge. This gave Norm a good chance to expand his sampling area while safely under their watch. Oreen carried the samples allowing Norm to pick at, dig or collect whatever he saw fit to test. The plan allowed them to approach several large rocks bearing the familiar phosphorescent yellow-green patches. Norm couldn't wait any longer to get a close look at the stuff.

Moses was nervous and concerned for safety first. Norm might wander off to follow some enticing geological phenomena, if he let him. The leader almost reconsidered letting Norm venture away from the base camp first. But Norm had Oreen as a controlling factor. She would not want to go very far the first time, and he could count on her sensibility completely.

"Good hunting, Norm," Roberto said as they waved and set out to officially explore. They moved away with caution; Norm beaming from ear to ear. Moses gave Oreen the thumbs-up signal, and she smiled a broad smile that was visible through her visor. The pair moved slowly along the side of the ridge closest to the DEV.

After moving about fifty meters, as Moses judged by steps, they stopped at an outcropping, and Norm began picking up samples and placed them in awaiting containers offered by Oreen. Moses checked his heads-up display. Distance, forty-five-point-eight meters. "Not bad," he muttered.

They followed their prescribed course with precision, taking only a few short side trips of just a few steps. Norm was piling on the samples and Moses began to feel a little guilty for sending her to carry the load. When they reached a rock ledge bearing the bright green material, Norm snapped several close-up pictures using his auto camera.

Moses instructed his voice-activated helmet receiver to display the image on his handheld. It appeared in a few seconds as a neon green gel-like blob coating the surface of the rock. The photo was excellent and showed what looked like a smear of yellow-green fluorescent toothpaste under a black light.

Norm began gently prodding the gel with his geologist's pick. A slight amount clung to the pick when he drew it away. He scanned it with his handheld analyzer. It looked innocuous enough. He asked Oreen for a plastic container and scraped several samples into it, closing the lid and sealing it. He began handing it to Oreen, but she stepped back and looked warily at it. He smiled and placed it in his carrier as they moved to the next collecting spot.

After about forty-five minutes, they returned to the workbench lab, and Norm began organizing his samples. He laid them out and recorded each sample. The location of each had already been precisely pinpointed and correctly oriented on the base map as it was collected. The others gathered around to watch and lend assistance. Again Norm boxed pieces of many of the samples, and Roberto immediately loaded them into the DEV storage hold.

Norm then removed the vial containing his precious cargo of the mysterious green material. He scraped some onto a clear slide and placed it under the optics of his microscope. He turned on the illumination lamp and bowed his head to look into the custom eyepiece, specially formed to exactly fit to his visor. He stared, blinked, and stared some more, rotating the focus and changing powers several times.

Oreen was looking back in the direction of the DEV. Roberto and Moses were hunched close to Norm, trying to get a look.

Norm turned his head and stated: "It's alive!"

"Let me see!" Roberto was trying to force his way to get a look.

Moses stopped him, "Easy, Rob."

"It's alive," Norm repeated, "and I think that it may be ingesting or feeding on the rock. Go ahead, take a look," Norm stated triumphantly. "Take a good look, and then go get me some more."

They each took their turns. Under the crosshairs appeared a tiny wiggling mass of activity.

"Definitely!" Roberto stated as he danced around the workbench. "Life! We've discovered life on another world, the ultimate dream of every explorer throughout modern history." The last words sounded almost like the lyrics of a song. They were all filled with an intense feeling of excitement.

Moses' voice cracked with emotion. "I'm going to send a burst transmission to the *Kat*. Norm you do the honors, you found it." Norm dictated a simple message to his waiting computer and then read the entirety on the handheld before hitting send. It stated: "Exploration EVA three in progress. Collecting samples. Will relay all computer-storage data following. Have discovered possible lifeform. Confirmed phosphorescent material appears alive and active. Will further assess." "Wait until they get this one. Are we gonna stir up some shit or what?"

— § —

Aboard the *Kat* the message came in clear within only twenty minutes. Rod was sitting at his communications console reading a book as the message began to form from bits and pieces on his monitor screen. He glanced at it and went on reading as the letters slowly formed. He was about to take a sip from his drink bottle when he saw the word "life". He dropped his book and straightened in his control chair. The final words appeared. He read them several more times, signaled the con and relayed the message, hitting the alert button.

"Incoming," he shouted into his communicator.

Jason was on the bridge along with Sergey and Doc. Phil Allen was sleeping. Jason whirled around in his captain's chair and looked at the words on his screen. He read the message and rose from his seat exclaiming one word, "Life!"

It became a moment etched in time. The relaxed atmosphere of the *Kat* was instantly replaced with feelings of awe and curiosity. Their comrades on the surface had made the ultimate discovery. They had instantaneously justified their entire mission. They had succeeded in securing a place in history and given the mission planners the ultimate satisfaction for their planning and foresight to push for this complex voyage.

Jason prepared to relay the message to Earth along with the data stream from the surface. He would add his personal comments and congratulatory regards. Now if he could only get them back from the surface he would feel successful, no matter what happened after that.

Moses and Norm laid out plans for the next brief sortie. It would involve following the backside of the small ridge, the side they now faced, the reverse side when observed from the DEV. A small valley led away from the Habitat work area in the same direction they had followed on the first collecting trip. Only this time the exploration would be taking place on the other side of the rocky ridge.

After considerable discussion, Moses agreed that Norm and Oreen would again be the collectors and Moses and Roberto would pack up the rest of the samples prepared by Norm and stow them. Since Norm wanted to make the selections, and since Oreen and he had a good system worked out already, the decision made sense.

Once again, the intrepid explorers boldly set off to forage for Norm's raw materials. They had not gone very far into the small valley when they began examining a deposit of some type of blackened crystalline material glistening in the wash of their lights. Norm pulled out a long telescoping probe and gently poked the material. It reacted, propelling his probe back and moving his entire arm. "Whoa," he proclaimed, startled.

Oreen looked from behind him, eyes wide. "I don't like that stuff," she said, pulling him toward her.

"What the heck was that?" Moses asked.

"Not sure," Norm answered. "But it's damn volatile. It may be a gas hydrate layer or something relatively dangerous. We'd better steer clear of this stuff." He leaned forward gingerly and extracted another small sample bottle from his carrier.

"What are you doing?" Oreen wanted no part of handling this new discovery and expressed it.

"We need a small sample to analyze so we know what to look for. If I can get a signature, we can program our handheld units to look for it and warn us. How would you like to step in a pile of that?"

She saw his point. "Just don't blow your ass up," she added grudgingly.

Norm collected his sample with delicate care. They decided to go no farther into the valley but to look around in the immediate area, picking a smaller side valley. They didn't spot any more of the shiny, black, volatile crystals, but they moved more cautiously now. Norm found some interesting layering and began seeking sample pieces.

Oreen began to turn over rocks. "Spider! Spider! Spider . . ." Oreen stumbled and began backing toward Norm, obvious panic on her face.

Norm sprang to standing from his stooped position as she backed right into his arms. "What? Where?" He looked beyond her at the point she had backed from and was pointing to.

"Right there," she pointed again shining her light at the place.

He saw nothing. He shined his light at the same point, traversing its beam back and forth. Nothing!

Oreen was upset. "I felt a presence that drew me to that small rock. It looked flat and maybe three inches across. I turned it over, and a tiny spider ran out!"

"What's going on? Are you two all right? It was Moses' voice in the helmet speaker. "What did you see?" he added, deep concern showing in his voice.

Norm coolly responded: "Oreen saw something under a rock. Apparently it ran off, or she scared it off. Did you get the description?"

"We got it. She said spider." It was Roberto's voice this time.

"It looked like one and ran like one," she insisted. "As soon as I turned the rock over it was gone. The light probably scared it."

The last thought stuck in Norm's mind. *The light scared it,* he thought over and over.

"Moses, I want to try a little experiment up here." Norm was thinking and planning as he and Oreen backed out of the small side valley. They were still only a little over eighty meters from the Habitat but out of direct visual range from Moses and Roberto around a slight bend in the valley. There was another small side valley directly across the main one from their current position. It was dark and not illuminated at all by their lighting.

"I want to turn off all of our light and check out another small side channel up here. We'll go to low-light night vision and look under a few more rocks."

Moses wanted them back with himself and Rob. "OK, Norm, but be careful and then get back here. You've been out there long enough. That is an order. Five minutes max."

They crossed the main valley without their lights, almost feeling their way. They entered the new side channel and ventured in only a few feet. Before entering, Norm had Oreen lower her flashlight to the lowest illumination value. It would be enough to see with the night vision equipment without being overwhelmed by brightness on the normal setting. She would switch it on at the first sign of movement. Norm lifted several flat shaped rocks straight upward. He and Oreen looked like two kids hunting for salamanders under flat rocks in a creek bed.

They found nothing, no sign of motion, no trace of anything except for more rock and sand.

Moses' voice interrupted their search. "Get back here. Your five minutes were up two minutes ago. Did you find anything?"

Neither realized that they had not uttered a sound since entering the side valley. Oreen was startled by Moses' voice and dropped her light.

"Nothing, nada. We're on our way," Norm said as they rose and switched on their lights.

In a few minutes they had rejoined the others, carrying another armload of samples. Again they separated and packed some of the samples aboard the DEV. Norm was meticulous in his procedure to catalogue and pack them. He would have plenty of material to evaluate for some time.

The battle plan for the next twenty-four-plus hours on the surface called for new procedures. Norm and Moses remained in the Habitat, working and resting there while conducting additional experiments. Roberto and Oreen returned to the DEV until the next exploration venture: a major exploration sortie away from the base camp using the rover, and a hike deep into one of the valleys.

Oreen and Roberto would be able to conduct additional limited experiments within the DEV. Their primary assignment was to assimilate Norm's observations and vocal descriptions of his work and re-transmit everything to the *Kat*. They didn't want to take a chance of losing a thing, no matter how trivial.

They all also felt it better to leave only two crewmembers outside, on the surface, for the duration of the ensuing scientific experiments.

Norm and Moses were to spend the next eighteen hours inside the Habitat analyzing collected samples; those that would not be returning to the *Kat*. Moses also planned to conduct several other experiments within the confines of the Habitat, using the makeshift lab. The occupants would be very busy and were completely prepared to eat and sleep within. Base Camp was now fully functional. If the entire operation continued as envisioned, it was possible that DEV Two could be used in the future to bring a second exploratory group to the site, upon the successful rendezvous of DEV One with the *Kat*.

Landing Crew One still had a long way to go before any decision would be made regarding subsequent operations by a second descent team. For the next eighteen hours, the distance between the DEV and the Habitat, the skin of the DEV, and the four plies of the Habitat separated the two pairs of explorers. In an emergency it might seem like miles.

Roberto and Oreen did not get much rest. They maintained a constant vigil watching the exterior and surroundings of the Habitat. In addition, one or both remained in nearly continuous voice communications. If or when the eighteen-hour Habitat EVA ended, Norm and Moses would return to the DEV at which time they all could then take turns at getting some additional and well-earned rest.

The eighteen-hour sojourn passed without incident. Moses and Norm completed their experiments. Norm finished enough of his planned duties to be satisfied and was ready to return to DEV One. He and Moses finished packing two containers of samples for loading in the cargo bay. Elated that things had gone so well, each picked up a box, preparing to evacuate the Habitat.

"Moses, how soon will you be out?" Oreen inquired.

"We're just getting ready to leave," Moses answered. "Five minutes and we should be ready to open the outer seal."

Roberto's voice cut off Oreen before she could say anything else. "There's another fast-moving storm line bearing down on us. It's coming in fast from the same direction as the other storm. Get out quick. We'll be ready at the pressure-lock hatch."

The sides of the Habitat started to move as the first winds began to kick up the loose dust and sand outside. Norm slid through the inner bladder and helped Moses through. They sealed the exit from the inner room behind them and began opening the second seal. The tent moved more rapidly as the taut exterior was shaken by the wind.

"Keep moving, guys. It's getting pretty windy out there." It was Roberto again with a tone of warning in his voice. "I estimate that you've got less than ten minutes to get back in here or turn around and ride it out from there."

Those words released adrenaline. They slipped back into their EVA suits and Moses pushed ahead through the second bladder; Norm wriggling through behind him as quickly as he could. They began undoing the third bladder seal as Oreen broke the silence, her voice raised, drowning out the sound of the increasing wind. "Bogey at six o'clock aft!" she shouted. "No, two, wait, three!"

Roberto switched his gaze from the windshield to the sweeping surface radar. Three blips were moving toward DEV One rapidly. He checked calculated target distance. They were coming within range of his lander lights. The outermost motion detector set off the warning alarms.

"Get out now! Emergency evacuation procedures! Drop everything, get in here quick!" He was shouting the order as he uncovered the main landing beams. Black dust, soot, and sand were beginning to swirl around in front of the craft. Roberto could not believe their luck. In a few more minutes they would have been safely back aboard.

The three radar pips were moving fast, and the weather was deteriorating rapidly. He strained his eyes to watch for his comrades. Oreen was finishing putting on her full EVA suit. He had not said a thing. She was preparing to enter the lock and open the outer hatch. She had the laser tool under her arm and said nothing as she closed the cabin door behind her. Roberto was alone now, their only eyes and ears at the controls.

Norm and Moses finished pushing their way through the outer bladder, ignoring the prescribed normal exiting procedure. They were greeted by nearly blinding conditions and a fierce head wind. Norm was still carrying a precious box of samples and refused to drop it. Moses moved ahead toward the DEV, leaning forward into the wind.

"I see them, just barely. They're out, Oreen." Roberto put on his helmet and used his heads-up display to aim his beams directly at the first approaching target. He activated his spots at maximum illumination. Norm and Moses were thankful for the extra light, since they could just make out the shape of DEV One. They pushed forward, straining against the ever-intensifying wind with each step.

The rapid approach of the unknowns stopped and they veered from the beam. Roberto removed his helmet, shocked by the speed of the maneuvers of his targets. He had watched the rear video monitor as the lights came on. The apparition he thought he saw stunned him. The turbulent storm debris had obscured it almost completely, but a haunting shape had appeared for an instant.

The blips were gone from the surface radar screen. He raced to assist Oreen. Norm and Moses scrambled up the exterior ladder and dove through the open hatchway. Oreen sealed them with a loud grunt. Norm looked at Moses and then at the converted laser tool standing alone in the pressure lock with them. "I wonder what that was for?" he asked.

— § —

When the news of the latest discovery reached Earth, it set off another wild round of speculation and wonderment. Newspapers around the world had the same headline in every major language: "Life!" Most followed that with something profound and original like: "We are not alone!" The slimy, green, rock-eating goo was an instant celebrity and was already somehow being equated with intelligent humanoid life. Ridiculous stories began to appear overnight based on nothing but rumor. The tabloids were having an absolute field day.

Anecdotes from many of the stories on Earth were relayed to the crew of the *Kal*. These were in turn relayed to the landing party. Upon hearing the results of their first announcement, the four on the surface universally agreed that no mention would be made of Oreen's little scare. Roberto had said nothing about his glimpse, and the videotape had been basically useless. Roberto sent the video capture to the *Kat* for further enhancement and analysis by David and Margie. They both had obviously seen something, but Oreen admitted to her three companions that it could have been a glint of light on her visor or some other sort of aberration. But she had sensed a strange, inexplicable presence too. The landing party wanted to send only accurate scientific data, so, at this point, they needed more to go on. They would seek corroboration.

17

EXPLORATION SORTIE

STORM TWO lasted almost two hours but was much less intense than the first. Base Camp weathered it well, with almost all of the lighting and the sensor array remaining operational. While the others watched the storm through the window ports, Roberto continued to scan the entire area with his landing beams for the full duration. They were all very tired, and little was said since Norm and Moses returned from their brush with trouble on the hostile surface.

As the storm suddenly abated, it was Oreen who questioned Roberto's intense surveillance of the surroundings with his lights. "Rob, what are you looking for? Did you get a look at what caused the radar blips?"

After a pensive moment, he answered. "Not really anything positive, just a large outline against the black background. It blended in and the blowing debris made it really faint. I sent the video clip to the *Kat* before the storm eased. Maybe they can make something out using the ultra-enhancement process."

"Rob, we need to turn off those lights. The batteries are getting low. Look at the meters." It was Norm's fatigued voice. Roberto checked his gauges and immediately deactivated his spots. "Damn, I wasn't paying enough attention. They are low. We all need some rest. When we take our exploratory sortie, we can shut off as much power draw as possible at Base Camp and recharge the entire system." The others nodded in agreement.

They put together an impromptu meal and drank badly needed extra liquids. They removed their flight suits and freshened up. Modesty was not a big concern in the close confines of the DEV. Feeling less hungry and more comfortable, Roberto and Oreen lay down to get some sleep. Norm and Moses had an hour or so of time to relax and close their eyes between experiments while in the Habitat. Oreen and Rob had remained vigilant. Each pair would now have the luxury to sleep at least four to six hours depending on the ability of the first pair to remain awake and alert.

At the end of this mandatory rest period, they planned to begin the fourth major EVA, which would be the first venture away from Base Camp. They would use the rover initially, with exploration and sample gathering on foot to follow. They were all eager to start the first major sortie, but were apprehensive about moving away from the relative safety and security of Base Camp.

— § —

The garbled bit of video feed arrived aboard the *Kat* as David and Margie were finishing their daily workout. It had been re-fabricated from the scattered bits of data and automatically fed into the computer enhancement program. Margie was proud of her own refinements to the already ultra-complicated software. She and David could make nothing out of the original completed images. The video was snowy, dark, and of poor quality due to the storm. Transmission during the storm and scattering by the atmospheric shell had further eroded the quality. With so little to work with, it was amazing the computer could decipher anything.

As an enhanced image began to form, the final product startled them. They both recognized similarities to an earlier equally controversial image. David called up the earlier picture from the computer memory files, and it appeared on the second monitor. The image was a photo taken by *Stealth Finder Two*, probe one from the surface—the photo with the bent twig-like object in the foreground. There were striking similarities between the two, even though the two objects were at vastly different scales.

The new single-frame capture from the video showed two of the jointed, elongated, cylindrical structures and a part of a third. Margie typed in several commands and figures and size dimensions appeared superimposed over the picture. The estimated object size read: 'Height – two meters, Width – five meters, Depth -?' It was big, whatever it was and they obviously only had a part of the total width.

Margie instructed the computer to do a best fit of the object to the library within the database. It began to scan the enormous files as they settled back in their seats to wait.

— § —

At Base Camp, the first two sleepers, Roberto and Oreen, awakened rejuvenated, refreshed, and recharged with renewed energy. The second two were barely able to remain awake through the five-hour rest period for the first pair. Moses and Norm welcomed their respite and were sleeping in less than five minutes. Fortunately for Moses and Norm, the calm, which followed the

EXPLORATION SORTIE

second storm, again was uneventful.

Roberto felt pretty good. Yawning and stretching, he shook his head to clear the vestiges of sleepiness. Then with Oreen, he began to assemble the necessary equipment for upcoming EVA Four, and spent several hours preparing for this next trip outside. Relaxing and eating took another full hour. Roberto spent considerable time examining and becoming intimately familiar with the laser cutting tools converted by Moses. Oreen prepared sample cases and photographic gear, all the while watching Roberto almost fondle the newly fabricated weapon.

"Be careful with that thing," she said continuing her work. "You're giving me the creeps," she added. "What did you see out there that has you so interested in that laser?"

He set the weapon down and looked directly into her eyes. "You tell me exactly what you saw, including what you felt, and I'll answer your question honestly and completely."

"You've got a deal." She stopped her work and moved closer to Roberto, checking to be sure that the others were still sleeping. "I told everybody what I thought I saw. Well, it's not 'I thought.' I did see something. It looked very much like a small spider, maybe an inch across, multiple legs and a center body. It moved way too quickly to see any other details. I'm sure that I saw it, and I knew that it was there. I had a feeling about looking under that specific rock and felt a presence again, but one that I have never sensed before."

"Why didn't you tell us all that you were sure?

"It gave me the creeps. I don't like spiders. When I was a kid, I was bitten by what they guessed was a brown recluse." She pulled the sleeve of her flight suit up exposing her forearm, pointing to a small pit in her skin. "See that? I still have the scar to prove it."

"OK, I already knew that you didn't like spiders. It was all in your training profile." Roberto seemed satisfied by her latest revelation. It was his turn. "I saw one too; no doubt about it. It was there on the radar screen, and I saw at least a vestige of it when I hit the high beams. Only this one was big. It had to be six feet high and more than twice as wide from the radar signature."

"Now I know why you're playing with that thing. If there are six-foot spiders roaming around out there, I want one too."

"We only have two and Moses will be carrying the other one." Roberto again picked up the weapon, tested it for balance and feel and placed it back on a seat.

"Why haven't we seen more of these creatures if they are out there?"

Oreen's question was answered from the reclined rear chair occupied by

177

Norm as he slowly sat up. "Because whatever they are, they don't like white light," he stated emphatically. "I'm convinced that it's a sensitivity to white light!"

They hadn't realized that Norm was awake or they had simply been too loud and had awakened him. He had been eavesdropping on their conversation.

"I think that you're absolutely right, Norm. We haven't seen anything else due to maintaining a well-lit landing zone and perimeter." Roberto nodded in agreement as Norm moved closer. Moses was still sleeping soundly, oblivious to their entire conversation.

"Now wait a minute," Oreen was pondering again as she began. "We're beginning to think that there may be giant spiders running around in the dark out there, and you want me to join you for a picnic in the rocks? We have some mighty flimsy evidence to go on. One: I think that I see a bug. Two: Rob thinks he sees a big ass bug. Three: I feel like there's something out there, and the radar shows some strange shapes that appear when the weather gets bad. You following me?"

She paused to watch reactions. "I think maybe there just might be something, but I'm not ready to conclude that there are little or giant bugs running around. We may just be hoping that there is something out there besides green rock-eating slime. We've been under a lot of stress, and none of us has had anywhere near enough sleep. We may be scaring ourselves, creating our own visions, wanting something else to be out there." She paused again for effect, waiting to see the initial reactions to her theory. Oreen clearly understood the effects of their situation on the human brain and physique and knew all about stress-induced delusions.

Neither Roberto nor Norm said a thing. Their raised eyebrows said that they realized the plausibility of what Oreen said. Norm ventured a follow-up statement first. "You could be right, Oreen. I haven't seen anything remotely bug-like yet. Not a piece of dead carcass, not a trace of feces, or microscopic remains or anything that looked even remotely insect-like."

"How about the pits in the soil? Could be tracks." This time it was Moses who interjected the comment after yawning audibly.

"Welcome back, Moses." Norm went on with his observations, "Could be tracks, but they don't have any particular pattern to them. Something walking would have a discernable kind of a repeating pattern. I've taken lots of photos of the pits and they sure don't look much like tracks, but that's not to say that they aren't."

While this conversation was going on, Oreen called up the video replay from the moment Roberto uncovered the high beams and aimed them. They all watched the short video carefully as she repeated it frame by frame. There was nothing obvious but a couple of crooked vertical lines.

"Not much," Roberto said. "Maybe I was seeing things. I was awfully tired. Maybe my eyes were playing tricks. We sent the video to the *Kat*. Let's see if they have anything." He sounded discouraged.

"All right crew, let's get ready for our walk in the park." Moses wanted to deflect interest from the subject at hand. He wanted their energies focused elsewhere. "See if they got anything, Rob. If there is something on that video, David and Margie can extract it and give us a tangible explanation."

Roberto was satisfied with that. He prepared the message and sent the inquiry to the *Kat*. They went back to work finalizing preparations for EVA Four.

When the incoming message was received aboard the Mother Ship, Rod Amerigo smiled. He had been about to send the analysis, prepared by Margie and David, to DEV One, and he responded by sending it immediately.

The landing party was surprised by the quick turnaround time of forty-five minutes. When the incoming report finished forming on the screen, they all crowded around the forward monitor to read it. The analysis was more revealing than they expected. It read: "Best frame contents yielded usable data. Vertical segmented section analysis: possible articulated appendage. Best fit: upright foreleg arachnid. Close match to earlier probe photo. Be careful!"

"Well, I'll be dammed." Moses looked at the rest of his crew. "We didn't say a thing about spotting any possible bugs. In fact we transmitted nothing else about this other than the video."

Everyone immediately realized the importance of this revelation. The *Kat's* computers had just concluded that the video did harbor a trace image of a possible arachnid leg. It had reached this logical and significant conclusion without other prompting.

All four crewmembers actually felt much better. Maybe they weren't seeing things. Now they had reason to be extra alert and had something special to anticipate.

Preparations completed, they were ready to leave DEV One in just over an hour. They opened the outer hatch and handed down the equipment with much more efficiency than before. Roberto proceeded to the surface rover under the watchful eyes of Moses, who was standing guard like a sentinel. Moses held his laser weapon in front of him across his body, at the ready, armed, safety on, and at full power. In his own mind, he had temporarily suspended the prime directive.

Roberto climbed onto the rover and backed it up to the awaiting explorers. He had remotely activated it and run a complete systems check. Everything looked fine, and he was ready to roll. They loaded the gear and each in turn climbed aboard, taking one of the four seats. Roberto turned on the driving lights, front and rear. Norm attached floodlights with adjustable narrow beam spots to their brackets atop the roll-bar cage.

The rover was equipped with flexible multi-layer sides of Tanaka's material, which could be raised for protection if or when needed. In addition, the rover had a winch, complete communications and radar center, multiple, redundant steering systems, an auger, mini-trencher, and plenty of survival gear. It was fully loaded with all four of them and their exploratory equipment but moved easily as Roberto released the brake, and they began inching forward

Oreen used her handheld remote to extinguish the DEV lights and all but two of the floods on the DEV side of the ridge. She switched off the lights covering the Habitat, and it disappeared into darkness. Lastly she switched on the rotating, red-and-green homing beacons.

They synchronized all watches and handhelds before embarking and tested all their many lights. The locator system and tracking systems were functioning to perfection. Weather conditions were monitored continuously. Each crew person was responsible for specific life-support readings. Ready and able, they moved away from Base Camp One with confidence in their equipment and a slight trepidation for themselves.

Roberto hummed a few bars of the cavalry charge and smiled at Moses beside him, riding shotgun. "Let the exploration sortie begin," he said as the Base Camp began to dim and disappear in near darkness behind them.

After traversing about one kilometer, they stopped at another rock outcropping. Norm and Oreen climbed out to obtain a few precious samples. Roberto planned to follow the original ridge to the right and a new ridge to the left began flanking them. The terrain was rising; they were definitely going uphill and entering a valley.

Norm procured one sample and returned to the vehicle with Oreen. "This part of the lava ridge is pockmarked with numerous small indentations and tubes, the appearance is almost honeycombed." None were sure if he was dictating into his voice recorder or conducting his own field trip. All listened as Norm continued. "The rock appears to be basaltic lava and a relatively recent flow. The tubes in the lava are approximately five centimeters or less in diameter, and most are lined with small traces of the green lifeform."

Ahead the valley rose steadily and began to narrow noticeably. The now common green slime glowed with greater intensity in the distance, its abundance adding an eerie glow to the landscape. While stopped, Roberto had input more surface terrain data and expanded their growing databased map. Their sinuous path was traced on the dashboard monitor in a pale yellow. Distance, elapsed time, and other pertinent data flashed nearby.

Roberto chose a route leading into the deepening valley, noting all potential obstacles in the rover's path. Norm wanted to head toward a particularly bright patch of phosphorescent green, which covered a considerable area in the distance. Once targeted, all Roberto had to do was steer—the completely automated rover would do everything else.

Silence was pervasive except for the crunch of the soil and rock beneath the rover's tires. Otherwise the vehicle itself was virtually silent. All four looked left as an audible rumble from the distant volcano disturbed the silence. An orange plume of molten lava spewed from an active vent, this activity added an eerie but beautiful red-orange glow to the otherwise ever-darkened sky overhead.

Rambling on into the narrowing valley, each was filled with awe and bewildered by the constantly changing landscape. Their headlights cast a white wash on a greening landscape. Neon-colored green slime was everywhere, concentrated in innumerable tubes of ever increasing size dotting the landscape. The ambient light conditions were gradually increasing, as the glowing lifeform became much more abundant.

They made numerous stops. Each time Norm tried to ferret out something new to sample and test, all the while having a great time, collecting invaluable data and leading an entertaining geological field trip. Oreen and Roberto were fascinated. Moses was listening, but his attention was more focused on their surroundings. He seldom did much more than glance at whatever Norm was pointing to or sampling, and was particularly on alert when they moved away from the rover for any reason. At those times, he would rise and continue scanning the area in all directions.

Since leaving Base Camp, the four explorers covered almost three kilometers. The going had been relatively easy, the terrain almost flat, but slowly rising, and not too rough. They reached their pre-selected target, which was as far as they could go using the rover.

It was time to recheck all systems and breathing mixtures and reverse the rover controls to expedite leaving. Roberto set a manual brake and lowered the intensity of his lights to half. He shut off the rover and picked up his handheld for one last check.

The surrounding black rock glowed a brighter hue due to the prevalent patches of neon green. Norm and Moses had tested the new lifeform and concluded that it would cause no harm to their suits, boots or gloves. Oreen had rigged up a unit capable of detecting the semi-explosive, sparkling gas hydrate. They only had to avoid one deposit of the dangerous material so far on their journey.

From this point on, they explored on foot, all remaining close together. Norm pointed out the steady increase in the size of the tubes and openings in the rocks. As the green increased, the frequency and size of the holes increased. Norm wanted to know exactly what formed the holes. Did the green creatures eat the holes and tubes in the rock, or did the green occur more abundantly due to the availability of more numerous openings to fill? Perhaps the green only enlarged pre-existing holes. He wanted to know.

They had not seen anything move during the entire trip. The sweeping surface radar detected nothing; its use now restricted by the closing landscape. Steepening ridges on both sides and an end to the drivable valley ahead surrounded them on three sides. A little to the right, but almost directly in front of the rover, a narrow green-lighted passageway seemed to lead into a broadmouthed cave. To Norm, it appeared to be a classic lava tube: a natural cave formed when the outside of a molten lava flow congealed, forming a hard outer crust. As the amount of molten material decreased beneath this hard outer shell or the source became diverted or was cut off, a hollow tube was left behind. He guessed that this was the case as he asked Moses about venturing inside. The opening was at least one hundred yards distant. It glowed with a partial lining of green, which beckoned him.

Visible gas or vapors rose from the top of the tube at its entrance, and they could just make out the shape of the entrance from only the ambient light cast by the green lifeform. Moses agreed to allow this target to be their destination for foot exploration. Once they had reconnoitered its entrance and determined the safety of venturing inside, he allowed that this would become the farthest point of the exploration sortie.

Moses wanted to conduct low-light experiments prior to leaving the rover for any reason. He needed to test the night-vision visors for their present surroundings. He wanted to turn off all white light for a short time and watch from the rover using only the night-vision receptors. If nothing happened, only then would he give the OK to hike to the cave opening and allow Norm to examine it. There was enough of a bright green glow within parts of the visible cave to cause him to consider exploring inside using the low light equipment.

Before switching to night vision, he turned on the spotlights and he and Roberto slowly scanned the entire surrounding area. Norm and Oreen used their spots to illuminate the closest jumbled, rocky crags. After multiple passes over the unchanging landscape, they switched to night vision while simultaneously lowering the intensity of their spots. The transition to night vision went smoothly as they marveled at the surrealistic panorama before them; an alien landscape with a beauty all its own.

They watched and waited expecting strange creatures to dash at them from the darkest recesses of the shadows, but the only things that dashed were the figments of their own imaginations. Nothing changed, and nothing moved. Everything was tranquil, but shimmering through their specialized visual equipment.

They sat transfixed for twenty minutes. Moses' hand twitched. His finger was on the trigger button of his weapon. Roberto's head swung around back and forth, his eyes darting from rock to rock. No one spoke for the entire twenty minutes. Instead they listened intently.

Moses broke the silence asking: "Anyone seen anything, any movement?"

"Negative," answered Roberto followed by the same response from Norm and Oreen.

"Me either," Moses added, answering his own question. "Oreen, do you feel anything strange?"

She answered without her normal hesitation. "Everything I feel is strange. For a moment I thought I was getting that same feeling I had before when I sensed a presence, but it isn't clear and the feeling isn't strong. It's just there, weak, but there."

"Tell me right away if you sense it, OK?" Moses was almost pleading as he asked. "OK, let's get ready for a little hike. Norm, don't try to carry too much."

They strapped on and attached additional lights, and another camera and prepared for a short march up to the cave entrance. Roberto took the point, with Norm behind, Oreen next, and Moses bringing up the rear. In single file they picked a path through the alien landscape, heading directly toward the opening of the cave. They were forced to use their light source twice. Roberto was careful as he chose each step, probing often with his telescoping walking stick. They moved forward, lengthening the distance from the rover while decreasing the distance to the tube. As they moved away, Oreen switched on a white marker light atop the rover behind them.

Arriving at the entrance in only a few minutes, Roberto moved cautiously ahead to examine the immediate area of the opening, returning to the others after a brief surveillance. "It looks flat and fairly easygoing inside. I'd like to light it up to be sure before we go in." Their helmet visors were sensor-controlled, meaning they could switch from white light to night vision without shock to the eyes.

"We can go in using our lights and switch to night vision once inside, if everything keeps going smoothly." Moses sounded more confident and comfortable than he had for a while.

By choice they switched to white light, and the visors made the automatic adjustments. Each turned on a handheld light and the helmet spots, and began shining their beams around the entrance and deep into the cave itself. The sound of loose rock clattering to their right startled them all, and they turned in unison to illuminate and locate the source of the sound.

Moses was jumpy again. He had a light attached to his laser weapon and moved between his charges and the direction of the sound. Each strained to get a glimpse of the cause of the noise. A small piece of volcanic rock bounced several times and came to rest about ten meters in front of them, just inside the cave. It was little more than a pebble. They stared at the path it had taken from a small recess up and to the right of the entrance.

They watched, listened, and waited. "Lights out," Moses ordered. "Let's observe with the low-light visors and see if anything else happens."

One by one their lights winked out. Oreen's was the last. She crouched between Moses and Norm, ready to flick it back on. Roberto turned with his back to Moses, watching the path they had followed from the rover. They waited again for several minutes. There was no repeat of the sound of falling rock, and there was no movement at all. The only sound was the occasional rumble of distant volcanic activity. A shimmer of red-brown lightning crossed the black sky above.

After what seemed like forever to Oreen, Moses announced that it was time to return to white light. She eagerly switched on her helmet light and her hand flashlight, with the others following suit, once again bathing the area in a wash of welcome illumination. Oreen could see well with the high-tech gadgetry, but preferred the security the white beams provided.

It was time to venture inside the lava tube cavern. Norm checked elapsed EVA time and air mixture status for all four explorers. The re-breathers were working well, but everyone was consuming more air than usual, due to the high level of excitement, and increased respiration was a natural result. He wanted plenty of margin for a safe return.

Moses inspected each of the others and considered attaching them all together in pairs with a loose tether, but decided against it. Moses and Norm moved ahead into the mouth of the cave. Oreen and Rob were to follow, but only upon his satisfaction of complete safety and his subsequent signal.

The cavern entrance measured approximately seven meters high and perhaps fifteen meters across at its widest point. There was very little of the neon green around the immediate entrance, but it increased in profusion with depth inside. About thirty meters within, the cave floor rose slightly, and was partially blocked by fallen rock debris. Beyond the rock fall the walls shined brighter with a nearly continuous coating of the green lifeform. Ambient light from that point on looked adequate for further exploration and sample gathering. Green features like stalactites hung from the ceiling. Norm wanted to determine the exact composition and cause of these features.

Moses planned to move far enough in to reach the rock pile. There, he and Norm would take gas samples and Norm could take photographs. Once they had determined that it was safe, Oreen and Roberto could move up to join them. Moses did not want to waste time, take any foolish risks, or stay inside any longer than was absolutely necessary to finish the collecting specimens.

He and Norm reached the rock fall with a minimum of effort. They surveyed beyond with their lights, probing every indentation in the rough walls with twin beams. Seeing only black rock and green coating, they signaled for the other two to join them, and in a few moments they were all peering beyond the present obstacle at the brighter depths.

"I kinda like this cave," Oreen said softly. "How often do you get to go in a cave that gets lighter the farther you go in?"

"And warmer." Norm added that observation as Moses again began to forge ahead. They had not noticed any temperature change through their thick EVA suits, but Norm had been monitoring it since they entered using his handheld unit. He followed Moses and moved steadily toward a second rock pile another thirty-five meters ahead.

Oreen suddenly tensed. Roberto stopped and watched her and noted her change in body language. Her semi-relaxed state turned into rigidity. She rose from a half crouch and was raising her hands toward her head.

"Oreen, what is it?" Roberto looked past her toward the sidewall of the tube. There was nothing there. "What is it? What's wrong?" He repeated. Moses and Roberto had stopped in their tracks, their minds forgetting the collecting and focusing instead on Oreen.

"We're not alone," she stated. "There's something else in here. I can feel it. It's a strong feeling, and whatever it is, it's close."

Moses' voice cracked with tension. "Oreen, Roberto, get over here with us. Let's stick close together.

Roberto grasped Oreen's shoulder and directed her to the rendezvous with the others, where they stood together beside the second rock fall, again traversing the entire inside of the tube with their lights. Norm had his camera ready and was taking a few shots of the nearest stalactite hanging overhead.

Moses flipped off the safety on his laser weapon. Roberto noticed and did the same. Oreen just stood and looked farther into the cave, saying nothing.

After a few agonizing minutes with no change in their surroundings, Norm suggested that they switch to the low-light gear and settle down and observe. Reluctantly they each switched off the white lights and stood with their backs together, creating a three hundred and sixty degree field of view. Norm spotted the movement first and elbowed his nearby companions, nodding in the direction of the shadowy movement. They watched in awe as a dark shape began to move from the deep shadows of a recess, directly ahead of them, just beyond the second rock pile. The object rose up on spindly legs, exposing a round, flat body between opposing sets. It appeared to be about one-third meter high and roughly one meter across. Norm snapped two photos using only ambient light, not wanting to scare it off with a flash. His video helmet cam was recording everything. The object began to move. It was no more than fifteen to twenty meters away and moving straight toward them.

"Easy does it, everybody. If it gets too close for anybody's comfort, hit it with your spotlight. I'll be ready to zap it if that doesn't stop it. We take no chances, but we don't go looking for trouble." Moses' voice was a barely audible whisper. In the time it had taken him to utter the words, the creature closed the distance to them by half. They got a good look at it. It was arachnid in shape, but was very smooth, with only legs and the central thorax-like body. There were no apparent eyes or antennae or a mouth or hair. It was smooth and dark gray-black.

Moses felt Oreen's fear as she pushed against him. He flipped on the light attached to his weapon and prepared to fire. The creature had closed to within less than seven meters and showed no signs of slowing down. When the light came on, the strange, spider-like lifeform reared on its hind legs and darted away at blinding speed. In a second it had vanished back into the recesses of the cavern.

They all sighed with relief. Roberto felt the rivulets of sweat running down his back. "The SOBs are afraid of our lights!" he shouted emphatically.

Norm followed that with his assessment, "They may be afraid or cautious or extremely sensitive to it for some as yet unknown reason. They don't like it, or maybe they just aren't used to it. We haven't seen anything on this planet that would indicate that there is any source of pure white light other than hot lava. Remember, we are the aliens here."

As he finished those words, the outline of a much larger creature caused movement in the distant, glowing, semi-darkness of the cave. It had the identical form as the first visitor, but this one was many times its size. They all froze with fear for one moment as it moved slowly at the edge of good illumination.

Moses ordered: "Take cover behind the rocks, get low and watch. Same procedure as before, and then let's get the hell out of here." He turned off his light and crouched down behind a four-foot high rock with Norm. Roberto and Oreen crouched low against a smaller rock less than one meter away to their right.

The eerie apparition moved steadily toward them, stopping for a moment, as if sniffing its surroundings. They watched with intense curiosity as it closed the distance to their hiding place. It looked enormous to the cowering Earth visitors. Oreen showed great bravery to not panic and run. Roberto aimed his weapon at the widest part of the body and took a deep breath. He wanted to hear something from Moses as the creature approached to within ten meters.

"Lights on, everybody!" Moses commanded. The strange creature was close enough, showing no signs of stopping again. They all shined their lights on it at once. It stopped, reared on its rear sets of appendages, and without warning, sprayed a stream of milky liquid straight at Roberto and Oreen.

Moses squeezed the trigger and, with a loud buzz, a stream of intense red light hit the creature square in the center. Roberto fired too, completely severing two of the creature's legs. It turned and tumbled away from them in a writhing fit of motion.

The spray of liquid originated from an orifice that appeared on the underside of the body. The rock in front of Roberto and Oreen was sizzling as if being dissolved by strong acid. Moses and Norm were unaffected, and Oreen was well hidden by the rock. The liquid had contacted Roberto on his legs and chest, and his suit was dissolving in places. EVA suits had patches and strips of Tanaka's material that seemed unaffected, but the fabric in between was dissolving rapidly.

Oreen began to frantically brush the solvent off of Roberto with her gloves. Moses surveyed the area again and Norm strained to assist Oreen. Their gloves did not dissolve, but Roberto was in serious trouble. He began writhing in pain as the suit was penetrated on his left inner thigh, and flesh began to burn. They furiously scraped off as much as they could, and Norm began wiping the remaining spots with his field wipes. Moses took his first aid kit from his EVA suit pocket and dropped it on Roberto's chest. Norm tore open several gauze bandages and wiped the burned area again as Roberto agonized, lying on his back. His suit was breached and his body exposed to the alien atmosphere, but that was the least of his problems.

Norm pulled a drinking water bottle from his waist belt, ripped off the adapter top fitted for consumption, and flushed the wound repeatedly, trying desperately to wash off the acid. They alternated cleaning the growing wound with gauze and water until both supplies were exhausted. Before they stopped the damage, Roberto had an inch-wide, inch-deep, over three-inch-long open gash in his upper leg. They packed the wound with antiseptic gel and gauze from a second kit and bandaged it.

The ugly and deep wound was bleeding, but they had controlled it. Roberto almost passed out from the pain several times. Oreen gave him two injections near the wound and then closed the holes in his suit with emergency tape sealer. "We've got to get him out of here and back to DEV One before he goes into shock."

They forced Roberto to his feet, and Norm supported him while they turned to retrace their steps out of the cavern. Oreen picked up Roberto's weapon and looked at Moses. "We're ready, Moses, let's go," she urged.

"Not so fast," he warned, pointing his light and weapon back into the cave.

Oreen turned to look as Norm steadied Roberto. As if searching for something, a dozen or more of the creatures were roaming about.

"Move out now! I'll cover you as you get Rob out of here. I'll be right behind you," Moses said.

"None of that hero shit," Oreen said as she helped Norm make a speedy retreat with Roberto, almost dragging him to the entrance, with Moses backing steadily behind them. Once there, they rested for a moment and watched Moses back toward them. He fired several times, each time scattering the arachnids. It was almost as if they were testing him.

As he approached their position at the mouth of the cave, he motioned them on with one hand adding: "Don't stop until you get to the Rover unless you have to."

Norm held up his handheld unit and used it to activate the front and rear headlights on the rover as well as both spotlights. They helped the now semiconscious hulk of Roberto move away from the cave.

Moses paused briefly at the entrance, and then turned and ran to catch up with them. He caught up about halfway back to the rover, but they were all still cloaked in near complete darkness. He turned to check the rear just in time to see a huge set of forelegs descending toward them. He fell to his back and fired continuously, blasting the creature to pieces. Milky acid landed in splotches everywhere around him. A piece of a leg landed hard on his chest. He pushed it aside and sprang to his feet as he heard the fire of the other laser weapon.

He ran like a madman, sprinting toward the position of the rover. As he rounded the last dark crag, the blinding lights of the vehicle greeted him. Norm and Oreen were pouring Roberto into a rear seat. Oreen aimed her weapon at the rise on the left and fired repeatedly.

Norm finished securing Roberto and dove into the driver's position. Oreen hopped aboard, and Norm started the vehicle and began moving away from Moses as he sprang into the rover, grabbing the roll bars. Moses rolled over into the second front seat and again raised his weapon to fire. He pushed the trigger button, but nothing happened—he tried again to no avail.

Oreen noticed his frustration. She had already dropped her weapon on the rear seat. "Use the spotlight," Oreen shouted. She was whipping the light from side to side.

18

THE SURPRISE

A S THE ROVER drew away from the narrowest part of the valley, Moses felt an incredible pang of pain in his shoulder. Searing heat burned as he sat down when the rover bounced over a large rock. Oreen almost toppled out, but her grasp on the spotlight saved her from falling.

"Slow down Norm," he cried. He punched a compartment in the side of the rover interior wall marked with a Red Cross, and a door flipped opened revealing a compact first aid kit. The kit top opened automatically, and he ripped the top off a box of gauze and wiped at his shoulder. Moses did not realize that acid had hit him until he felt the intense searing pain.

Norm noticed his actions and slowed the rover down. Oreen saw what Moses was doing too. She sat down behind Moses and shined her light on his shoulder and the melted material of his suit. He needed assistance; that was obvious.

"Roberto, can you keep your eyes open while I help Moses?" Roberto was jostled by a bump and looked like a rag doll in his harness. "Roberto, please," she pleaded.

Roberto raised his head and said, "Go ahead Oreen. I can handle it." He was groggy and in obvious pain, but he straightened up and picked up the weapon beside him. "Got you covered, Norm."

Oreen went to work on Moses' shoulder, cleaning and bandaging. Loose wrappers blew from the vehicle. She tossed out an antiseptic squeeze tube and mumbled something unintelligible. *Humankind's first careless litter on the new world,* she thought, *and I don't care.* She was frustrated and angry. She marveled at Roberto. He was scanning the area to either side of the rover and turning to check to the rear. She knew that his moves had to be causing him tremendous agony. She didn't have the heart to tell him the "weapon" he was aiming was completely discharged.

Oreen stabilized Moses and gave him the same antibiotic, bandaging, and the same suit patching treatment she had given to Roberto. He thanked her and took up his guard position, wincing in pain. He refused the painkiller. Moses wanted complete control of his stimulated senses and could not afford to have his wits deadened in any way.

Moses did a quick inspection of the other converted laser tool and checked the settings on his own too, knowing what he'd find. It was empty, discharged by the bursts he had fired. The transformed cutters, the weapons he had fabricated, packed quite a punch, but the available energy did not last for very long.

"The other one's empty too," Oreen offered. Roberto looked at her in disbelief, sickened by the thought.

"I've got one recharged pack for mine and one for yours." Moses elicited an immediate smile from his crew as he ejected the power pack from Roberto's weapon and clicked in the new one. "Now you're cooking with gas, Roberto," he said. He turned and replaced his spent power pack too. "We are ready to kick some ass," he shouted as they bounced through a rut and swerved around more debris.

The first kilometer seemed to take forever. The rover was too slow for them now even at top speed, and Norm could not afford to make any driving errors. The valley was widening again and the terrain was starting to flatten out. Moses was watching to the left, Roberto to the right, and Oreen to the rear.

Norm looked forward at their path and glanced when he could at his terrain identification tracking display for assistance in picking his route. He was trying to follow their first track as close as possible to return by the exact same route. He had not been watching his other radar. He glanced at it in horror. The now familiar signature of one of the planet's blinding black storms covered nearly half of the screen, and they were driving straight into it.

Norm slowed the rover to a crawl drawing the attention of his crewmates. He pointed to the radar screen, and they all showed realization of the problem at hand. Just then a wisp of wind provided a tangible signal of the coming tempest.

"We'd better put up the sides and top and batten down as best we can," Moses urged.

When the rover rolled to a stop, Moses and Oreen climbed out. Moses was suffering in obvious pain—each motion requiring extra effort. Oreen tried to do most of the task, but he insisted in doing all that he could. Norm stood up to help raise the sides and pull the ultra light, super-strength material over the roll bars and secure it in the middle. It took less than two minutes to secure the sheltering shell on the rover. The combination window-door openings on each side were zipped shut when they were all back inside. Another of their host's ominous black storms swept over them kicking up sand and dust.

In a few minutes they were inundated by the storm, the wind whipping the sides of the rover turning semidarkness into complete darkness. Visibility dropped to near zero even with all of the driving lamps and searchlights on high. Their precious radar became useless once again. They were vulnerable and at the complete mercy of the elements.

"We should have gotten a message to the DEV for relay to the *Kat*," Roberto reminded them. The four had not thought of it in their haste to make a retreat. It was now too late because of the storm raging outside their tiny wheeled shelter. Several strong gusts of wind shook the rover, and one large piece of storm tossed debris hit the front and creased the fabric top as it whizzed by. They settled down to wait and ride out the tempest. For now, there was nothing else they could do.

When the raging winds subsided, Moses decided to take a look outside. He unzipped the top zipper at the center after knocking wind-deposited sand and dust from the covering. He unfastened just enough to stick his helmeted head through and was appalled by the poor lighting. The rover lights were covered with the sticky soot and nearly obscured. He slowly rotated in a semi-crouched position in order to survey the entire circumference of his surroundings. After turning about three-quarters of the way around, he stopped, startled, helmet to leg with an arachnid appendage. It was covered with a profusion of small circles somewhat resembling a compound eye, but yet somehow different. He slowly brought his laser up to his side and prepared to thrust it through the zippered opening beside his head. The appendage was only inches from his visor and probably would have crushed him if it had come down a meter lower. It remained close to him for a moment, and then retracted away. He pushed the gun through and reached with his uninjured arm to wipe soot off of the spotlight already pointed toward the creature. It was huge, standing next to the rover and dwarfing it. When the light illuminated its side, the creature moved slightly but did not rear up or run.

"We have a visitor," Moses whispered. "A big friggin' visitor sitting right next to us. Get out the other side behind me as quickly and as quietly as you can. Right now! Go!"

Norm and Oreen moved fast to unzip the other side and slipped out, Norm taking the laser gun. Roberto could hardly move, so he just lay down on the floor between the seats, and surrendered the weapon to Norm. Moses continued to watch the lifeform, unsure of exactly what to do. He waited. They found it incredible, but the enormous creature also did nothing. After a few minutes it moved slowly away and then disappeared into the darkness.

"We were dead meat," Moses lamented. It could have crushed us or sprayed that acid stuff or done anything that it wanted to. It just left." They all wondered why.

The wind died down, and the air cleared. The storm moved on. Norm wiped off the lights and prepared his vehicle to move out. They all pondered the significance of the encounter and wanted some reason why the creature did not attack, some reason for the behavior during this encounter, and they were all looking straight at Oreen.

"I don't know," she said, reading their minds. "I don't have any idea why what just happened took place. I'm baffled, but I think that I have an idea. Maybe it didn't feel threatened or something like that."

Norm asked the logical question. "That implies intelligence of some sort doesn't it?

"Yeah, I guess it does," Oreen answered. Then her eyes rolled back and she collapsed into Norm's arms. He was startled and almost let her fall to the ground.

"Oreen, what's wrong? Can you hear me?" Moses was concerned and struggled to her side, peering at her though her visor.

Her eyes returned to focus, that much he could see. "I'm OK, I think." She didn't sound groggy and appeared to be regaining her complete faculties. She straightened up and stood for a moment before saying anything else. "Something is happening to my feelings and perceptions of things nearby and visions from afar. I know I was exposed to the nanos and now perhaps I'm beginning to sense effects. My mind can see things now, things I've never perceived before. When I can make some sense of it myself, I'll let you all know, share any details, but for now, let me work on it. If I seem preoccupied, you will all know why." Oreen did not want to convey the troubling feeling of foreboding currently bothering her. Something somewhere was not right but she could not get a focus on it.

"Let's get the fuck out of here!" Moses didn't care whose ears he'd burned. All back in the rover, they started it up, dropping the covers to where they could just see over them. Concealed together in the close confines of the rover, the four rode in silence. They bumped along over some rough terrain. Their tracks from the trip in the opposite direction were just about gone; obscured and erased by the wind. Norm attempted to contact the DEV at Base Camp but was having trouble getting through. When the communications computer on DEV One acknowledged receipt of the message for the *Kat*, he was relieved. The message read: "Trouble during Sortie One. Roberto hurt. Returning to Base Camp ASAP. Will advise more once in DEV." When he tried to get the computer to relay the message to the *Kat,* he received an error message: "Communications Error, Explanation: Antenna Failure."

"The storm must have knocked out the burst antenna. I can't get the computer to send our message to the *Kat.* I'll try using the ship's antenna, but it may not get through." Norm informed the computer how to circumvent the problem and hoped that the message was at least sent using the lower-power DEV antenna.

As they rounded the last corner leading out of the valley, they strained to see the beacon marking the location of Base Camp. It was there, welcome and rotating slowly. The light from the floods, left on when they departed, was hardly visible. The lamps were covered by soot, knocked over by wind, or dimmed out due to low power.

They were getting close. Moses used his handheld remote to turn on the other lights. What he beheld in the distance turned his blood cold. His stomach tensed, and he tasted bile. Base Camp was a shambles and DEV One was listing badly to starboard. There were pockmarked pits or tracks everywhere around the lander and Habitat. The back of the Habitat was flattened. The scene looked like one of devastation from this distance.

They stopped for a moment to survey the situation and then, with caution, the rover proceeded into Base Camp. Norm drove forward with grim determination. Moses stood up on the right front side holding the roll bar with one hand, brandishing the weapon with the other. Oreen stood next to Moses to steady him.

Roberto's will to fight and his energy were gone, but if looks could kill, Roberto was seeing a lot of dead aliens. They had not noticed any more creatures since the post-storm close encounter. None were evident around Base Camp, but their handiwork was very clear.

What they could see from the distance in the dim lights looked even worse when they pulled up beside the crooked DEV. Norm circled the vehicle and stopped to park the rover between the Habitat and DEV One. Norm was most interested in the antenna, Roberto the DEV, Moses the lighting and sensors, Oreen the crushed Habitat. There were remnants of pockmarked pits everywhere, undoubtedly the tracks of the arachnid lifeform.

Roberto struggled out of the rover and, though in great pain, forced himself to inspect the damage. DEV One had suffered a lot of damage. One landing strut was collapsed, the wing buckled and bent. The entire vehicle was leaning to the right more than ten degrees. There were two jagged holes more than a foot across in the far side. Both the exterior shield and part of the inner skin had been breached, but fortunately the inner pressure hull remained intact.

After a cursory inspection, Roberto leaned against the base of the ladder and eased himself down to a sitting position. His helmeted head flopped against the ladder and he looked very uncomfortable. Norm finished his inspection of the antenna. Oreen returned from a quick look at the Habitat. Moses watched them and stood guard while they inspected, then gathered them together at the base of the DEV ladder for their collective assessment.

Roberto! "You first, Roberto. He jostled him back to consciousness. "Then we get you inside." Moses was devastated, and although he tried to hide it, his voice betrayed him.

"We can't fix it, at least not without a lot of time and serious effort. We won't get back even if we could fix it. A lot of fuel has leaked out of a broken line from the wing tank. The tank is probably ruptured. I think that we are stuck here. I can't do much to fix it anyway." His head drooped forward.

Norm was next. "The antenna is damaged, but I can fix it. The cables were ripped loose, but Oreen and I can get it working again within five or six hours."

"Fix it, Norm. Start now." Moses turned to Oreen. Oreen spoke evenly, reassuringly. "The Habitat can be fixed if we have to use it. It's just knocked crooked. Some braces are bent but can be straightened up."

"Forget it, Oreen. Let's concentrate on the antenna. We need it the most right now. I don't think that we have any fire danger, but I'm going to foam the underside to be sure. Open the hatch, Norm. Let's get Roberto inside. The strut will hold up OK."

The hatch opened easily, but it took a great deal of effort to get Roberto in. They did not bother with the isolation stay, preferring to get Roberto out of his EVA suit and check his wounds. Oreen would stay with Roberto while Moses and Norm attempted to erect and rearm the burst antenna. Norm found spare cable connectors and would make a temporary splice. Without having to fabricate or modify the connectors, they could have the antenna working again soon.

Moses and Norm returned to the surface to complete the work. They each carried a weapon and replacement parts. Norm also carried the last replacement lamps for the lights that were down and broken. While Norm replaced nearby lamps, Moses opened a small hatch and pulled out a hose, which he used to foam the area around and below the broken wing. When he finished, he knew for sure that they were not going anywhere. He and Norm then began working on the cables and antenna that was misshapen and covered with sand and soot. They stood the antenna up and straightened it as best they could. Norm replaced the connectors and reattached the cables after making a clean splice. With a little luck on their side, their repairs would have it working again. At this juncture, the landing party was in dire need of a little luck.

Oreen helped Roberto out of his EVA suit and tried to get him to lie down on the reclined rear seat. He was reluctant but finally relented due to weakness and exhaustion. She redressed his wound and tried to make him comfortable. Next, she attempted to send a distress call to the *Kat* using the onboard transmitter and antenna system. She knew it was improbable that the message would go through, but she had to try, some of their first ones had made it. Instead of putting her helmet back on and using voice commands, she typed her message with the keyboard. She was glad to have the helmet off for a while. The message was sent as a distress call and read: "Base Camp partially destroyed by arachnid life forms. DEV One badly damaged, not flight-worthy. Roberto's injury very serious. Moses also sustained injury to shoulder. Restoring antenna, power low. Situation serious but not critical. Please acknowledge ASAP." She almost added request assistance but hesitated. She would wait until they acknowledged and then send a SOS.

Norm and Moses finished the exterior repairs and powered the antenna and booster. The first attempt ended in a shower of sparks, and Norm began to worry that Moses was in too much pain. He could barely lift his wounded arm. They reconnected a blackened circuit board and tried again. This time the control panel winked to life and the system powered up correctly. At least now they could communicate again. The four were fortunate that the repairs worked because Oreen's first message did not go through.

Norm again assisted Moses back through the hatch. Once inside, Oreen helped remove his EVA suit. When she removed the suit from his wounded shoulder, he cried out in pain. The entire inside of the back of the heavy suit and the sleeve were covered with blood. His wound was oozing blood, and it was obvious he had already lost quite a bit. Chills of fear and hurt for Moses ran up and down Oreen's entire body. She quickly went to work on him and jabbed an IV into his arm. Moses slumped before her—a broken, disheartened leader, but his bravery had been inspirational. She loved him and now worked feverishly to save him.

Norm saw Oreen's message on the monitor screen. It had been almost two hours since the first attempt to send it. There had been no response, no acknowledgment. He switched over to the exterior antenna and increased power to the system. He typed in SOS followed by the original message prepared by Oreen.

"That's all we can do for now," Norm said as he turned away from the system. He also checked the radars, which were still operational, and began running a complete diagnostic analysis of DEV One. He noticed the food and water set out by Oreen and picked some up as he flopped in the copilot's pivoting chair.

"How bad is it?" he asked Oreen.

It was Moses who answered the question. He said, "Real bad! We can't fly, power is getting low, and they don't even know about our situation on the *Kat*." He was dispirited. He was also still in tremendous pain and had lost a lot of blood. He finished by adding facetiously: "The locals prepared quite a greeting for us, didn't they? That was sure one hell of a surprise."

Oreen had to do something to restore his confidence and keep him focused. She said, "Norm means how's the shoulder, not how bad is this craziness. You and Norm already fixed the antenna, and we've sent a message. It's time we all said thanks to God that we're here, alive, and we should ask the Almighty for a little help."

— § —

The crew of the *Kat* was already worried. Bits of the message sent from the rover came through as indecipherable, and there had been no communications from the surface for too long. If the first message had been received, they would have moved to full alert. Instead they were standing by aboard the *Kat* and waiting nervously. Rod had tried to send a message but received no confirmation of receipt. He assumed that it was the same problem they had before with the surface storms and reported the problem to the Commander.

When parts of a message finally did come in, the first three letters were all he needed to see to know that the landing party had serious problems. Rod was just leaving the gym. Commander Kidd and Doc were entering to begin a workout. When they used the gym together, the rest of the crew accepted that it was "do not disturb". Rod hit the open communication line announcing, "Captain to the bridge. Urgent information from surface." He wanted Jason to be the first to know the true seriousness of the message prior to informing the rest of the crew and NASA. He knew that the captain would want to assess the contents of the message and then take appropriate action.

— § —

In the conditioning room, Jason and Doctor Ann Pritchard were just finishing a rigorous workout, including a few minutes of very close physical contact. They were relaxed and feeling the warm glow of their private intimacy. Jason was startled by the message from Rod, but not alarmed because Rod had alerted everyone else aboard at the same time. He toweled off, kissed Doc a quick goodbye, and headed for the bridge.

Rod met him just outside the hatchway to the conditioning module and handed him the partial message beginning with the old, traditional-but-universal distress signal, SOS. He apologized for disturbing them, but Jason waved it off as he surveyed the brief message. He could also make out the words *camp destroyed* and *DEV damaged*. Jason stopped in the corridor outside the gym when Doc appeared in the hatchway, concern showing on her face. He tapped a button on his communicator, immediately patching his voice through to the ship's system and announced his orders to his crew. "A partial message has just come through from the landing party. They are in distress, and DEV One has been damaged somehow. We will attempt to ascertain the exact nature of the problem and get a more detailed report. In the meantime, I want everyone at alert stations, and fully prepare DEV Two for immediate launch. I want a continuous full report on the weather below and any potential targets for penetrating the shell. Get to work, people!"

He and Rod hurried to the communications center. They prepared a reply for the landing party just as the computer assembled the entire inbound message. They were now sure that the four on the surface were in real trouble, but they needed to know more. Jason prepared the reply, and Rod began transmitting it. All they could do now was prepare for a rescue launch if a confirmed request came through for one. DEV Two was ready and being prepared for move out.

— § —

Norm was pleased for the first time since returning to Base Camp when they received confirmation of receipt by the *Kat*. He relayed the message to the others. All Jason needed was a more detailed assessment of their situation and an official request for assistance. The four talked it over and decided that the only choice they had under the circumstances was to request immediate extraction from the surface by the use of DEV Two before anything else jeopardized Roberto and Moses. Roberto needed much more medical attention, his condition was deteriorating at an alarming rate, though he insisted that he could handle it. Moses was weakened by the loss of blood, but still showed formidable strength and resilience. They would send the request immediately and then sit back, hope for no more trouble, and wait.

Norm attempted to send the second message, but the antenna was acting up again. He looked out through the side port with powerful binoculars and saw a new tiny scorch mark on the recent connections he had completed. He would have to make another repair if they had any chance to get the message through. Moses agreed that he could watch things inside and Oreen could help Norm by standing guard while Norm made the repairs.

Norm said simply, "No way." He wasn't about to let Oreen go out there with him. They needed her inside. He could facilitate the expected repair by himself and be back inside without exposing anyone else to risk at this point. Norm suited up and carefully looked over the laser weapon. Moses was hesitant but did not argue. Norm found another circuit board and a few jumper connectors and prepared to leave DEV One. They checked the radars and surveyed the perimeter as best they could through the soot-covered windows. He planned to clean the outside view ports as best he could on the way back in.

The motion-detector system was now useless. The visitors had ruined it too. Norm would have to rely on his comrade's eyes and ears and his own ability to complete the repair with only one eye on his work. He would stay low, move fast, and work as quickly as possible. He didn't relish the idea of being outside on the surface, alone and preoccupied, with the spider-like life forms wandering about.

As he exited the hatch, the radar showed clear atmospheric conditions; no storms coming at least, and the surface-sweep radar detected no unidentified blips. He slid down the ladder, brought his weapon to his hip, and surveyed the entire area around the DEV before proceeding. He had new batteries in the light atop the weapon and saw nothing unusual. Satisfied and nervous, he shuffled straight to the antenna and again stopped to look around. He felt his heart pounding when he removed the circuit board and inspected the damage to the precious antenna. His assessment of the problem from the lander proved to be correct. He popped out the old board, replaced it with a new one and bypassed a fried wire with his clips. He held his breath and pressed the recessed button marked manual power. A few lights blinked on the control panel, and the burst antenna came to life once more. Norm continued to hold his breath, waiting for another short or problem, but the system continued to operate.

He again surveyed around him and checked with Oreen, who was watching him from the side port window. She gave him a thumb up signal and said, "Everything looks OK from here, Norm. The antenna is working within tolerances, and you are clear to get your ass back in here. Pronto!"

He was about to rise from his crouch to leave when a spray of liquid hit him directly on his helmet visor. He was so shocked that he slipped backward and landed firmly on his rear end. He saw the culprit through the droplets of acid on his face shield. Had he not had the helmet on, his eyes and probably most of his face would now be dissolving.

Norm reached into his belt pack, still attached to his EVA suit, and extracted a small plastic sample bottle. Removing the lid, he rolled to his knees and reached around behind the tiny arachnid creature with the bottle. He was trying to capture the critter using the technique he had used as a kid to catch bugs. It worked. Before the lifeform could flee, he had it sealed in the bottle and began looking around the antenna for more.

Oreen's view was partially obscured by the soot covering on the view port but she watched his antics and could not believe what she witnessed. "What are you doing, Norm? Moses wants you back in here. It's an order, Norm."

"I got one," he answered. "I've got a bug in a plastic sample jar. The little SOB sprayed me right in the face. I see another small one and have another bottle. If I can't catch it on the first try, I'm out of here." He lunged suddenly from his position toward the rock behind the antenna. "Gotcha, you mean little shit," he said as he rose and trotted back to the DEV, ascending the ladder and opening the outer hatch in one continuous motion.

"You aren't bringing some of those things in here, are you?" Oreen was perplexed and very displeased by his actions. The thought of those creatures inside with them caused her unusual anxiety. She did not like the strange feeling she had about them, but again made no direct comment to the others for her own unsure reasons. Norm calmed her by saying the samples would be needed for scientific scrutiny, and the creature's acid spew did not dissolve the sample bottles. He assured her that he did not need a larger one, but if they decided to get one, she could have the honor of catching it. Oreen accepted that but assured Norm that, if they did need a big one, Norm would make excellent live bait.

Once Norm was safe back inside the disheveled confines of the DEV, Oreen began sending details of the injuries to Rob and Moses for Doc to evaluate and then sent her formal request for rescue. Norm watched his bugs through the translucent sides of the sample bottles. He wondered how long they could survive in the sealed confines of their prisons. He lamented about all the work they had completed and the stores of samples and data he had collected and now possessed. If they could be rescued, would he be able to take any of it with him? For a scientist, the thought of abandoning everything was clearly unthinkable. But he knew that he had to put those thoughts aside. Thinking about their survival needed to take precedence.

19

RESCUE

IT WAS SEVERAL nerve-wracking minutes before the computers deciphered the fragmented message from the marooned landing party. There was no doubt in anyone's mind that a rescue would be implemented. Jason relayed the messages to Mission Control but did not plan to wait for permission to mount an immediate rescue effort. His superiors at Mission Control might want to delay or, God forbid, decide to not risk another surface mission and the additional lives it might cost.

Jason gave the orders to begin unloading all unnecessary gear from DEV Two. The second rover, permanent weather station, communication relay system, and other specimen containers were removed. An extra internal fuel tank and extra booster system were installed. These modifications could be made in only a few hours and were already under way.

Jason had a difficult decision to make about the crew for a rescue mission. The landers carried a maximum of six crewmembers. With four to bring back from the ground, he could only send two down. As he saw it, crew two consisted of Sergey Vosorov, and David or Margie. He had to keep Sergey as pilot. Though capable and strong, Jason did not want to send Margie due to her emotional tendencies. David was the logical choice. He was trained to handle emergencies and weapons, could think on his feet, and remained cool under stress. David would accompany Sergey to the surface in order to facilitate the rescue. Decision made, Jason was satisfied.

After working with his crew for almost two hours, the commander then turned his attention to the information before him and a plan for the rescue. The detailed transmission from the surface alluded to large spider-like life forms. It suggested attack by these creatures and the method of defense employed by the landing party. Roberto and Moses had used the converted cutting lasers to good effect. They had plenty of scientific samples to bring back, and his landing party had accomplished ninety percent of their planned mission. They had never anticipated hostile natives, but now they had to face that problem too.

Finding them on the surface would not be a serious problem, no matter how dark it was. The homing transponders would lead DEV Two directly to the landing area. Getting through the shell was the first major hurdle. It had gone well for DEV One, but the eye of the storm they dove into had been one of the best-formed and most open features they had seen in the shell, since they left. Assuming the second crew could get through, how much fuel would they have to use to get to the point on the surface occupied by the first lander? Then they had to land, load, and transfer the scientific materials, take off and fight their way back through with a full load. Jason feared that he was sending these people to their deaths, and wondered if they did have a real chance of getting back. This question began to haunt him, and Jason felt the burden of command.

He called a crew meeting to inform Sergey that just David would be ac-companying him. The others all understood, though Margie felt tightness in her stomach. As soon as the modifications to DEV Two were completed, Jason said they were free to go. Dismissing the rest of the crew, Jason sat alone to speak to David and Sergey. "They had to fight down there and have put up with some serious storms," Jason began. "David, you need to be prepared with the same kind of converted laser. How many have we got, and can you rig them up?"

"We have one more, sir, and enough parts for another. Sergey and Margie converted the one we had and built the second and I installed the first in the DEV. It can be lowered with the forward video and radar systems and aimed using the video camera. I can fire it with a joystick we rigged up inside. The other is a shoulder-pack mount similar to what Moses fabricated. It's the best we could do. They use up juice pretty quick, but we rigged up stronger batter-ies and they still work fine, maybe pack a little more wallop. We'll be packing heat." David's seriousness and complete determination showed on his face.

"How soon until you two can be ready?" Jason asked, watching their eyes.

"Within the hour, Commander," Sergey responded.

"Go get them!" Jason said the words and rose to salute them. They turned and headed for DEV Two.

More than six hours passed before the launch crew had DEV Two prepared for move out. Margie was ready at the controls, David and Sergey were seated in the craft, and all of the modifications and unloading were completed. Jason and Phil were scanning the stormy shell below, watching for the first signs of a suitable vortex. *Stealth Finder Two* had detected two possible targets, but one had quickly dissipated, and the other was very small and too tightly spiraling. The remaining crew wanted to give David and Sergey the best possible target, the greatest chance to reach those trapped on the surface. Margie was reciting a short prayer for them over and over.

Jason gave the order for the move-out maneuver and Margie opened the outer doors and began the tedious task of freeing DEV Two from its hangar. In twenty minutes DEV Two was at the end of the fully extended manipulator arm and ready for release. With the push of a button, Margie disconnected the umbilicus, turned the craft loose, and began retracting the mechanical arm.

Sergey powered up his engines and moved at low thrust away from the *Kat* to a safe distance astern. There they assumed the nose-down attitude for orbital extraction and awaited the occasional tiny opening in the swirling maelstrom below. Sergey used his main engine to drop three thousand meters below the *Kat* and began the wait.

Jason sent a message to the surface that DEV Two had launched and was awaiting a suitable opening in the cover. He knew that they would be glad to hear that news. Jason also figured that their message to Mission Control had gotten there and that life at NASA was now chaos, and that they were likely expecting him to wait for orders before attempting any rescue. He would face that hurdle if or when it presented itself. In the meantime, he was hoping that DEV Two would already be well on its way prior to his receipt of suggestions or orders from Mission Control.

Sergey and David said very little as they waited. They studied the monitors, which showed the ominous clouds full of turmoil below them. Their vigil was interrupted by the beeps from the computer as it picked up incoming data from the distant *Stealth Finder*. It had detected and was now actively tracking a small circular vortex less than one hundred kilometers from their orbital path and a little more than two hundred kilometers to the rear of the *Kat*. David drew connecting vectors on the screen, and the computer went to work computing an intercepting course, trajectories, engine-burn duration, anticipated fuel consumption and other pertinent computations needed for an attempt to enter the vortex.

To hit this first potential target correctly, they needed to make a quick but very precise decision. They had watched the dive of DEV One on the screens on the *Kat* and had a basic idea of what to look for. They also had studied numerous vortex types and shapes since DEV One had left for the surface, assimilating all pertinent information on these features into the ship's growing database. Computer simulations or models of a variety of vortex types were now available to them; at least they had more data than the first group. But none of this mattered once they made the decision to dive into one. Then, only luck and great piloting gave them any chance for success.

The detected approaching feature did not look too promising. It was small and the entrance was very narrow. It shifted wildly like a newborn tornado. After studying the shape for a few moments they decided to pass on this first opportunity. It ended up being a smart decision because the feature broke up and was swallowed by the tumult at what would have been a point just after their dive into it had begun, a probable point of no return.

They waited for another two hours with little of opportunity appearing on the screens. Finally the computer began tracking a second eye. This one was different again, with a wide opening and slanted sides piercing deep into the shell. The lower half of the computer-generated model of the feature was narrow and nearly vertical. This target looked much better than the first, and their model placed it within acceptable parameters, so David set the course, and Sergey activated his main engine and aimed his craft. They had some distance to cover to rendezvous with the target. David signaled the *Kat*, and they began their orbital extraction fire and dove at a shallow angle in the direction of the fast approaching funnel.

When they intercepted the target, the thought of diving into and taking the unknown chance of getting down through the feature seemed rather ludicrous to both. Finding a way back through when returning never entered their minds. They were frightened, and there was no way to hide it. Sergey chose his moment, fired his thrusters again and screamed, "Geronimo!" followed by a quieter, "As you Americans are so apt to say." In seconds they were entering the wide, shallow whirlwind, nose down, plunging at outrageous speed.

David wanted to close his eyes but forced himself to watch the gauges and controls. The windshield cover was secured, so they watched the video monitors, following their path while the cone narrowed.

Sergey gasped, David tried to swallow, mouth dry, there was no opening ahead in the vortex, only horrendous wind. The bottom of the funnel was gone, swept to the side and into the torturous clouds. Sergey leveled out as quickly as possible, following the now horizontal end of the cone into the surrounding hell. He swung the craft in a wide arc and almost completely reversed their course when he ran out of room and hit the wall of the vortex at a low angle. DEV Two was slammed hard by the wind shear and thrown to the side violently. Sergey had no control, and he was stunned momentarily by the storm wind's impact. David grasped his redundant controls and attempted to reduce their spin as the side of the cone hit them again. This second brush with the wall of wind saved them. DEV Two was hurtled forward in the correct direction to save them from potential disaster. David glanced at the monitor and saw that the craft was facing toward the widening part of the sloping vortex. He hit the emergency open button for the protective windshield cover, and fired the main thrusters. Sergey shook his head and regained his wits. They pushed the craft hard, trying to escape the clutches of the closing cone of wind around them. They climbed almost straight up, David now guiding the DEV back toward the entrance and watched the sides of the vortex sweep in like a closing eye. Their faces strained in terror, the walls of that eye closed down upon them. The cone on the monitor was almost gone, and the end of the tunnel ahead was rapidly disappearing. David pushed the engines to the limit. They strained in their chairs. DEV Two broke clear of the shell, and the eye dissipated and disappeared behind them.

David and Sergey were in a state of cold sweat. Sergey grasped David's shoulder and hugged him, feeling sure that they had come very close to being destroyed by the shell. Their brief elation, felt after a close brush with death, lasted only seconds, interrupted when David looked at fuel expended. He was a little dismayed to see the level of only eighty-three percent. Their escape had expended too much fuel and they could not risk a second attempt to reach the surface without refueling. They would have to return to the *Kat*.

When they signaled the *Kat*, Jason told them that the crew had watched their path until they were inside the funnel and cut off. He was shocked by their reappearance and said that he wanted them back and refueled for a second attempt. There would be no rest for the weary rescuers, and none was expected. Jason was leaving them no time to reflect on their harrying experience.

After refueling, trying to be calm and as macho as possible, and pretending to regain their composure, the two were ready to try again. The previous experience had been terrifying. Those on the *Kat* knew that to do it again took real courage. DEV Two was undamaged and quickly readied for a second attempt. Sergey moved away from the *Kat* and again positioned his craft for the dive maneuver. Another seemingly endless two hours passed before they acquired a new target. This one was different again, with a narrow opening and steep, harsh sides. It was well formed and penetrated the foreboding cloud layer as far as they could detect without appreciable narrowing. It looked like a good target. They locked in the coordinates. Sergey fired his thrusters and once again began his intercept maneuver.

David relayed the message. "Commander, this one looks pretty good, and there are no other targets detected. So, we are going for this one. "We'll signal you when we have made contact with DEV One." His voice cracked on the last sentence.

"Good luck, and bring our folks back," Jason countered. "Your target looks good, and you are go for insertion and landing."

"I love you, David. Watch your fuel and be safe." It was Margie's voice. She was with Commander Kidd, and her voice gave him strength as DEV Two rocketed into a shallow dive and began closing on this second sinister-looking orifice in the shell.

Sergey guided the craft into the black eye of the omnipresent tumult of roiling clouds. His chosen path placed them dead center in the mouth of the vortex. In less than ten minutes they were swallowed up by the rotating funnel and plunging nose down toward the surface. All that David could do was watch the monitor tracing their path, keep one eye on a few critical gauges, and pray out loud. Sergey concentrated on his flight path and joined in the prayer.

David finished his verse and squeezed out the words: "We are dropping like a rock and rocking." It was smooth sailing through the wide eye for more than one third of the way through. At about the halfway point, the smooth ride ended abruptly. They could see the turbulent atmosphere boiling ahead on the monitor. There was no way to avoid it and no way to estimate its thickness or true intensity. The tiny craft plunged headlong into it at tremendous speed. They braced themselves as best they could and hit the layer head-on. Turbulence pounded the craft with unrelenting ferocity. DEV Two was knocked sideways and began spinning out of control.

There was almost nothing they could do. Sergey was barely able to maintain consciousness, and David was shaken so hard that he came very close to blacking out. The shaking and pounding on the exterior of the craft were merciless. They both expected the lander to be pulled apart at any moment. It lasted for several minutes and they became totally disoriented. The computer system began to fail. One monitor went blank. Without the system, they were lost and would certainly perish. David was too paralyzed to check if the backup system activated.

Sergey was somehow able to withstand the forces and was trying desperately to regain control when they broke through to smoother atmosphere. David was sick and vomited in his suit and helmet. He would just have to put up with it and function if they were going to make it through. Sergey noticed his problem but could do nothing to help. He had expended considerable fuel to regain control and was fighting hard to maintain it. He needed David's assistance. Another wall of wind was blocking their path not very far ahead.

Sergey saw a sliver of less turbulent air between his craft and the wall of the vortex and made the split-second decision to steer for it. The maneuver worked. They slipped past the worst part of the turbulence and again broke through into smoother atmosphere. They were now more than three-quarters of the way through and again diving toward the base of the shell. The spiraling eye was still open all the way to the base, and David counted off the seconds in his head as they sped toward the exit from the hellish shell layer.

When they broke through, there was no sense of jubilation, only a sense of thanks for having survived again. They stared at the main monitor. The tiny cursor, shaped like their craft, exited the cone and began decreasing in dive angle. It was over, and they were badly shaken, but through.

David was uncomfortable but began his tasks of monitoring the ship's systems and preparing to locate his comrades on the ground. They ran the mandatory atmospheric tests and determined that it was safe to open the shield covering the front windows and look at the new world for the first time. The heat shields had functioned well, and DEV Two was still intact, with the exception of one computer system and several cracks in the exterior ceramic coating. Fuel consumption was nearing twenty percent, meaning they had little extra to use to locate DEV One.

They switched on the locator system, which immediately began the search for the signals from DEV One. It picked up the weak signal more than seventeen hundred kilometers away. The situation could have been much worse; they were very close considering the circumstances. But the distance necessitated using more precious fuel to get to the landing area.

David locked in the coordinates, and Sergey lowered his glide angle even more. He needed to conserve fuel and wanted to coast as far in the direction of the landing zone as possible, but they were dropping rapidly. David switched on the communication system and attempted to raise the marooned landing party.

He was elated when Oreen's shaken voice came on and said: "We are sure glad to hear from you. Thank God you made it. We have a problem here. Another storm is moving in, and you definitely don't want to try to land in it." Her transmission started to break up. The new storm began to sweep over the Base Camp. "Don't last long . . . it's over . . .will advise . . ." The signal faded out.

Sergey leveled off at thirty thousand meters and throttled back on his engines, which he had just fired up. They switched the surface radar to long range and activated the ground-acquisition system for approach and landing. The interference caused by the storm ahead and below allowed David and

Sergey to locate the worst part of the alien weather phenomena while they closed on its position.

— § —

At Base Camp the surface team began preparing for the arrival of DEV Two. There was a general feeling of relief, and spirits were immediately raised by the thoughts of being able to leave this inhospitable dot. They were apprehensive, watching the new approaching storm, when David's voice penetrated the silence and lifted their declining morale. Even Roberto forced a smile. But the new storm would interfere with any landing by DEV Two and with a possible rescue from the damaged craft.

Norm and Oreen now understood that unlike storms on Earth, which sent creatures scurrying for cover, the storms on Enigma brought the menacing creatures out. Oreen's perceptions of her new surrounding were growing clearer with each passing hour. She began to feel that same sensation that she had in the cave, but kept it to herself. The last thing any of them wanted was more damage from the curious or malicious beasts before they could get the heck out of there. One thing was sure to the four marooned explorers; they somehow needed to keep the intruders at bay and make certain that the creatures caused no more damage or threat before they could be rescued. The crew of DEV One also wanted nothing other than the storm to cause any delays in the landing by DEV Two.

Norm cooked up a little surprise for the spider-like life forms that might venture too close. He received Moses' blessing to institute a defense plan. Norm had devised it himself and would carry it out by himself if the need arose. He unpacked the emergency, high-explosive plastique and fashioned several bombs with detonators and tiny timers. He packed them carefully in a shoulder pack clipped to his EVA suit. The plan was simple. He would leave the lander alone and position himself with his back against the remaining good landing strut and blast anything that got too close. He would use the handmade grenades if the weapon failed to keep the creatures away. Norm's bravery was beyond anything the others had ever imagined. He was prepared to stand alone to protect his wounded comrades and would not allow Oreen to join him.

Norm put on the heavy EVA suit and slipped into the outer lock without saying a word. The storm began to intensify outside. The remaining lights were brought to maximum illumination. He slid down the ladder and took up his defensive position under the wing. It wasn't long before Oreen informed him that, as predicted, the surface radar showed several incoming objects of varying sizes. They were well outside the illuminated area around Base Camp. As the storm intensified, the lumens given off by the lights began to decrease, and the intruders began to circle closer.

Moses turned on the landing beams, but power was getting low, and they needed it more for other essential systems; so, he made the decision to use them only as a drastic measure. Norm could not see much; the storm winds kicked up sand and fine debris. The onslaught of black silt made visibility even worse. The creatures crept closer as the light and visibility diminished. Norm armed his weapon and set three of his makeshift bombs on a protruding part of the landing strut. He wiped his visor with his free hand repeatedly, training his weapon level with the other hand.

— § —

Aboard the approaching lander, David and Sergey could only wait for the storm to dissipate. They were forced to circle to the rear of the storm and burn precious fuel. Oreen tried to communicate and had better luck now due to the close proximity of DEV Two. She kept them apprised of the situation while both landers tracked the storm. Oreen described the approach of the arachnid life forms and patched the location of the creatures to the computers on DEV Two. She was continuously feeding the information to Norm through his heads-up visor display and handheld unit. Even if Norm could not see the creatures visually, he could locate them precisely using the indirect detection and identification provided by the radar in conjunction with the computers.

As the creatures closed the distance between Base Camp and themselves, at the height of the storm, Oreen and Moses felt they were close enough. Moses instructed Norm to fire a burst in front of the largest approaching spider form as a type of warning shot. Norm carefully aimed at a point a meter in front of the creature and fired. The resultant blast was weakened by the intense storm but zapped the ground next to one of the creature's legs. It did not hesitate but continued heading directly for the craft-and Norm hiding beneath it.

Moses yelled: "Eradicate that thing, Norm! It's huge!" Norm gave his weapon full power and fired repeated blasts at the creature, which was now almost on top of them. He scored several direct hits, and the spider withdrew leaving smoldering pieces behind. Several others of various sizes replaced it. Norm picked his targets and fired away in a blaze of red blasts. As he hit one creature it was replaced by several more. He let his weapon fall to his side, picked up an explosive device, pressed the preset timer, and threw the bomb. Before it exploded, he was tossing the second, and when the first went off, he threw the third.

Three very loud explosions rocked DEV One. Moses hit the landing spots. Norm was preparing three more bombs. When he looked up he could see several pieces of exploded aliens and many more advancing over the carcasses. He fired several more bursts and laid down a continuous line of fire until his weapon was empty. The creatures were heaped in dead piles, but more kept coming even with the dying lander lights turned to full brightness.

The storm was passing, and the soot-filled air was slowly clearing. The lights were of limited value due to their new coating of soot. Norm threw his remaining bombs in different directions. He could now make out the closest creatures clearly, and there were many behind them. The three new explosions filled the air around the lander with new plumes of dust and arachnid parts. Norm knew that he could not escape and had nothing left with which he could defend himself. At that moment there was a glint on his visor and he saw the blazing red of the other laser weapon stop a large charging beast dead in its tracks. It was Oreen standing on the wing above, blasting away. She was frantically shouting for Norm to clear out from under the wing. He charged out and twisted up the ladder in one move. They retreated together toward the hatch.

As the second weapon ran out of power, they were about to close the hatch, when a streak of movement passed over the lander and the familiar blazing signature of the laser weapon strafed the ground to the rear of the craft. Creature parts flew everywhere as the high-powered weapon devastated the ranks of arachnid life forms. It was DEV Two, and it was ripping the creatures to shreds. The storm was nearly over, and the creatures began to beat a hasty retreat back toward the canyons from which they mysteriously emerged.

The sight of the second lander brought the crew on the ground new hope at a time of near desperation. DEV Two was a welcome sight and at just the right moment. Moses likened it to the cavalry charge to save the wagon train in the old-time westerns. When he recognized the sound of the lander he shouted: "Hallelujah, man, what timing!" The sound of DEV Two returned again along with the report of the laser cannon. The craft made a second strafing run and swung in a wide arc to survey the landing zone.

The area around DEV One and the entire Base Camp was now littered with carcasses of dead arachnid forms. So much for establishing no-impact safeguards for any new lifeform discovered. The human impact on the local fauna had been tremendous. The impact on the alien human visitors had been near disastrous. One look at the flattened Habitat and mangled lander told the story. Whether because of curiosity or planned aggression, the local inhabitants had proven to be hostile and destructive.

There was not a lot of room in the proximity of DEV One to set DEV Two down. Because of the acid and acrid fluid spewed by the creatures or spilled from their broken bodies, the area was not very safe to move about. Norm returned to the surface and checked on the condition of the rover. It had been pushed sideways and bent up pretty badly, but it still worked. Norm used it to push carcasses aside and clear an adequate area adjacent to DEV One. The second lander was still consuming its vital fuel supply, and Sergey was now very anxious to get on the ground.

As soon as Norm had pushed aside enough of the debris and cleared a suitable place, Sergey began the hovering maneuver. He slowed his forward speed and rotated the engines for landing. David counted off the feet until touchdown, and the second lander began to descend to the surface. When dust rose from the surface, David braced for landing, but Sergey set the craft down so softly that he was not even aware that they were actually on the surface until the power to the engines was being cut.

DEV Two landed at the end of a battle against giant silvery smooth "spiders". To David it seemed like something out of pure science fiction, but he was now right in the middle of it. They secured the vessel and looked out of the window at the filthy figure of Norm Mailor, who was hardly recognizable in his blackened EVA suit. He was waving to them. They waved back.

David looked forlornly at the fuel gauge. It read forty-three percent, definitely not enough to get back to the *Kat*. They rose and headed for the door. Norm was banging on the side of DEV Two. His voice through their helmets kept saying: "Get a weapon out here."

20

ESCAPE

M OSES SENT a message to the *Kat* confirming the second DEV's touch-down and describing the latest round of combat with the strange creatures. After this last confrontation he wanted them all out of there as soon as was physically possible. Roberto was now very weak and feverish. The potential problem of a secondary infection was almost certain. His wound was serious, and his condition was getting worse by the minute. He was stable, but they had to keep him sedated due to the severity of the gash in his leg and accompanying unbearable pain.

Norm had impressed them all. Moses had never personally witnessed valor of the type that Norm had shown. He withstood the onslaught of the alien beasts by himself and continued protecting them until he was out of power and explosives. Moses knew that he would have tried to fight them with his bare hands. Moses had not even noticed Oreen go to his assistance. He was thankful for the timely arrival of DEV Two. He could only imagine what might have happened if they had not arrived when they did.

Moses watched Norm while he waited for the hatch to open in the side of DEV Two. Norm was atop the ladder as soon as David opened the hatch and grabbed a new power pack for his weapon. The stark contrast between Norm's soiled EVA suit and David's white one was shocking. They shook hands and David used a clean cloth to wipe Norm's visor.

Sergey and David were taking no chances on polluting the inside of DEV Two with any kind of contaminant from this weird world. Sergey would remain onboard, at the controls, if possible, for the duration of the material and human transfer from DEV One to DEV Two. The fresh batteries and clean lights of the second lander bathed the area in a fresh wash of pure bright white light. Sergey had seen enough of the creatures below to know that he wanted no part of another confrontation with them.

David brought some special medicinal bandages and additional painkillers and antibiotics for Roberto. He wanted to get them to him as fast as he could.

David climbed the ladder and placed the supplies in the pressure lock. Oreen was waiting at the inside hatchway to DEV One. She looked through the inside window into the chamber and said: "Are we ever glad to see you. Thanks for coming. We are sorry about the reception. The locals crashed the party."

David was thankful to see that she was still in good spirits. He closed the outer hatch and surveyed the area from the platform atop the ladder. It looked like a battle zone, with numerous pieces of strange looking angular debris. He could see the remains of the Habitat behind the rock ridge. It was flattened and the bracing bent or broken. The trailer for the rover was on its side and crushed. It was all to be left behind, but no one had ever expected it to be demolished. DEV One had sustained heavy damage. The broken wing sagged pitifully, and it was obvious that his comrades would have been stranded if he and Sergey had not come for them.

Norm was talking to Sergey through the communication link provided by their helmet systems. He wanted to know how much collected material they could carry on DEV Two. Norm wanted to take as much as possible. There were still many secrets to be unraveled concerning the new world and its inhabitants. Norm knew that his samples could be invaluable to scientific research and further evaluation of the Stealth Planet. Sergey wanted his craft to be as light as possible for the flight back and rendezvous with the *Kat*. The two sets of desires were diametrically opposed.

For the present, the weather was once again clear and the winds were near calm. The active surface radar systems spotted no wandering life forms or activity of any type. David and Sergey began an exhaustive evaluation of DEV Two. They needed to make the second lander ready for takeoff as quickly as possible. The main computer system was non-functional. There were several cracks in the outer ceramic coating that needed to be repaired. None were structurally serious, but all were bad enough to need patching and sealing. David began this process first. The fuel gauge on DEV Two read only forty-three percent. They would have to transfer fuel from the remaining good tank on DEV One. The tank in the broken wing had leaked and could be contaminated. Between the remaining wing tank and the tank in the fuselage, there would be enough to fill everything aboard DEV Two, including the extra tank added before departure, if they did not waste any.

Transferring the fuel was the tricky part, and a time consuming process. They had trained for this eventuality and knew exactly what to do, but it was still a dangerous process and could not be performed unless constant conditions were maintained. One thing they all agreed to, they wanted to begin the material transfer first and, when complete, finish by transferring the fuel. While this last process was taking place, they would not be able to load equipment or samples, fire laser weapons or use explosives, and they would be forced to power down many critical systems.

Moses discussed the number of procedures they needed to complete before departing with Sergey and David. They set up a step-by-step process and sequential order, a process that of necessity had to be most efficient. David would repair the DEV cracks as soon as the system checks were completed. Norm and Oreen would bring Roberto to DEV Two and place him in the decontamination lock. They would then clean the windows and lights of DEV One and run a power cable between the two landers. This way all lights could be brought to full power in hopes of keeping any potential visitor at bay.

Norm and Oreen could then begin transferring Norm's most important samples and materials from his experiments, packing them carefully in the cargo hold of the second lander. They would have to weigh and clean each container. Moses and Sergey would monitor their two crafts and keep a very close eye on the weather and the immediate surroundings. When David finished the repair work, and if all systems checked out fine, he would then set up the fuel conducting lines and prepare for the vital transfer.

As bad as he wanted to get out of there, Norm hoped that it would take David a while. He and Oreen had a lot to do, and they were both just about exhausted. Neither had gotten a chance to eat or rest in quite sometime. Both were running on adrenaline, and their energy was giving out.

Moses wanted to help them, but his shoulder was far too sore, and he was still feeling weak. He packed up Norm's things that were still in DEV One and prepared what he could for exit. His preparations also included getting out food and drinks for Norm and Oreen. He knew that they were running on borrowed time. Moses tried to force Roberto to eat something, but he could not, so he gave him essential fluids. Oreen redressed his wound and prepared him for his move to the other vehicle.

Sergey was impatient but satisfied by the schedule set up by himself and Moses. The clock was already running. David scrambled all over his lander, ferreting out cracks large and small. The repair process was going very well. David was full of energy, in stark contrast to the crew of the other lander. Moses and Oreen assisted Roberto from lander to lander and looked completely worn out by the time they helped him into the pressure lock.

Sergey said, "I'll take it from here." They wearily departed to begin transferring boxes of samples.

There was no longer any reason for any of them to worry about remaining in the lock on DEV One. The crew of DEV One went inside for a few minutes and rested while they drank and ate. They also took just enough time to regain some energy and then suited up again to begin the task of moving, weighing, cleaning, and repacking the cargo. The schedule did not call for time to rest, but they had no choice. By the time they were ready to begin the actual packing of the first few boxes, David was close to finished with the repairs. Moses suggested that he take time to help clean and pack the cargo. Sergey did not object. He knew the scientific importance of the materials. His main concern was cargo weight, and he could not afford to be anywhere close to overweight at the time of takeoff.

— § —

Aboard the *Kat*, everyone was ecstatic to hear about the safe passage of DEV Two through the shell and the subsequent rendezvous and landing. They were dismayed by the news of the storm and attack by the alien creatures. No one had ever seriously considered or thought much about this eventuality. It was more like a surrealistic dream to all of them.

Jason still had his apprehensions, even though, to most of the rest of the crew, they were halfway there. He knew that the unknown tough part still lay ahead. Getting back was the most formidable obstacle to the success of this entire mission, and now the lander would attempt to return with six instead of four and the extra weight of their many samples.

Commander Kidd had received an official directive from Mission Control at almost the same time as DEV Two disappeared into the eye in the storm clouds below. He read the latest message half expecting to see a *wait for more information* attitude. Instead, the message gave him permission to mount an immediate rescue effort using the second lander, if, in his discretion, he though it was a tenable objective. He was surprised. He had underestimated his superiors' ambitions. They had tremendous faith in his abilities and those of the entire crew of the *Kat*. At least he had already done the right thing in their eyes too.

According to the report from DEV Two progress on the surface was very slow. The first message from the new landing team had shown the low fuel problem and need to transfer fuel from the first lander. Roberto needed more help, but he was hanging in there. The lander was intact and surface conditions favorable. They had a lot to do, but Jason had faith in their training and abilities. Now all he and the rest of the crew aboard the *Kat* could do was to stand by faithfully and hope for the best.

— § —

David finished the repairs to the exterior surface of DEV Two ahead of the time allotted for the job. The repairs had to be sufficient for the ascent. Sergey summoned him before he could join Norm and Oreen to load the collections and samples. Sergey wanted to switch out the main computer system from the other lander. He could not get the main control computer on DEV Two to function correctly. It had sustained too much damage, and he did not want to be dependent on the backup system alone. David and Moses would remove the main system from the first lander, and Sergey would install it in DEV Two. This would delay things, because like everything else that would be in the flight cabin, the computer had to remain in the decontamination lock too.

Moses insisted that he could remove the computer without David's assistance. No one knew if or how he was going to accomplish this with only one good arm. Moses was not even sure if he could do it, but he wanted to give it a try and thus allow David to help Norm and Oreen. David went to work with Oreen, and they instructed Norm to sit down and rest. He did so with little resistance. David was amazed at how much they had already finished and was eager to work loading the heavy cases. They tallied the total weight so far and were pleased that they still had room and were well within the allotted weight limit established by Sergey for crew and cargo.

Norm was pleased because he knew that he would even have room for some of the cases of samples abandoned within the Habitat. If they still had room and time, he wanted to make an attempt to retrieve a few of these. Sergey would make that decision when they completely finished the job at hand, and they still had a lot to do. Norm was so fatigued that he was struggling to lift his arms.

Sergey checked the time and decided that Roberto had remained in the lock long enough. He assisted him through the inner hatch and out of the lock. Roberto was groggy from the painkillers he now needed, but acknowledged the help and fell into Sergey's arms. He wanted to help, but Sergey directed him to a rear chair and attempted to sit him down. Roberto would not sit, but instead pointed to the copilot's chair and insisted that Sergey seat him there. He pushed the seat back and propped up his leg. "Sergey," he said, "I'm not useless yet. I can use my eyes as a lookout and watch the screens for visitors. I've got a bone to pick with our friends out there, a little score to settle if they come back again. I'm not dead yet." He slurred his words and they faded out at the end.

Sergey thought for a few seconds and agreed to Rob's wishes. Rob did not look good and the size of his wound was made obvious by the size of the dressings and bandages. Sergey knew that Rob was in serious shape, but he could use the extra eyes, and Rob had finished a good nap in the lock. For the moment Rob appeared to be semi-alert and he insisted on helping in some way. He looked and acted uncomfortable, but under the circumstances, any help was welcome. This would free Sergey to set up for the fuel transfer. By the time David and the rest of the crew were ready to begin transferring fuel, he would be fully prepared on the inside.

Moses struggled mightily to extract the main computer from its mounting brackets in the cockpit. He was unable to free it completely and began to feel his wound start to bleed again. Oreen suspected that something was wrong. She heard his forced breathing when she tried to get a progress report. Moses sounded bad, almost as weak as Roberto. She could sense that something was not right. Her sixth sense could feel his struggle and extreme discomfort. It was as though she could feel something strange outside of herself, within him. Then she knew what it was; Moses' wound was infected, and the infection was alien. She felt these new enhanced sensations very strong, with a certain conviction. Oreen also sensed changes within herself, nothing like those within Moses, more akin to subtle perceptive ability increases, greater mind awareness of the entire scene around her. At times she felt almost like she was looking at the scene around her from a nearby viewer's perspective.

She stopped her work with David. "Moses is in trouble and overexerting in there," she said. "I've got to go help him right now. It can't wait"

It was Norm who stood up and sent her on her way to the ladder. "Go Oreen. We can finish this. You help Moses before he messes himself up even worse."

She moved to the ladder and climbed up, opened the hatch, and clambered through. "She looks tired, too," David remarked after watching her effort.

"I'm fine," Oreen responded. "You two just finish that. We'll get the computer." In a few minutes she emerged from DEV One with the computer system neatly wrapped in plastic sealer. Moses was close behind, now almost gasping with each movement. "I patched him up again and can't get him to stop working," she stated. They helped her down the ladder with her load and waited to assist Moses.

"I'm still commander of this landing party and, as such, I will continue to help in any way I can until I pass out or die. Is that clearly understood?" Moses stood firmly and shook off the assistance. "I will stand guard until you are finished loading. They helped Moses down and got him to sit down on a small portable chair beside the landing strut, where he could lean back and at least look comfortable.

Oreen made several more trips into the first lander to gather a few remaining personal items and then sealed the hatch. They stowed the unneeded items in sealed bags in another small cargo hold and went to work to finish loading all gear from DEV One. Moses sagged into the portable chair, but remained vigilant at guard with the laser weapon lying in his lap.

Another full hour passed before everything was cleaned, weighed and neatly stowed. The time had come to begin the fuel transfer. David, Norm, and Sergey removed transfer hoses from each lander and connected them with care to one another, and then the two ends were attached to each lander. Sergey checked the system and began the transfer of the vital semi-liquid propellant. The process of complete transfer and balancing the fuel tanks would take a couple of hours.

Moses could not do anything else outside, so he was moved to the pressure lock along with supplies and the extra computer and awaited his move to the inside. Norm collapsed in a heap and sprawled out to rest on one of the lander wings. David sat cross-legged on the other wing with the laser weapon at the ready. Oreen sat below the wing, watching her handheld connection to the surface radar, also checking on the fuel-transfer line. They had to power down several systems. They all prayed for no storms and no visitors at this critical juncture.

Oreen was nervous and still sensing things unnatural to her. "David, you see anything move?"

"No Oreen, nada, nothing. I've got one eye on the radars on my handheld and one on the local landscape. You let me know if you get the feelings like you said you had before." Oreen had told David about sensing the alien life-form since landing. They passed the next few hours thinking and watching. Few words were spoken.

The entire transfer process went without a single hitch. By the time it was completed, Moses was safely moved to a somewhat more comfortable position inside DEV Two. Norm had gotten a little rest, and Roberto at last relented to lying down when Moses moved to his seat. With the tanks on full, Sergey set to work installing the computer removed from the other lander. As soon as it was operational, they would be ready to leave, and none too soon, as far as Sergey was concerned.

All external hatches to the cargo compartments on DEV Two were closed and secured, except for one that could be closed from inside. David disconnected the fuel lines and stowed them in lander one. Any extra weight was discarded and placed inside DEV One. When Sergey finished installing and testing the replacement computer, the nonfunctional system was jettisoned and placed in a hold on the disabled lander. Every nonessential item was left behind in order to make their load as light as possible.

Norm pleaded for a chance to retrieve the other containers from the Habitat. He now had that chance. Sergey powered up his craft and all working systems in preparation for the earliest possible departure. During the power down for fuel transfer, several blips were detected on the radar screen during a brief period of surface winds. They had not come very close, but instead had roamed around, just out of the reach of the lander's powerful spotlights.

Sergey, Moses, and Roberto were safely aboard and as prepared as possible for the strains imparted to their bodies during liftoff. Moses gave the go ahead for a quick trip into the Habitat in order to retrieve a few more important samples and data files. They planned to open the bladders and keep them open for a quick exit. The inflation system worked but would barely hold the damaged structure up long enough for Norm to slip in, get what he wanted, and get back out. David would stand guard, holding a flood light, and Oreen would help Norm as he passed the cases out.

The lander beam provided just enough light to illuminate the Habitat behind the rocky ridge.

The small valley, into which Norm and Oreen had ventured on their second look around, stood silent and foreboding while they watched the Habitat inflate. The Habitat structure was a mess, having been literally trampled. Just as the Habitat was filling up, and Oreen and David trained their lights on the entrance, a flash of movement caused Norm to freeze and duck. The foreleg of a large spider-shaped beast came down between him and Norm. David staggered backward. Norm rolled to the entrance of the Habitat, barely escaping being crushed by the leg. Oreen's blood-curdling scream reverberated through their helmets. She moved back behind David, who almost fell to the ground. He had the laser gun slung over his shoulder. The beast had appeared without warning and surprised them completely. Oreen ripped the gun from David's shoulder and trained it on the creature just as it made a second attempt to crush Norm. The scientist dove headlong through the opening into the habitat. The arachnid reared, threatening with its forelegs to crush David and Oreen or spray its acidic expectorant on them.

Instead of firing the weapon, Oreen pulled David violently toward her and fell backward while rolling toward the rock ridge. She narrowly escaped hitting her helmet on a rocky protrusion of the volcanic material. A spray of sticky chemicals spattered the ground to their left. This time it was David who rose with the weapon. He pushed Oreen behind the rock. He fired the laser as the beast fired back. David dove to his right, rolled and fired again drawing the huge spider from behind the rock. He wasn't able to score a disabling hit. Suddenly a blast of red passed over his shoulder, and the powerful laser mounted on DEV Two slammed the beast. Moses was zapping it and not letting up. It reared again and was flipped to its back as leg parts were ripped from its dying body.

It was a narrow escape, and this time the creature had appeared from the shadows during calm conditions. David and Oreen swept the area behind the ridge with their lights. There was no more obvious movement, but they both heard the sound of scurrying feet in the dimly lit valley beyond the Habitat. The rocky ridge had been just high enough to prevent detection of the creatures and Moses had blacked out for a few minutes. Oreen had suspected nothing. The situation was bad and deteriorating if somehow these creatures could sneak up undetected. David called for Norm through the headset and was greeted by: "Thank you, that was close. I've got two containers here and three more to get. That's all."

Oreen and David could not believe it. While they were fighting for their lives, Norm was crawling around in the Habitat finding his scattered sample and data cases. He handed them out, and David and Oreen each grabbed one. Norm put one under his arm and struggled to drag the others to the lander. In another five minutes, David and Norm loaded the last cases while Oreen stood guard. They were finished and had completed loading, and were still under the maximum weight allowed by Sergey and Moses.

Norm decided to ask for one last chance to pick up a few pieces of arachnid carcasses before they lifted off. Sergey ordered Oreen to enter the lock and at the same time toss out the grimy EVA suits. The second landing party supplied the original crew with new ones. As each entered the lock, they stripped from the old suit and left it behind in the lock. They entered the cabin shivering and naked and put on the new suit there. David and Norm also changed in the lock and discarded the old suits. They made all practical attempts to minimize the amount of potentially contaminated material brought aboard, now showing no regard for how much human refuse they left behind on this unkind planet. All the rules were broken and a struggle for survival had rendered the prime directives all but obsolete. Further decontamination of themselves and all of their new cargo would take place on the *Kat* during the return voyage, if they now could just have the skill and good fortune to escape and get back to the mother ship.

The only problem with having Norm and David take a last look around to procure a few more samples was that both copilots were now outside. Sergey did not like this arrangement, but he could lift off with them in the decontamination lock and they could pass through more quickly if circumstances forced it.

Norm and David circled the DEVs and picked up as much Earth material—the discarded EVA suits, bulbs, batteries, and broken debris— as possible. They placed it in the first lander and sealed it up. They were able to restart the battered rover, climbed onto it, and drove around the perimeter of the area, picking up a few pieces of broken creatures and putting them in bio-isolation containers for future analysis. Norm also gathered some new soil samples and was astounded when he found another lifeform, a tiny wormlike creature, apparently feeding on an arachnid carcass. He quickly placed it in a sample bottle and sealed it in another container. Norm finally had enough; he was ready to go. They parked the rover, looked around once more and headed for DEV Two.

While Norm and David were making their last brief sortie, Sergey and Oreen were studying the latest data relayed from the *Kat*. It was information concerning the last plotted positions of any vortices or openings in the stormy shell layer. There had been few if any in the close-range area of the *Kat*. Several small eyes had been detected in the layer at great distances, which made complete analysis of the features impossible. The time delay for deciphering the messages also complicated finding a suitable feature for their exit. After considerable review and computer estimation of the present position of the best target, they selected the one with the most potential and locked in the intercept coordinates.

It was mostly guesswork. The eye might dissipate or change direction by the time they got to it. As soon as they lifted off, they would begin scanning the underside of the shell looking for other potential targets. As far as Sergey was concerned, they basically had one chance and had to make it on the first try. It was possible to make two attempts, but dependent on total fuel consumption.

The last thing that David and Norm did was to place a small time capsule, a United Nations flag, and a plaque on the rock ridge beside the lander. Oreen turned on the floodlights to illuminate them, and Sergey recorded the brief ceremony for posterity. Norm uttered the final sounds from the surface, though as he looked around he had a hard time mouthing the few words. Norm said simply: "We came in peace, and we leave in peace." The words seemed hollow and unreal as he surveyed the destruction around him. *If this was some more intelligent lifeform, what it would think of their visit?*

With the ceremony completed and feeling rather sad about the confrontations with the planet's inhabitants, they climbed the ladder, said goodbye and closed the exterior hatch behind them. DEV Two was now ready to lift off with them within the safe confines of the lock, but it would be better to wait, if possible, until they were inside the cabin with the others.

That meant another one to two hours for complete decontamination and final change to the new flight suits. The only lights illuminating the landing zone and Base Camp area were those of DEV Two. All of the other lighting was extinguished. The radar screen showed considerable activity surrounding their position. As long as the visitors kept their distance, there would be no further confrontation or destruction.

The laser weapon beneath the fuselage could not cover all approaches to the craft, but the spotlights could. Oreen continuously rotated the spots toward the closest blips on the screen. Sergey would aim the weapon when he could. The creatures were out roving without a storm, and they were getting braver or more tolerant of the white lights. This was their most nervous and alert passage of time waiting until the last of the crew and lander were ready for lift off.

Two of the creatures suddenly made a charge toward the craft. Oreen hit them both with the high beams, but they stopped only briefly, and then proceeded to move forward toward DEV One. Sergey did not hesitate. He could get the first one in his field of fire, but the second one was just out of effective range. He fired two quick bursts. One hit the creature, and it backed away at high speed. The other backed away more slowly.

The blasts awoke Roberto and startled Moses, who had been nodding off. Shouts of: "What's happening!" echoed from the decontamination lock.

Oreen studied the screen and looked at Sergey. Another group of three or four smaller blips was advancing from the right and two large ones began moving in from the left.

Moses looked over their shoulders in the front row and pointed to the weather radar screen. "There's a small storm moving in again. It's still about thirty minutes away at its present speed and direction, but I say let's get the hell out of here."

Sergey did not wait another minute or attempt another shot. His engines were rotated for takeoff and he had warmed them up. He shouted, "Buckle in," to his crew and warned David and Norm to secure themselves with the mesh restraints in the pressure lock. Oreen made sure that Roberto and Moses were secured in the back seats and strapped herself down. The nearest two creatures were only a little over one hundred meters away and closing.

"Stand by for lift off!" Sergey increased power to his engines steadily and large plumes of dust began to rise around the craft. He counted down: "Five, four, three, two, one."

As he reached one, Oreen shouted: "Go, go, get us out of here!" The nearest creature was charging the lander. Dust covered its approach.

DEV Two rose rapidly under full power. The engines roared, and the searing heat kept the huge creature from dragging the lander back to the surface. "Damn, that was close," Oreen said, watching the rear video and altimeter as they climbed through one thousand meters. "I hope I fried that thing," Sergey added.

The DEV climbed steadily toward the threatening shell layer far above. At ten thousand meters Sergey slowed their ascent and leveled off. He wanted his copilot beside him so that Oreen could concentrate on nothing but the shell layer above. They had been in the lock for just over an hour and were safe enough for now.

David and Norm removed their soiled EVA suits and left them behind in the lock. The entered the main cabin and put on fresh flight suits for the trip back to the *Kat*. If they made it, they would go through intensive isolation and decontamination again there anyway. David assumed his position in the copilot's seat, and Norm took up position in the second row to assist Oreen. They were ready for the climb out and the search for a way back through the frightening shell layer.

The crew had another good look at the dimly-lighted scenery below. Jagged mountains were discernible only because of the orange glow of scattered lava flows from the active volcanoes. The dendritic patterns glowed with pale neon-green hues, winding through sinuous valleys, now rapidly disappearing below. The contrast of subdued colors against the background of perpetual darkness looked inhospitable for life. But they had found it, a lifeform unfamiliar with—and unfriendly toward—the visitors from Earth.

Sergey guided his craft skyward, accelerating again, distancing them from the surface below, while pointing straight toward the menace above. David and Oreen scanned the foreboding ceiling overhead with the multiple radars. They could paint a useable picture of the underside of the barrier but could not see through it. To escape they had to find the base of one of the vortex openings. Any attempt to penetrate the clouds directly was suicidal.

DEV Two climbed at a steady rate. Sergey followed the course set by the computer for the planned intercept with the tracked vortex. It was still a fair distance away. David watched the fuel gauges, and noticed that Sergey kept his eyes on them as much as any of his many instruments and controls. They were all uncomfortable being pushed back in their seats. Oreen was concerned and worried about the additional discomfort that she knew Roberto and Moses had to be feeling.

When they approached what should have been the rendezvous point with their potential exit, the monitors and radar screens showed no target. Either the eye in the clouds had dissipated, or it had changed directions. For whatever reason, the path through the cloud layer was gone. The only thing evident on the monitors was the terrible turbulent tumult before them.

A search for a new target was necessary, but would waste their limited supply of fuel. Any wait or delay would produce the same result. They needed a quick solution. To continue to cruise around risked running out of fuel and dropping back to a certain death. Even if they could land again, their supplies were limited and the reception committee left a lot to be desired. If they flew directly into the layer, the ship would be torn apart. Their choices were extremely limited, and the finality of the results very definite. They had to find an opening, but where?

The situation was beginning to turn desperate when Oreen began rocking in her seat and started to remove her helmet. The cabin was pressurized and filled with a safe breathing mixture, but the helmets were always worn at such a time. She removed her helmet and shook her head and hair as if freeing it from something. Her eyes were closed, and her face had the look of a person in a deep trance.

Oreen felt a strange surge of energy deep within her brain, a feeling unlike any previous. She became cognizant that her senses knew that the nanos were working inside her. Long ago she had stopped worrying about their presence in her system. Knowing she had been exposed to them and inhaled them, Oreen always recognized that they were there. Now she was more keenly aware of them and knew that they were doing as programmed, improving whatever they worked on, and making most essential repairs. Oreen's own brain seemed to be programming them in much the same way as the mainframe onboard supercomputer controlled them. Her perceptive abilities were exploding; she felt out-of-body once again.

Standing ridged in the cabin, Oreen removed one glove revealing a slight iridescence on her fingertips, perceptible in the low ambient cabin light. She raised the ungloved hand and pointed, her eyes still completely closed. Oreen passed into a deeper trance. She pointed and mumbled something unintelligible to the others.

Sergey turned the nose of the lander in the direction she pointed. Oreen's body turned as she re-aligned her arm up with the nose of their craft. She again moved slightly to her right, and again he turned until she lined up with the front of DEV Two. She pointed upward, and he began climbing more. Oreen never uttered a word but continued to point and seemingly direct the craft from an unseen force or sense of direction.

They climbed and followed her directions for more than ten minutes. No one questioned her or said a word. Suddenly she spoke and pointed without opening her eyes. "There," she said and then repeated, "There." At almost the same moment the computer detected a potential target and began depicting an upward-sloping funnel in the ominous layer above. They were fast approaching it, but the opening was still several minutes away.

Moses spoke through strain and pain. "My God, she's found it. She's found our ticket home! Thank you, Oreen, and thank you God Almighty."

Sergey pushed his engines to maximum thrust shouting, "We're not there yet!" Oreen collapsed back into her seat. Norm quickly checked her face and eyes. Oreen acknowledged that she was all right with a strained-but-broad smile as Norm assisted her back into her helmet. They were again pushed back into their seats. Sergey had a course set and the computer took over. He accelerated and they chased the hole in the shell. They closed the front view port cover and prepared for the encounter with the wall of darkness and turbulence ahead. As they approached the opening, a better picture of the shape and degree of penetration of the layer began to emerge. The eye was formed by a narrow cyclone, spinning incredibly fast, piercing the layer completely. The cone of more stable air within thinned from the top and bottom, resembling an hourglass shape. The waist or narrowest point was almost midway, but it looked wide enough for passage.

Sergey hit the target dead center on the way down to the surface. David remembered the horror of their first attempt to penetrate the layer after leaving orbit. Everyone realized that all of their efforts would be for naught if Sergey made a mistake this time. The pilot was cool and collected, total concentration on his craft and flight plan.

Roberto was now semi-awake and following Sergey's every move with intense interest. He was fighting the numbing discomfort and effects of the painkillers and medicines in his body. The six space travelers were on edge and concentrating on the final maneuvers, which would reunite them with the *Kat*—or spell their doom.

Oreen's energies were spent. Her mental and physical fortitude on the surface had been heroic and tireless. Her uncanny gift of inexplicable sensory abilities had guided them to a potential escape route. She was now overcome by complete exhaustion, the tension and fatigue evident on her face. If they ever did make it back, they all recognized her special contributions to this mission. Jason's choice of her as the fourth member of the first landing party had already proven to be a masterful decision.

The monitors showed their craft starting into the narrow tunnel twisting wildly before them. To Roberto, the entrance looked very similar to the vortex he had entered with DEV One. He remembered the way the funnel had moved and closed in on them as they had made contact with the wall of high-velocity wind.

Sergey had chosen a course heading up near the left side of the whirlwind. Roberto interrupted the silence. "Sergey, go for the starboard side. Stay away from the left." Sergey didn't hesitate and immediately steered the lander to the right side. Roberto's intuition or experience was proven correct only seconds later, when the storm twisted again, and closed in rapidly from the left. It happened so fast that Sergey would have had no time to react. Roberto struggled to say more but could not. The G-force was just too great in his weakened condition and his breathing was becoming quite labored. Fear began to replace the adrenaline rush of escape and the gut-wrenching terror of not finding a way back through. Roberto still had optimism for their return to the mother ship, but he was losing hope that he would make it alive.

Several thin layers of unstable atmosphere shook the craft violently and began to impede their speed and upward progress. Sergey fought for control as they approached the narrowest part of the hourglass. Fingers of swirling tornadic winds lashed at the craft from the narrowing sides of the bleak storm wall. This was the moment of greatest danger. David's white knuckles held his redundant copilot controls as he watched the cursor enter the narrowest point. The sides of the funnel were almost touching directly ahead. All that Sergey could do now was aim as best he could, hold on and hope for the best.

They grazed one side and then the other. DEV Two began to spin wildly around its long axis. They were spun forward, propelled like a bullet fired from a rifled gun barrel. The spinning, shaking, and pressure on their bodies were very close to unbearable. It lasted only a couple of minutes but left them all ragged and nauseated. Now they were more than halfway through and rising through a steadily widening cone of more stable atmosphere.

David was able to maintain consciousness. They had lost some cabin pressure. When he looked at Sergey he was shocked. Through his clear visor he could see Sergey's eyes were bright red. Blood was streaming from his nose and running from the corner of one eye. David realized that he could hear absolutely nothing. He could taste blood and bile.

David looked around the cabin. The spinning slowed and Sergey regained control. Oreen was unconscious. Moses was awake but grimacing in obvious horrible pain. Norm looked OK, and he was speaking, but David could hear nothing he said. Roberto looked pretty bad, grim in fact, and appeared to be unconscious. There was nothing else anyone could do for him at present. Suddenly Sergey gagged and slumped forward toward the guidance controls before him. He had held on as long as he could, but conditions had overcome him.

The lander began to change attitude. David pushed Sergey away from the controls and struggled to keep him back and redirect the craft. Norm forced himself to reach around and hold Sergey as David took over to fly the craft. Norm continued to speak, but David did not acknowledge. He checked the communicator's links, and they all looked normal. David could still hear nothing.

They were now three-quarters of the way through the layer, and David opened the view port cover. The DEV was again jostled several times by crosscurrents and pockets of unstable air. When the window covers moved aside, David could see stars twinkling ahead.

They had expended more than ninety percent of their fuel and were still at maximum thrust. The gauge continued to drop steadily as they approached the top of the stormy layer. DEV Two still had a sizable distance to go to obtain orbit, but they were going to make it through.

Norm suddenly realized that David could not hear. He pointed to the fuel gauge and held up three fingers; meaning only three percent of the fuel remained, including the added reserve tank. They could both sense the diminishing gravity pulling at them. It would be close, but they had momentum and were reaching orbital velocity and distance from the planet. Norm pulled off his glove and crossed his fingers. David acknowledged by nodding his head. Norm's glove began to float in front of them.

As the lander slipped into a low orbit the engines began to sputter out. David quickly switched them off, with the digital fuel gauge reading less than one percent. Norm grasped David's shoulder and said, "Nice going, David. You did it. We are in orbit." David did not hear a sound and only acknowledged with a slow nod. Moving his head hurt with intensity.

DEV Two had attained a very low orbit. The six knew that orbital decay was now the most serious problem and their major concern. They had to be picked up by the Kat before their orbit decayed and DEV Two began being pulled back. The gravity pull was inconsistent and only a fraction of Earth's, but they were not free from the clutches of the Stealth Planet yet.

David signaled Norm by hand that he could not hear. Norm typed a message onto the monitor screen for David indicating that he would signal the

Kat, while David began to assist his fellow crewmembers. Norm prepared a message and fired it off to the *Kat.* Next he tried direct-voice communications and checked to see that all the locator transponders and lights were working. While he waited a reply to his voice hail, he began calculating how long they had before they began falling back.

— § —

Jason and Rod could not believe it when Norm's voice broke the radio silence. Norm clearly stated that they were through the barrier and had attained a very low orbit. His final words were, "Out of fuel; crew in bad shape; help us quickly; we need your assistance ASAP."

"They made it!" Jason screamed. "Action, stations, full alert! We're moving out now!"

Alarms went off throughout the *Kat.* Crewmembers dropped what they were doing and scrambled to action stations. Phil Allen began the propulsion systems startup. Margie hastened to plot a course to the source of the voice transmission. She located the emergency position finders within minutes and cross-plotted the location of DEV Two with the computer's assistance. Phil was pleased when Margie reported that they were not too far away and still on the same side of the planet.

Margie finished calculating their location and fed the information into the main guidance system. She also sent the bad news to Jason. "Commander, the lander is a little over nine thousand kilometers distant and in a very low orbit. They made it through the layer, but just barely. My estimate is that they are going to start losing their orbital position almost immediately and start falling back in about one hour."

Phil Allen had already brought the *Kat* about and was heading back toward the position of the lander at a speed that would put them there in about one hour. Jason thought over Margie's message and made an immediate decision. "Phil, put the pedal to the metal. If Margie's calculations are correct, we have about an hour to get there, find them, latch onto the DEV, recover it and get back to a stable orbit. Normal recovery alone takes over an hour. Let's get there as fast as possible and start figuring out a way to make an extra speedy recovery."

Excess velocity and acceleration while in orbit would make controlling and stopping his craft more difficult. Phil began to speed up as soon as Jason gave the order. Jason sent a message to Mission Control indicating that the rescue from the surface had been a success; the flight back into orbit a success, but the recovery of the landing craft and crew was going to be tough. He ended by giving them a few details of his unfinished plan to intercept and snatch them from a decaying orbit.

Jason wanted Margie ready with the manipulator arm. He was afraid that they might only get one chance. As a backup he planned to have a tethered space walker attach a heavy tow cable and drag them higher if need be. If that failed he was not sure what they would attempt next. Other suggested ideas from the crew were a little too dangerous, but at this point, desperate measures might end up being the only choice.

In forty-five minutes, Phil had closed the distance and was forced to begin deceleration. Aboard DEV Two the crew members were suffering from various aches and maladies but were much more concerned about their worsening orbital situation. They were already being pulled back toward the surface slowly but measurably. Norm and David were feeling bad but could handle the situation. Oreen was weak, Moses pale and sweating, and Roberto's condition was grim. Sergey was dizzy and disoriented but helping as much as possible.

David made the decision to fire the engines for one last burst in the direction of the fast-approaching mother ship. He informed Phil Allen of the decision so that Phil would not have to drop any lower. The *Kat* could also compensate for the movement of the lander toward them and try to not overshoot the target at such a critical time. Norm and the rest of the crew felt and heard the last engine fire and listened as it sputtered out all the while watching the view ports and monitors with a sense of desperation, hoping for visual contact with the *Kat*.

The mother ship looked resplendent with her running lights aglow when they first saw her. It was a heartwarming sight. They watched the braking retros firing and they stared, the ship growing steadily larger. The *Kat* glided into full view. The familiar voices of their crewmates filled their helmets with words of encouragement.

Nearing each other, large hangar doors opened and unfolded. The mechanical manipulator arm was already extending, and a tiny figure with a jetpack was moving out of the hangar at the end of a fine line. Rod was not considered for a descent mission, but he was determined to secure the lander—even if he had to grab and hold it with his own hands.

Both vehicles were precariously close to the stormy layer below. It and gravity appeared to be pulling both vehicles steadily downward. Neither was entirely out of danger, but the smaller vehicle now had no power and was drifting helpless. Phil was maneuvering the *Kat* dangerously close. He would be forced by circumstances to demonstrate his greatest piloting prowess.

Margie's mechanical arm appeared to be extended to the limit, and the tiny space person was moving beyond its reach. They heard Jason warning Rod to be careful. One small mistake could be fatal, but he ignored the warning and moved ever closer. Phil brought the *Kat* masterfully as close as he possibly could. They were attempting a first, an extremely dangerous running catch. Officials at NASA would have had a fit and would have never allowed such dangerous action. Jason was gambling on the skills and desires of his entire crew.

Distance figures were counted down. The commander watched in near awe, as the tiny figure of Rod slammed hard into the side of the lander, but somehow hung on tight, and began the task of frantically pulling in the heavier cable attached to his tether with one arm, and then somehow managed to pull the cable to him and attach it to the lander in mere moments. Miraculously and against good judgment, a cable now coupled both craft. Margie began to move the manipulator arm closer.

Phil informed Jason that they had to pull out now. Jason just kept watching the arm and ordered Rod to get back inside the hangar. He jetted away from the lander, waving to her comrades inside. Margie only had one chance to hook onto and start pulling in the lander. She skillfully moved the arm toward the coupling connection and closed the gap to inches. Instead of the customary slow, meticulous methodology, the arm swerved toward the coupling socket and engaged it in one motion.

"I've got them!" Margie shouted in a high-pitched, excited voice. She had tried something warned against and entirely wrong, and it had worked. She was already pulling them toward the hangar bay.

Jason breathed a huge sigh of relief when the lander moved even closer.

"We've got to go!" shouted Phil.

"All right, move out at slow speed as she brings them in." Jason had won this round against his Stealth Planet foe and was not about to lose another. Moving during recovery was also not even in the book, but in this case they had no real choice. It was move or face disaster. The *Kat* had dropped much too close to the turbulence below. Margie was bringing in the lander many times faster than the prescribed manner for normal recovery. As she neared the hangar doors she said: "Commander, you must cease acceleration. The vibrations may cause me to hit the side and damage the doors or knock the lander loose."

Jason knew that they had gained some altitude. He signaled Phil to stop acceleration. Margie took her chances. Everyone stared at the monitors covering the recovery as she gently swung the lander into its berth, bumping one side once and hitting the near side twice. But the lander was in, and Jason ordered the doors closed and secured, and told Phil to get to a very high orbit and cruise there.

The impossible had just been accomplished. Jason had both landing parties back aboard, as well as a treasure of samples, and they would soon be safe again in a stable orbit. To this point, the mission had been disastrous—but successful beyond their wildest dreams.

Though battered and wounded, his landing teams were secure. They and their craft would be quarantined in the hangar for the prescribed period for complete isolation and scrutiny. It would be tough on everyone, but the precaution was necessary and absolutely mandated. Doc, Jason's new love, had volunteered to join the landing parties and remain in the hanger and board the lander alone to stay with them and care for them. This was not mandated by the prearranged protocol and it was controversial and dangerous, but the injured needed her.

Jason planned to have a gala celebration when they did emerge. They would have plenty of time to dictate a full report while confined. He also already planned to recognize and recommend the highest awards for their stalwart efforts and service far beyond the call of normal duty. They had truly personified "all the right stuff".

21

REUNION

FOR THE FIRST TIME in over a year, Jason felt a little more relaxed. Throughout the preparation and journey, he never had much time to reflect and unwind; to escape from near continuous worry. There were days of tedium and days of excitement, but he had always been on edge and ever watchful. With his full crew back aboard and the eventful-but-successful landing now behind him, he was more than ready to kick back a bit.

While Doc assessed the conditions of the landing parties and formulated her prognoses and diagnoses, the Commander began to formulate his report for Mission Control. His superiors and support personnel were eager to receive his official mission status report, complete with his comments and personal observations. Jason was a stickler for details. He had fed them a steady stream of timely reports, but this time he planned to let them anticipate and wait for the next one.

During the haste to rescue their comrades, Jason sent no word of their actions or progress to Mission Control. Jason needed to further assess the situation and was not planning to prepare his report until he had a much better idea about the condition of the crewmembers now sealed in isolation.

Doc had gathered everything she could to evaluate the returning group when she entered the hanger bay. Now back from her tethered space walk, she waited for the doors to close and the hangar to repressurize.

Jason was worried about her. He watched as she waited to enter the lander through the isolation lock, realizing now that she would be exposed to any dangers brought back aboard from the surface before the prescribed isolation period had expired. Her medical equipment and supplies were unwieldy loads, and he wondered if it all would fit in the lock with her. He watched her enter the blackened lander when the hatch opened and felt sadness as it closed behind her. Doc was inside with the crew and Jason understood just how dependent the returnees were on her skills.

Inside the lander everything was already crowded and in shambles. Instead of caring for the worst-off first, Doc decided to try to get Norm and Oreen into shape to help her. Norm was white and dizzy, but he was able to help her as soon as she finished checking his vital signs. Oreen was still weak but also somehow able to help her organize the cramped interior and begin cleaning up the mess. They were hungry and thirsty, but Doc thought that they better wait to eat until the inside of the DEV was checked for contaminants. Eating would wait until later, even though they needed the energy. The doctor prepared some supplement and vitamin booster shots and gave them to the entire crew.

Sergey was her next target, and she had him feeling more rejuvenated in only a few minutes. He would have red eyes for a while, but he appeared to be in good shape. David had ruptured eardrums and possible other inner-ear damage. He would have hearing and potential balance difficulties for a while, but she could find no other major problems. She administered some medication to relax his nauseated stomach and digestive tract and checked him over as quickly as possible.

Doc drew blood, collected other samples and set them all aside for analysis and then she went to work on Roberto. She marveled at the wonderful job that Oreen and Norm had done to patch up his wounds. From the outside things looked all right, but she gasped as she removed the last bandages. The large gash in his leg was open and oozing, but the blood vessels were sealed and he was losing only traces of blood. It was a miracle that he had not bled to death. That was the good news. The bad news was the obvious sign of infection beginning to form in places within the wound.

Doc picked up some swabs from her medical kit, dabbed gently at the wound, and looked to see some telltale sign, but what she could see with the naked eye told her nothing. Roberto was oblivious to her actions. She attached leads and a finger cuff, and began further assessing his condition. He was showing signs of shock and his vitals were not good. His condition was already critical. She worked over him feverishly. "Roberto, Roberto, can you hear me?"

"Doc, we pumped him pretty full of painkillers. We didn't overdo it did we?" Oreen was concerned that she had overdosed him.

"No Oreen, he's not OD'd. If you hadn't blunted the trauma, he'd be dead. He's in shock, and I don't like the look of that leg at all."

Doc cut away more of the uniform, completely removing the bottom in order to see how far the burn-like damage continued. She checked his genitals, finding another burned patch on the rear of his scrotum. Trauma to the leg was severe and finding a way to save the limb became her chief priority.

The antibiotics administered by his crewmates may have slowed down the infection, but there was no doubt that Roberto was in extreme danger. She gave Roberto even more pain medication but nothing else. She had to slow his metabolism to a crawl without killing him. She had no means to chill his body while in the DEV, so drugs had to do. Doc then removed several small tissue samples to go with her swabs for analysis and scrutiny under the microscope. If Roberto had an infection from Earth-based microbes, she knew pretty much what she was up against. If an agent from the surface of the planet below had caused his infection, she was dealing with something completely new.

Roberto had been through a lot, and considering the severity of his wounds, he was lucky to still be breathing on his own. His pulse was weak and his breathing now uneven and strained. He had an elevated temperature and erratic blood pressure. It was unlikely that he would regain consciousness even without the painkillers. She had a very sick patient and did not have the luxury of her hospital module for treating him. His condition was critical, and her resources for treatment limited in the confines of the lander. They would need to get him out of there as soon as possible if he had any chance to survive.

Oreen was sick with worry and grief for Moses as much as feeling bad from her own physical condition. Doc recognized that fact too. Moses had regained consciousness with Doc's assistance and insisted that the rest of the crew be checked out first. Moses was tough, but he was almost as serious as Roberto in some ways at this point. He too had a fever and was sweating profusely. He was given a little water, and an IV was already adding liquids to his badly taxed system. He was awake but still a little incoherent.

The reclining back seats became hospital beds for Moses and Roberto. Every nonessential object in the lander was packed in bags and placed in an empty cargo hold through an internal hatchway. Oreen set up a small lab for the blood work and analysis of their body chemistry. The data was fed directly to the ship's main computers.

Once Doctor Ann Pritchard got them all comfortable and as stable as possible, she went to work to evaluate the lab data. Oreen prepared the initial samples with professionalism. Doc began the methodical evaluation of their chemistries and biological factors. She was particularly interested in the blood work from Roberto and Moses to see if the computer identified any foreign antibodies or agents.

It did not take long to get her answer. Roberto had a very high white blood cell count and very strange antibody traces. His body was at work trying desperately to fight off some type of infection but was not doing a very good job. In fact, from what she could tell, it was losing the battle. Something was attacking his white and red blood cells and beginning to devour them. Deprived of a percentage of his essential white and red blood cells, he was losing a continuous and ever-intensifying battle against an unknown invader.

Doc checked Moses' blood samples, expecting to find the same thing. Her suspicion was confirmed. She held her breath when she checked the next sample that was Norm's. He appeared to be the healthiest at the moment. As she scanned the slide holding his sample she breathed out a huge sigh of relief. There was no sign of the deadly activity apparent in both Roberto and Moses. Norm's blood sample looked normal. She felt better. Norm appeared to be shaken but fine. Doc went through the same procedure with each of the samples multiple times, using both Norm and Oreen's assistance for the additional screenings. The tests confirmed that the pest was restricted to Moses and Roberto so far. Given a few days rest, unless infected, the other members of the landing teams would make complete recoveries.

Doc decided to let Jason know as soon as the initial evaluations were completed. She gave him the bad news directly and made no attempt to hide it from the rest of the crew. They would have to remain in quarantine unless things took a big turn for the worse. She ordered a bio-isolation shield for the infirmary and a corridor leading to it. If they had to move Roberto or Moses soon, she wanted to minimize the risk of exposure to the remaining crew of the *Kat*.

Jason dozed off while waiting for information from Ann. Hours passed. Her report put him temporarily back on edge. He received a communiqué from Mission Control inquiring as to progress with the landing-party recovery. He sent a terse response that the lander and all crew had been recovered, and that Doc was evaluating their condition. It was brief and to the point and sure to disappoint his compatriots at Mission Control. Jason was in no mood to deal with bureaucratic paperwork and reports at this moment. He knew that his new change in attitude was the result of the psychological letdown induced by the fact that the prime part of the mission was now over.

David, Sergey, and Norm wanted out of the lander. Oreen was content to stay with Moses. Norm wanted to begin preliminary evaluation of some of his samples. The materials could be safely moved to the isolation lab once they could open the hatch and begin decontaminating the exterior of the storage containers.

Norm could do little else but wait with the rest at this point. He remembered the last sample containers with the live, captured, arachnid creatures. They had been sealed in the bottles since capture, and he was sure that, if they were like Earth creatures at all, they had consumed their entire breathable atmosphere and had perished in the bottles. It was too bad that he would not be able to observe a live one up close.

Norm checked the storage locker inside the cabin where he had carefully placed the two bottles. He opened it and retrieved one translucent plastic container holding the captive.

Oreen recognized the container and expressed her complete disapproval. "Norm, if you open that thing in here you're going to need a pry bar to get my foot out of your butt."

"Cute, Oreen," Norm responded, "I can definitely tell that you're feeling a little better."

David could not quite make out what they were saying, but he could tell by their actions that something was brewing. Norm removed the plastic bottle from the storage space and examined it. David watched in mild amusement when Norm pretended to open the container.

Oreen's face never changed. Either she knew that he wasn't that stupid, or her sixth sense was back in working order. Norm held the bottle in front of one of the overhead lights and saw that the little creature looked very much like a dead counterpart back on Earth. He shook the bottle very slightly and was amazed by the instant flurry of activity inside. The tiny creature sprang to life and darted around inside the bottle. Norm shielded the bottle from the direct light and placed it back into the darkened locker.

Everyone saw the arachnid movement and Norm's haste to put it away again in the storage vault. "Wow," he said as he turned away from the small door. "It is still very much alive and hopefully still will be when we get out of here. Doc, what can you do to get me out of here soon?"

Norm did not have to plead his case very long or emphatically. Ann was an excellent physician as well as a scientist at heart. She recognized the value of obtaining information from a live specimen of the lifeform. After studying Roberto and Moses' situation in detail, she made a difficult but necessary decision. Regardless of what the mission directives stated, she had to end their isolation. She would have a much better chance to further evaluate and counteract the mysterious infection now carried by Roberto and Moses with the use of the Kat's main medical facility. Without immediate additional treatment, both infected crewmen might not survive. Their chances of survival were many times better in the infirmary.

Doc signaled Jason and decided on a private conversation, at least from his end. It would be difficult to prevent eavesdropping in the lander, and she did not want to keep her conversation secret from the isolated group. Jason usually went by the book. His military background strongly influenced his decision-making process. But he had launched the rescue mission on his own initiative. If he had waited... The thought chilled her, for she knew that the six patients around her would all now be dead.

"Jason," she began, "I want to get Roberto and Moses out of here ASAP. I will take full responsibility for the decision. I cannot give them adequate attention here, and their condition warrants immediate transfer to the infirmary."

"It's very noble of you to take the responsibility, but it is your call, Ann. I will back your decision fully."

"There's another reason," Ann continued. "One of Norm's bugs, which he captured alive, is still very much alive." The commander then heard Norm's excited voice in the background. "Jason, if you get me and this critter out of here, I may be able to duplicate its atmosphere in the bio-isolation lab. I know that this is against most basic rules, but we have prepared for this contingency and are trained for it."

"I already have the rest of the crew making the preparations," Jason said. "Leaving all of you in there is not going to be part of the plan."

The group in isolation was already tired of the cramped conditions within the crowded lander. Doc was grateful for the answer until she looked at the tissue samples for a third time. They had changed. Under the scope the first tissue sample from Roberto was smaller, as if somehow shrinking or being consumed.

"Oh God! Jason. We can't come out of isolation. This stuff looks nasty, and I still don't even know if it's infectious."

"Ann, we have another problem. Casey just went into contractions. She's having some problems."

"Can't help you there, Jason. I can tell you all what to do, and the rest will come naturally."

"That doesn't look like a viable option, Doc." It was the voice of Margie. She was with Casey comforting her and helping her breathe. Rod was with her too, deep concern etched in his face. "Doc, something's not right, she's having real problems, bleeding, and in horrible pain." Doc could hear her irregular breathing. She was in early stages of labor with obvious overtones that should not have been there.

Doc faced a real quandary. Her mind raced as she pondered her options, and she felt her own elevated pulse rate climbing.

"Margie, you will have to deliver that baby." Her statement was almost an order.

"Doc, she will need a C-section, and none of us are qualified surgeons except for you."

"Margie, I can talk you through it or someone on this crew must deliver the baby.

"I don't know nothin' bout birthin' no babies." Margie knew she could not.

"I'm dead serious, Margie."

"So am I doc, she needs you, not one of us."

"Crap, I can't be in two bloody places at the same time." At about the exact moment she finished uttering the words, all of the alarms on the monitors attached to Roberto went off. Doc responded at once. Roberto was in full cardiac arrest. His eyes were rolled back, and he was not breathing. The situation quickly got worse. Frenetic energy replaced conversation. They attached a defibrillator and began heart massage. Tracheal tubes were inserted and oxygen pumped into his lungs. When nothing happened, Doc removed the tubes and started full CPR to no avail.

"Ann, what's wrong?" Jason was pleading for information.

"I'm losing him. I shouldn't be, but I am." She resumed her work, turning over the CPR to Norm.

They struggled for another fifteen minutes. Doc slumped over Roberto and asked: "Why?" She added: "He's dead." Her pronunciation had finality to it. No one could believe what had happened. Moses was awake, looking much like he had just seen a ghost. Eyes wide, tears running, he already mourned for his close friend and compatriot.

Jason was stunned, speechless, and profoundly shaken. What had been the complete joy of recovering his crew was replaced by a hollow melancholy. His grief was short lived as an agonizing wail from Casey filled the entire ship. Things were coming apart at the seams; a sudden nightmare was swarming up around him. One thing was certain, either Doc was coming to Casey, or Casey was going to Doc.

"Crew, we must complete the bio-secure transfer chambers from the compartments adjoining the quarantine returnees and Doc. We will place Casey in that area so that they can open the quarantine area and bring her in. It's that or watch her die during delivery and lose her the baby too. Doc, you will bring her in and do the delivery. That is an order; get to work!"

Doc closed Roberto's blank eyes and covered his face. "We need to get him in a suit and zip it shut and seal it. We can't contain this for long, with things happening like they are, but we can isolate and eliminate as much as possible."

Both separated sections of the crew went to work to finish clearing and sanitizing for as "clean" a transfer as possible. When finished, two compartments adjoining the hanger were empty, and Casey was moved to the one closest to the isolated hanger. An empty compartment separated Casey from the healthy crewmembers. Once secured and cleared, Jason gave the OK to the quarantined group to go get Casey. Norm and Sergey had her in with Doc in less than five minutes, and none too soon. The risk of infection to the baby and Casey would have to be taken. Casey's baby had already been exposed to nanos and now would be subjected to the new menace too.

Doc went to work assessing the situation with her new patient. Casey's pleading look through grimacing eyes told her all she needed to know. She administered a local block type of anesthesia and prepared for an emergency delivery. Doc did not have the luxury of much time to do a more thorough examination of her new patient. Casey was conscious, which was a surprise to her. The unborn infant was showing signs of acute stress. Sylvia and Rod had taken blood samples for her and had fed them into the medical computer system for detailed analysis. The results were not good. Ann had two new patients in very serious condition.

One thing was certain to Doc; she had to take the baby by c-section immediately, or she would lose the unborn child. Casey was stressed, but mothers were known to survive incredible trauma, if the child was not stillborn. Ann scrubbed up again, while Oreen disinfected Casey's lower abdomen and prepared to make the necessary incision.

In less than five minutes, without further apparent complication, Doc handed a tiny pink form to Oreen. She frantically hurried to stop local bleeding and close the incision. There was no movement from the infant. It lay in Oreen's arms, motionless, no cries of newborn lungs gulping in their first sweet breaths of air. Oreen did not panic. She cooed while she cleaned the child, carefully wiping away anything from the baby's airways. In one swift motion, Doc swept the baby from her arms and blew in its face, suspending the child upside down to pat its back. Nothing happened. She began gentle CPR and urged the child to breath. Casey's eyes looked like they were about to glaze over, when a tiny cry delighted the crew. A chorus of weak newborn screeches followed, in sync with cheers from the crew.

"It's a girl, Casey, a beautiful baby girl." Oreen was at her side comforting her, encouraging a response, while Doc held the baby near Casey's face. Casey managed a very weak smile, as Doc brushed her cheek with the wailing infant, holding the two together, hoping that the mother-daughter bond would give her strength and a will to live. The child was saved, the mom alive, but Doc knew that neither was even close to being out of danger.

"Rest, Casey, she's here and needs a mother." Doc and Oreen then began assessing the newborn, checking the tiny squirming figure, counting fingers and toes, when Doc stopped to look close at the miniature digits on her right hand. Oreen could not help but notice it too. The little girl was born with silver-purple sheen on her fingertips, the now unmistakable signature of nano exposure and ingestion. Analysis of the infant's blood before birth showed the signs of nano activity in the blood shared with her mother. The quasi-luminous fingertips, undetectable before birth, were an overt sign of nano presence.

Once the newborn was stabilized, Doc began to do what she could to bolster Casey's waning energy. She was completely exhausted from the pre-birth struggle, her body limp and drained. Oreen sat down by Moses and it was not long before the doctor faced another serious problem. Moses was delirious, burning up with fever, coughing deeply and agonizing with each successive chest heave. Doc had been forced to ignore him while Sergey and Norm wiped his brow and did what they could to comfort him.

The baby cried incessantly, needing the touch of her mother, flailing her tiny arms as if reaching out for contact. Doc placed the child on Casey's chest, above the incision and put its lips to her nipple. It worked. The baby began sucking and quieted after only a few seconds.

Moses' state was a quandary, his condition perplexing, and the exact cause of his malady unknown. A diagnosis was easy, but a treatment a total unknown. There was nothing Doc could do to stop the foreign infection that was destroying his body in an insidious manner. She had already lost Roberto, and knew that Moses would not be far behind if she could not stop the deadly progress of the disease.

"Jason, I think that the baby is fine, and Casey will make it if she doesn't slip any further. I can't do anything more for Moses. Right now I'm just terrified that Casey and the baby are in here with us. Moses is getting worse and coughing all over in here."

"Ann, you've done a fine job. We'll take it one step at a time." The commander's voice was strong, his words deliberate and vehement.

Oreen was horrified by the doctor's last words, her faced drained of emotion, a longing in her eyes. "Doc, I think that there is something we could try. I have an idea and a feeling that the baby could be our answer."

Over the next few hours, everyone rested and tried to ingest a few calories. Casey stayed the same, the baby fell fast asleep, and Moses continued to decline at an alarming rate. Doc monitored the infant the closest. She aimed a camera so that Rod could view his daughter and Casey. Probing the innumerable computer files, Ann found nothing to match the symptoms and devastating rapid effects of the new menace killing Moses.

"Oh no, the last blood test shows that the baby is already infected with the alien disease." Doc blurted it out without thinking; she was so shocked to see the result.

Everyone showed the same dismay, except Oreen. She was now staring through the eyepiece, squinting at the activity on the freshly prepared slide. Her eyes beheld something unusual, not noticeable on first glance. She turned to grin at Doc, the others looking at her in disbelief, wondering how she could smile at such grim news.

22

ISOLATION

AFTER DOC STUDIED the slides and several more blood samples from Roberta, the name chosen for his new daughter by Rod, she listened carefully to Oreen's ideas, and pondered the possibility of the concept, and the chances of success. The theory made perfect sense, and with the help of the main lab, anything was possible.

The baby's blood held the key to their plan. Nano activity in the child's blood impeded activity of the virus-like infection. The nano presence in Roberta, working directly with her brain as a substitute computer, initiated a type of defense against the consuming ability of the new invaders. It was almost like the tiny replicators were building a minute screen around each invader, causing them all to move harmlessly to the kidneys for expulsion. If they could isolate and concentrate these factors, they could theoretically create their own serum, inject it into each crewperson, and inoculate them all against the new peril.

It was worth a try, and Ann had no other good ideas. The plan she and Oreen improvised meant they would all suffer the risk. Doc would have to go to the lab to create the antidote, but that meant leaving quarantine, and the potential to spread the infection. Her last communication with Jason had confirmed it. She was infected; the alien disease was active in her blood. Sergey showed traces too. It was spreading. Moses would be dead in less than four hours, a prediction from the computer.

The entire crew of the *Kat* had actually trained for the eventuality of necessary early release from quarantine several times during the voyage. Their removal would not be much different from the prescribed exit from decontamination except for leaving much sooner and having one dying crew person, one weakened new mom, a baby, and one corpse to transport. They also now had a new overriding fear of additional deaths from the alien infection.

Doc, Oreen, and the two patients were ready to move in less than one hour. An immediate shift to the on board hospital was their only chance. David and

Sergey would help move Moses and Casey to the hospital module, and then return to help Norm and to close down DEV Two and secure the hangar. Everything that came back from the surface and was not of use for scientific evaluation or research would be jettisoned to space. Some of Norm's samples and materials were left behind in the cargo holds of the lander. A select few cases of his bounty were taken to the lab and placed in isolation containment there for his immediate and future evaluation.

Casey, as the ship's biologist, had been anxious and eagerly looking forward to joining Norm in the analyses of the new life forms, until her difficult final days before the delivery. Now she was fighting for her life.

Margie was also anticipating getting her hands on some of the photographs and video from the surface. The landing party had attempted to transmit some of the digital pictures from the surface to the *Kat* with fair-to-good success. Since their return, a veritable treasure of digital photos and video had already been downloaded to her system from DEV Two. Margie was also waiting for special cartridges of film taken by the low-light equipment. She and David would have plenty to keep them busy for a long time on their trip back to Earth—provided any of them survived. Margie could hardly wait to hug David. She had almost lost him. She knew that and had hardened herself for that possibility. She thanked God and her lucky stars that he was back, safe and close by again.

The crew of the *Kat* quickly completed all preparations to isolate the parts of the ship through which Doc and the landing party would transport the two non-ambulatory members. It took less than five minutes to actually move them.

Once Doc Pritchard had Casey and Moses secured in her hospital, she asked Oreen to stay and sent David and Sergey back to the hold. There they finished their task of securing DEV Two and returned with Norm and his samples to the lab, one compartment away from the hospital module. The module next to the lab and the hospital became their home during another period of quarantine isolation. At least they would all be more comfortable in this situation. The hangar and the compartments through which they passed were sanitized and vented to space.

David had the computer to use to communicate and to begin working with Margie on the volume of photographic data. Oreen could fuss over Moses, assist Doc, and look over David's shoulder.

Norm and Sergey were like the proverbial kids in a candy store. The crew had set up most of Norm's onboard evaluation apparatus in the lab. There was a bio-isolation unit, and he could barely wait to get to work. While Sergey bathed and cleaned up, Norm began attempting to create a blend of gases suitable for a breathing mixture for his captives. He also wanted to cool things down to a more suitable temperature in the unit. He worked with determination, though a little preoccupied and distracted by Doc's latest challenge. Norm had peeked again at the captive creature before bringing it to the lab, and it had again shown signs of activity, though far diminished from the last time.

Most of the rest of the non-confined crew were scrutinizing everything Norm did. Margie made several suggestions, and Norm thanked her for the assistance. He desperately needed to rest but wanted to keep the captured lifeform alive if there was any possible means to do it. Margie wanted to be in there with Norm but knew very well that Jason would never allow it.

By the time Sergey had cleaned up, Norm had a reasonably close mixture ready and filled the isolation unit with the gases. He prepared a small container into which he transferred the bug. Norm took the precaution of adding a darkening film to the container and placed it in the isolation chamber.

Doc and Oreen continued tending to the patients and working on their experiment. They stopped work in the hospital lab for only a moment to join Norm and watch the release. The doctor also needed to find out if the sputum from the alien creature was the source of this insidious malady infecting them. David was next to clean up, but he wasn't going anywhere. He stopped typing at the terminal in the lab and also turned to observe. Norm placed the plastic bottle holding his prize inside the bio-isolation unit and sealed it in. In addition, he placed a small container of the planet's surface material in the unit. He then reached in, using the thick-gloved handholds, and opened the container of surface material, pouring some into the creature's new home. Lastly, Norm prepared to release the arachniform into his mini-environment. Carefully, he unscrewed the lid and tilted the bottle into the new container. The small beast rolled out looking very much as if it had expired.

Norm was crushed. He was exhausted and ready to drop. The look of dismay on his face was replaced with elation as the bug-like lifeform began to move and immediately scooted to the darkest recess of its new home. He wanted to let the small creature acclimate itself to its new surroundings, but he also wanted to maintain continuous observation.

Oreen made the first comment, "Where's the fly swatter?"

Doc returned to the hospital module and began a more detailed analysis of her patients. The toxic form of life had infected Roberto and Moses and had now spread. Maybe she could create an antitoxin. They now had a live creature from which they might possibly extract or cultivate a cure. She needed to know a lot more about the nature of the affliction affecting her charges. She also had to try to keep the others from contracting it, though her chances seemed small.

The creature could not hide completely. Norm and the crew could now observe and study it on their terms. Its simplicity and strange beauty impressed Norm. It was obvious to all why the computer had made the best-fit description an arachnid. It had eight apparent legs, all shaped the same and a central oval body with no segments, other protrusions, or ornamentation. As rugged and uneven as the planet's surface had been, the arachnid lifeform was the complete antithesis. It was smooth and an almost dull metallic color with no rough edges or other exterior features. With no eyes or antennae or distinctive body parts, it had no front end or head. It was just a smooth rounded body with eight equally featureless legs. The legs appeared to be non-jointed tubes with simple bends. There was no sign of the orifice that spewed the noxious chemical spray.

Even though the landing party had numerous encounters with these creatures on the planet's surface, they had never had a chance to study one up close. All previous encounters had been in storm-cloaked darkness or under extreme duress. Moses had the most extreme face-to-face meeting with an appendage but had remembered little real detail except the strange looking features on the ends of the legs. Now they could all take a close look and scrutinize the "bug" as much as they desired. Everyone wanted to know a great deal more about these unfriendly adversaries.

Norm had to keep everyone away from the creature's new habitat while he prepared another enclosure for the second captive. He wondered if the other spider-like lifeform also still survived. Memory told him that the second captured creature was slightly larger than the first, and it was in an even smaller sample container. He could only hope that it too survived.

David and Sergey helped improvise another suitable enclosure. Norm removed the second plastic bottle from the dark carrying case. This time he did not have to shake the bottle to see action inside. The arachnid sprang to life as soon as the dimmed light in the makeshift lab illuminated it. It scurried around inside the bottle with amazing dexterity; ending up hiding as best it could in the recess of the cap and neck of the bottle. Norm was quick to place it in an area shielded from the lab lights. The creature could move with incredible speed. Transferring it to its container home would need to be done with extreme care.

They were all also awed by the fact that the creatures had survived unharmed in the bottles for quite a long duration. An equivalent sized spider from Earth, in an equivalent sized bottle, would have already used up its air and suffocated. Taken from approximately minus-eighteen degrees Celsius or zero Fahrenheit, the creature had even been able to stand the changes in temperature to its ambient surrounding in the warm-blooded earthlings' vehicle. Norm had not put the bottles in any kind of refrigerated receptacle due to their haste to leave.

Oreen was observing the entire process while Doc continued her analysis. Oreen quickly pointed out the fact that the cave had gotten warmer as they went farther in and there had been lots of those bugs' brethren in there.

Norm acknowledged her astute observation with, "Why didn't I think of that? Man, I am tired. I need some rest."

Sergey helped Norm transfer his other visitor, and then he and Norm decided to allow the creatures to acclimate themselves for a time, while they both took a much-needed rest. David seized the opportunity to take his turn to clean up and get rid of the odor from when he became sick going in for landing. He had freshened up as best he could upon landing but had recently received a number of comments about getting new cologne.

When Sergey and Norm woke up two hours later, Oreen was out cold, and David was ready to take a break too. He remained awake working with Margie on a few of the photos. Oreen lasted a while longer after Norm and Sergey crashed, but she finally relented to bathing and getting some sleep, but only after orders from Doc.

Jason checked on them all repeatedly by telescreen. Casey and Moses were still sedated and their conditions remained unchanged.

Norm added some of the phosphorescent green slime-like lifeform to one of the containers holding the arachnids. He intended to continue to make the creatures' surroundings as hospitable as possible, hoping that they would continue to survive. He placed a container holding some of the slime into the bio-isolation unit, opened the container and transferred some to one of the small habitats. It took a few minutes to prepare the transfer from a small vial of green glowing goo to the arachnid's abode. Sergey helped in every way possible to make a smooth transfer. Once completed, they planned to sit back to wait for a reaction from the creature, but the reaction was immediate. The arachnid literally pounced on the green slime and settled into it with the lower center of its body.

"Look at that!" Norm exclaimed in triumph. "I think that it's famished and diving in for a good meal."

"Could be," Sergey added with encouragement. "We will know for sure if part of the material disappears due to being ingested."

Doc came in to announce that the monitors and her observations indicated that Casey was stable but Moses' condition was now beginning to get even worse. She had isolated the toxin in their systems as a type of alkaloid poisoning working in conjunction with rapid tissue destruction—a double-edged sword. The only way to produce a remedy was to create anti-venom similar to that synthesized for poisonous spider bites on Earth. They had two specimens.

To produce a single dose of anti-venom for normal spider bites, many spiders had to be milked of their venom. But the poison affecting her patients was not concentrated venom injected directly into the victim. In the case of her dying subject, the venom was absorbed into the wound in a low concentration, and its effect was taking place slowly. Doc hoped that they could produce an antitoxin from a small amount of material.

She needed a sample of part of the creature or some of its acrid spew. Norm pointed out that in their very last reconnoiter of the surface around DEV Two before leaving he had gathered a few broken pieces of the creatures. They both knew that this would help them to determine if the body parts carried a possible ingredient.

Norm brought the three cases holding the lifeform parts into their isolation area as the last load from the lander. He knew the cases because they were unlabeled, due to their haste to leave the surface. They were stacked with several others along the side of the lab module. Inside the cases, the body parts were enclosed in sealed bags that did not dissolve.

Norm tried to remember what he had picked up. He had been careful to stay away from the larger carcasses and the dangerous semi-liquid from within them. There had been a leg part, almost a foot long, severed from a one-meter specimen. He was sure that it was in the bottom box. His recollection told him that the middle box, in the stack of three, from appearances, held two chunks of ripped exterior body cover. The top box carried a more rounded piece of the lifeform, which he had hoped was perhaps some type of internal organ. Norm had picked it up last and wanted to be sure that it was properly packed anyway. So he selected this box to open.

As a precaution, Doc returned to the hospital module and closed the hatchway behind her. David and Oreen were in the living and sleeping module to which the door was also closed. Sergey would help Norm extract the creature part and secure a tissue sample for Doc. Norm moved the sample container to the lab bench, and he and Sergey put on surgical gloves and masks as a further precaution.

Norm opened the seals and began to raise the lid. At just that moment the hatch to the darkened sleeping module opened and David moved through, yawning and stretching. Norm and Sergey were distracted just enough to miss the initial flurry of activity. Several small arachnid forms scurried from the opened lid and leaped to freedom. David almost gagged on his yawn. Norm dropped the lid and attempted to reseal the box. David saw the blur of one to two inch "spiders" running wildly, he jabbed the button to close the sleeping module behind him. He was not sure if any of the creatures had gotten by him, but he attempted to determine where at least two had gone.

Sergey was swinging wildly at one. It leaped away from his attempts to smash it with a seat cushion. Norm covered his face as a stream of fluid shot from one of the beasts and splashed on the lab wall. David dove for cover. The lab became a scene of pure pandemonium as the two scientists attempted to battle the tiny creatures and fend off their toxic sprays of liquid.

David crushed one in a corner, but the others were just too quick. This time, they were fighting the creatures on their own turf, in an Earthlike breathing mixture, and the creatures were still surviving. David was able to grab a hand-held unit and activate the alert. He had to wake Oreen in case one or more of the creatures had gotten past him and into the darkened sleeping area. He knew how much Oreen disliked spiders, especially now, after the encounters on the surface of the Stealth Planet. Next, he had to quickly figure out a way to stop the arachnids and save himself, Norm, and Sergey from any serious harm.

David grabbed a breathing unit and tossed a second to Sergey and a third to Norm. At least the masks protected their faces and eyes. The light flight suits they were presently wearing were of limited value for protection. At least the creatures were seeking places to hide rather than attacking. They moved about with apparent ease and comfort. The simulated, partial gravity of the *Kat* was closer to their native gravity than to that of Earth. Both sides were in full retreat and taking defensive postures within the limited confines of the temporary lab module.

Oreen had awakened in a start when the alarm sounded and the lights came on. She heard David's brief warning and at first was unsure if it was real or a dream. Whether by her unnatural instinctive sixth sense or by simple fright, she froze. She could feel the presence of one of the life forms very close. Oreen turned her head very slowly and deliberately to the right and surveyed the area outside of the sleeping pod. There it was, only inches away, hiding in the dark beneath her crumpled flight suit. She was wearing only a thin T-shirt and issued briefs. There was no way to cover up more without alarming the creature, which she knew moved much faster than a human. She could not even tell if it was facing her or facing away; it looked the same from any direction.

David spoke to Oreen as he squinted and noted where he thought several of the "bugs" had gone. "Oreen, we have several loose arachnids out here. Have you seen any signs of one in there?"

"Oh yes! I have a visitor. He's almost eye to eye, and I don't like it at all." She was furious but speaking slowly with forced control. "Somebody get this thing away from me, or the somebody who let it out is in mighty big trouble."

Doc was taking in the entire scene through the portal in the hatchway. Jason and much of the rest of the crew were watching in disbelief on the monitors. The privacy setting in the sleeping module was hampering anyone from visually helping Oreen.

Norm had made one serious miscalculation. He had not sealed the sample bag properly, but he was not worried about that fact at the moment. He knew he would receive his lambasting later, if and when they took care of the present situation. It appeared that he brought a type of egg sac or repository for juvenile life forms aboard, and now several were out.

Jason suggested that David, Norm, Sergey, and especially Oreen, not move or attempt any other activity for a few moments to see if the creatures would settle down. He got no argument from Oreen, who was steadily becoming more upset about the situation.

The primary problem at hand was determining the exact number and how to either recapture or eliminate the creatures. They were loose in the modules and had sprayed several blasts of their acid, and David had crushed one. Containing their potential germs, toxins, or any dangerous substances was now a moot point.

Doc was now in an even worse dilemma. Moses had awakened with chills and convulsions, and he was now in even more critical condition. She had to do something fast; if not, she knew that he would probably succumb to his illness first or die from shock.

It was Rod who came up with a simple possible solution. He had been observing everything that occurred in the lab. Jason had pushed the illumination within the lab module to maximum in hopes of forcing the creatures to seek darkness. That idea had worked. They had also raised the temperature. Rod suggested preparing a small, dark, chilled container, and placing some of the glowing green lifeform in it as bait, then dimming the lights, and placing the container near one of the life forms to see what would happen.

Sergey and David remained stationary while Norm prepared a small dark box and placed a smear of phosphorescent goo in it. Moving slowly and alert to any movement, he squeezed a chemical chill pack and used it to cover the bottom of the box. The plan was simplistic but worth a try since it could be instituted so quickly. When he was ready, Norm placed the box near the lab bench. David lowered the light intensity to very dim. Before their eyes could even adjust, the first small spider form was inside the enclosure, pressed into the green slime. One by one the others followed suit.

Oreen was perspiring profusely and still watching her new neighbor out of the corner of her eye. She had been amazingly patient, considering the circumstances. Without warning, and before she could inquire as to progress in the lab, the creature darted toward her, ran up her face and hid itself in her dark hair. She had all that she could stand. In one motion she rolled from the sleep pod, shook her head, and screamed a blood curdling, "Let me out of here." She also clicked off the privacy switch and stood before the hatchway pleading to leave.

David moved swiftly to the hatch to the sleeping area. Norm carefully closed the container and moved it into the bio-isolation unit. David brightened the lab and sleeping module to full illumination. They had seven captives so far. As soon as David eliminated Oreen's little terrorist, they would set up to see if they could locate any more.

Without warning and to everyone's disbelief, Doc opened the door to the infirmary. She barged into the lab and scraped up the crushed bug as well as the expectorant on the lab wall. Without a word she returned to her work area in the infirmary. No one said a thing.

Jason, observing the activities from the bridge, just cringed. It was the commander who had laughed the most after the last onboard creature escape, the little escapade with Orion, when he had gone AWOL early in their voyage. He was not laughing now, but instead, thanked Rod for his quick thinking and great idea. Jason was composing a new message, and would be sending one very interesting report to the folks at NASA and Eurospace.

David entered the sleeping area, allowing Oreen to exit past him. He carried a powerful flashlight and a small box filled with a plastic-covered cold pack and a dab of the green lifeform. Oreen pointed to where she thought she had seen it last and exited, trying to compose herself, and went straight in to assist Doc. To Jason and the others watching David from throughout the *Kat*, the image of the Security Officer trying to coax the arachnid lifeform out of hiding and into his box, as serious as it was, painted an amusing picture. To David, it was anything but amusing. He was deadly serious and taking no chances. He had the box in one gloved hand, his breathing apparatus mask on, and a hard plastic pad, as a shield, in the other hand.

The "bug" in the sleeping area was soon entrapped, and no others were found after an exhaustive, time-consuming search of that module. Sergey and Norm found one other live one hiding in the lab, but it was obviously dying. They also found one other tiny one, which was already dead. The creatures obviously only lasted for a finite period of time without their own breathing mixture. Norm and Sergey made this assumption and arrived at this conclusion after examining the expired specimens.

It was an exciting and dangerous time for everyone confined to isolation. The entire situation mandated extending the period of time the crew would have to be separated. But they had won another round against the alien creatures with no more casualties so far. Doc had also procured the needed specimens and materials from which she and Oreen could potentially extract a serum to treat the afflicted, but Moses' time was running out.

Norm was now in the commander's proverbial doghouse. Jason ordered him to abandon his experiments for the present, to do a thorough clean up of the lab, and then to get some additional rest. There was no argument with that directive, and Norm began the task of cleaning up the mess caused by the incident with the arachnid escapees. Sergey felt the same guilt for the mess and was eager to assist Norm. When finished, they double-checked to see that every box and container was secured. Satisfied with the check, Norm and Sergey entered the sleeping area and ate a snack before resting again.

Doc Pritchard and Oreen tried several extractions and mixtures to treat the infection. After many attempts they came up with a chemical extract that seemed to hinder the growth of the malady in a mini-culture medium. They immediately set about creating more and refining the mixture. Moses was no longer breathing on his own. Their progress finding any form of treatment was just too slow. Oreen could no longer be patient with their present attempt to save the man who had first stepped forth onto a new world, the man she loved more than anything she had ever known. Doc was doing the best she could but it was not enough, and Oreen now knew it. They were going to have to try something very soon or lose Moses for sure and probably Casey too. Moses was simply not responding to any of the treatment administered to this point. They had not slowed the advance of the disease at all, but as weak as she was, Casey's body seemed better at fighting it off—and Oreen knew exactly why.

Jason finished his report up to the present moment and sent it to Mission Control. He knew that it would keep them busy and entertained for quite some time. If he had been required to make up an adventure, he would have been hard pressed to come up with anything as interesting or entertaining as this truth.

Doctor Ann Pritchard's skills as a physician and diagnostician were pushed to the limit. Without saying anything to Doc, Oreen began typing at the computer terminal in the lab. Doc looked a little bewildered but continued her work unassisted. Oreen jumped up from her seat at the console and wheeled Casey against the lab module wall, placing her in close proximity to the nano vein running through this compartment.

"Oreen, what are you doing?" No answer. She repeated the question, concern on her brow. "Oreen, I need your help. What are you doing?"

"I'm gonna try something, Doc. I have an idea and it may be the only hope for all of us." Crewmembers seldom questioned Oreen's motives, but Jason wondered what she was up to too, but he held his question and just observed. They followed her progress by watching what she did on the computer. After a few moments, horrified, Jason ordered her to stop. "Oreen, you can't do that! You don't have any idea what might happen!" She ignored him and just went on. "Oreen, stop, that's an order!" he shouted.

Doc was not aware of what Oreen was doing; she was too busy with her own work, and could not take the time to evaluate it. She was disappointed that Oreen was not helping her, but David had begun assisting her as they tried different solutions and began to concentrate a potential anti-toxin. They did not know if the serum they were working on would work, or what concentration to use, and a large part of what they were doing was guesswork, but they had to try something.

Oreen on the other hand seemed very sure of what she was doing. Jason typed a command into the computer to stop her actions but nothing happened. "I can't let you stop me, Jason. We have to try this, and I feel that it will work."

This time Doc stopped to look. "Mr. Security Officer, stop her at once." Jason's order was direct.

David left Doc's side and moved to intervene in Oreen's endeavor. Oreen started to block him, but stepped aside when the room came alive with activity. The computer followed her plan. Tendrils sprang out of the nano caring tube on the wall above Casey sending smaller tubes into her mouth, branches to her nostrils and ears, and another branch to her vagina. She shook on the gurney and began to glow with iridescence before them, eyes wide. Shocked crewmembers grimaced with total horror. Her eyes closed gently, and pain slowly drained from her face. No one knew if it was a reflex of death or sleep, an end or a new beginning. Only Oreen knew the significance. She alone realized that the nanos would try to build a more perfect human being, fix what was wrong—mankind had just taken an evolutionary step.

The key for Oreen had been the baby and the reaction to the foreign invaders in her bloodstream by the nanos already there. Casey had them too, but the reaction had not been the same. Oreen had needed the commands from the main computer and a direct link to Casey to attempt her unprecedented cure.

Moses cried out in pain from the other side of the chamber. Oreen, renewed fear in her eyes, agonized for Moses, understanding better than anyone exactly what he felt. With her extended sensory powers she could literally feel Moses' discomforts.

Doc rushed to Casey's side to check her vital signs again. A cursory look revealed that Casey was fine, in a deep sleep, and her brain activity was much closer to normal. "Jason, she is resting much more comfortably. What Oreen did definitely helped. Will it work for Moses, too, Oreen?"

"Not the same way. Moses doesn't have nanos in his system, but we can put some there." They began the process and could do nothing more but wait. Moses would at least have the benefit of the experimental procedure on Casey.

23

DEPARTURE

THE SURFACE EXPLORERS and rescue team had been back aboard for less than two full Earth days, but so much had happened. Jason was now awaiting a response from Mission Control from his most recent transmission and was hoping, like the rest of the crew, that Doc and Oreen could work their miracle. He wanted to wait until the sick and injured of his crew were reunited before they began the rapid acceleration phase of the return voyage.

Margie prepared fresh food, or at least more fresh than their rations, and left several meals in the sleeping area for each of the isolated crewmembers before they moved in. They all enjoyed these meals, but as they ran out, the isolated group would be forced to return to the pre-prepared food. The final decision on how soon the isolated members could intermingle again with the rest of the crew would be made by Commander Kidd and Dr. Pritchard, acting as the life support decision maker, if and when they deemed it safe.

— § —

In Houston, Hank Wadkins and Lawrence Greenbaum were the first to receive and review the inbound report of the rescue and subsequent activities. Hank read the report from a hard copy downloaded from his computer as Greenbaum looked over his shoulder. Lee Tanaka was on his way up, but they were too interested in the contents to wait for his arrival.

Everyone at Mission Control was still ecstatic about the fact that the mission to the surface had succeeded. The details of new life forms and alien attacks were fascinating and almost beyond credibility. If the messages had not come from Colonel Kidd, and been authenticated by Communications Officer, Rod Amerigo, they might have thought that the crew was suffering from some type of space sickness, dementia, or delusions.

There was extreme concern at Mission Control about the sick crewmembers and the chances of contamination of the entire vessel Moses Brown was the current Neil Armstrong of the entire space-exploration program. His death now, after the incredible escape from attacking creatures and the hostile surface, would be a true international tragedy.

The entire interested world was eagerly awaiting information of any type from their space heroes. News of Roberto's death and the severity of Moses' condition had not been released. Mission Control did not even know the full story on what had happened and of Casey and Moses' prognoses for survival. Hank and Larry knew that they had to prepare a press release as soon as the last report from Jason was distributed to the various members of the program. The press contingent was camped outside Mission Control and circling like vultures for any tidbit, any update.

Just as Hank got to the part of the report that discussed the escape of the arachnids, Lee Tanaka burst through the door into Hank's office like a whirlwind. "You've already got it?" he exclaimed more than asked.

Larry answered the question, "Yes, and you're not going to believe it." Hank continued to read on. At this point, he was not about to start over. Lee swung into a chair beside his desk and began listening intently without another comment.

Hank read the report in its entirety to his captive audience of two. When he finished they all just looked at each other for a moment.

Lee Tanaka scratched his chin and remarked: "And we thought that they were going to get a little bored. Wow, that is an amazing piece of information, and I missed the first part."

Larry Greenbaum looked at Lee and said, "You still have not heard how they were able to rendezvous with the *Kat*. The best decision we ever made was to put Oreen Nadu on that crew. We have a space-exploration vessel filled with heroes and invaluable scientific materials and data. We need to do everything possible to make sure that we get them all back here safe."

The "Green Bomb" was famous for his understatements. He picked up a second copy of the report and began to read it again to himself. Tanaka had already swiped Hank's copy and was reading it through at rapid speed. When they had all read and absorbed it thoroughly, they began the task of preparing a press release. The only details they were hesitant to release immediately were the severity of the conditions of the two and the potential contamination problems, since these details were very sketchy. The rest of the story was about to cause a feeding frenzy at the next news briefing, scheduled for later that afternoon.

— § —

Aboard the *Kat*, Jason could only sit and wait for the response to his report, while he awaited news from Doc regarding the condition of her patients. So far, no other dangerous contaminants had been identified within the confines of the isolation area. He hoped that this would continue to be the case, since he wanted to end the quarantine as soon as possible.

It had been more than eight hours since Oreen and Doc started the revolutionary treatment. Ann had steadily increased the concentration of nanos injected into Moses to create the possible antidotal reaction manifested in Casey. She watched carefully for reactions. Nothing had changed perceptibly in the current condition of Moses, and the computer had yet to initiate the obtrusive connection it had made with Casey. Since his condition was no worse, that fact alone fostered a sense of hope that maybe the process was working. Oreen simply said: "Give it time," and settled to maintain her vigil by his side.

Casey's color had changed from a sickly, pasty white to more robust. Her improvement was very noticeable, and Doc was becoming optimistic for her eventual complete recovery. The baby was also resting more comfortably, almost like she sensed that Mom was getting better.

The crew worked without rest and the ship was readied for the return voyage, except for the infirmary and isolation areas. Jason received a return message from Mission Control, confirming the receipt of his report. He did not have much to add for now, so he passed it along to the crew. Several leading Earth-based toxicologists were working on the problem for Doc, since Jason had attached some of her chemical analyses of the poison to his initial report. Little could they imagine what Oreen had conjured.

Jason, his crew, and the *Kat* were now almost prepared to embark on the long journey back to the familiar surroundings of Earth. As the Stealth Planet's ominous skies rotated below them, Jason again thanked God that they had made it this far. The turbulent looking, foreboding black ball had turned out to be a formidable adversary. Future exploration, if there was ever to be any, would undoubtedly have to take on a very different complexion. As they prepared to leave, Jason felt a certain sense of good riddance. It would still be a very long time before any of them could sink their toes into fresh soil or enjoy a good steak dinner, but at least they were about to start in that direction; they were homeward bound.

When the computer finally initiated the connection to Moses, everyone left the module except for Oreen. She stayed with Moses, though Doc ordered her to not hold his hand or get too close during the process. Just like Casey, the nano caring tubes branched to him and entered his orifices. The connection lasted almost fifteen minutes, and Moses looked like a limp rag with no facial expression when it ended. The results were not as dramatic or obvious as Casey, but a subsequent blood test showed frenetic nano activity in his system. Voracious nano builders had begun blocking the infection. It looked like the process was working.

When Oreen emerged from the module, Doc gave her a lasting hug. No words were spoken but emotion washed over them both and they lingered together while the others watched in silence.

After another full Earth day, Doc downgraded her patients from critical and pronounced them fit enough for the rigors of accelerated travel. No one wanted to stay in close proximity to the planet any longer than absolutely necessary. Casey was awake, smiling, and adoring her beautiful Roberta. Moses was more stable, still unconscious and breathing with assistance, but seemed to be steadily improving. Oreen felt a squeeze of her hand once while she talked to Moses. She wept openly when she perceived the first palpable response to her encouraging words.

Jason gave the official order to proceed with the extraction from orbit maneuver and to begin moving away from the Stealth Planet. Jason, Phil Allen, and the rest of the team made all of the final preparations. They loaded the pertinent information into the main computer for the return trip to Earth. Mission Control gave their full blessing to leave this macabre world behind and to begin the long voyage home. Departure held no special significance, no fanfare, only a combined, shared sense of relief. They moved out slowly on the planned trajectory and began accelerating.

24

RETURNING

WHEN THE RETURN journey began, Jason had time to reflect on the incredible amount of diverse activity that had filled his life for almost
two and a half years. His existence had been a pitched battle of emotions.
This entire adventure had all begun with the discovery of a distant, well-dis-
guised solar object, Enigma, the Stealth Planet. That had been in July of 2029.
That discovery led to the greatest technological creation in the history of
the Earth, the creation he commanded. Almost seventeen months of planning
and additional development had resulted in the assembly of his crew and this
magnificent vessel known simply as the *Kat*.

To Jason, the launch on December 25, 2030 now seemed so long ago. He
and a crew of seventeen highly-skilled individuals had guided the ship nearly
three billion miles to their distant target near the edge of the solar system, arriving a mere 297 days after launch on October 16, 2031. That fact alone still
amazed him as much as getting there. They had spent a week of preparation
in orbit, and then his landing party had set down on the surface on October
23, 2031, what would now be a long remembered date for Earth history. A
mere eight days later, on Halloween of 2031, they had already abandoned orbit
and were heading home. To Jason, the time in the proximity to their goal had
passed like an instant, and so much had happened.

They now faced the trial of the return journey. The ship, healthy crew,
and even those recovering were still performing admirably. He hoped for a
non-arduous journey back to Earth with few problems. If or when they did
make it back, Jason decided that he would retire from command, and that he
would never let Ann Pritchard out of his sight for a very long time. At least he
would have her wonderful company for the long return trip. They had already
agreed to get married as soon as their feet were on terra firma again.

— § —

During most of the last two days before departure David stayed too busy to think much about Margie. He had been sure that he and Sergey were going to die inside the vortex while descending to the planet's surface. He had thought of his love for Margie then, in abject fear that he would never see her again. When he communicated with her by computer to check out a couple of new photos, David had an extreme desire to touch her.

He wanted some time to work on his diary. Every crewmember kept a daily or at least an occasional-entry diary. Most kept one for personal reasons, but it was also a mandatory part of their routine. David kept two, one for himself and the requisite one for NASA. His personal one was filled with his own insights and feelings garnished lavishly with sensual references to his beautiful wife,

David enjoyed the exhilaration of the last two years. Since the discovery, his semi-laid-back lifestyle had changed dramatically. His life had been a tremendous adventure and challenge, but at this moment, he felt drained. The previous months had also contained an incredible stress load. His mind and body had handled it well, but right now his persistent headache was pounding, and his ears were constantly painful.

During the rampage of escaping arachnids in the lab module, he had again reacted instinctively, but even if someone had shouted instructions, he would not have heard them due to the condition of his sense of hearing. But somehow he had heard Oreen.

Though during the journey to the Stealth Planet their comments were often barbs or almost adversarial, they were never antagonistic toward each other. Over time they had become quite good friends. David began to wonder if Oreen had somehow reached him with her special powers. He tested his own hearing again, but the silence continued.

The monitor screen in front of him blinked, and Margie's bright smiling face appeared. It immediately uplifted him from his painful doldrums. She could do that to him. He was not too tired to think about some of the other wonderful things she could do too. Margie typed a message. "Hi, love, that was a great job you did in there."

"Thanks," he said. "Duty called. Actually, I was scared of those little things."

"You scared?" Margie interrupted, typing quickly. "I was petrified. You already have enough troubles with the hearing problem. For a ship full of heroes, you are the best. Commander Kidd was proud of your actions too. He told me."

"And how is our commander?" David spoke, wondering to himself if he was too loud. Margie was typing in a reply when David thought he heard something again. He turned from the computer in the lab in time to see Oreen approaching him from the hatchway to the infirmary module. Had he heard her or felt her presence? It bothered him because he did not know.

Margie stopped typing and watched the scene from her monitor. Then he heard something again. He was watching Oreen's lips move and had definitely heard the words come out. Oreen was beckoning him to assist her or accompany her back into Doc's module. He was now sure that he had actually heard her for just a moment. He touched his ears, smiled at Margie's pretty face on the monitor screen, and followed Oreen.

Margie understood his meaning and was so pleased for him.

"I heard a little," he said following Oreen through the connecting hatchway.

Upon entering the hospital module, David immediately saw the problem and raced to assist Doc. Moses was arched up and straining mightily against the restraints keeping him in place. Doc was struggling to contain him and force him back. The three of them had to use all of their combined strength to push Moses back down again.

Moments ago, the semi-comatose patient had been resting peacefully. All had changed in an instant. Doc was alarmed that it was a fit of body contractions prior to death. She had been working with Oreen on additional ways to make Moses more comfortable.

David looked at Doc's face as she turned to pick up a hypodermic syringe. He saw a look of real fear and near panic. He then looked at Moses' face and saw a grimace of pain and bewilderment. When he and Oreen first entered the module, for a moment, David had a flashback to a scene from an old movie about aliens, where one of the creatures suddenly burst forth from the chest of a space explorer. That scene was eerily reminiscent of his present surroundings.

Moses' eyes were open, questioning, afraid and in pain. He had not uttered a sound, and before Doc could inject him, he began to settle back and relax on his own. His pulse and respiration had spiked wildly during the convulsive behavior, but now they became steadier, though subnormal.

"He's breathing on his own!" Doc shouted. "I thought we had lost him, but he may be coming out."

Hang in there, Moses!" Oreen shouted.

"Stay with us, Buddy," David said softly.

By late that day, Moses began to respond to the medications and stimulants, while the nanos within him continued to engulf and expel the foreign invaders. The level of tension began to subside throughout the vessel. Norm and Sergey took more time than they were allotted to get some additional, badly-needed, rest. When it was David and Doc's turn, they snoozed for hours. Before retiring, Doc left orders to be awakened in two hours. Oreen woke her but only to tell Doc that everything was fine and to go back to sleep. At the end of the second two hours, she ignored the orders and just let Doc rest.

Jason would not allow Norm do anything else in the lab except for screening for contaminants in his isolation unit and keeping an eye on the beasts contained therein. This he declared a day to rest and to give thanks for the continued improvement of Casey, Roberta, and Moses, and perhaps even to pray a bit for their safe journey home. Moses was responding, doing a little better, and continuing to breathe on his own. Though still on basic life support, he was steadily gaining strength. Everyone was delighted when Doc reported that his prognosis had greatly improved.

Oreen was maintaining a near constant vigil over Moses. His condition had worsened to very near death prior to being connected to the unknown potential of the nanos. Doc had considered asking Oreen to leave the hospital module but knew that it would be futile. Oreen maintained continuous contact with him, always holding his hands or touching his brow. She had been of tremendous assistance to Doc and was not really in the way or interfering at all. Besides, Doc liked the company and moral support.

The third day since the rescue became the fourth with little other excitement. By midway through the fifth day, Moses was much better, and the spread of the infection had been halted and its effects reversed. He was coming along fine. No other strange maladies or complications appeared. None of the others in confinement developed any symptoms or became ill in any way.

Between the evaluation by the crew of the *Kat* and the work done by the group in quarantine, several potentially dangerous contaminants were identified. Each one of these was isolated, tiny samples preserved for research, and the remainder eliminated as much as possible from the environment of the quarantined modules. No other containers of samples from the surface would be opened until placed within the true lab module of the *Kat*, rather than the makeshift lab in use. There was just too much unknown risk.

Jason wanted to reunite his crewmembers at the earliest possible opportunity. Messages concerning this subject passed between him and Mission Control several times. He yielded to their demands that he maintain the quarantine as long as it was practical. The quarantine was not lifted until the end of seventh day after leaving orbit.

Doc Pritchard finally had a chance to complete a thorough review of her analysis of the malady and of the other foreign contaminants. She compared her findings with Margie and the report from the scientific medical team at

Mission Control. They all agreed that any present danger was evaluated and alleviated or at least could be controlled. Any future problems could and would be handled in unison with Mission Control during the remainder of the return voyage.

Casey and Moses were recovering very well. Casey was trying to do some work in the hydroponic gardens and spending a little time working on biological data from the planet and crew. The gardens had been neglected during her period of incapacitation. They required a delicate balance for proper health and growth and this had not been maintained as well as she would have done. Rod had done an adequate job, but he just did not have Casey's touch, and had to cover multiple duties. Some food in the contaminated areas had been condemned and jettisoned as unfit for consumption or recycling. If the gardens failed, their food supply would surely run short.

Casey did not wait to inform Jason of the impending problem. She and Rod worked together to calculate growth and usage rates for the food, and to inventory every edible item on board again. The results were not good. They would run out of food stores well before their calculated return date, so it was mandatory that they rendezvous with the supply vessel.

Jason was troubled and the consequences were frightening. He instituted an immediate rationing system. Nothing would be wasted. Following mission procedures, Roberto's body was placed in one of three specially designed containers and exposed to the cold of space to freeze it. Under 'survival contingencies most extreme', in an obscure part of the mission plan, was the possibility of using processed human flesh for consumption. The Human protein could be processed through the ship's systems and turned into a survival mixture. It was not quite pure cannibalism, but it was borderline. At this point it was still unthinkable, and this contingency was almost unimaginable, but every possibility had to be considered, and a struggle to survive against starvation was a very real possibility. The size of the ship allowed only so much food storage. If their gardens failed to produce enough extra, the problem was exacerbated.

Time passed quickly, and constant cleaning kept the entire isolated group very busy. David's hearing started to return on one side. Doc had done as much as she could to save his one eardrum. Only time would tell if the other one would heal properly. Margie and David had a field day reviewing the huge volume of photographic data. When Jason decided to allow it, Sergey and Norm were ready to work on the lifeform analyses and to gather much more information concerning the creatures' habits. Nurse Oreen continued ministering to her patient like a mother hen hovering over her chicks.

When Jason, Doc, and Mission Control all agreed that the isolation could be ended, the announcement brought joy to the entire crew. Moses was sitting up, though still very weak. Rod wanted to hold his baby for the first time and to hug his future wife.

The connecting compartments were re-pressurized and filled with fresh atmosphere. The hatches were opened at the end of the infirmary and connecting module, and the happy crew exchanged hearty greetings and innumerable hugs and handshakes. Once again, Rod Amerigo prepared to catch the entire scene on video for posterity, especially the scene of him, Casey, and the baby. Only Phil was at his duty station. Everyone else gathered for the reuniting moment with Commander Kidd's complete blessing. For most of the remainder of the journey home, the *Kat* and its array of sophisticated computers would take over the majority of the guidance work.

Each of the crew presented small gifts to the landing party, rescue team, and to Doc Pritchard. Smiles, cheers, and tears were exchanged between the two separated groups. After a moment of silence and contemplation for Roberto, Jason called for a ship-wide celebration beginning with a double-ration feast in the dining area. Moses was assisted to the dining module. The commander wanted everyone together to enjoy a moment of triumph against the incredible adversity and the rigors of the mission. Rod had fermented his own home-brewed wine in the galley for this moment, and was ready to see it sampled. After the brief greeting celebration, David and Norm supervised the movement of the bio-isolation units to the permanent lab. Jason wanted to be extra careful until all surface samples, life forms, and cases were safely stowed in the lab, which was, in itself, one large bio-isolation unit. When this was completed, the temporary lab module was resealed.

Jason delivered a short speech and notified each of the landing party that special commendation and various other honors were soon to be bestowed upon them. In his own words, he reviewed what he believed to be exemplary service, far beyond the call of normal duty, displayed by each during the landing, rescue, and return.

Jason had carefully reviewed the debriefing reports completed by the group while in isolation. From the debriefings and his own observations, he included special recommendations in his ongoing status reports to Mission Control. Jason was not one to brag, but his pride in his crew was obvious to everyone who read the report.

Within a few hours of being reunited, the group meal and Rod's interesting wine concoction were consumed. Personal stories and anecdotes were told and would be retold for days to come. Morale reached another peak in the roller-coaster emotional world that was now a part of their daily routine. David and Margie were overjoyed when finally reunited. Doc and Jason were now bonded for life. Moses and Oreen were almost inseparable.

Though the crew realized that things were bound to get a bit routine for a while during the return voyage, they now could look forward to the luxuries of life on their home planet so far way. With an abundance of material from the surface of the Stealth World, their curiosity for scientific endeavors would be well-sated. Every member of the crew would get to spend time in the lab, caring for the surviving life forms and working on the evaluation and assimilation of volumes of scientific data.

Pilot Phil Allen placed the *Kat* into its extreme acceleration phase as soon as the celebrating was over and everything was secured again throughout the ship. The Stealth World finally disappeared behind them.

Phil and Jason abandoned their chess matches for a few days so that Phil could spend time playing against Moses to pass the time while he healed. Roberto had always looked up to Phil, as his inspiration and mentor, and Phil sorely missed his copilot friend. Playing chess against Moses took his mind off of the loss of his "wingman, Orbit" and kept Moses' spirits lifted. With Oreen there, Phil heard Oreen talk about her perceptions on the surface. She told them of her feelings when the alien bugs approached. Often transfixed by their stories, Phil had a hard time concentrating on the games, but he also thought less about Roberto. Phil noticed subtle changes in Oreen, and at times he felt like she was reading his mind. He also observed that she played both games, from his and Moses' point of view, and anticipated their every move. He even wondered if maybe Oreen and Moses were somehow communicating by mind. Phil was a very skilled player, and Moses was a good player, but not as veteran. But their games were incredible, and Moses was now a stalwart competitor.

The folks at Mission Control and throughout the respective space agencies had piled on the accolades after the crew was reunited. There was a constant flow of messages between the space travelers and their Earth-bound comrades. Personal messages from family and friends brought news updates and reports of reactions to their extraordinary exploits. The world was preparing for the much-anticipated arrival of their heroes.

— § —

During the first weeks of the voyage home, with Margie's assistance, David finally broke the code. He had been working on the Ishmael mystery whenever he had time, and now he had plenty. The fire in the supply module was no accident. Their exposure to nanos had been premeditated and programmed into their vessel so incredibly well, that it took them months to work out the answer. Clues were everywhere because the circumstances of the onboard fire during the trip to Enigma and the subsequent exposure of some of the crew never did add up. They searched and searched and at last found a most diabolically ingenious code within code that made itself transparent unless one specific numeric sequence was triggered. And David had traced its origin from the point of combustion back through the data files to before launch, and Margie found the link. Ishmael had taken it upon himself to be God, a creator of a new subspecies of human, one with nano builders programmed to mesh with the body and brain. Consequences yet unknown, and against both law and common sense, were their reality. It was all there, all in the computer database. No one was to know. Ishmael planned to observe and record the results for himself and worry about the ramifications later. They were his guinea pigs in the completely controlled environment of a spacecraft, locked away for two years. It was almost perfect.

Anger was the initial reaction but it was soon replaced by fear. Margie and David also found out what would happen if someone did discover and somehow break his code. David had taken the precaution of downloading everything about his investigation onto his laptop and handheld. He had even removed any modem or means of connection by anyone or anything. He felt secure that the secret was safe for now, but if Ishmael found out, or if they had missed something, they also knew the consequences.

If discovered, Ishmael had devilishly planned their demise, an accident in space, and erasure of their existence. David discussed it with Margie and they decided that they could not even share the information with Jason, but both knew that Oreen would figure it out, that she would somehow know. They went to work on a way to keep it from Ishmael without making him suspicious. No exposure to anyone of his diabolical plan could take place until they could confront him with their evidence face-to-face. He received all mission information; he had to, NASA needed that, needed him to be aware of every bit of data so that he could monitor his nano-assisted creation.

25

HERO'S WELCOME

DAYS PASSED into months, and the distance between the ship and Earth began to shrink. The crew and the vessel were encountering few problems. Food supplies and all essential materials for life support were still strictly rationed but were diminishing too fast. They had lost, used, and consumed more than had been expected.

Their mission was proving that in some ways, the outer reaches of Earth's solar system were still poorly understood. While approaching the Stealth Planet, the *Kat* had encountered broad belts of radiation, dust and gaseous zones and passed through meteor belts of debris; from sand-sized particles to huge, tumbling rocks. They had traversed all with no serious concerns or problems. Unlike the close-spaced objects popular in Hollywood's great space epics, debris and objects in the meteor belts were, in actuality, thousands of miles apart. Most were avoided by minor course changes, initiated well in advance by the scanners and navigational computer, and imperceptible to the persons on board. Margie and Phil were in charge of watching for these zones on the return trip.

The planned course for the homeward voyage was different from that of the outward trip. Movement of the celestial orbs around the sun necessitated the new route.

Her computer warned Margie well in advance of the positions of any potential obstacles in their path. It was capable of detecting large objects at a great distance. As the object size diminished, the distance at which an object could be detected decreased in proportion. There was no way to completely avoid the more dangerous debris belts due to their vast expanse. Large objects were easy to avoid and the least dangerous. Tiny objects were hard to detect, but because of their speed, they were potentially just as deadly. Most off duty crewmembers spent time monitoring the scanners with Margie while within the belts. Several took over whenever she bathed or rested.

Her long-range visual and sensor scans yielded no initial clue to the danger ahead. They were between one-quarter and one-third of the way home, when the computer set off the danger alert. Margie was sound asleep in front of her console. David, who was with her, sounded the alarm. Margie opened one eye and swung around to confirm the message on the screen. The computer had just detected an object in their path big enough to set off the alarm. Anything larger than a walnut was capable of causing catastrophic damage to the *Kat's* external systems, especially if it impacted the wrong spot, and because of the distance reading, this piece of space detritus was much larger.

Margie suddenly realized that the *Kat* had just completed an acceleration phase and that they were still moving at near maximum speed. Even a very small object could cause considerable damage under these circumstances. She calculated the distance, size, and vector data for the object. Her eyes widened, and her fingers began to fly over the keyboard at her console. Panic gripped her as she read the analytical data again on the computer screen.

Jason Kidd's voice filled her ears. "What have we got Margie and how far? What set off the alarm?"

She knew that the data on her screen was not appearing on the captain's. Margie had set it up that way, just in case the scanners made mistakes, as they were so apt to do. He was not aware of the problem.

"Just a minute, Jason, while I recheck the data." Margie was afraid; beads of sweat on her forehead evidenced her fear, but her nerves remained steady.

Oreen heard the tone change in her voice, and sensed her trepidation. The ship-wide channel was open to everyone when the alarms went off. Oreen felt the anxiety of danger and set off at once for the photo and astronomy module. Margie ran and reran the scans. David gripped her shoulder. As she turned to him, Margie looked into his eyes and uttered, "Shit!"

"What do the numbers say, honey?" David inquired, glancing at the screen and then back to her face.

"It's a cluster of objects! I can't be sure yet if it's actually a grouping or a wide area of smaller rocks, but one thing is certain, we are on a dead-certain collision course with them."

David checked over the data and the intercept warning vectors on the screen while Margie opened the statistics box on Jason's screen.

They both heard the exclamation of expletives from Pilot Phil Allen after he saw the data and understood their predicament.

"Of all the rotten luck." Jason muttered to himself, but they all heard it. "Phil, can we avoid it?" Jason asked, but he already knew the answer.

"If it's one or just a few objects we probably can and will, but if it's what I think it is, likely not, sir." Phil answered in a formal tone that he reserved for difficult situations. He had not had to use it for quite some time. At this point, he was very serious and already double checking the computer produced collision avoidance vectors. "We may be able to avoid it, but we're moving so fast that it won't be easy."

The computer had already started rapid deceleration and laid out the best fit for avoiding the objects ahead.

Oreen joined Margie, David, and now Sergey in the photo lab area. As she appeared, the commander noticed on the two-way visual communications screen and summoned her to the bridge. "Oreen, we may need you up here far more. Please come to the bridge."

"I'm on my way, Jason. I don't like the feel of this." Oreen patted David on the shoulder and gave the other two occupants a wary glance as she exited the module and headed for the bridge.

Oreen traded concerned looks with several of the crew on the way to the command module. Jason was studying the screens with Phil and Moses when she arrived. Moses had been on the bridge ready to make his next chess move and Jason asked him to stay. Everyone else was busy securing the ship and taking up his or her assigned positions at emergency alert stations.

Phil and Jason were already planning their next action and did not even look away when Oreen joined them. Margie had trained the onboard optical and specialized telescopes on the fast approaching objects, but they were still beyond visual range, hidden in the overpowering darkness surrounding them. The *Kat* was equipped with conventional thrusters. In an emergency, these could be used to initiate a rudimentary collision avoidance system, for single, widely-spaced objects. As they neared the debris belt, more and more scattered tiny objects were detected, littering their path.

As the marked objects appeared the sizes decreased from basketball size, to softball, to fist, to walnut, smaller and smaller as resolution increased. Most of these rocks were labeled as bogeys and marked by small pips on the video screen. The great spaces between most created no immediate threat, but as the distance decreased to the closest, more and more tiny ones began to appear and to fill in the gaps. Attached to each tiny pip was a flag, which would open an individual information box, attributable to that particular piece of debris. As more appeared, the computer automatically and systematically ranked each by potential threat. Because of the wide spaces between most, few were of any real consequence to the *Kat*, but several were going to pass too close for comfort. Suddenly, the computer shifted into high gear adding minute blips to the pattern at an alarming rate. In the area of the first and largest ones detected the screen depicted a myriad of micro-bogeys, one centimeter or less in size. Kevlar and Tanaka's material in the *Kat's* skin could deflect glancing hits, but high speed head on or direct impacts with even these very small particles were still very dangerous—potentially deadly.

Jason, Phil, and the computer system needed to make a series of instantaneous decisions and course corrections. Minor variations as speed decreased were possible and mandatory, in order to vary the angle of intercept slightly and to avoid contact with the largest of the objects. At least the *Kat* was in its most compact form during the acceleration phase, and they had already reduced forward speed by more than forty percent. Contact with one or more of the smallest pieces of the space debris appeared to still be unavoidable.

Jason ordered the computer to secure all compartments of the ship and to prepare for possible collision. This would make certain that the nano transport system was ready for hull repair and any emergency pressure loss. All crewmembers donned their pressure suits and readied their helmets. Casey put Orion in his bubble and sealed herself in the garden compartment. Norm secured the lab and scooted his two live specimens into the small tubes he had used to bring them from the surface.

Excitement and fear replaced the pleasant atmosphere of the last few days of the return trip. The crew continued to function well, the high level of competency and training apparent. Everyone moved from relative lethargy to action stations in only seconds. All attention became focused on the fast-approaching, imminent danger.

Moses began rubbing his lucky metallic mission shoulder patch, removed from his old landing suit. It had probably saved his life by protecting part of his shoulder while deflecting some of the spray of arachnid acid. He wanted to feel its luck now.

Jason and Phil chose a combination of firings of the positioning and maneuvering jets to try to move the *Kat* out of harms way, away from the largest of the objects. Phil was given flight system control by the captain again, flying with only minor assistance from the computer control and guidance systems. Jason was doing what he could to help. Sergey was not on the bridge when the warning sounded. He had assumed a position in the backup command module.

"Rod, fire off a message to Mission Control regarding our present situation. Then everybody get ready for trouble. Please fully suit up if you haven't already done so, and it is time to put on your helmets and re-breathers, and make sure that all modules are secure. Ladies and gentlemen, the captain has turned on the seat belt sign." Jason did his best to lighten the mood as the debris field closed in around them.

It was time to initiate rapid thruster firings and pray that they worked. With the computer picking the most suitable path and Phil concentrating on the data, Jason asked Oreen which of their few options she felt had the best chance for success. Without hesitation she answered that the best plan was the one that took them left and below the largest nearby object. To Jason and Phil, that direction put them in the path of more scattered debris and appeared to be the poorer choice. They wanted to go above and to the right of the field or larger pieces. Jason looked at Oreen's face once more for her assurance and saw the determination there. He instructed Phil to make the maneuver she suggested.

To have come this far and to have gone through so much, to now be ripped apart by space debris seemed so unfair to David and Margie. Suited up and ready, they were alone in the photo-astronomy module. A look of gloom was now pervasive among the crew. Everyone but Oreen had a look of uncertainty, but conviction that one more crisis could be averted. Those who had been with her on the surface of the planet sought hope in her face.

Debris was now visible. The powerful shafts of light extending from their ship, like silver-white fingers, reflected back their first glimpse. The sensors had long ago created a computer-generated image. Now human eyes beheld the danger lurking ahead. It looked like a miniature version of the star fields from sci-fi movies, numerous dull colored rough shaped objects illuminated by the beams. Their sensory array told them that they were solid and metallic, a ferrous metal. If they contacted any of the larger pieces, even at this reduced speed, the collision would be fatal to the *Kat*. Intercept with the minute ones would be like being hit by buckshot at many times the speed of the fastest bullet.

Sergey and Phil continued to slow the *Kat* down as much as possible. The entire crew felt vibrations and heard the maneuvering retros firing. In the present ship configuration, they were not only much safer, but the ship's overall profile was at least much smaller. In the vastness of space, they were gambling with inches.

It would be over in seconds. A direct impact with multiple rocks, or a mass of minute grains, would be instantly fatal to all of them. The lives of all aboard were now in the hands of Air Force-decorated Pilot Philip Allen, NASA's best. Mission Commander Jason Kidd switched off all autopilot functions and let the computer guidance systems give only minor assistance to his pilot. Phil was using a heads-up display and flying by feel.

They again felt the abrupt movements of the *Kat* as various thrusters fired and the sounds reverberated throughout the silent ship.

The voice of Oreen in prayer drowned out the rumble of the jets. "Dear God of us all, deliver us now." Followed by: "Right, Phil, right and down."

More loud sound, and the *Kat* swayed again as fist-sized chunks of rock whizzed by. Moses declared that he thought he saw sparks. Incredible as it seemed to the crew, Oreen did it again. The crew knew that someday there would be legends told about this fine lady, that is, if they made it, or perhaps even if they did not.

Another sizeable rock went by above and to the right. Margie closed her eyes and hugged David as more rock and small debris loomed ahead. She held on with all her might, waiting. It was David who screamed, and for an instant she knew it meant death.

It was a scream of pure joy. The mass of material all missed, and in an instant it was behind them. Jason opened his eyes, looked through his visor, and saw trickles of sweat pouring from Phil Allen's shocked face. He had been making his piece with God, accepting his fate. They missed. Rod had soiled his suit. The remaining objects ahead were far enough apart that the *Kat* and Phil should have no more major problems.

The shrill pings and sounds of decompression were unmistakable.

"I didn't even see them," Phil yelled apologetically. It wasn't his fault. He had already done a superhuman, computer-busting, and divinely guided task of avoiding instantaneous death. Would they now be killed by an undetected micro-debris version of what was behind them?

Transfixed, David realized that he had seen this all before. It was a classic case of deja vu. His security officer persona clicked in automatically when the decompression alarms sounded the first warning of a space explorer's greatest nightmare. They had already experienced the second during the fire in the storage compartment. The worst fear was that of any uncontrolled depressurization. The blinking warnings signaled and coincided with the instant pressure balancing of the rest of the ship. When the penetration of the hull took place, the *Kat* was already secured. Depending on the severity of the problem, this fact, coupled with the programmed repair work of the nano system, could be their salvation.

David read the status report on the screen before him in total disbelief. Margie was also staring at it, trying to help him evaluate the extent of the damage. The *Kat* had been impacted and pierced in at least six places by pieces of the space debris. The computer confirmed that much. One module had multiple penetrations and, from the initial reports, was badly damaged, maybe gone. The computer screen also indicated high levels of nano activity in the damaged areas as expected, and one glaring problem. Ishmael placed finite amounts of nano builders into the nano transport tube system prior to launch. These were always monitored and now the numbers were rapidly dropping. The tube system had been compromised by one impact, and because off the size, the nanos were losing the battle to repair that breach and were being lost into space.

David recalled the chilling drill from training when Doc's module was depressurized during a simulation. The drill had seemed so real. His bad dream had just happened again, except this time it was real. Doc's personal module was highlighted as the most severe impact. Photo recon was only two modules away from Doc's compartment.

David ran a quick scan of the bio-locators. Eleven crewmembers and one baby were accounted for. The grim question was where was Doctor Ann Pritchard? As it had during the drill, her locator placed her in the infirmary beside her personal quarters. At least it appeared that she was not in the compartment destroyed by the rapid decompression.

Jason's voice broke the silence. He and Phil were on the bridge and had been too busy with their immediate problems to check much else. Jason wanted a damage control report. He still was not aware that the impact was in the infirmary area. "How bad is it and where, Mr. Security Officer?"

Margie answered for David as he opened the compartment hatch and left her behind. "Jason, the impact was in Ann's compartment, but she was not in it. She was in the infirmary unit. David is on his way to assess the situation."

It was a difficult decision and order, but Jason said it anyway. "Stop where you are, David. Don't open any more sealed areas at all. We are not out of the woods yet. There is still a lot of debris ahead. If she needs assistance, I cannot allow you to reach her yet." Then Jason tried to raise Ann directly. Everyone else onboard had already checked in. There was no response. Either she could not answer, or there was some problem with the communications. The latter was very unlikely.

Video feed from the infirmary area had been knocked out. Margie switched to the backup and was about to patch it through to the ship-wide system, when the picture before her took her breath away. The insides of the infirmary looked normal except for a large smear of red down the wall, obviously blood. Warning lights were flashing everywhere. Margie panned the room with the remote camera, and there was Doc. She was struggling to put a bandage on her own head and was bleeding profusely. Her helmet was off, smashed, and she was obviously incommunicado. Margie used the handheld voice relay, and Doc looked up at the monitor and saw Margie's questioning face. Then Margie understood. Doc was cut and bleeding and also trying to seal the door between her and the destroyed compartment. The hatchway was closed but definitely lacked a perfect seal. If it failed further, Doc and the infirmary were history.

Margie relayed the picture to David on his handheld. David was only one compartment away from the infirmary now. He could be there in seconds, but it meant disobeying orders. Margie relayed the information on the situation to Jason. He had another tough decision. Margie had already relayed the information on the failing hatch seal to Jason. Now Margie gave him the news of Ann's injury and perplexing situation. They were almost clear of the debris zone but had been repeatedly pummeled by more fine debris.

Before Jason could say a thing, hatch-opening indicators showed that David had disobeyed a direct order. If the infirmary hatch seal failed while David had another section open, the integrity of the entire vessel could be compromised. Rapid decompression explosions were violent and dangerous. Multiple compartments bursting at once would be catastrophic.

When the hatch behind David sealed, he began to open the one to the infirmary. Now he was disobeying the order twice. Jason shouted at him to think of the danger, but his communicator had somehow become switched off. Ignoring the danger and the orders, he forged ahead with his plan to aid Doc.

When the main hatchway to the infirmary showed a green light on the status indicator indicating that David was sealed inside, they all felt a little better. David first helped Doc to finish the bandage and then began to assess the problem at hand. Doc explained that she had just come back from her sleeping compartment with her helmet when the piece of junk ripped through it. She had waited for the light to come on indicating a good seal. A split second earlier, and she would have been caught with the hatchway opened. The sudden shaking of the ship had thrown her head first against the bulkhead, which had caused the lacerations to her neck and forehead.

It took David almost ten excruciating minutes to obtain a safe reading on the hatch status indicator. He and Doc succeeded in making it seal thus preventing further damage.

Nano builders succeeded in sealing five punctures within seconds. Only Doc's destroyed personal compartment was a casualty of the debris penetration, and its destruction was total. The nanos were able to seal the tubes leading into and through the area, but could not repair the massive damage to the multi-layered skin. Many of the builders had been lost into space in a futile effort to seal the large breach. The *Kat* was damaged, but its structural integrity was still intact. Nanotechnology had again proved to be invaluable.

Without a doubt, it saved the *Kat* that it had helped to build.

Jason said nothing about the disobeyed order, though he did plan to discuss it later in private with David. They cleared the debris field, which had proven to be another major obstacle to their return.

— § —

Once again, Mission Control was awed by the report of the latest incident. They were more impressed by the performance of their crew than anything else.

Ishmael was delighted that his creation had worked well and proven to be another decisive factor contributing to the overall success of the mission. He alone carried the nanos within his body on Earth, the result of the careless accident in his secret lab. The subject of nano-human interaction was as controversial as cloning humans once was. He was very pleased that some of the crew were now hosts for his great technological breakthrough; his planned next step in human evolution. He could not wait to examine the entire group and to study the physiological changes he alone anticipated. The whole venture had gone better than he had planned. Rod had been the perfect scapegoat for his devilish, but necessary, little plot to expose one or more of the crew to his builders. It had been a bold plan, but well thought out. Oreen's actions to save Casey and Moses had been better than a he could have dreamed. He was as giddy as a child with a special secret when he considered how well his side experiment had worked out, and no one, absolutely no one, had caught on. He patted himself on the back with tiny silvery-purple iridescent fingertips.

— § —

But Ishmael did not detect that David had figured it out. At the right time, David planned to expose him, to turn over his findings to those who would do something about it, but David also knew that the only reason they might make it back to Earth was because of Ishmael's tiny helpers and Oreen's brilliant use of them.

As they approached the inner planets, the travelers became more and more anxious to get home. They were also beginning to run out of food.

Two unmanned supply ships had been sent out on an intercepting course to meet them. The chances of a successful rendezvous were slim. When they passed the three-quarter mark of the return voyage, they had not detected a sign of the first one. Regrettably, NASA had lost contact with the vessel too. No one ever was sure as to exactly why or what happened to it. The second small craft was hurtling in their direction sending continuous telemetry data. They were able to track and set a minor course change for a rendezvous with it.

The gardens did not remain fresh and viable for the entire journey. Casey was able to grow a fair amount of edible foodstuffs, but the technology needed more study. She did a marvelous job of preparing interesting, palatable meals, but her ideas and variety of choices were running out too. They would be near starvation without re-supply, one of the problems of such a large crew. Jason began to worry about the Roberto contingency. He said nothing to the crew but began making plans to supplement the dwindling food supply with his remains, a thought that revolted him. He held two secretive brief meetings with Casey to discuss the eventuality. She listened and in a shocked voice said: "With all due respect commander, you're crazy! I won't do it." Jason just looked at her and said: "You will if I order it." Jason was upset by the near insolence, said nothing and scrapped the idea. They were all about to lose even more weight.

After only brief discussion with his crew and the directors at Mission Control, they embarked on one last adventure. The *Kat* had to attempt to intercept and dock with the drone supply vessel. They also needed some other supplies from the transport ship almost as much as they needed food. Once the decision was made, the crew was ready for the challenge—and a break in the return travel monotony.

They were nearly eighty percent of the way back when the meeting with the supply ship took place. Slowing down and finding the craft took time and added to the overall duration of the return voyage. The supply vessel was a tiny speck in an empty void. The planners did their job directing the vessel on an intercepting course extremely well. The locator beacons emanating from the supply drone were strong and easily tracked. Once the guidance systems of both ships were locked on to each other, it was a matter of allowing the computers to finish the task. Pilot Phil Allen coordinated these using a little of his own piloting skills to close the final gap.

The countdown clock to re-entering Earth orbit showed fifty-eight days when the actual rendezvous took place. Empty stomachs added to the intensity of the task. Rather than attempt a dangerous docking maneuver, Jason and Phil made the decision to launch the DEV vehicle again and simply tow the supply ship back to the *Kat*. Then Margie could use the manipulator arm to latch onto it and swing it into the empty uncontaminated lander bay that had originally housed DEV One. The supply vessel was designed to fit in this bay and could ride back to orbit with them or be jettisoned. NASA had a reason to want the supply drone back because it also carried several sensory arrays and was gathering data.

On the day of the rendezvous, everything started out well. Sergey did a masterful job of using the *Kat's* multiple propulsion systems to bring their vessel to the general vicinity of the small supply ship. When he turned the *Kat* over to Phil, he closed the final distance with precision. Margie swung the lander out of its storage bay with Sergey and Rod at the controls. The pair truly enjoyed their brief chance to pilot the DEV and bring back the prize.

In only a few hours the deed was done. Sergey moved the DEV out, and Rod made a perfect hookup with the floating, shiny NASA drone. They towed it back to the *Kat* and made a complete circle around the mother ship to survey the damage from the impact with the space debris, now a distant but frightening memory. Sergey lined up for Margie's skilled retrieval. Once Margie moved the manipulator arm to capture the supply vessel, the DEV released the tow cable. Margie took her time and moved the vessel into the hold without a bump or touch.

While she did this, Jason allowed Sergey and Rod to have some fun with the DEV at a safe distance from the *Kat*. Doc and Casey had stowed away for a ride in the DEV with the Commander's complete blessing. Flying in formation with the *Kat* was exhilarating and thrilling for the four onboard the lander. Margie had wanted to go too, but Jason had decided that four crewmembers on the Lander were enough and he needed her skills with the mechanical arm.

Jason had already made another decision that Margie, Rod, Casey, and even Doc if she wanted to, would lead them into orbit aboard the lander upon their triumphant, and much anticipated, return to Earth's orbit. This was not in the book and not an anticipated part of the mission forecast or script. Jason had conjured up this idea himself as a personal addition to the mission plan. While slowing for final capture, they would unexpectedly deploy the DEV and use it to photograph and record the entire process from their own perspective. It was their little surprise for Mission Control. They would make it their personal statement, and undoubtedly ruffle a few feathers, by buzzing the space station in the blackened, battle-scarred lander. The press was going to eat it up. It was probably frivolous and somewhat dangerous, but they had all agreed that the unexpected escort would be worth it. The boost to morale would not hurt anything either.

That evening they dined, or perhaps gorged, with pure abandon. The prepared and sealed turkey dinners from home tasted wonderful after weeks of rations. It took time to retrieve the lander, and then to initially unload the supply vessel, but it was well worth the effort. By the time they were done, everyone was satiated. For the rest of the journey, they would all eat well and probably regain some weight. Returning to full gravity could end up being a real challenge to their weakened legs.

By the end of October 2032, the weary, homesick crew was on the final leg of their arduous journey and fast approaching a growing blue ball. Daily communications with families and friends were now becoming a routine. A fairly harsh restriction was placed on communications with the media until a debriefing meeting planned for the second day back on the International Space Station. Discussing mission particulars, even with families, was still not allowed.

The media representatives were already assembled like a pack of hungry wolves. Lee Tanaka likened them more to a school of piranhas. In actuality, they were behaving very well and yielding to almost all of NASA's restrictions without dispute. There was already enough red carpet rolled out to reach to the moon and back.

President Walker was still very securely in office and enjoying an approval rating among the highest of any United States leader in history. He was well liked and respected on an international basis too. He and various other heads of state were competing for the biggest chunk of the publicity associated with the heroes' return. None wanted to overshadow the true importance of the crew and their achievements in any way.

The president assigned his personal secretary, Liz Rainwater, the task of coordinating the planned celebration in Washington, D. C., when the space travelers attended their official national welcome back ceremony. He had plenty of other staff members to handle the task but none better qualified or more liked than Liz. Her years of dedicated service to him brought her status and respect among his entire staff. She was absorbed in the task. Her attention to detail and phenomenal memory served her well.

Even upon their return to Earth's surface from the Space Station, the crew-members were going to go through another incredible battery of tests and physical examinations. Getting re-acclimated to Earth gravity would take some time too. The actual celebration was to take place almost a week after their return. Subsequent public appearances and travel would be up to the explorers themselves. They were NASA's to control for a few weeks of quarantine and evaluation before being turned loose to do as they pleased. At any rate, they were now all celebrities, under a constant spotlight, no matter what they decided to do. Few people ever fully believed that they could complete the entire journey and mission successfully. Even though everyone had sent them on their way with great fanfare, most had some lingering doubt that they would ever make it back.

— § —

Now their return was imminent. The slowing process had already been started, and preparations for the return were also in full swing aboard the *Kat*. The *Kat* would make one broad turn around the moon and then slow and move into position for orbital capture. The crew was finishing their diary reports and packing up a few personal items.

Norm and Moses worked tirelessly to make final preparations for the transfer of their most precious cargo. They had lost most of their arachnid captives but had managed to keep the original two alive. They finally opened the box from which the group had escaped. In the protection of the main bio-isolation unit, they discovered that most of the creatures in the box were dead. There were more than one hundred still in there. Amazingly and inexplicably, another four had somehow remained alive. Norm was delighted to have so many to continue his work.

The two original arachnid forms had consumed most of the green lifeform, but it too had continued to flourish in captivity in the controlled environment of the isolator. Most astonishing was the tiny wormlike creature collected by Norm just before leaving the surface of the Stealth Planet. It had not survived the lengthy captivity before its enclosure was finally opened. They preserved the dead example but were in for another surprise. At the bottom of the box, which had contained the hoard of arachnids, were several of the worm life forms feasting on the dead arachnids. Where they had come from, or how they had appeared, was a mystery for future scientific evaluation. Norm and Casey were just pleased to have additional live examples.

Casey brought Orion to the lab one day to see his reaction to the new life forms. She had placed him in the unit in a clear plastic container. When the lights were brightened, he tried to bite at one of the wriggling worms placed before him, probably thinking it was food. Orion was a very lucky tortoise that he had not become food when stores ran out. They had all gotten a kick out of his floating antics when the near gravity was turned off and enjoyed his company as ship's mascot. Two arachnids had attacked the clear box holding Orion with amazing ferocity. The poor tortoise was terrified by the creatures. It was one more important lesson concerning the aggressive new species.

Norm had plenty of time to catalog many samples in his collection. He also did more complete evaluation of many of the rock, soil, and soot samples. He had already amassed a huge volume of data, and more than half of his collection was still in storage. Each sample was very carefully sealed for transport and additional work by eagerly waiting scientists back on Earth. He found several other traces of life forms in the rock record. There were a few fossils and vestiges of some other highly unusual life forms, comparable to nothing on Earth, past or present.

Margie and David assembled a fantastic collection of photographs and beautiful images from the entire mission. They were confident that it would make one intriguing show when it was all finally released. NASA had allowed just enough to be released to pique everyone's curiosity and whet appetites for more. Their collection started with the earliest smudged image noticed by David on that fateful summer morning. It would end with the beautiful bluish planet ahead of them, framed in the *Kat's* front view port. In between were the most original images ever captured by a camera lens. The times and events recorded in these images covered the most unforgettable moments of the voyage.

In a few more hours the *Kat* would, once again, glide into position beside the enlarged International Space Station. The crew was more than ready. The space station was a bustle of activity. The entire world had again focused its collective attention on a tiny spec approaching the space station.

Jason had DEV Two ready for his little surprise. It was charred and ugly, and hardly the candidate to be leading the parade, but they did not want to clean it off. The inert soot was another valuable piece of material for scientific scrutiny.

NASA wanted them to arrive at the International Space Station during prime time for the U.S. East Coast. Jason thought it ludicrous that someone really wanted them to do this, but he decided to cooperate and therefore make their little surprise even more outlandish. He discussed the approach with Phil and Sergey. Phil was turning over the controls of the *Kat* to Jason so that he could pilot the DEV. Orders and common sense called for the utmost in care, but Jason knew that Phil would give them quite a show.

— § —

At 4.00 p.m. EST on November 17, 2032, the *Kat* glided quietly and serenely into the grasp of Mother Earth's awaiting gravitational arms and began coasting toward the ISS on the other side of the globe. As they neared the station during this first orbit, and in full view of satellites monitoring the return, the hangar doors of the *Kat* opened wide, and a small dirty craft appeared moving steadily outward on the well used mechanical arm. At the arm controls this time were the less skilled hands of Sergey.

Watching in wonderment from several angles, the audience of viewers was amazed to see the lander released and its engines glow to life. It moved away and in front of the *Kat* and began twinkling with a cover of tiny flashing lights. Clearly visible on the front of the lander was one four-letter word, home. Hanging from the rear of the craft and suspended by a wire was a small banner reading, "Earth or Bust." Jason had not been informed about the banner.

This development caused a real stir at Mission Control. As the craft moved away from the *Kat*, another craft moved into view to one side. It was a space plane with a large flashing sign reading, "Welcome home."

All communications channels were opened when Jason made his official request for docking clearance from the ISS. "Commander International Space Exploration Vehicle *Kat* to Commander International Space Station. We respectfully ask your permission to move into the docking space for our craft."

"Permission granted, Jason, and welcome home." The spontaneity of cheers from within the *Kat*, the DEV and the ISS was almost overwhelming. The normally stoic captain had tears streaming down his face. Jubilation ran rampant. The world rejoiced in a miracle of pure science and determination. The culmination of billions of dollars in expenditures, countless man-hours, and a journey of two years was drawing to a close.

The station's highest-ranking inhabitant was a non-military scientist from Germany. It was obvious to all viewers that he was truly relishing this moment. The military decided to have some of its top brass take part in the welcoming ceremony on the ground. Lee Tanaka was on the ISS and could hardly wait to say hello and then begin an assessment of how well his material had fared. Except for one damaged section, which he already knew about, it appeared that the skin of the *Kat* was in good shape.

Phil Allen and his crew had a great time on their brief but surprising foray in DEV Two. They sped ahead of the *Kat* and circled the ISS twice before waving the short wings and heading back to the hangar. The maneuver left a lot of folks at Mission Control scratching their heads. It had captivated and enthralled the vast television audience.

Their little excursion was over almost as quickly as it started. Phil skillfully maneuvered the small craft back to the *Kat*, where everyone watching thought that he was about to fly it straight into the hangar. He moved in close, too close for Sergey's comfort and came within meters of bumping the manipulator arm. From Jason's vantage point it looked as if he hit it. Sergey did not even get nervous. He latched onto the vehicle and retrieved it so fast that even Margie was impressed with his expertise.

The crew sped out of the lander vehicle and hangar as soon as they could.

No one wanted to miss the docking with the space station. Once they were back inside the hangar, and the doors closed, they moved through the pressure lock and were out of their helmets and space suits, and changed back into the lighter flight suits. They left their now soiled space suits behind in the adjoining compartment and sealed them in for techs to decontaminate later. They had their uniforms looking spit-shined for the reunion, which was about to begin.

As if in slow motion, the *Kat* gracefully neared the docking position. There was a contingent of floating space walkers waiting to attach lines and secure the vehicle at the end of the docking umbilicus. Eyes peered from every possible view port on the station. Others peered back from within the *Kat*. David shuddered inside when he saw Ishmael's same tiny, helmeted figure, staring from the same view port, just as it had during initial launch.

Docking would prove to be a tedious task due to the sheer size of the two space exploration platforms. It took over an hour to make everything secure giving the four who flew the DEV time to rejoin the others.

A part of the ISS had been cordoned off for the greeting party and the crew. Greeters knew that they too would need to be briefly quarantined along with the arrivals. The crew was now experiencing complete weightlessness since the partial gravity generated by the *Kat* was shut down during slowing and approach. For their stay aboard the ISS they would be weightless. It was almost a cruel trick to return to weightless conditions just prior to returning to the now unfamiliar pull of Earth's gravity.

They would spend several days under intense scrutiny in orbit receiving their preliminary health checks and evaluations. During this time they would also go through a short debriefing. This would be followed by a short trip to the surface and another period of isolation, tests and questions. None of them were looking forward to this part of the itinerary very much. Most of them were looking forward to seeing their families and just enjoying the sights and sounds of the planet they missed.

Jason, Moses, Oreen, and David were waiting on the *Kat* side of the docking pressure lock when the ISS technicians finished their preparations and began to open the hatch. They could see a least one face through the tiny glass portal in the hatch. Jason recognized the face, even though he had never met her. It was Margie's little sister holding onto one side of the flexible umbilicus and holding fresh flowers in her other hand. Jason immediately ushered Margie to the front of the group waiting eagerly inside the *Kat*. She moved to his side with a quizzical look, having no idea why. Jason knew nothing about her selection to be the official greeter. Jason purposefully blocked her view until the hatch creaked and slowly swung open. He found out later that day that President Walker had personally chosen Margie's little sister. President Walker's greeting words from his office in the Whitehouse were simple and brief, a mere paraphrase of a another great man's words from the pre-space exploration era. But he found the statement so fitting to the occasion. He said simply: "Never in the field of human endeavor was so much owed by so many to so few." His words were from 1940, borrowed with only minor modification from Sir Winston Churchill.

Margie shrieked when she spotted her sister. They met in the middle between the ISS and the *Kat* and held up the entire welcoming process while hugging and sobbing. Margie was so pleased that she forgot everything else around her for a few minutes. When order was restored, Jason just smiled and said a simple hello to the station director.

When they entered the ISS through its hatchway, the red carpet was really "rolled out" for them. Upon passing through this very portal before departing, the pictures of several of the greatest space pioneers had been placed strategically above the hatchway where none of them could miss it. This time, above the portal was a block-lettered sign reading "Heroes Return." Around this sign were individual pictures of the entire crew.

As Jason passed through the opening, and Margie and her sister followed closely, David lagged behind. He had never thought of or pictured himself in the same company as those intrepid pioneers. Even Rod passed through before him, taking photos and videos of everything. David stood and stared at the photos and the sign for a moment. His thoughts turned to the next group of explorers who might pass through this same portal. He imagined for a moment the crew and their feelings. He hoped that their destination would be a return trip to the mysterious Stealth Planet. They would be better prepared and would be able to more fully explore his discovery. A sense of pride filled him.

A technician who had opened the hatch had his personal camera attached to his suit. As David paused beneath the archway of the hatch, looking in awe at the sign, this amateur photographer snapped one innocent picture of David's face in profile, jaw dropped, staring at the sign. This one photo would one day win the tech photographer a Pulitzer Prize.

He slipped past David through the hatchway. David passed through last, a fitting end to the incredible adventure his discovery had triggered. They were home at last. They were true heroes. The world would celebrate them and not soon forget.

Ray Blackhall is an independent earth scientist and the founder and president of Cosara Energy Company. As a geologist, Ray and his company are actively involved in prospect generation and exploration for oil and gas and participate in the drilling of numerous wells along the Texas Gulf Coast. He is an active community member and is an officer and director of several local and national professional organizations. The author's intense interest in reading, research, and meshing scientific fact with contemporary fiction has resulted in realistic, topical, full-length novels.

Ray is a graduate of Syracuse University with a B.S. in Geology and received his Master's degree in Geology from Miami University. He has been happily married to his wife, Sally, since 1980, and they have one son, Colin. Born and raised in Buffalo, NY, the author currently resides in Houston, Texas.

REVIEW COPY
Dusty Spark Publishing